"Deftly weaving together elements of a futuristic thriller, a family drama, and an ode to illuminated manuscripts, *Forget I Told You This* follows lonely scribe Amy Black on her quest to discover the mystery behind tech giant Q, a local resistance group seeking her help, and ultimately, herself. The prose is gorgeous, the plot tense, and Amy is a wonderfully flawed and sympathetic character whose intense battle between her artistic ambition, the demands of her family, and her own need for love form the beating heart of this gripping and imaginative novel."
—ERIN SWAN, author of *Walk the Vanished Earth*

"*Forget I Told You This*, Hilary Zaid's portrait of the artist as a face-blind queer scrivener obsessed with ancient texts takes us to the back alleys of Oakland and the secrets rooms of a social media giant that is god-like in its omniscience and omnipotence—a world very much like the present. In this literary thriller made up of shifting identities and realities, where nothing and nobody is as they seem, one thing is a constant: the penetrating insight and elegance of Zaid's prose."
—LORI OSTLUND, author of *After the Parade*

FORGET I TOLD YOU THIS

ZERO STREET FICTION

Series Editors | Timothy Schaffert
SJ Sindu

Forget
I Told You
This

A Novel

Hilary Zaid

UNIVERSITY OF NEBRASKA PRESS · LINCOLN

The University of Nebraska Press is part of
a land-grant institution with campuses and
programs on the past, present, and future
homelands of the Pawnee, Ponca, Otoe-Missouria,
Omaha, Dakota, Lakota, Kaw, Cheyenne, and
Arapaho Peoples, as well as those of the relocated
Ho-Chunk, Sac and Fox, and Iowa Peoples.
This book was written on the past, present,
and future homeland of the Ohlone People.

Library of Congress
Cataloging-in-Publication Data
Names: Zaid, Hilary, author.
Title: Forget I told you this / Hilary Zaid.
Description: Lincoln: University
of Nebraska Press, [2023]
Identifiers: LCCN 2022056838
ISBN 9781496235367 (paperback)
ISBN 9781496237354 (epub)
ISBN 9781496237361 (pdf)
Subjects: BISAC: FICTION / Erotica /
LGBTQ+ / General | FICTION / Women |
LCGFT: Queer fiction. | Novels.
Classification: LCC PS3626.A62539 F67 2023 |
DDC 813/.6—dc23/eng/20230112
LC record available at
https://lccn.loc.gov/2022056838

Set and designed in Janson by N. Putens.

For L, R, S, and G—you are my alphabet

and in memory of
Karen Augusta, Mel Zaid, and Rhonda Kim
who created beautiful things

We're writing these things that we can no longer read, and we've rendered something kind of illegible, and we've lost the sense of what's actually happening in this world that we've made . . .
—Kevin Slavin, "How Algorithms Shape Our World"

In black ink my love may still shine bright.
—William Shakespeare, "Sonnet 65"

FORGET I TOLD YOU THIS

1 The Letter

IN THAT EARLY EVENING HOUR, AS MEN AND WOMEN poured from the Q shuttle bus up Telegraph Avenue, I plunged into the stream of bodies congealing into darkness and pressed toward the small curiosities shop where, once a season, I was paid to ink handwritten letters.

That fall, planned blackouts blanketed huge swaths of the city in shadow. But at the mouth of Temescal Alley, a smart blue postbox shone wetly in the gathering dusk. I didn't know why the U.S. Postal Service had decided to take its last stand in that enclave of digital hipsters. No one in the instant, frictionless world wrote letters. But I missed them. I missed the paper and the ink and the longing. I missed the unfathomable distances. A witty graffitist had tagged the postbox in white paint: "This is not a postbox." Clever. Turning object into art with words. I brushed my fingers across the stenciled letters the way I had once seen a woman skim her fingers against a doorpost and then touch them to her lips. Six weeks earlier, I'd dropped a letter in this box addressed to Q, Department of Arts & Letters, a plea to be chosen for an artist's residency at the social media behemoth's most elusive division. I'd never heard back.

My phone buzzed twice in my hand. A message from my mother: *When are you coming home?* An equally urgent notice from 1-800-Flowers.com warning me that I had just seven days left to send an arrangement in time for Connie's birthday.

It was October again. The season for haunting.

I deleted the ad, texted my mother *Don't wait*, and threaded my way to the shop.

Set back from the corner of 49th Street, Crimson Horticultural Rarities was warm and close, its shelves creeping with exotic plants, driftwood shadow boxes, glittering square-bottled perfumes, a small blood-colored shop smelling of candle wax and mineral earth. Customers floated among the tentacled plants, fingering volumes of botany. There was a density to the air, the soft gauze of spices brushing your cheeks. I found it deeply soothing.

"Amy!" Greer waved a sheaf of printed pages. I recognized her by her nose ring and her asymmetrical hair, dyed, this season, cerulean blue. "I set up your table in the back." I glanced through the list of late fall stock—Tillandsia and succulents, cedar eggs and sandalwood soaps—names I would scribe across ivory card stock in my careful, fifteenth-century chancery hand. The hand-scribed cards were part of the vibe, charmingly irregular, a promise of something real. I could have calligraphed Greer's cards at home in my room, or at the Hawk & Pony, but Greer didn't like keeping the shop open at night. Years ago, in her first college apartment, she'd been raped by a man who had climbed through the window. Now, along with tech stocks and rents, crime was up. The curbs of Telegraph Avenue glittered every morning with broken glass. Greer wanted me in the storeroom so that, on that Fall Festival night, the first night of the year that she stayed open after dark, she wouldn't be alone.

I didn't fear either darkness or solitude. In the tiny, cramped storeroom of Crimson Horticultural Rarities, my sense of purpose and my present tense for once slid into alignment: I slipped back into an Age of Letters, the era in which I should have been born.

The storage closet was hardly the medieval scribe's public square, but that's what the internet was for. I live-tweeted my location from @illuminated and ducked through the curtained doorway into the cramped storeroom where anyone who wanted my services could thus easily find me. An old card table had been squirreled away among the shop's overstock. Grabbing a spare drape from a shelf, I spread the swatch of velvet over the table to veil the spidery legs and arranged the tools of my trade across it: a sharpened quill, four square cut-glass bottles of ink—indigo and sepia, emerald and black. A set of votive candles. Next to them, I set out my pasteboard placard, penned in clear, black ink: *Love Letters, Hand-Scribed.*

The room was no more than a closet stuffed with boxes. But behind the doorway's velvet curtain, with candles glowing, I imagined myself in one of the small, dark cells of the medieval monks and scriveners, content to do the thing I loved, if only for myself.

And then, suddenly, I wasn't alone. Like a thought forming into words, a man in narrow jeans and a tweed vest pulsed through the curtains. A glistening beard and mustache clung to the man's face like a mask. The flames twitched. A drop of ink dripped onto the crimson cloth and quivered before the velvet drank it up.

Could I say I was surprised, when the thing that had just happened was something I'd imagined long and desperately enough to feel at that moment like a wish come true?

The man seemed nervous. His dark eyes flicked at the shelving, at the walls and boxes over my shoulders. In the warm, waxen light of the votives, his forehead shimmered with sweat. The shops on the alley had been stables once and, at that moment, I imagined I could smell the muscular heat and grassy breath of horses.

The man's eyes fell on the pasteboard sign at my elbow. He hesitated, fingering the chain that hung from the watch pocket in his vest. "I'm disturbing you." He nodded at the pages spread in front of me, the bottles of ink. In the silhouette he cast on the wall, his heartbeat jumped in his neck.

"No. Please." I smoothed the velvet with my palms and pointed at the empty folding chair opposite mine. Suddenly, I felt shocked by my own audacity. I'd never actually written a letter for another person, for a stranger, for money. I spoke quickly to hide the tremor in my voice: "Sit down."

He glanced over his shoulder, but the curtains had already settled behind him; the parted waters had closed. His hips slid around the folding chair, a fluid, serpentine movement, like an animal slithering through a hole. As he sat, he braced his palms against the table, but he misjudged its solidity—it was only a card table, covered by a rag. The ink bottles chimed against each other and his fingers scrabbled to silence them. Living with my brother in the house, I was used to small, abrupt catastrophes. I put my hands over the bottles, stilling them, and smiled. I offered him my portfolio. (I had never handed my portfolio to anyone and, for a fleeting moment, I shivered with the fear of a new mother handing her baby to a stranger, the terror that he would flee. Silly, I chastised myself, considering the storeroom packed tight with boxes: Where could he possibly go?)

He considered the brown leather cover. On the front, a craftsman had hand-tooled a capital *A* in the Insular style—*A* for the beginning of all letters; *A* for Amy. A long time ago, it had been a gift from Connie.

We'd met in college, Beasts & Bestiaries, Medieval History. When Professor Lindgren turned his back, Connie tore the corner carefully from the top of a page and folded it into a tight square she pressed to the back of my hand. (She was a chemistry major, used to minuscule notation. *Subscript. Superscript.*) I had slept with girls before. But none of them had ever written to me. We all have a medium through which the world makes sense, through which it *means*. It might be music, poetry, or paint. A medium through which our experience of life is the most perfectly apprehended. I unfolded the note. I straightened my spine against my seat. In the outstretched arms and legs of her *W*s, I saw that we would become lovers.

As much as I had once missed Connie herself, I still missed *that*: crabbed handwriting and bright, square envelopes; lined notebook sheets; dark, bottled indigo. The kind of love that could dye your whole world midnight blue. I still kept Connie's first note in an antique pewter snuffbox, the only letter between us I hadn't burned.

The man in the tweed vest leafed through my pages with square-trimmed fingers. He paused over the illuminated letter *I* in one of my father's many letters from Golden Gate Tool & Die, letters I copied because they proved that even from something banal, I could make a beautiful thing. As he looked at them, I suddenly wondered if they were, in fact, beautiful, or if they just looked old, clumsy, and sad. Amateurish. This might be the moment in which someone said it out loud: *You can't write. You can't draw.*

That newly familiar heat flooded my face, my chest, the skin at my throat, the careless crank of the thermostat all the way up. I reminded myself: I had someone at my table, looking at my work. Art without an audience is a letter that never gets sent, a voice crying into the dark.

The man in the tweed vest gazed at the page more intently than a lover. If I could have cast silken threads across the table to catch him there, I would have done it. He was a stranger. He owed me nothing. But he had already given me this.

He cleared his throat. "What determines which ones are made like this?" His finger tapped an outsize *B*, its curves the dull gold of harvest moons. His curiosity touched me, his queer, shy interest. He spoke oddly, without using the word *letters*, but he was clearly referring to the illuminated initial capitals in which I took a particular pride.

Throughout history, scribes have employed a variety of techniques for setting apart initial letters—the letters that appear *initialis*—at the beginning. They can be red (*rubricated*) or dropped lower than the baseline of the rest of the text or simply larger than the others. In the seventh century, the Insular ("island") style of Anglo-Saxon and Irish book art introduced the decorative capital, patterned with shapes or twined with animals. My own capitals were never peopled and rarely animaled. I preferred the elaboration of color and shape, light and dark, landscapes with nobody there.

I found the man's manner strange, but it occurred to me that maybe that was just me, what had begun to feel like midlife's widening gap in understanding other people. "Well . . ." I hesitated. I wasn't used to talking about my work. "I suppose you could say there's an algorithm." *The Algorithm* was a phrase murmured at the Hawk & Pony like the name of a god. I smiled, a flickering smile meant to show that, though I was bookish and odd, I could speak the lingua franca. But, at the word *algorithm*, the man in the tweed vest rubbed his forehead as if in distress, and his distress encouraged me to think that he might be more like me than I had dared to hope.

He held the book closer to his eye, inspecting my very untraditional illuminations, bricolages of stamps and tickets, found objects layered with color and ink. He was almost sniffing the page, the tang of paper and tannins, iron and wood. Then, as if satisfied, he patted down his chest like someone thirsting for a cigarette but, instead, fished a silver watch from the small pocket of his vest. A pyramidal prism flashed from the cover. The Q logo. I'd seen it on the Q app, on bus shelters, on billboards and banner ads, on commercials between binge-watched episodes. But I'd never seen it on an object like this.

This was a real watch, an analog. I wondered where he'd gotten it. It seemed like something only an insider would have, someone important at Q. Inside my chest, I felt a long-barred door opening up, a door I hoped to walk through. At a press of his thumb, the watch cover sprang open. A bit of fluff drifted onto the tabletop—a bit of bluish down that looked at first like a fingerprint but turned out to be a feather. He looked at the watch. "Those must take a long time."

I swallowed hard. That was the reason people had stopped writing letters in the first place: they took too much time. My eyes fell to my portfolio, which he had discarded. *This*, I thought, *is the moment he leaves me*. I slid my book back across the table, prepared to fold my desires and aspirations back into the pale envelope of myself. He pressed the watch cover into place and slipped the watch into its pocket.

Then, without warning, he closed his eyes, blank spots, suddenly, on his darkly masked face, reminding me how quickly a person could feel alone. "Please listen," he whispered, pleading, a live wire jammed straight into my brain. I was so shaken it took me a second to realize he was dictating a letter. The light winking through my bottled inks could not have been more beautiful to me than it appeared in that moment. I grabbed my quill and began to write.

> I know we've hardly met, but would you believe me if I said that I know we were meant to help each other? Right now, being with you is the most important fact of my life.

Maybe it wasn't the most original thing to say, but the language of love is repeated because it moves us.

As I watched the ink ribbon from nib to paper, I thought about how many times, after Connie, I had lain in bed with a perfectly sweet, attentive lover, and sighed into the dark for a different kind of desire. The way my hand knew its way across the surface of the page, this dark effluvium—this was the form in which my body most intimately knew love.

It was claustrophobic inside the tiny back room of Crimson Horticultural Rarities, warm. The man across the table was sweating profusely now, salting the air with urgency. My fingers flew across the page. I was trying to listen as I imagined a real scribe would, as a conduit, nothing more. (After Connie, I had often felt that way, staring at the faces of the people I knew— like a piece of glass through which light passed.) But the heat off his arms and the passion in his voice made the hair at the back of my neck rise up. Who wouldn't want to be spoken to in a voice like that?

I didn't imagine he was speaking *to me*.

I imagined his voice was *mine*.

Every so often, he tapped the page where he wanted me to leave space for a decorative capital. Then he raced on: "Everything depends on you," he said. He swiped his hand across dry lips, and then the man in the tweed vest leaned over the paper until his dark curls brushed my forehead: "I need you to make Tal forget me."

Forget me?

A drop of ink trembled at the tip of my quill, a dark crystal, quivering with light.

Questions swirled inside it. Who was Tal? I'd assumed I was writing a love letter, but now I wasn't sure. Tal must be a former lover. Then to whom was this letter addressed?

The man gazed quietly into the darkness behind me. He didn't seem to notice that I had stopped writing, or that the drop of ink on the tip of my quill had splashed next to the letter *T*. His wide, dark pupils reflected the flickering candles. Maybe it was the intonation I had heard in his voice when he whispered Tal's name, the tenderness that had become a softness in the shape of the *l*—but I had the impression that he felt pain for Tal. That he still loved her. (In my mind, she had already become a woman.) I pointed to the spot at the top of the page where

I had left a space for the name of the recipient. "Who—?" I began. His desperation had sparked a wildness in me. I needed to know who this letter was for. I needed to know how a woman had made a person feel this way. I needed to remember how to conjure that magic.

But Greer hissed my name through the curtains.

"*Amy!*"

Her voice was sharp with fear.

"Excuse me—" I unfolded myself from behind the table, careful not to jar the flimsy legs, the bottled inks, the candles. Careful not to let this delicate, fevered world collapse. The velvet brushed my forehead as I swam through the curtains, then closed up behind me.

Behind the counter, Greer stood as unstirring as the bottled roots and herbs. Above her, three Edison bulbs hung bare in the warm night air. I itched to get back to the man at my table, my scriptorium, but I tried not to sound impatient. "What is it?"

Like an animal that holds still in order to avoid catching the eye of a predator, Greer didn't turn her blue head. But she raised an eyebrow toward two men crowding the shop's front door. Blocking it.

One, a thick blond, had wedged his back against the doorjamb. He was facing out, scanning the traffic as it funneled through the narrow passage from the alley to the street. The other bent to his phone, his broad back straining against a too-tight sports coat. Their body language was tense, their tight suits the wrong kind of tight suits for this neighborhood, their pants too wide around the calf. Were we being robbed?

As if, despite our stillness, he had caught our scent, the man with the broad back marched to the counter and thrust his phone under Greer's nose. "Have you seen this man?" It was a photo: the usual, dark punctuation of a face, the indistinct braille of eyes, nose, mouth. When the broad man pressed the phone closer to Greer, I looked away.

There was a young woman growing up in India who didn't realize she was blind in one eye until she was twelve years old. Sitting with her father before a pile of his lawbooks, she grinned: "Wouldn't it be cool if we could read with both the eyes?" His face collapsed in her monocular blink.

We experience life within the limits of our own senses. From inside the closed bubble of the self, it's almost impossible to appreciate that those senses don't mirror the way other people see the world. Until some shock of disconnection. The bubble bursts. You understand; you're different.

I had never been good with faces.

At first, there was nothing odd to me about the way I saw other people, the hot-pink-and-brown blur of them. The human brain instinctively finds ways to adapt. I had always recognized my childhood best friend Callie by her strawberry shampoo, by the brass buttons on her blue, wool coat. I felt no self-consciousness, no awareness of difference. Then, one day, I stepped into Mrs. Lim's kindergarten coat closet, looking for my rain boots. A child's head floated between the hoodies and coats, a visitation from another dimension. I stared intently. "Who are you?"

"Amy!" Callie struggled out from between the heavy coats. "It's me!" she laughed. But that moment just before she laughed, as she hovered behind the coats—in the hesitation that edged her cry, I could hear that she had fooled me and *she couldn't believe it*. That was the first, sharp prick to the thin, rainbowed sense bubble. At that moment a gap opened between myself and Callie, between myself and everyone. What did it mean to be like other human beings? And what if I wasn't?

The mind quickly seals over unbearable gaps.

Outside my circle of intimates, other people remained somewhat distant and mysterious. Blurred. I understood this as something flawed in my relation to others. An insistence on loneliness. An introversion. The strange, numb twin of the thrill of recognition I felt in a line of handwriting. They were married, already, the sense of absence and its antidote: the thirst for letters. The thrill I'd felt when I met Connie.

Recently, this tendency of the smiling face on the street to feel unplaceable had grown more inconvenient. I was dating again. At the end of the summer, I met Jaqueline, an industrial designer whose ability to fuse art and technology I found mildly thrilling. I was still imagining that I might find myself *with* someone. *Meet me on the platform,* Jackie texted as my train pulled into 19th Street Station. It was six o'clock, a game night in Oakland, a sea of green and gold caps and jerseys transferring en masse to the Coliseum-bound train. I saw a woman lift her hand to me, my date, a petite blond in a summer dress, one of the few people in the station not wearing baseball insignia.

"*Buonasera, principessa,*" I murmured into her hair, remembering our long afternoon in her studio, the late summer peaches. I tucked her small hand into my pocket and leaned into her mouth.

The high bleat of the inbound train skipped toward us as her head twisted violently from mine. "Excuse me?" It took me a moment to register her confusion, a slow moment of mortification to understand my mistake: I had just kissed a stranger.

Jackie, who had been watching for me, had seen everything.

Now, when I heard my name at Berkeley Bowl among the avocados and oranges, the smile I hoped looked friendly was pasted across my features. Along with a blossoming need for reading glasses, I accepted this new fuzziness around things that used to have sharp, clear edges as *becoming middle aged.* But the truth was more complicated. I'd spent the previous eighteen years not looking up. Before that, I'd had Connie. And with Connie I'd always had letters.

I didn't want to be alone. But now that handwritten letters had faded from history, I could not know another person intimately. I had come to accept this as a fact. Until that night. Until the man in the tweed vest sat at my table.

I itched to float back through the velvet curtains, to the word *Tal*, to the man and his letter.

As the broad, blond agent peppered Greer with questions, I cast my eyes around the nearly empty store. In the far corner, a woman hovered at a table crowded with succulents. She wore a sweater and knit cap the color of the plants called lamb's ears (*Stachys byzantina*)—a soft, furred sage green. The sweater and cap matched the plants beside her, soft green mounds of vegetable flesh. She glanced from counter to door. When the bright bits that were her eyes caught my glance, they flicked away. Even I could see: she was a woman trying not to be noticed.

"What about you?" The bulky man in the gray suit shook the screen in front of my face. "Have you seen this man?" I squinted at the dark spots floating on the screen, the five holes of the human head.

"Sorry." I stepped back toward the storage closet, where the man in the tweed vest filled the room with his hot breath, warming my bottles of ink.

The other agent launched himself from the doorway. "Where did she come from?" He was pointing at me. (In a trice, the woman in the lamb's ear sweater slipped behind him out the front door.) His eyes fell on the doorway behind me, and, in a second, both men tore through the velvet curtain. Above them, four green letters glowed *EXIT*.

In their hurry to get past me, they knocked me to the ground.

My wrist ached. But that wasn't what hurt. Just moments before, my skin, my throat, my veins had flushed with the urgent murmur of a human voice. But now a cold despair rushed from my head into my stomach, into the suddenly cold tips of my fingers. All the cues I'd read from the man in the tweed vest as emotion—his profuse sweating, his leaping pulse, his juddering heel—had nothing to do with that letter. He'd been hiding out in the back of the store, a criminal who'd taken advantage of my vanity to occupy a secret space. The room in which I'd left behind my portfolio!

I rolled to my side and pushed myself off the floor, careful to spare the injured wrist. Above the doorway, a taxidermied raven glared at me with glassy eye.

In the back room, I found my card table shoved aside to reveal the emergency exit. The candles sent up slow, gray ghosts. The man in the tweed vest and his pursuers were gone. A blizzard of papers littered the room—my portfolio, my loose sheets lay in drifts across the dusty floor. I bent to peel my father's Golden Gate Tool & Die carbons from the scuffed cement, the once-bright pages dull in the gloom. They rattled like fallen leaves in my hand. I shuffled the sheets together until the corners met and wondered about all the hours I had poured into them, hours I might have spent programming databases, or writing code—earning my place in this world. I didn't bother to dust them off. I turned one of the scattered sheets over to the fresh ink of the letter I had just been writing. He'd left it behind.

So, it hadn't meant anything to him after all.

I sighed and wiped my ink-stained fingers against my skirt; I began to gather my things.

That's when I noticed that my quill and inks had been set neatly on a shelf, not thrown across the floor with everything else. It was hard to imagine the two men in suits pausing to take care with my things. I thought again about the emotion in his voice when the man in the tweed vest whispered *Everything depends on you*, the way the vein in his temple pulsed. The way he'd touched his fingers, gently, to my words. I studied the chaos of pages still spread like tea leaves on the floor, the letter that had been tucked facedown among them, and then the little tableau of writing implements on a shelf behind where he had been sitting, and wondered: Was this carelessness, or was it art? If you wanted to hide a leaf, where better than among the fallen leaves?

Voices thundered back toward the emergency exit. I let my pages fall back to the floor. A moment later, the men in the suits blasted back in. Shoulder to shoulder, they pressed me to the wall of the dusty little storeroom. "Did he give you anything? A phone? a flash drive? Did he ask you to give something to someone?"

"No." My skirt swayed over the loose sheets scattered across the floor, where the man in the tweed vest's love letter lay faceup, a letter among a dozen letters. "Nothing."

Hiding that letter was as reflexive as curling my head from a blow, my solar plexus, my heart. Everything in the world had told me that my one, innate organ for apprehending intimacy had shriveled and broken off. (*People don't read. People don't write.*) Except this man. Except his letter. Except his love and sadness for a person named *Tal*. I'd felt them both flow through my hand, the love and the sadness. Why did he want Tal to forget him?

(Everything might have been different if I hadn't decided Tal was a woman who had been left behind, a woman with too much to forget.)

As soon as the man's thick pursuers evaporated into the dark, I slipped through the back door to find him.

Night had fallen—instant, black, October night. In the cramped passage behind the shop, I had to blink hard just to see that I was there. I followed the seams of the brick wall until I came to a door. It was locked, immovable but humming. I pressed my cheek to the cold metal. It smelled the way I remembered coins used to smell and I imagined it would taste the same against my tongue: like cold, and electricity, and blood. I could just make out the burr of voices under the low thump of a bass drop. I pounded, but no one heard me, or no one came.

Greer stood in her back room, surveying the mess. "I'm closing."

I started to protest, but Greer waved her hand, as if the man in the tweed vest had come there because of me, as if my being there had made the whole thing happen.

But, feeling his letter pulsing through the covers of the notebook into which I'd slipped it, I thought: maybe I had. Clutching the notebook, I stepped onto Temescal Alley, determined to find out who Tal was and what the man in the tweed vest wanted her to forget.

The alley was hobbit-like, two rows of corrugated-tin storefronts once built to stable horses. The local barber pole spun lazy blue ribbons and light blazed from open galleries. The narrow passage bustled with people pressing from bright doorways, people rushing to catch rideshares somewhere else.

Self-conscious, as always, among strangers in a crowd, I pushed through the perfumed bodies as aware of the letter tucked into my satchel as if it were throbbing against my chest, visible in an instant to the people who could instantly recognize me: the men in the too-tight suits, the man in the tweed vest.

Head down, I started toward the open shop next to Crimson: the barbershop with the blue-striped pole. Straight razors hung in thin, bright lines along the walls, glittering like rows of teeth. At each chair, a bearded man stood grooming a bearded man, a razor at his throat. Hip-hop bubbled vaguely from an old-fashioned black radio in the corner, under the bass of male voices. He could have been any one of them, and I wouldn't have had a clue.

I watched a barber line his blade against the pale underside of a man's exposed throat. For the first time since I'd stepped out of the shop, it occurred to me that the man in the tweed vest was someone I should be afraid of. Plainclothes agents of the law were looking for him. He was a criminal. When the man in the tweed vest discovered me between himself and the back door to the alley, I might have easily been slit from breast to belly. In the doorway, a man with a pale, freshly shaved jaw pressed past me, smelling of shaving soap and limes, a neat white line cut into the hair at the nape of his neck. The whites of his eyes glowed in the night. What color were the man in the tweed vest's eyes? I couldn't remember.

I ducked out of the hot, pomaded air and into the dark, warm night. Along the alley, bearded men in lumberjack shirts and plain white T-shirts swarmed the doorways, men in jeans and men in narrow pants and men in chinos and loafers, men with shining, dark heads of hair and hidden faces, any one of them the man who thought I could identify him to the police.

I hurried out of the crowded alley toward Telegraph Avenue, where horses once clopped trolleys back and forth from Idora Park. A figure loomed there in half-dark: a woman, alone. Her hand glossed the graffiti on the mailbox. I knew what it meant to be a woman alone. And on that night so close to the end of October, those letters on that mailbox were a talisman to me, summoning all I still wanted. A connection that could only happen through words.

She poised on the curb in a knit cap, her head tilted, birdlike, looking, listening, peering into the dark. Out on the street, the darkness thickened, heavy with the Diablo wind. I knew as I felt it: I wanted her to be Tal. Who else would be flickering there in the darkness so close to the place he'd just been hiding, wanting to get closer?

A halo of fine, soft wool rose along the arm of her sweater. When she held her hand up to her forehead, like a sea wife scrying the horizon, the wide arm of the sweater slid back, revealing a glinting gold tattoo: a naked female figure suspended inside a leafy O against a spangled sky.

I'd created a conduit between Tal and the man in the tweed vest. And I wanted to open it. I reached for my bag.

Not quickly enough. As the headlamps from a Google Street View car foamed at her feet, she surged into the faces flooding from Temescal Alley. But before she stepped into the darkness, in the pale gold lamplight, I saw that her sweater was a silvery, lamb's-ear green.

2 *Nocturnes*

IN MY NARROW EDWARDIAN ON 49TH STREET, MY mother perched on the wooden piano bench kneading out Chopin while my father nodded on the couch. It had been ages since my son, Tristan, or anyone else had played the upright my parents had bought him. The little plastic busts of the composers ranged on top of the piano—Schubert and Schuman, Chopin and Liszt, scowling, armless—mocked the droop of my father's head.

My parents and my brother were sheltering at my place for the duration of a planned blackout. The local power company had an unfortunate history of not maintaining their lines, which sometimes, on blustery days, set entire towns on fire. Now when the forecast threatened wind, Pacific Gas & Electric simply turned the power off in the hills, carrying my parents down from my childhood home and here into my living room.

My mother's playing was a good sign. A concert pianist turned piano teacher, lately she only played when my father was too spent from eating, shuffling, and breathing to need her help. Today, she had made it through the long afternoon with enough will left for music.

My father jerked awake when I kissed him, a bead of drool glossing his cheek. For an instant I remembered the drop of ink before it sank into the velvet tablecloth, the smell of candle wax and sweat, and shivered at the letter in my bag.

"Amy!" my mother complained. "We've already eaten." It was a statement of fact—I'd have to get my own dinner—but also an accounting: family life had happened without me. It didn't matter that I had lived without them for years. For the moment, my family were back. "Were you with someone?" My mother had stopped playing; her question hung in a silence still thick with the reverberation of strings; it hummed with the theme that had become the background score of our every conversation: the fear that I would stay single—like my brother, someone my parents would have to worry would survive them alone.

Never mind that I had an eighteen-year-old son. Tristan was the magical creature in our family, the bright young person designated to go live his own life and be free.

"I had to work late. Remember?" I hadn't told my parents that the planned power outage that had swept them from their home had also shuttered my job. I couldn't handle endless hours alone with the two of them and Fox News while my brother went to work. (The power in San Francisco where he worked as a guide at the California Academy of Sciences hadn't been affected.) I dug my mother's phone out of the couch to offer proof of fidelity, apology, though I wasn't apologetic enough not to flee. Every other morning, the visiting nurse came to the house to bathe my father and shave him so my mother could go get food or get her hair done or breathe. I also needed to breathe. In the face of my father's senescence, I needed to remember that though he was old and ill, I was still alive. I shook the phone at my mother: "I texted you." A silver-topped Golden Girl peered out of my mother's phone with concern; just that morning, I had reset her lock screen to an image of turquoise, tropical waters, and already it had set itself back to an ad for MedicAlert; we'd talked about ordering one for my father to wear around his neck. I showed her the message. But my mother rarely picked up her phone. Her hands were full with my father. Two nights before, he'd fallen off the toilet.

"It's awfully late," my mother protested, and who could blame her for resenting being left alone, and not even in her own house? The power outages were capricious and uncertain and, even despite them, distant towns might burst into flame. "Don't your bosses know there's a crisis happening?" She meant the blackouts, but she could have been talking about their lives. My mother's cheeks rouged with anger: though she had never wanted me to live a *bohemian* life, recently she resented my job, not because it was sucking away the last of my life for something we all knew was pointless, but because it kept me away from them.

Guilty, I offered a morsel of confession: "I was with Greer. In the shop." My mother's flushed face paled and contracted. She remembered what had happened to Greer. And though she may have wanted something more for me, she had never wanted that: an odd girl doing odd things in an oddities shop. I shifted my bag on my shoulder. "I was hired to write a letter." Despite what I thought she might say, I felt my pride rise up.

My mother, who had turned to wipe the spittle from my father's chin, fixed me in her bright eye. "A letter?" My parents were a decade apart, my mother a music student when they met and my father a sales rep for Golden Gate Tool & Die. At the back of her closet, tucked into an old, satin-covered hatbox, my mother kept ribbon-tied bundles of their letters, mementos of his many travels, the lifeline between them when they were apart, thin blue skins papered with stars and flowers, presidents and princes. I thought she would be pleased. "Who would hire a stranger to write them a letter?" Her narrow face folded inward.

"A letter? Of the alphabet?" My brother, Michael, appeared in the living room, cradling a mug, his voice bright with hope. Michael lived with my parents, and when they became power outage refugees, he was part of the package, the one unadulter-ated bit of joy. Solid and cheerful with his thumbprint dimple and his eager smile, my brother was that much younger than I was, not to associate *letter* with *mail*. He was a person people called *disabled* but who was, above all, exuberant. He was still in the bow tie he wore to the Academy, the job he loved because he got to talk with so many people, and where, for the most part, people were kind to him. They treated him as if he were an endangered rain forest animal, which, in a way, he was. There are a million people who would give anything not to have a child like Michael, who *had* given something not to have a child like Michael—a genetic test, an outpatient procedure, a pale-pink tablet taken right away—and those people would never have a clue that, for all the money and the specialists and the fear for his future, a son like Michael would be the balm of their old age. Michael carefully wrapped my father's shaking hand around the mug of lukewarm tea.

Nearly a decade younger than I was, Michael was a child of technology, a person of a different time. That he wasn't familiar with letters was not a symptom of his disability, the limits of which he had far exceeded, but a reminder that distances did not exist for him. He had bounced radio signals off the moon. "Here—" I slipped my letter out of my bag and was about to hand it over.

My mother gasped—"My goodness, Amy! A letter is personal!" Her thin fingers flew wide, a gesture of surprise more meaningful to me than any expression on her face might have been. (Sometimes, now, I wonder how much more my mother knew about me than I understood about myself. Though whatever she knew would hardly have mattered: my parents vehemently rejected labels when my brother was born with one.) My mother, whose people were British, had a strict sense of propriety about certain things—eating dinner on time, dressing for international travel. Not reading other people's mail. She had caught me, once, at the bottom of her closet, sifting letters from that hatbox, and blazed a handprint against my face.

My mother was right: I had undertaken a confidence. I slipped the letter back into my bag.

Down the hall, my parents' old grandfather clock mourned the half hour. (Tired of having to wind it, they had given it to me and Connie as a "wedding" gift more fitting than they could have known.) Before Michael was born, on the nights of my childhood when I found myself awake in the odd hours, the dark chime of that clock through the quiet house had always sounded to me like the loneliest note in the world.

I missed Tristan. And, because I missed Tristan, because missing him was still so raw, for the first time that evening, I missed Connie, though it had been so long that missing her had become an idea separate from what loving her had been.

When he saw I wasn't going to show him the letter, Michael plopped down and fiddled with the dials on the ham radio that was his obsession, as happy as ever with one earbud dangling from his ear. My mother rearranged herself on the couch, careful not to disturb my father's humped ribs, and steadied his hand around the mug.

When I was in elementary school, collecting toy mice dressed in vintage top hats like chimney sweeps and grooms, fur mouse ladies in silken nightcaps and lace, my father brought home a tiny little screwdriver and even teenier metal screws—screws as slight as eyelashes. Screwing a jeweler's loupe into the socket of his eye and pinching the eyelash of a screw between his fingernail and thumb, he assembled my little mouse bride a brass, four-poster bed.

Now my father just managed to bring the mug underneath his trembling chin. As narrow as my mother's face was, my father's was round, his hooded eyes round under his heavy brows, his cheeks full and now almost waxen, his mouth pursed. He paused over the steaming tea and cleared his throat, a harsh, wet cough that could only clear so much: "Why do you have it?" His other hand, crooked in his lap, pointed, shaking, at the letter.

The two of them, my father with his typewriter and his sheaves of carbon paper, my mother with her thundering fingers, had always seemed so powerful. Now, clutching each other in the middle of my living room, they looked so small and so old.

I wasn't about to tell my parents that the man who'd written that letter had fled the police. I wondered suddenly about the men in the too-tight suits: Had they *said* they were police? Or FBI? Had they ever shown a badge? "I needed more time for the decorative letters," I fudged. My parents huddled on the couch, uncertainty crowding their eyebrows. The two of them had so adamantly discouraged me from spending Saturday afternoons in high school alone at the kitchen table with a penknife and bottles of ink, it was hard to remember that what they wanted most was for me to be happy. It was hard for them, too.

Though I may have wanted to spite them once, years ago, I didn't want to hurt them anymore. "The man I wrote it for works at Q." I remembered the watch he'd pulled out of his vest and decided it had to be true. "An engineer." I didn't know anything about the hierarchies at Q, but even my mother knew that Q's engineers ruled the company. They ruled the economy. You could credibly say they ruled the world. "A software engineer."

My mother played her fingertips against my father's knuckles, a little riff that might have meant a melody, if I could have understood the notes. "Is this about that art studio?" In her voice, I heard that hum again: the hope that I would be happy.

Ever since I'd read about it on a computer terminal someone had forgotten to log out of, I had fantasized about earning a coveted residency at Q's enigmatic and legendary Department of Arts & Letters. Q was the largest social media site in the world, yet where Google touted its biggest number-ness and Amazon announced itself the world's largest river of every consumer good imaginable, Q had assumed its place in the alphabet as one small letter, one of the most unloved. (In Scrabble, Q's high value derived from how difficult it was to use. It was so hard to place, the Scrabble dictionary adopted foreign uses for it: *Qi* for *chi* was one of my father's favorite words.) A circle with a tail. A zero turned into something different. A cipher.

It was a blazing fall afternoon twelve years earlier, stifling into the late-afternoon hour between scheduling conferences and managing fish sticks and five times tables and getting ready to do it all over again. Tristan was in second grade. Smutch-fingered, a jumper off couches and bookshelves and ledges. That afternoon, I let myself linger before rushing to pickup, a pause under the Main Library's vaulted white ceiling. I liked to come here to stare at the endless spines of books on the wall. I could just as easily have pressed my cheek against the cool wood tables, but I knew if I did, I would fall asleep, so I jiggled the mouse and turned my eyes to the computer. Someone had left it tabbed open to a photo of a Soviet propaganda–style poster with the caption: *Produced by Q, Dept. of Arts & Letters, whose coveted silk-screened posters disappear as mysteriously as they appear on the walls.* A long-expired Reddit thread told the legend of a secret screen-printing press, the light box fueled by burning wood from the desks of former employees. When I looked up, the golden glow had drained from the walls; I was late to pick up my son.

Six years later, a Google Alert brought news of an artist-in-residence program at Q. There were no instructions for how to apply. I scoured my social networks for someone who might know someone who might know someone. (Connie would have known people.) Six years after that, two months after Tristan left home, I inked my letter of supplication in my best italic minuscule, sealed it with a drop of crimson wax, and deposited it into the graffitied postbox on Temescal Alley.

"The Artist's Residency." I smoothed my fingers against the black nap of my skirt.

There it was again, the hot flood of hope, rising up in the face of all my objections. I admitted it only then to myself: As soon as I saw the man in the tweed vest's watch emblazoned with the logo, I thought that Q had at last sent someone to find me. Isn't that what we all want? To finally be recognized as the person we were meant to be?

My mother seemed relieved and so did my father. Now that their power had left them, they needed to believe in something, and why shouldn't it be me? Even Michael seemed excited. "Did you see him, Amy?"

"The engineer?"

Michael frowned. He flapped his loose earbud in his hands. (My brother often grew impatient with what he perceived, rightly, to be *my* delays.) "The terrorist!"

My mother's narrow face grew narrower still. "Michael, what do you mean?" But my father began to cough and then to choke, his tea splashing over the rim of his mug, darkening his lap, so she didn't hear the answer.

"They were looking for him in Temescal Alley." Michael nodded, not raising his eyes from his radio, as if reading the text off a ticker. "A terrorist!" He gaped, squinting behind his glasses.

I pressed my fingers into the tenderness at my hip. "Are you sure it wasn't ICE?" I kept my voice low while our father gurgled. (It was alarming, but we'd both grown used to it.) I remembered the man in the tweed vest's tawny fingers. Terrorists were the world's great boogeymen, cover for government roundups of the undocumented. Michael glanced at my father's teacup. He screwed his earbud deeper into his ear and leaned into the radio. "I don't think they said ICE." He shook his head. "Sorry, Amy. They didn't say ICE." It would be easy to imagine that my brother, with his small nose and thick glasses, had tuned into the ham radio world because he was lonely, because he wanted to listen in on the world from which he was in many ways excluded. But the truth is, he had made himself the center of a community that thrived in the shortwave hours of the night, as he had at the museum, waving people into the huge open gallery of bones with an inexhaustible smile; my brother was the most extroverted, the most unlonely of all of us. "Did you see that man?" he asked again, encouraging me once again to take part in the world, like him.

"No." I held my breath until my father stopped choking, until his face faded from deep crimson to its usual, waxen hue. "I didn't."

But I had seen the woman who loved him. Tal was the woman who had been standing in the shop, just outside the curtain, waiting, hovering, listening. She was the same woman who had been waiting at the mailbox. I *knew* it was her. I'd seen her. I was sure that I had. I *needed* to be sure that I had, because I needed my art to mean something. I needed to know that a letter I wrote could still move someone, if not for myself, then for somebody else.

I glanced down at the coffee table, at my father's *Wall Street Journal*, his half-empty mug. I had no idea how long my parents would be living with me—as long as the power was out. But as long as the power was out, I had time to find out who Tal was and to get that letter into her hands. I kissed my parents good night.

Over his thirty-five years at Golden Gate Tool & Die, my father came home every night smelling of carbon paper and oil, earning the kind of living that, in those days, secured a mortgage and a family. My mother played with the Berkeley Symphony and was on call for the San Francisco Symphony Orchestra until Michael was born; afterward, she taught piano. I'm sure opening the door for students at four o'clock in the afternoon with a package of chicken breasts thawing on the counter wasn't the life she had imagined for herself. But with a house in the Berkeley Hills, they had enough. More than most people in my generation. More than enough.

Then my father got sick. Michael's physical and occupational therapists and private school, an adjustable-rate line of credit that had gone haywire, and a pension fund that had gone belly-up had left little padding. At this point, my parents had two sets of stairs my father couldn't climb; monthly drug costs totaling $1,200; and debt from a reverse mortgage equal to a shocking percentage of their home's enormously skyrocketed value. In their old age, there would be no smiling attendants bearing colorful drinks, no bridge games overlooking the whitecapped bay. They would hunker down at home as long as they could before surrendering to my care. It was always the plan that Michael would eventually move in with me.

My mother told me all of this in late spring. I was boiling water for Trader Joe's white cheddar shells, a late, hurried dinner after Tristan came home grass-stained and sweaty, before I opened the bills. The mourning doves were lowing under the eaves, or maybe the neighbors' rooftop pigeons. A chair scraped the floor over the kitchen table, one of the Ecuadoran exchange students who rented my upstairs rooms.

Five months later, my tenants returned home together to Quito, grateful to escape a nation hostile to immigrants, and Tristan left home.

Then came the blackouts, a wave of darkness washing my parents down from the hills, and I found myself climbing the stairs to my student rental room with its narrow student bed. It was strange, but no stranger than Tristan's leaving, which had flayed me, leaving me sobbing into his pillow, staring at the blue-and-white walls of his childhood bedroom. In light of his leaving, it wasn't so bad to have my parents here for the time being, my brother next door. There was a symmetry to it, a return to the way things had been before. The illusion of going backward in time, instead of toward loneliness, and mortality, and loss. A way of pretending that I didn't lack a life of my own.

I threw my bag on the single bed, its narrowness a reminder of one more thing I wouldn't have again. The quilt that hung against the wall—an interpretation of a sixteenth-century French tapestry, a woman with a unicorn at her side—made the room feel cozy; the windows got southwestern light. I'd moved my drafting table up here when my tenants moved out. Now I was trying to feel at home.

The minor chords of a Chopin Nocturne drifted down the hall. My father had turned on the television. Q was in the news again, something about the election; China had crushed another protest; people were losing their minds.

I propped my laptop open and sat on the bed. The turquoise beach scene I'd put on my mother's phone had spawned, striping my own phone with tropical waves and round-trip prices to Kona. Without rental income coming in, those banner ads would have to be my Kona. I Googled "terror" and "terrorist" and "Temescal Alley." But nothing turned up. I went into Google Maps, typed in *Temescal Alley* and *Crimson Horticultural Rarities* and even the intersection of 49th Street where the blue mailbox squatted. But there wasn't anything. The mailbox wasn't even on the Google Street View photo.

A strange lightness peppered the top of my scalp. Everything that had happened that evening suddenly felt like a dream, like a wish that had started right and then gone wrong, like something that might not have happened at all. I wondered if this could be some other figment of aging, a reminder that, even though I was going to sleep in the room next to my brother's, I was getting old. Then I told myself to stop being melodramatic. My *parents* were old. My father, disabled. I was forty-six. The bruised purple notes of a Nocturne bled through the walls.

I fished through my bag for the half-finished letter. *Being with you is the most important fact of my life.* His voice had thickened with regret.

Despite being thrown to the ground, the letter still looked clean. Only the last, fresh drop of ink had smeared. Fine lines trailed from the "l" in *Tal* like kite tails in a high wind, like they were in a hurry to run off the page, like the man who'd left it behind. As I should also hurry away: from him, from his letter, from the thick men in their suits, from the word *terrorist* and *thief*. But when I remembered that hour in the dark, candlelit room, an hour that flowed without self-consciousness, without worry for my mother and father, when I stared at the beautiful, hand-inked letters and the smooth, white sheet, a quiet calm fell in my mind. It draped the thump of Michael falling into his bed next door, the surging and falling notes of the piano swelling and tugging down the hall; it fell over the electric hum of the Teslas as they floated down the dark, Oakland streets, and over the pop from the corner that might have been an M80 or might have been a gun. It blanketed my mind with a curtain of darkness and quiet. In the light of the bedside lamp, I felt the old, familiar romance of letters inked along a clean-ruled page.

I unpacked my quills and lined up my bottles of ink on my drafting table and began my bricolage.

A discarded library copy of Audubon's *Birds of America*; a brochure full of paint chips in purple, violet, and blue; an antique book of sheet music (Berlioz); a three-year-old *National Geographic*. I cut and pasted, layered and glued, behind, over, and around my own, hand-lettered initial capitals, part modern, part medieval, most unusual.

By the time I noticed that the hall was quiet, a shower of swallows sprayed from the capital "T" in *Tal*; the thumbnail of a moon shone bright with a moth's wing of silver leaf.

How often did life strike these little sparks of incandescence?

I remembered the gold tattoo, a naked female figure against a spangled sky, the bare forearm of the woman who'd glittered at the curb.

What right did I have to want that?

From inside the pewter box I kept behind a stack of linen, I pulled out Connie's first note, folded so often that the seams had worn through like pinprick stars. I hadn't opened it in years. But then the man in the tweed vest showed up, just days from Connie's birthday, and he'd asked me for a letter. A letter like that had made me want things. It made me remember what wanting feels like. And I wanted to feel like that again.

The paper smelled like cedar and ink and too much time. *Walk with me?* I had stared at them so many times, the words had stopped meaning, the crabbed, blue script, a faded spider web spun so many years ago by her pale, bitten fingers. I stared at it the way people stare at the photograph of a face. Once upon a time, Connie had been my partner in this thing. Once upon a time, she had introduced me to magic.

The first time we met outside of class, she led me through the redwoods to the triple arches of a red-roofed building in the old white-walled Spanish style, up to a golden oak door. It was early spring. Mock orange sweetened the air. A red-winged blackbird played his little piccolo in a tree somewhere. Students were whirring by on bikes, people we sat with in dim lecture halls, laughing and calling out, faces up to the sun. They all fell miles away when I pressed my palm against the door, which was carved with circles bigger than dinner plates, *Mining and Metallurgy* writ in beautiful, Beaux Arts capitals over the top. It might have read *Magic and Alchemy* for the way those golden panels simmered with syrupy, pollen-specked light.

Connie had been talking to me about the two summer internships she'd won, one at a campus lab, one at a pharmaceutical company. Even at nineteen, she had a firm fix on her future. I liked her certainty, and the sturdy way she walked. When we slid into the sliver of shadow at the edge of the golden doors, Connie stopped talking. Coolness bathed our shoulders. We stood in a long, narrow hall two stories high. Huge, milk-colored domes suffused the room with milky light. The perfect geometry of the oculi, the globes of light: I felt like we had stepped inside the illumination of a letter, the ornate and gilded world inside a page. We stood silent and looked up, the hairs on our arms just brushing, just close enough to bridge a spark.

I refolded the note carefully and shoved the pewter box back behind the linen. Then I picked up my phone and tapped open *scizr*, flicked through the inscrutable faces in the cruising app. I was thinking that night of *Tal*, looking for a warm body, but seeing only already-familiar screen names. Then I hit *18*. Not a name, but a number, attached to a profile picture neither smile nor cleavage, but a human hand, fingers curled over palm. The hand was tea-colored, well proportioned, symmetrical, and strong. I put on my reading glasses and swooshed the image larger. A writing callus pebbled the middle finger.

I double tapped.

The app chimed back.

A match.

I stared at the screen. Then I typed:

What are you doing right now?

A wave of heat spread through my head and neck. They had been coming on since late September, just shy of my forty-sixth birthday. I got up and opened the window and leaned out, looking across the rooftops, bathing in the night air.

I was leaning against the sill, waiting, when my phone rang. It was Michael, sitting on his bed in the room next door, waving at me on the Q Video Messenger. "Amy! It's Michael!" His voice vibrated through the wall between us a half second before it echoed from the screen. He could have knocked on my door or stuck his own head out his window. But my brother with his ham radios had always loved technical forms of communication. "Are you going to sleep?" His face filled the screen.

I wondered what Tristan was doing right then. He was wandering the world, out of range, too far away to reach.

I leaned out the sill toward the flat roof of the house next door. Working upstairs over the past few weeks, I'd notice that some afternoons and evenings a neat, narrow man stood out on the graveled roof in a T-shirt and cap, tending to a wooden hutch mournful with the lowing of doves. Some nights, when I was working at my drafting table by lamplight, when I looked up at the low, liquid sounds in their throats, he tipped his cap to me. That night, the rooftop was quiet and dark. I imagined standing out there in the dark, apart from my family, above the streetlights, a joint in my hand. The man in tweed had made me restless; his letter had made my blood itch for blood, my skin for skin.

I turned back to my brother: "Soon."

My phone thrummed again, impatient with desire. My *scizr* match had messaged back. *18.* I sucked in air and blew it out again. "Good night, Michael."

"Good night, Amy!" Michael's cheerful good night filtered through the wall. A second later, the Michael on the screen smiled and waved and said good night.

Downstairs, my father had gasped and wheezed himself to bed. My mother shook a tumbler of ice in the kitchen. For the moment, they didn't need me.

It was very dark outside. The night was warm and breathing. A man was on the loose, running from love. I glanced at my phone, a silver brick. I looked back at the letter on my drafting board, tattooed with longing. Then I pressed the window sash up as high as it went, I hitched up my skirt, and I jumped.

3 Unreal City

ALGORITHMS ARE NOTHING NEW. THE WORD COMES from Al-Khwarizmi, the ninth-century Persian mathematician famous for his book *The Algebra*. Algorithms are nothing but a set of rules for making choices. In computers, algorithms process enormous calculations; they also put apparently unrelated things together.

Near Fruitvale Village, spotlights dipped the wide-feathered palms into black relief and hollow-eyed *calaveras* glittered from lampposts, grinning, twined with roses. I arrived at the address she gave, a blank-eyed warehouse, and stationed myself in at the door cut into the corrugated siding, meeting the eyes that glittered past, searching, waiting. She surprised me, catching my arm from behind: "*Ink?*" My *scizr* screen name. Her voice, smooth and low, slid like warm water down the nape of my neck. (That was a relief. Profiles never mentioned voice, and a high, childlike chirp or a sullen drone could ruin an evening.) I turned to a woman my height—petite, with short brown hair clinging to her head; clear, parchment-colored skin, very smooth. Her shoulders were small and round.

The telegraph office of my nerves had begun to jump with frantic signals, *dash dot dash*—but there was no one there to transcribe them. Just adrenaline. Just nerves.

She stared at me longer than was polite, as if asking *Are you sure?* Or maybe she wanted to say *I'm not sure.* I could tell from the clear, smooth skin stretched tight across her cheeks, the clear skin on her hands, from the way her body carved the air, she couldn't be over thirty-five. Could she see the dark vessels flushing with blood, wide against the pale skin of my throat? I angled my neck into the breeze coming through the door.

She tilted her head: "Do you want to talk? Get a coffee?"

There was the silence again, pulling between us like a ribbon of ink. I considered the cut of her jaw, the smallness of her shoulders, the wideness of her hips. The warm air that enveloped both of us smelled of old newspaper and paste and metal scorched to melting. It smelled like the heat off my skin. I hadn't leapt out the window and down the neighbor's trellis at ten o'clock at night to get a coffee. "No."

A working of the strong jaw, a movement of the lip. "Okay." She offered her hand, the same pale, tea-colored hand I'd seen in the profile image for the username *18*. The bones and ligaments folded in on themselves like a complicated puzzle I might never unlock. Pale bands crossed the backs of her knuckles—ring finger, middle finger, thumb—where sunlight had tattooed light stripes, the photonegative of rings, a semaphore of absence. They appealed to me; I didn't want to know what they meant. At the tip of her thumb bubbled a clear, smooth blister. "Call me *Blue*."

For the first time since my son boxed up his vinyl records, since I'd started tapping *scizr* once and twice a night, a small bird thrashed in my throat. I took the offered hand. It was pliant, warm. She smelled like night jasmine and something dangerous, like gasoline. Behind *Blue*—she could call herself whatever she wanted to call herself; that wasn't her name—through the warehouse door, an enormous papier-mâché man walked an enormous, papier-mâché dog. Behind the dog, a flesh-and-blood woman bowed a cello beside a flesh-and-blood man in a porkpie hat, plucking a big, brown bass, rubbery, loping notes like a bouncing ball. In time with the music, in time with the fingers of the cellist, up and down the neck of the cello, Blue's fingers slid up and down mine, investigating the skin around each knuckle, as if she might find her own missing rings on my fingers. She had a light touch, a shower of silver glitter up and down my arms and legs. I gazed into the shadowed warehouse. "Blue. Is that the color of 18?"

She blinked.

Her mouth bowed down at one corner, up at the other, a gesture I told myself I would commit to memory, along with the dark wet of her eyes. She kept drawing her fingers through mine, like someone quietly stroking a cat. And there was that voice, low and smooth as charcoal on paper, shades of black and gray: "Let's see what else you know."

She led me by the hand up a crude set of wooden steps that wound into the upper reaches of the warehouse like planks laid out across the air. The boards flexed and juddered alarmingly under her small feet, her hips broader than her shoulders, a surprising roundness on her small frame, a metronomic sway that blended pleasantly with the mild shock of terror at each jounce that the staircase might come tumbling apart.

Underneath us, the cello and bass wove their net of looping notes. She hadn't let go of my hand.

The ceiling, an enormous panel of corrugated metal, floated atmospheres above us. The lower floor, where the musicians still played, a slab of slate-colored cement vined with electrical cords, receded, cold and far below. I stopped for a moment on the rickety stair and stared at the cellist's head, shrunk to the size of a pea.

She turned. "You're not afraid?" Provoking.

Her lips parted, revealing teeth that glowed like the whites of her eyes. She could have meant the bowing pine planks tacked haphazardly together, or our distance from the floor below, or our proximity to the room to which she was leading me, or to what we would do there. "Be careful." She bent her knees and straightened up with a jounce. Under our feet, the wooden staircase bounced a little; small bright lights twinkled behind her in the darkness like ships at sea; my breath caught in my throat. I didn't say anything, but she settled my two hands on the back of her waist and I followed her up into the air.

Upstairs, twinkle lights garlanded the doorways of makeshift lofts, thin walls draped with heavy carpets to muffle noise. The floor felt solider up here, at least, and I was only half-alarmed by the sight of a piano—a black, squat baby grand, like my mother's—under the scales of a wire-frame dragon. Around us, pressing close against our skin, all the warmth of the warehouse gathered like a thick blanket, heavy with weed, cut with the sharp tang of electricity and Blue's midnight scent.

She led me into a glowing doorway, a tiny improvised jewel box just big enough for a small nightstand and a double bed. Chinese lanterns, gold and red, clustered in the high corners, the golden light heavy against the flimsy walls like ripe fruit bulging against a paper box. In the window above the bed, night had flattened itself against the pane. The room didn't have a door, just a curtain—velvet, like the curtain on the back room of Crimson Horticultural Rarities. The velvet curtain, the close, warm smell of her perfume, the light seeping like golden liquid from the lanterns—all of it brought his words whispering again into my ears: *Everything depends on you.*

I examined a bruise-colored fingerprint someone had left on the wall.

Her breath steamed my ear. "What did you say?"

In an instant, she had grabbed both of my hands and pressed her face into the bones at the top of my spine. I could feel her breasts against my shoulder blades, the tension in her abdomen against the muscles of my back. Without letting go of my hands, she wrapped her arms around my waist until they crossed like the straps of a straightjacket. It was a small room, high up in a vast, rattling warehouse. If I screamed, no one would hear me; I was very far away.

Her warm hands held my arms fast against my navel. The strong jaw moved against my neck: "Is this what you want? This?"

When you feel outside of the world half the time and swallowed up by it the other half, you need something, someone to push against. To feel the surface of your skin meet the surface of the world. Someone to push into.

I breathed against the bonds of my own arms tight around my ribs. "Yes."

When I submitted, she turned me toward her, exposing the blue veins in her neck.

Heat radiated from the pores of her throat, from her collarbones, from the smooth skin at her ribs. The skin was soft where my mouth found her navel.

"Come back." She pulled me up by my elbows. She ran her hands up under my shirt, worrying my ribs the way she'd worried the joints on my hands, as if she were trying to count and measure my bones. Maybe she was. Downstairs, the cello and bass started up another tune, a song I'd heard on the radio at night, a love song filled with sadness. She pushed her hands into my hair. "Okay?" She reached for the comb gathering the hair on top of my head. She wanted to undo me.

I hadn't grown up with consent, Heidi Chan pressing me into the back of the art closet in high school, no words to say what we were doing, unhooking each other's bras while the radio played. But I liked it. My hair spilled in black waves across our shoulders.

*Yes*es steamed from head to toe, a blazon of desire, until the corrugated metal ceiling high above us clung with drops of wet.

Then—"Ow," I wrenched my hand from the vice of her legs. "My wrist."

She stepped back, unbuckled, half-zipped, and released me from where I stood pinned against the thin white wall. We were both askew, my skirt up my thighs, my hair a wreck.

She explored my hand between hers like she had before, stroking her fingers along the joints, stopping to worry each knuckle like a rosary bead. "Did I really hurt you?"

I wanted to shake my hand out, but I let her keep it. "I fell." I turned my words sideways, didn't say anything about the men in gray suits, the man in the tweed vest.

She dropped my hand and raised my skirt farther up my legs. "Yes, you did." A dark bruise spilled across my upper thigh. She winced. "This isn't what you mean by *Ink*? You don't expect me to—"

I shook my head. "It's just a bruise. But I use that hand—" I stopped. She waited. She knew what I'd just been using my hand for. "To write."

There it was, after all this time and still so unexpected: the way sex opens a woman up. After all the coolness with which I'd lain in lovers' beds, nuzzled hidden places, said polite good nights, I was shocked to discover that this could still happen. This was the true sex, the true undoing. I stood next to the wall in my skirt and boots and bare breasts, suddenly self-conscious, and waited for her to say something, to react in some way. (*People don't read. People don't write.*) I reached to pull my skirt back down over my knees.

"Sit." She patted the bed with her free hand. Holding my hand again in one of hers, she backhanded the hair from her forehead and wiped the sweat from her lip. "Tell me everything," she said. And then, to make sure there was no question about whether this was a good idea, she unzipped herself. Pants and underwear puddled on the floor. She pulled her tank top and shirt over her head and flung them to the ground. Her skin was tawny, marked here and there for emphasis: the dark scribble between the legs, arches marking the wet surprise of her eyes. A line of real India ink tattooed the crest of her hip; it wrapped around her leg and stretched down the insides of her thighs.

Tattoos were the one place people still liked their ink, sometimes words—BELIEVE, or HOPE, written in feathers—but this was something different. The lines of her tattoo rippled across her inner thighs like a set of combers on a shallow bay. Signs and symbols, letters or numbers, danced around the edges. I touched the top of my head, unconsciously reaching for reading glasses. She grazed my fingertips gently against her thigh to feel the subtly raised skin, the faintest of embossing, black as the Lava soap my mother used to buy to scrub the ink from my fingers. Spreading across her thighs, they seemed to spill from her; they seemed to flow back inward.

Downstairs, the cello bowed a sinuous tune. The quiet intensity of the man in the tweed vest flickered in my memory like the candles that had trembled at his breath.

I pulled her down onto the bed. "Let me see." Still half-dressed, I found the line on the crest of her hip with my tongue. I pushed her thighs apart, revealing a bathymetric chart of depth, thin, annotated lines of ink radiating out from her center in shockwaves. It stunned me how much I still loved it, the hot wet of my mouth on the hot wet between the legs, the sharp charge. Heidi Chen in the art closet, underwear looping one shoe, pushing my head down, pushing me past fear, showed me what my mouth already knew, this instinct, this supple turn of the tongue, serifs and finials, descenders and bowls, not to speak but to write.

Afterward, Blue licked my lips. Her body had gone languid, loose as a cat. "You like ink. Do you have any?"

I shook my head, but I didn't protest her sitting up, reaching around my waist to unbutton my skirt, the quick tug on my underwear. Purple spider veins traced the top of my thighs; they had a tendency, these days, to ripple like the face of a lake on a windy day. If she said *You're beautiful*, I'd know she was lying.

"There." The word bloomed over our heads like a pin on a map. Marked by that imaginary star, we lay side by side, two naked strangers.

I let my eyes wander the blank white walls. "This isn't your room." I knew people her age disavowed possessions, but this was extreme. The walls didn't even reach the ceiling.

"It belongs to the Slumber Artist." She rolled onto her back and stretched an arm up over her head. "Did you know, when we sleep, a network of hidden waterways opens up inside our brains, secret canals the cerebrospinal fluid can flow through? Our dreams flush out our poisons." The rumpled white sheets smelled of lavender and sweat, of smoke and sleep and last night's sex. I turned onto my back and stared up past the golden lights into the darkness where she was staring and saw the jellyfish of thoughts and dreams pulsing through velvet waters. It was easy to imagine that coming to this bed could flush out the effluvia of disappointment and loss. "It's really quite beautiful," she said. The tin ceiling was humming faintly with the notes of the bass, big, loping, notes like someone skipping. It had been a very long time since I had felt like skipping. Her fingers trickled up my thigh, across the bruise. "Who did that? What happened?"

For eighteen years, I had been the one to ask these questions: *Are you hungry? Are you tired? What happened?* And now, for who knew how many more: *Do you need your pills? Are you thirsty? Are you hungry? What happened to you, Dad? What happened?*

I saw myself balanced on the wall at the top of the room, falling over, falling off. "It's a long story." I pressed a hand across my thigh, at the bruises still blooming on the bones of my forearms. She turned her free hand palm-up: *All the time in the world*, it said. "There was a man." Her mouth folded and unfolded. In the glow of the red and golden light falling from the Chinese lanterns I was back at Crimson Horticultural Rarities, transcribing the names of succulents. "He asked me to write him a letter."

"A letter?" Under my fingers, her flesh tightened around her ribs, holding in breath. I could tell she wanted to know what it said. That's how it is with letters. That itch. My mother had gasped when I offered to show Michael the letter. *It's intimate!* she'd protested. But wasn't this also intimacy? Didn't *I* deserve intimacy, at least for an hour or two, with another adult human being, intimacy that wasn't finding the notes my mother left for herself on the little desk in the corner of the kitchen—*Breakfast pills, Lunch pills, Dinner pills, Bed pills*—, intimacy that wasn't kissing a cheek or tucking a spoon between lips or wiping my father's pale, wrinkled bum? My son had left. My lover was gone. I didn't need anyone. I didn't want to want. It was his fault, the man in the tweed vest, for filling my head with language, for flooding my belly with the desire for desire. *Make Tal forget me* he had said, sweating out the marrow of some poor lover's forsaken heart. He owed me this.

I said, "A love letter."

"*Love?*" She closed her eyes, humming. "That sounds serious."

The silence pooled between us. *Love* was a hole with no bottom, a deep pit to fall in. A word not to say in situations like this.

"So they say." With the fingernail of my free hand, the nail bed still rimmed with black, I drew pictures across her skin: a shower of swallows, a thumbnail of moon. I wondered if she would think it was beautiful.

She exhaled to the ceiling as if emitting a stream of smoke and smoothed her palm against the side of her head. "So. You've managed something rare: to be taken seriously as an artist."

That surprised me. I started to protest. I was invisible as an artist. I had no life in the world as an artist. *That's not it*, I started to say. *That's not it at all.* But she pushed the heel of her hand against my lips. The taste of salt. The smell of smoke. "There are a lot of artists around here who are known, you know, in our little world." Her eyes glittered in the lantern light. "But your work has meaning to someone outside of you."

Yes, I said. *Yes*.

This time, we kissed slowly, kisses that blazed into summer nights—hillside blue inking into black—baked dust and dry sage and white sparklers crackling in the street. Inside the vaulting darkness, the warehouse began to swell with music and voices, the rasp of the bow back and forth against the cello strings. Outside, an October wind rattled the roof and the eaves shook as if the warehouse itself would fly apart.

Afterward, I felt like myself again, and not who I had become.

Afterward, she fingered the pale scar at the top of my pubic bone, the soft wreck of my belly. Then she turned to the little bedside table crammed against the wall—she twisted to reach it without turning her hips, her legs fused with mine. I wasn't looking for anything beyond the moments we had already shared, but I noticed that: how she didn't pull away. She drew out a fistful of pencils and some paper; a bright orange strap-on; a packet of cigarettes. She offered me a cigarette and tapped one from the packet. In the golden light, the orange strap-on throbbed.

She tucked a cigarette between her lips, then shook her head: "I always forget I can't smoke in here." That she smoked helped remind me that we didn't really know each other.

"Do those belong to the Slumber Artist?" I nodded toward the strap-on, the pencils and paper.

She glanced at the odd assortment of things. "I like to be prepared." The cigarette stuck loosely to her lower lip.

My fingers traced the bright orange dildo, the pencils. "Are you an artist?" Her papers lay open in the golden dusk of the small, white room, half-scribbled with numbers and drawings like the one spanning her hip.

The voices that had gathered in the ground floor were rising like heat under the wide, tin roof of the warehouse, expanding in the golden and shadowed air of the Slumber Artist's room. I wondered what it looked like, what color and shape it was, how it moved, the art we had committed here in her bed.

"Depends." She shrugged and tapped the curling pages. "Depends what you call art. It doesn't matter." Her drawings, if that's what they were—pencil whorls like the elevations on a topographic map—meant something, I could see that, but nothing to me. "We're performing," she pointed up, toward the music swelling the air. "This weekend at the old 16th Street Station."

Was that an invitation?

Blue tilted her head and cupped one of my breasts in her hand. If she could have weighed that breast against the breast it was at eighteen or thirty-six, she would have felt how much heavier it once was, how much more elastic, how the density had run out of it along with my faith that I could do anything. It barely clung now, flattened, to my ribs.

I gathered it up in my hand. "This was nice." What an idiotic word. *Nice.* A word made of cardboard and glue.

She pulled the unlit cigarette from her lips again and pursed them, blowing the smoke that didn't fill her mouth up toward the ceiling. "Same." I had been watching her mouth, the way the skin of her lips clung to the cigarette, the paper tugging the plump flesh until the moment of release, and now I felt the tug in my own flesh as she pulled her leg from between my thighs with a sound like peeling tape. The air felt cool against my skin. She stood, holding the unlit cigarette against her blistered finger like a pencil. Then she was pulling her underwear on. With a quick *zip* her pants sealed back up like time going backward. She bent to pick her shirt off the floor and disappeared into the black fabric and, with a wriggle so suggestively sinuous, for the flash of a second before her head reappeared, I expected the person who popped through the head hole to be the man in the tweed vest.

I shuddered.

Misunderstanding, she tossed me the blanket. "Hey, look at that!" The warmth had rushed back into her voice, something unguarded. I glanced at the wreckage of our evening—papers covered with topo maps, two yellow pencils, a white blanket puddled in my lap.

Whatever she saw there inspired her to grab one of the pencils, one of the sheets of paper. She shook the pencil across the page, etching lines that angled like wind-blown sheets of rain. Then she stared at it and licked her lips and said, "Okay. Okay." She folded up the paper and stuffed it in her pocket. Connie used to say that when I wrote, I disappeared into another world. I didn't know why it bothered her; she got lost in her work, her formulas and equations. But this was different, this leaving, Blue's an absence so complete it was an intimacy, leaving her body behind like that for me to look at.

I was still looking when she picked up the tank top she'd been wearing earlier under her shirt and pulled it over my head. "Here." Her warm breath wet the fabric as her lips pressed the spot where she thought my lips would be. By the time I pulled my head through the hole, she was gone.

The music and voices swelling from the ground floor hit me like a wall of water as I stepped through the curtain into the hall. Out in the warehouse, jewel-colored gels cast purple, red, and orange light up from below. I felt like an eel buried in the depths of an ocean strobed with colorful fish. I flushed, remembering what she and I had done in the bed of the Slumber Artist.

I hadn't learned her real name. I hadn't told her mine.

The rickety stairs suspended above the distant warehouse floor felt more precarious without someone to hold onto. Bodies pressed past me, red plastic cups in hand, forcing me to the edge of the wooden steps where they dropped into thin air. I tiptoed down them as quickly as I could, not looking over the side.

Down on the first floor the combustible smells of alcohol and gasoline mixed with the fermented sweetsour of sangria, warm scents vying to survive the warm October winds gusting through the open warehouse door.

Out of habit, reflex, inability to be with others, I pulled out my phone and checked my notifications, my *scizr*, my Q feed. At the center of my feed, Q nudged three faces into view: dark eyes peeking out over the mask of a dark beard, every one. Above them the label: *People you may know.*

I clicked *X* so fast the line-up disappeared before I realized I should have written down their names.

4 *The Huntress*

IT IS BETTER TO HUNT THAN BE HUNTED. OR AT least, so I imagined the lusty fourteenth-century pilgrim and Christian mystic Margery Kempe opining as I headed out early the next morning to the Hawk & Pony, where riders bound for Q gripped paper cups, cradled pastries in white paper packages. As I hung back near my usual, quiet table in the gloom, I watched them swivel their hips away from the counter and looked for the man who had moved his hips just so in the back room of Crimson Horticultural Rarities.

Outside, the Q shuttle wheezed to the curb.

During Connie's post-doc, she presented a paper at a conference in Paris. After three wet fall days circling the *arrondissements*, we packed *pain au chocolat* onto the TGV to Nice, where we had a bed for five nights and no obligations. After the gloom of Paris, the brightness of the Mediterranean made us giddy. In Saint Paul de Vence, Connie pulled me into a cottage garden. Behind a row of bitter orange trees, she pressed my back against an old stone wall while chickens high-stepped past with darting glances. Public sex, trespassing, getting lost—we would never have done such things at home. But we weren't at home. We were outside of our country, our continent, our lives.

At the curb, I watched slender, bearded men float, trip, and bound up the steps onto the bus. One narrow,

46

bearded face after another. My boot hit the top step; my hand gripped the rail. Nobody asked who I was, what I was doing. No one stopped me. If Tristan hadn't left, I wouldn't have done it. If Tristan were still home, I would have played it safe.

It was a quick step between messenger bags and I was at the top of the aisle, staring down rows of motorcoach seats too high to see over, and another few quick steps back to peer between the rows. I had jumped out the window for sex. I would have pulled a stranger by the hand behind a garden wall, I would have jumped on a bus to anywhere without thinking about it twice. The trees on the sidewalk outside began to move as the bus lurched onto Telegraph Avenue.

It was a clear, bright, October morning, the Mission spattered with protest signs, bent posterboard, and broken sticks, the littered emptiness of streets after the party's over. I pressed my nose to the cool window, disappointed not to see the scrim of activists from the evening news swarming the Q bus, the protest dancers flexing and stretching in their parti-colored Spandex suits, the enormous banners, hand-painted and bright: *Fuck off, Q! Evicted!* I had felt a surge of joy at their boldness.

And yet, as I trundled toward Q with a busload of tech bros, I found that I wanted to number myself among them: the purposeful, the well-paid, the appreciated. Couldn't I claim it was subversive that I wanted to ply my trade at one of the world's richest tech companies, a resident artist in the perhaps ironic Department of Arts & Letters? It was obvious enough that one day—when the culture at large decided it wasn't trendy anymore to be artisanal or lettered—the department would vanish without a ripple. But wouldn't it be grand, at least for a moment, to be a part of it all?

I was thinking about that—being a part of it all—as the bus rolled into the Q compound and the khaki-covered riders rolled off like an army of pale, thin Oompa Loompas disappearing behind the factory gates. The air even swirled with the smell of melted chocolate—chocolate and coffee. The warm, rich smells, the sense that I could be a part of it all, the letter glinting with gold leaf in my shoulder bag like a golden ticket, sent me marching after them with more confidence than was rightfully mine, past the bistro cafés, the dry cleaners, and the barbershops that lined the Q quadrangle like the square of a small village, into the shining glass and chrome entry tower, where I shuffled myself between them and queued to get in.

I had the vague sense, as I glanced at the security kiosk ahead, that I didn't belong here. But I moved forward, sandwiched between the people ahead of me and the people massing at my back, with an even stronger sense that I was crowding the turnstile to some grand exhibition of this new era of human life, like a visitor to the World's Fair with its moving pictures and brightly strung electric bulbs, courtesy of Mr. Edison.

The people who had designed this place seemed to imagine it that way, too. Shuffling forward, I turned my eyes to the vast hall beyond the turnstile and spotted the pale architecture of a mammoth, the thick, yellowed bones floating beneath the glass ceiling like the big Blue Whale hanging at the Museum of Natural History. For a second, I expected to see Michael there at the entrance in his jacket and tie, smiling and waving, Tristan sitting in the humid biosphere, staring up at the butterflies, his face luminous among the slick, green leaves.

My phone chimed: I checked to make sure it wasn't a message from my mother or my son. But it was just another ad for flowers for Connie's birthday I clicked into the trash.

I was almost at the guard booth.

When the man ahead of me stepped forward, the turnstile admitted him with green light and a chime.

Beyond the turnstile, I spotted a too-snug gray sports coat

drawn tight across a broad back. My body instinctively reversed—pressing me into the messenger bag across the chest behind me, which was pressing forward to get in. Of course: the man in the tweed vest worked at Q. They would be looking for him here. *I* was. I clutched my bag tighter under my arm, his letter inside of it. I struggled to move backward, but there were dozens of people behind me in the narrow entry gate; it was no use, we were cattle in a chute.

The man behind me coughed. I could actually feel the heat of his forearms against my back, the restraint required not to push me. Counting on his impatience, I twisted toward him, smiling. "I forgot my badge. Swipe me in?" Why shouldn't he? I thought of myself as harmless. I allowed myself to forget for a minute that we are a nation of armed lunatics intent on blasting each other to bits.

The man pointed to a spot near the scanning pad, a shiny coin of glass that pulsed with blue light. An icon beneath it illustrated the whorls of a thumb. *Biometrics.*

Well, *fuck* me.

The man in the too-tight gray suit had not turned, but, if there were a commotion, he would; the muscles of his back hunched visibly under the fabric, like the muscles of a snake squeezing beneath the skin. I could see the silver moonlight seeping from the letter in my bag, the swallows flying off, twittering alarm. I stretched out my thumb, set it lightly on the glass, and braced myself for the light to flash red, the alarm to howl.

The man behind me jostled closer.

I looked up. The kiosk had chimed. The light had turned green. The sound of the hall came rushing into my senses, which seemed to have turned off for an instant, like a moment between sleep and waking. I hurried through.

"Miss—"

I pretended not to hear the man in the guard booth calling out. "Miss!"

It was the morning rush. Bodies kept chiming through the portal; bodies flowed behind and beside and around me, and, happy for once to be caught in the flow of so many people, I hurried past the man in the gray suit and under the flat glass panes of the roof and the curved yellow bones of a long-dead animal, and felt more pleased with myself than I should: The guard hadn't called me *Ma'am!*

I was there to find the man in the tweed vest. But I had to see the art studio. Something had unknotted in me the night before in the Slumber Artist's bed. *Your art has meaning*, my lover had said.

I had no idea where I was going or what I was looking for, exactly, but I thought I would know what it was once I found it, so I just kept walking, across high, glassed-in bridges between buildings named for the colors of the rainbow—Yellow and Orange and Green—until I came to an entry marked *Indigo* in purple-blue neon light. The air here was different, dark and cool. I smelled the faint intoxication of mineral spirits and ink—familiar smells, art studio smells.

The crack and clatter of pool balls rattled through in the empty breezeway, where someone had tacked a poster to the wall: a screen print, a brand-new one, in the style of a '60s concert handbill. Capitals fat and warped as clouds of weed smoke announced the Q *All Hallows' Ball*, which would take place on campus on Friday evening, October 31. *Performance, magic, midnight spirits.* The text was framed inside a giant smoke-ring of a *Q*. I drew my fingers across the thick scrim of the ink and thought seriously about swiping it.

Instead, I moved through the open doorway into a rec room with a pool table, the colored balls scattered motionless across the felt. In an adjoining room, a tall figure slouched on a stool, a black pool cue pointing up at his knee, his torso long and lean in a pale pink polo that made his smooth, brown arms look like summer.

He was wearing madras shorts, his legs, too, long and brown, his whole persona altogether nothing like the pale, bearded tech bros I had seen in the halls in their khakis and fleece vests. Pink chalk dusted the fingers of his right hand. I watched as he lifted his index finger and thumb to his mouth and neatly licked them clean.

Pregnant women eat chalk. They crave it. Connie was lying in bed in a white tank top and white underwear I used to tease her were *grannypants*, reading from a pregnancy book, when she told me that. Connie didn't like the idea of craving, as a rule, and this idea of craving something that could make you sick—chalk or mud or laundry soap—put her distaste at odds with her chemist's brain, which told her that the body's desire for a molecule that gave no pleasure or sustenance must be driven by some kind of necessity, if only we could figure it out.

"Hey," the long, lean figure drawled, watching me watch him, "Feeling lucky?"

"Sorry?" Like the licking of chalk from his fingers, his question surprised me, the intimation of sex from this man with his catlike languor.

"If you think about it," he spoke through a hand half-covering his mouth, "all we really want is the freeze-dried marshmallows. But if the box came with nothing but marshmallows in it, it would be too shameful to buy." The thing I heard in his voice was not seduction, I realized, but loneliness. I looked down at the mug he was holding, printed with the words *I can has cheeseburger*. It was full of Lucky Charms.

I could hear my mother, chastising me when I pulled on Doc Martens: "Amy! You're a middle-aged lady!" As alien to me as if she'd exclaimed: *You're the Bishop of York!* "Can I have some?" I asked my new friend, who reached across the bar for another mug and nestled it under one of the clear plastic columns full of rainbow-colored cereals striping the wall. I dropped my bag on the floor and climbed onto the stool beside him.

"Do you know an engineer here with a dark beard?" I asked him.

"Do I know an engineer here *without* a dark beard?" He pushed the dark frames of his glasses against his cleanly shaven face, his voice sanded flat with boredom, and handed me the mug. "Jae," he held out his soft, long-fingered hand. His ID badge read *Jae Kim, Cueist*. He rocked the pool cue beside him with the tip of a finger. His eyes scanned my chest, slowing at the place where my Q ID badge should have been.

I smiled and tried, in my black skirt and boots, my black turtleneck, to look harmless. It was obvious to both of us I didn't belong there. "Amy," I held out my hand and waited until he took it. A breeze coming from a nearby doorway carried in the acetylene vapors of solvents and glue. And, then, before he could ask me what I was doing there, I set down my mug. "I'm just headed to the art studio."

His eyebrows lifted behind his glasses, but all he said was: "Enjoy."

The crack and rattle of pool balls followed me down the stairwell; the smell of pulp and paste and printers' ink—the smell of the high school art supply closet in which I used to make out with volleyball team captain Heidi Chan—old, familiar spirits, rose up to greet me.

Down at the bottom of the polished-cement stairs, the studio was an echo of Eichler. Mid-century cement-and-glass, with a sliding glass door onto a cement patio; outside, a neat square of blue loomed over a blue-green patch of grass, like a 1975 backyard, and as lonely. A neon sign poked like a fingertip above the rooflines of the campus, a glowing pink intensity that hummed over the big Quad like a *(No) Vacancy* sign outside a cheap motel, burning one word against the October sky: *LOCKDOWN*.

I had traveled with Connie to her childhood home only once, to help her pack it up when she was much too young to have done such things. Her mother had died—uterine cancer at age fifty-two. Her father, an alcoholic, might have been alive or dead. We flew back on a Southwest flight to Tucson in the fading pink light of dusk. The house was a post-war, mid-century modern in a sub-division of similar mid-century homes whose uniformity promised community and family and dreams that for the Austins had stopped coming true. Connie pulled the heavy brass key from her wallet, where it had worn a blackened outline against the grain.

In the den, her father's college tennis racket still clung to the wall alongside a dark rectangle from which a photo or certificate attesting to his existence had been removed. A wide glass slider led to the cement-and-grass patio on which Connie had once drawn foursquare grids in colored chalks. We stood in that den, in front of that glass slider, breathing in the must of a house that had not been opened in over a year—her mother had traveled to Houston for treatment—looking out at the dried, brown scrub grass and a string of colored lights that still webbed the space between two palms. *This is the old door* Connie pressed her finger against the cool pane of scratched glass, stuck all over with decals of faded dragonflies. *This is the new one*, she tilted her head toward a double pane of glass tinted slightly blue. Then she explained that this was the pane of glass that had needed to be replaced after her brother James had gone through the old one.

It was late one evening during one of their parents' legendary cocktail parties, James still laughing at some joke a friend of their mother's had told, her cocktail glass in her hand. He was already moving forward before he'd turned his head toward the door, doing a little dance step, when he went right through it. Connie pirouetted gravely. *It doesn't shatter the way you think it would.* Connie was taking an advanced class in physics the semester her mother died, studying energy and waves and the laws of motion. *Bits and showers and sparkles.* James lay on the floor in disbelief, a shard of brightness wedged in his neck. When she got to this part of the story, Connie blanched and had to squat with her head between her knees, her hand against the cool glass, though she had been too young to stay up, and was asleep during the party while the *bossa nova* played on.

Then she clenched her fists. "She left me." Connie, who always saw the best in anyone, who forgave everyone every-thing, who believed people were fundamentally good at heart, sounded sharper than that piece of glass. I was shocked. Connie and I hadn't been together long then, but this violent emotion wasn't something I'd known her to be capable of, and it scared me. I reminded myself: Her mother had died. Anger was one of the phases. "Not now," she sat up abruptly and pressed her hot hand against the pane. "When my brother died. And I will never forgive her for that."

Connie, Connie. Every October, Connie. Usually, I just deleted the ads. What was it about the letter in my bag that suddenly made her so hard to forget.

I stared out the sliding glass doors onto the blind cement patio, then back up at the pink neon sign crackling *Lockdown*. It was cool in the studio, subterranean and old and familiar. Outside, the hot Diablo wind yellowed the grass.

I turned away from it to face the room. On a poster tacked to the wall, a pair of Q patriots, male and female, drawn in the stylized blockiness of a bygone era, gazed into a vast Milky Way whose brightest stars spelled out in subtle constellation: *Q*. Underneath it, a honeycomb of cubbies held more posters. *Loose Lips Sink Ships!* and *We Want You!* Patriotism and agitprop.

There were big white tables scored with Xacto lines, and bottles of printer ink, and the menacing curved blade of a paper cutter sitting on a shelf. I had been in art studios like this before.

There was nothing particularly special about it, after all, just a room like other rooms I had been in, no more, no less.

That's what I told myself.

Upstairs, in the Cereal Bar, music seeped from the pores in the concrete, the weird stretchy cries of the Mellotron in "Strawberry Fields Forever." Jae Kim, *Cueist*, leaned against the pool table in his creamy pink top and shorts. "You've tried the Dictionary?" He pointed over his shoulder, where an enormous LCD screen clung to the wall. "For your engineer?"

He pointed to my bag, slouched under the bar, a piece of oat cereal crushed to powder beside it. "Don't forget your things."

Out in the passage, the Dictionary hung from the wall like the Arrivals and Departures monitor in a vast airport. The huge, touch-screen monitor offered a thousand ways to search and browse: alphabetically by first name or last; by specialty; by department. I didn't know any of those things about the man in the tweed vest. I poked and swiped at the screen, scrolling through department listings—there were so many types of engineers: database, software, full stack—squinting at headshots, zooming them larger, pinching them smaller. I was never going to find the man I was looking for this way. We hadn't finished his letter: I didn't even know his first name.

In the corner of the screen, a *Q* spiked with arrowheads pointed to all four cardinal points, a compass rose. Touching it summoned a map of the campus. There were the color-coded buildings: *Yellow, Orange, Red*. The buildings and the lines between them seemed to shimmer with life. Pinching and swooping, I zoomed in closer. Under my thumb, little red, green, and blue dots circulated through paths and buildings like blood cells. I touched one: a face, a phone number and a department hovered into view. You could find anyone here, walking around the campus in real time, if only you knew who you were looking for.

I zipped my fingers across the map to the cereal bar, located the pool table and, sure enough, right next to it, a pink dot blossomed with the words *Jae Kim, Cueist.* I felt like a god, peering through a microscope at the creatures in my ken.

But what about me? I zoomed in on the spot where I stood and nothing was there. Of course. I wasn't carrying a badge.

I should have felt canny, like an invisible person. But at the moment when the map of the hallway where I was standing came into view with no one in it, my stomach rose up in my throat with that strange, dizzy sensation that maybe I really *wasn't* there. It wouldn't have been the first time since Tristan left that I'd felt this way. Unreal. A ghost.

Slowly, a white circle hove into view on the screen before me: inside the white circle, a pale face with dark hair knotted at the top of the head. I studied the features in that face: the teeth my parents had paid to straighten, the two cat's-eye moles above the eyebrows that made me know the person I saw in the mirror when I brushed my teeth was me. After a long moment of hesitation, the slot began to quiver, a blinking emptiness like the expression of a computer thinking. And then my name appeared. *Amy Black.*

I'd always loved my last name, grateful that the word (not a color, but a tone) almost always matched the color in which it was printed. People experience terrible dislocations of perception when forced to read color words printed in the wrong color—Orange, for example, written in green ink. They can read the word orange. But ask them what color it's written in, and there you have the problem. A hiccup. A pause. The instinctual brain at war with the decoding brain. But not for me. On paper, I am identical with myself.

I pressed my finger against the words. I wanted to see if they might come off on my thumb. I wanted to lick them. My bubble wobbled. How had I materialized inside of this machine?

I studied the photo more closely. At the neckline on my photo, a strip of blue showed that *Amy Black* wore the same peacock blue shirt I happened to be wearing under my black sweater, which she was wearing, too. The same strand of hair I could feel drawn across my forehead spun across her forehead, too. I inspected the monitor more closely. I couldn't see a camera anywhere. But the Dictionary must see me. Anybody there could see me. At least as long as I was parked in front of it, anyone looking at the Dictionary could see me. Well, fuck. Zooming out, I located the largest concentration of engineers on Q's campus and hurried away.

On the third floor of the Yellow building where the dictionary had suggested engineers would be, rows of human-sized orange, pink, and turquoise cylinders filled a wide, shaded alcove like a grove of space ships or MRI machines or sarcophagi. They would have been frightening, if not for the candy-coating colors. Though what seemed like all the blue dots in the Dictionary swarmed at this spot, I didn't see or hear a soul.

I stepped toward one of the pods, a pink one, its surface lightly pebbled. Although these were some kind of technological invention, they had obviously been designed—the textured surface, the gracefully contoured edges. And though I expected a great whiff of plastic, the cylinder smelled instead refreshingly of grapefruit. Hesitant, thinking of aliens, I balled my hand into a fist and knocked.

A muffled voice roared back: "Fuck off!"

I pictured a body locked in a magician's trunk. I knocked again, more briskly. "Hello!"

This time there was no mistaking the reply. "Fuck! What the fucking fuck!" The top half slid back just wide enough for a pale finger to poke out. It pointed to a large glass lightbulb hanging from a rope above it: "Napping!" Then the finger withdrew and the cylinder snapped shut.

I looked up at the bulb and back at the sealed space pod, once again shut tight. Then I cast my eyes out across the entire sea of pods and noticed for the first time that bulbs hung over all of the pods in the grove. The orange glow of the single bulb hanging over the pink pod reminded me of the light suspended over the ark in my childhood synagogue, the mysterious, flickering light that never went out. I'd never understood the light, or the ark it hung over, or what was inside. I didn't know what was happening here, but was it possible that someone thought that it was something holy?

A small, muscular figure brushed past me, beelined to one of the unlit sarcophagi, climbed into it, and slid the hatch shut. After a moment, the lightbulb suspended above it flicked on.

During one of the late, long afternoons we spent in slatted shadows in front of the television, Connie and I watched a movie in which giant cocoons marinating at the bottom of a swimming pool turned old people young again. Hurrying through the pod forest for a cocoon over which the light had yet to shine, I found a pale turquoise tube and climbed inside.

I slid the hatch shut. It was surprisingly quiet in the heart of the pod, surprisingly dark. Sunk into silky microfiber cushions, I could see nothing, hear nothing. I felt, myself, a nothing.

In the collection of the British Library sits the oldest intact book in European history, a copy of the Gospel of John. Thirteen hundred years old and counting, it survived the first five hundred of them buried in the tomb of Saint Cuthbert, famed healer and converter of the pagan Anglo-Saxons. Five centuries in darkness at the head of a saint. Though it was entirely dark inside my sarcophagi-shaped-space-capsule, I closed my eyes. But in my mind's eye I kept seeing the other pods stretched out around me, like ranks of headstones at the battlefield in Normandy, and this sense that others were around me while I was still completely alone, a sepulchral and a too-familiar feeling, left me unsettled.

As a wave of heat washed through the skin on my chest, I started to feel like I would suffocate. Scrabbling for the edge of the door, I slid the hatch half-open and it stuck. It was heavy and harder to manipulate from the inside, a little sticky on the tracks.

I banged against the door. "Help!" I squealed, knowing that the microfiber cushioning would disappear my voice.

But the hatch rushed open with a shriek.

"Claustrophobic?" A strong, thin hand reached into my pod, pulling me half-out. My wrist winced, still creaky from the violence and the sex the night before, as my head emerged from the hole.

The hand shoved my hatch forward more firmly on its tracks. From my prone position, I saw shiny loafers, khaki, then a full, luxurious ruff of hair, a thin woman of average height, long of leg, planted firmly on the ground. "Coming?"

I considered the confident stance of the person standing in front of me, the boldness with which they'd opened my pod. It seemed perhaps the jig was up. A part of me wanted to slip back into the tube and shut the hatch. "Do I have a choice?"

Her laughter slapped the curves of the colorful nap pods like bright waves lapping the shore, scattering pink and orange and aquamarine lights around the room, scattering brightness. I swung myself to sitting, straightened my skirt, and took a better look at the thin person planted on long, thin legs in front of me, hands on hips, one of those people who would meet you at the top of the boulder, or down at the bottom of the cave, and they'd beat you to it, a person who was up for anything. She thrust out her hand. "Sandy Jensen. Evangelist."

Sandy Jensen, whose hair was, aptly, a sandy shade of blond— thick, a little messy, longer than her shoulders—and whose voice, too, rasped with the mild roughness of waves against sand, propped her hands back against her hips. Her hands were large and thin-fingered and bare, her hip bones thin and sharp.

I could feel the force of her curiosity between us like a magnetic field, waiting for me to respond. Staring at a stranger in the halls of Q and not looking at their badge must have felt to Sandy Jensen like having her cell phone buzz in her pocket and not checking for messages, a practically epic test of will. I held her gaze, daring her to break it. Were her cheeks flushing against the pale, downy hair? Or was it the reflection of light off a nearby tangerine pod? I felt guilty. It wasn't her fault I wasn't supposed to be here.

I stood up: "Amy. Black." It hadn't even occurred to me to lie. At least my name was common enough to spawn a few dozen doubles. Sandy Jensen crossed her arms, shifted her hips, nodded. She was waiting for me to give my title. I fumbled, trying to come up with a title that matched Q's twee vocabulary—*Cueist*, *Evangelist*. Thinking about the residency I'd wanted so badly for so long, I coughed: "Art-ist."

Sandy Jensen propped her hands on her hips, elbows out, angles everywhere. "You're awfully early for the ball."

Ball? I smiled and turned to fish my bag out of the pod. It was time to make my escape. "Sorry—I'm in a bit of a rush—"

"Me, too." Sandy fell into step beside me. "Come on."

The quickness of my step as I hurried to keep pace with her storkish stride matched the quickening in my veins at the certainty that I was being marched back to someone's office, marched to security, marched straight off campus, and told never to return. Or worse.

We entered a large atrium in which two men were playing a game of chess with pieces as tall as a five-year-old atop a holographic chess board projected onto the floor. Sandy confided: "Once, very late at night, I saw a group of women in here using it as a Ouija Board. You should have seen the way they jumped when I came in! I'd been eating a powdered sugar doughnut." She laughed again, that scattering of colored petals.

Walking through the halls that morning, I hadn't so much as seen two women together. I wondered where these witches had come from, and whether they were an incarnation of the mysterious Department of Arts & Letters. I imagined the atrium floor awash with moonlight, a coven of women circled around a huge plastic pointer picking out letters until they spelled out a message from the dead. "What message did they receive? H-I-R-E M-O-R-E W-O-M-E-N?"

Whatever I had to lose, I'd probably already lost it, so what was a little cheek?

Another gale of laughter burst from Sandy Jensen's thin frame, a bold note from a reed. "You're funny." But her face pinked up in a way that made me wonder what it was like for her to be a woman there. Light from the open ceiling was twinkling off her hair and her badge and her shoes, and now it winked off her glasses, hiding her eyes. Though I didn't know her at all, I felt bad for her. I wanted to hear her laugh again.

I nodded toward the chess board: "I'm one of the witches. Don't you recognize me?"

I'd asked Connie once if she thought I was a flirt. She didn't answer me out loud, but picked up a pen and scribbled in the margin of the book she was reading: *It's much more serious, darling. You're a romantic.*

Sandy Jensen's fingertips brushed my arm. "I bet you are."

What if I was flirting? We were strangers; it was a lubricant. With any luck, she wouldn't ask me any more questions and maybe I could still get away without a fuss. At the end of the atrium, a wide hallway beckoned, and a set of doors, and whichever direction Sandy Jensen took, I planned to take the other. In the meantime, I would flirt.

I dropped my voice and Sandy leaned a little closer, as if she were prepared to cradle any word I uttered in the delicate cup of her ear. "I'm the spell keeper. I write them all down in teeny, tiny letters and use the letters to make pictures, so no one will notice them, even when they're out in plain sight." One day, after hours studying the beautiful illuminations in Hildegard of Bingen's book of visions, I had been stricken with a vague sense of disloyalty about being moved by Christian religious art when I wasn't a Christian. That day I'd Googled *Jewish writing* and discovered this: a ninth-century Jonah walking a gangplank into the mouth of a fish—man, boat, and fish all strung from lines of tiny letters. *Micrography*, the entry said, *the only original Jewish art form.* The art of scribes.

I was just flirting. But I hadn't learned how to flirt without substance. I felt heat rush to my hairline.

Sandy stopped walking. She looked me up and down, black turtleneck to black skirt and boots. I took the opportunity to look her up and down as well: a thin person, she was taller than I was—average-height taller, but her long, thin legs made her look longer, like a long-legged bird. She wore glasses, clear glass circles floating on a pleasant, pale flatness, the white half-moon of a smile, reflections in a pond. "Micrography? Is that what you do?"

We had reached the far side of the atrium; we stood submerged in the thick, golden light that gathered there like water at the deep end of a pool. Sandy spent a long minute studying my face, as if the two moles over my eyes, the feathered lines of my eyelashes, the dark curls of my hair had all been penned in micrographic letters, too. "Don't look so surprised, Little Witch. It's my job to know everything." She tugged the badge on her lanyard. "Are you coming?"

Over our heads, a brash *Awooga!* shuddered through the atrium, the klaxon of a submarine, the warning of a dive. Above and beside us, monitors flashed ALL HANDS! I winced, the word *terrorist* still fresh in my mind. Double doors behind Sandy burst apart, releasing an entire phalanx of humans. They pushed past and through and between me and Sandy Jensen, streaming and pressing through the hall, whirlpooling together and apart, heads and legs and arms, a blurring of bodies.

I hated crowds, avoided crowds, went out of my way to stay out of crowds.

"Hey! Jensen!" a chorus of voices called out over the heads between us. People swirled around us, checking phones, talking loud and fast, calling out.

For a moment, she was distracted. This was the moment to escape.

She knew *micrography*. My fingers plucked the sleeve of Sandy Jensen's sweater. "I'm coming."

Sandy Jensen swiped me into a room as smooth and curved as the inside of an egg. As soon as we entered, the door disappeared behind us, white on white, sealing us in. I was playing a dangerous game. I'd read once that Q had sued a trespasser for theft of intellectual property—just someone who'd walked through the Quad. It wouldn't matter that I hadn't stolen anything, I was being ushered in to some inner sanctum.

The room filled with sound: a siren-like drone rising slowly under a volley of twangy notes like fingers plucking a very loose string. I should have known better than to ask questions, to learn anything that could be considered *proprietary*. But I had never been good at keeping my thoughts to myself. As the keening rose higher and higher, I joked, "Someone left the kettle on?" I was trying to keep it light, but I was starting to sweat. The rubbery tangs ponged faster and faster; the single note arrowed higher. I had no right to be here.

Sandy Jensen tilted her head, listening to the shrill report, the rising chaos. When it cut to silence, she pumped her fist: "Yes!" She pointed to a placard mounted on the wall: *The sonification of climate change from the Middle Ages through the year 2016.*

I clutched my bag tighter under my arm. "*Sonification?*" The white walls curved over us like the apse of a cathedral, clean as the inside of a hollowed skull. No wonder I hadn't been invited to become a Resident Artist: paper and pens versus *sonification?* I wasn't technological or fancy. The thing that I loved was simple and old.

Sandy thumbed a remote control the size of a credit card. "Turning data into sound. In this case, average world temperature and CO_2 levels, annual. People have a hard time with numbers, but this really brings it home, doesn't it?" The siren flared again.

It was as amazing as it was horrifying. This is what people did here?

Sandy Jensen grinned. She pushed a button and the siren cut out, replaced by the plink of small shells through a rain stick, the notes of a ukulele, infrequent at first, then swelling into song. "And *that*—" Her hands lifted to the ceiling, "is the sound of people around the world connecting with each other on Q, from 2004 until the present. Super cool, no?" A choir rose over the sound of strings. "A whole world of organic connections!"

I closed my eyes and listened and thought about my mother, my father, Michael, and me. I wondered where Tristan was at that moment. He didn't have a Q account. He and his friends denounced Q as *social media for Old People*. "I see why they call you the Evangelist."

I wanted to believe in it, Sandy Jensen's world of connections. After all, it was the man in the tweed vest, and then Blue, and even Sandy Jensen, who together had somehow brought me here. I thought of Connie, then, the sadness of a string plucked once a year, but I let it go, let the orchestra of other strings swell and lift me up. I let myself believe that I belonged.

Sandy Jensen pointed to a livestream of the entry hall at Q. I recognized the mammoth hanging from the ceiling. "An installation from one of our recent resident artists uses facial recognition, Q's database, and satellite mapping to plot spidergrams of everyone who walks through the entry hall." She sounded like a docent at the Museum of Incomprehensible Notions. I squinted at the screen more closely, noticing a cat's cradle of red lines stretching out in all directions. "I guess it does seem a little ass-kissing. But you won't have to worry about that." Worry? Sandy Jensen tipped her head back and laughter poured from her throat, as if this were all some fantastic lark. She almost made me feel as if I were in on it, too.

But as I followed her through another door, the hard knobs sliding up and down Sandy Jensen's spine counted out the reasons I had not and would never get a residency here, where art meant *sonification* and *spidergram*. Sandy Jensen tossed a glance over her shoulder. "Hurry up, Amy Black. We're just getting to the secret spells."

I was just shy of ten years old when my father took me to J. Paul Getty's *Villa dei Papiri* on the Malibu Coast, the oil magnate's lavish recreation of an ancient Italian villa that once stood in the shadow of Mount Vesuvius when the mountain erupted. Its name means "Villa of the Scrolls." My mother had just told me she was pregnant and then suddenly my father was packing me off to Los Angeles. There were three mornings of brown and orange carpet and IHOP pancakes, and three long afternoons reading *Watership Down* at the edge of a too-small pool. Then, on the afternoon of the fourth and final day of the West Coast Tool & Die Manufacturers' Association meeting, my father told me to put my book away. I could tell from the way he kept saying *Chop chop!* that he was pleased with himself, and I began to dread that we were going to Disneyland. I'd heard about the log ride that made you wet if you sat in the front. "We have to get there at two!" he said, *Chop chop!*

My mother wasn't with us, but her hand was at work.

Since I was seven years old, I had been in love with the word *antiquities*. Marking off intervals between each short *i*, the crisp *t*s sounded to me like Time itself, ticking away. But nothing could have prepared me for the Getty Villa. It wasn't the smooth, Doric columns and fat, fruited pomegranates, the beautiful stone bodies and marble faces with the noses smashed clean off—though these were wonderful. I loved the idea of Etna's poison gas paralyzing everyone and everything in place, of the falling ash petrifying all of Pompeii. I loved the way the eruption held it all still, right there, *before* and *after*. Here was the beautiful villa with its long blue pools; here were the statues that had fallen when the ash showered down; here was a young girl of Herculaneum, cinching her tunic, turning to stone.

Years later, when I brought Tristan there, I loved it more. The beautiful remains of everything broken.

Sandy Jensen led me into a chamber filled with cooled air and golden light. A central atrium lit the room with sunlight and sky, blue and gold echoed in domes whose interiors had been variously gilded or painted azure. Patterned marble in the Byzantine style mazed the floor beneath the white marble columns that ringed the room, interspersed with hanging pots of Spanish moss and a sculptured tree leafed in bronze. A clockwork bird perched among the leaves chirped a tinny, ancient tune. The air smelled heavily and sweetly and darkly of books, the thick, animal smells of leather and parchment, the dusky vegetable smells of paper and glue. Familiar, comfortable, library smells. It surprised me, that there were books here, a small library of leather-bound volumes, dozens of tied scrolls, even more manuscript boxes lazing against each other on a shelf along the wall. But it surprised me less that a library at Q would look like Villa dei Papiri. Hack, for all his jeans and hoodies, clearly fancied himself an emperor.

Sandy disappeared through a doorway while I considered spines embossed in different languages, curved scrolls, flat boxes of the kind in which you could find a large, framed wedding portrait. I don't know why I thought of wedding portraits. This was something Connie and I hadn't done. Impetuous, maybe, or careless, for people who were trying to have children.

Sandy reappeared, flourishing a postcard-sized sheet of thick white paper mounted on black matte. "Look." She set it down and we bent over it together. "It's Hack."

Q was the brainchild of thirty-six-year-old M. David Hacker. He went by David, and by the time he had dropped out of Princeton, M. David Hacker had gone from David Hacker to *Hack*. As if, the more success and money he had, the less name he needed. The image on the desk was a hedcut of Hack: a three-quarters photo-realist image in the stipple engraving that was the signature portrait style of the *Wall Street Journal* and dollar bills. The unprinted whites of his eyes stared into the future. It wasn't the subject I would have chosen, but the print was neatly executed. Sandy Jensen's hair brushed my shoulder. "So?" She turned into the side of my face.

I bent closer to the surface of the page, careful not to touch it. Under the circumstances, I wasn't sure I should break it to Sandy Jensen that tiny dots and dashes were not micrography. On the other hand, I wouldn't have been who I was if I didn't care about such things. I shook my head, just barely.

Nothing seemed to phase Sandy Jensen. "You can't see it?" I didn't realize that she was toying with me. A large magnifying glass perched like a cricket over the edge of the table. Sandy pulled the glass down until it was directly over the paper. "Look now." Inside the dots and dashes, the blurry whorls of finger-prints. I bit my lip.

Laughter spilled from Sandy Jensen like a fistful of coins. "Me neither." Then she scooped the page up with the tips of her fingers and carried it to a glassed-in cell set into the wall. There was a rack in front of the cell, like the rack that holds LPs in a Select-o-Matic jukebox, and Sandy slipped the illustration into a slot on the rack. "We got lucky. The scanner's not busy. Usually, it takes at least an hour to get into the scanner, even if you sneak something to the front of the queue."

"Do you do this all the time?" Slipping books into a scanning queue seemed more like the work of an archivist than an Evangelist, but Sandy had already surprised me with the library.

"Me?" Sandy Jensen laughed again as if I'd said the funniest thing in the world. We both watched as a metal arm slid out of the wall and plucked the picture from the rack.

On the other side of the glass, in a white cell bathed in bright, flat, white light, the robotic arm set the card delicately on a platen, the hulking machine pincer gingerly caressing the piece left and right until it aligned perfectly with the center. It was like watching a robot cradle a butterfly. A complex apparatus hung suspended above the book, a network of lenses and boxes positioned at various angles over the surface of the page. Sandy handed me a headset: "Put these on."

I flinched when the glassed room grew infinitesimally brighter. But nothing exploded. Instead, a screen on the back wall of the glass cell filled, pixel by pixel, with the high-res. image of the page in crisp, clear detail, down to the millimeters' changes in thickness where the stylus had pressed the rag. The machine was scanning it, like a big, digital Xerox machine. After a moment, the image on the screen refreshed, this time with annotations. "M. David Hacker," a box beside the image read. A photo of Hack appeared inside it, along with a long biographical entry. As a human being who struggled to recognize real people in the flesh, I was impressed. I wondered if they had an app like that you could put on your phone. I had just turned to Sandy to ask when a blast of curses poured through the headset: *Capitalist motherfucker*, a neutral male voice recited, *Wanted for crimes against humanity; Big brother hacker liar.* The phrases flew into my ears faster and faster, a chorus of derision. Seeing my confusion, Sandy pointed me back to the screen, on which the stipple portrait had been magnified one hundred and then one thousand times. She was right: it was micrography. Micrography on a scale no human being could ever attempt with naked hand and eye. This was a portrait of Hack, created by a digital artist who hated Hack's motherfucking guts. The scanner was reading the minuscule words out loud!

Sandy Jensen shrugged, the fat headphones hugging her face. "Fucking artists, am I right?" She winked and peeled the earphones from her head and I followed, the library quiet again, the only sound the quiet tick of the bronze leaves. "He's got an agent now in New York. They always come for our Residents." She pressed a button and a robotic arm slid the print from the scanner into a slot in the wall. "Good riddance!" A flourish of her hand summoned another gentle wave of laughter.

I tried to imagine actually having a place in this weird, techy art world that could have been my stepping stone to somewhere else, but I so obviously didn't belong.

In the cell next to us, a robotic arm pulled an entire book from another rack and set it on the platen, opening it gingerly to the first page. Projected onto the screen above: a page of illuminated sheet music. You could see the invisible depressions where the printing plates had pressed the staff lines onto the paper. Despite my mother's attempts, I had never learned to read music, or to play, and eventually she'd given up on me and found a more willing and accomplished pianist in Michael. Half notes, whole notes, demisemiquavers, those flags rising from a line of skipping black balls were another alphabet that never spoke to me. I slapped the headphones on in time to catch the dark murmur of distant voices rising up as if from the depths of a well.

But it was the illumination that struck me: a golden serpent carrying a monastic little flautist across the sea of blue; silvered musical notes dotted the waves like bits of foam. On the screen above, labels appeared over each component of the image: *serpent, wave, monk, flute.* I admired it, even though I knew the computer didn't *understand* what it was looking at. There was no real artificial intelligence. There were just digital automata, clockwork dolls scratching hollow fingers across a virtual page. A parlor trick by a machine. Then a high, bright tune chimed through the headphones, a scattering of clear notes like birds breaking away in the dusk; the hair pricked up along my arms.

"It's the flute." Sandy Jensen peppered her fingers against the glass, little raindrops against the pane that drew my eyes to the silver musical notes dotting the azure sea. "Those are the notes the flautist is playing." I didn't know that much about scanning books, but I thought that scanning a page meant making the whole thing into one, big graphic file, a photograph of the page and all the words and symbols on it. But the Q scanners interpreted and translated everything.

"What kind of library is this?" Glancing around, I saw that the entire room was ringed with glassed booths just like this one, a hive of robotic worker bees in their cells all transforming the pollen of books and pages into some kind of rich, digital honey. But why? I knew about Google's intention to scan all of the world's books, and I'd trawled the collections of the libraries who'd converted their manuscripts to digital collections. But why would Q be scanning books? In the cell next to us, a robotic arm picked the last page of an unbound manuscript off its pedestal, stacked it neatly with the rest of the pages, set the entire stack neatly on the stainless-steel tray of a carousel and turned it quietly into the wall. The robotic arm swung around, picked up the next manuscript, and started the process again.

"Ah!" Sandy thrust a finger out. "Google was scanning all the books that exist. That got them into much too much trouble. This is a library of books that *don't* exist!"

She pointed to a display stand set between two scanning cells. On it stood a leather-bound manuscript with a large *V* tooled into the cover; the font style was a little different and the book was thicker, but the size and the shape of the manuscript cover looked a lot like my portfolio. *Very* much like. "Don't be fooled by the cheap cover," Sandy Jensen said, setting my face ablaze. I was glad Sandy Jensen hadn't seen my portfolio, didn't know that Connie had handed me the bundle wrapped in linen and raffia on Christmas morning, eyes glistening, and said *I had this made for you.* You could hardly tell them apart.

Sandy Jensen slipped on a pair of white cotton gloves and opened the simple leather portfolio to a manuscript page like no manuscript page I had ever seen. Dyed the deep purple of twilight sky, the page twinkled with letters of silver and gold, beautiful, uniform capitals that looked almost Greek. They were the kind of letters that belonged inside an ancient treasure chest; those brilliant letters sparkling against the purple depths of the parchment were moonlight and stars on the surface of the sea.

Sandy Jensen replaced the manuscript on its stand, the cover open. "*Codex Argenteus.* The Silver Bible." Sandy pointed to a placard marked 526 CE. "The Bible disappeared for a thousand years. When it turned up, nearly half of the folia were missing. Until now." Sandy looked up and watched my face. "Once we scan these pages, the Silver Bible will be complete again for the first time in over a millennium." She grinned. "Midnight, All Hallows' Eve."

The manuscript glittered in the museum spots, a time machine. Silver letters shivered on the surface of the wine dark sea, pale ghosts, missing for a thousand years. And here they were. "Jesus Christ." I had never seen anything so extraordinary, so precious and rare.

Peeling the cotton gloves from her hands, Sandy Jensen nodded at the book. "I believe he's mentioned." Then she laughed out loud, those bright peals that lapped against the turquoise domes and licked at the marble floor, limpid as water.

By that time, I had spent almost all of my adult life working at a job I had chosen only to support myself and my child. I'd had a passion but I hadn't used it. I hadn't made a life out of art. I looked around the Q library, at the shelves lined with scrolls and manuscript boxes, the purple page glittering with mercy. I took a deep breath, filling my lungs with old paper and ink, glue and cardboard and the purple pigment of snails that had been dead for over two thousand years.

From out on the Quad, an amplified voice reverberated among the buildings like the voice of a distant god. Something, once again, was happening here that would reshape the world. Something, like the art of the *Codex*, I would never be part of.

"So, you've seen what we're capable of." Sandy Jensen turned her gaze on me, assessing me, measuring. I took in the eager tilt of her head, which mirrored the tilt of the odd mechanical bird perched in the bronze tree behind her. "Do you think you can compete?"

I stared at Sandy Jensen in a way I supposed would be called *blankly*. Did she mean the spidergrams or the mechanical bird or the fifteen-hundred-year-old Bible itself? "Compete with the *Codex Argentus*?" I said.

A flock of bright birds flew from her throat, another gale of laughter. "You've got a sense of humor! Most people shit their pants at a chance to win an artist-in-residence position at Q. Not to overstate Q's weight," she shrugged. "But." She peeled her glasses from her face and wiped them with the edge of her shirt, exposing a flat strip of bare belly. I was curious about it, seeing another woman's bare midriff so soon after Blue's bare skin. I wanted to see what Sandy Jensen's navel looked like, but with a cool, satisfied want, devoid of desire. "Anyway, I can't wait to see you knock it out of the park here on Halloween night. And don't worry. I haven't given you any kind of advantage by showing you all this. At the Halloween ball, you're on your own."

My mind was racing, spinning out tendrils of ink in all directions at once. Q was hosting a competition for its next artist in residence and I had been included—or had been mistaken for someone who was. Did it matter how I got there, as long as I won?

I could hear the man in the tweed vest whispering *Everything depends on you.*

I smiled.

"So." Sandy Jensen glanced at my chest and pulled her phone from her pocket. "Let's go pick up your credentials."

Pliny the Elder referred to the red lead used in early Roman illuminated manuscripts as *flammeus*, the color of flame; more commonly referred to as *minium*, after its origins in the river Minius, the red pigment used to set apart capitals and versals, paragraphs and headings, was also sometimes called *stupium*. Pricked by the hard start of that word *credentials*, I felt both: stupefied and aflame. There were certainly no credentials waiting for me at Q.

Approaching the glassed kiosk that stood between the turnstiles going In and Out, I considered a dash through the gate, but my hip still bore the ache of the last night's rooftop jump and, anyway, I doubted I would make it. Instead, I approached the booth, Sandy's hand firm against my back, telling myself that my parents and brother would be okay, wondering who would pay my bail.

The guard, a short man with dyed black hair and a New York accent, stretched his hands across the counter. "Ma'am, please open your bag." *Ma'am.* I missed the other guard, the one who'd called me *Miss.* I clutched the bag tighter under my arm, the letter inside it alive with danger, bright birds restless with song.

Sandy Jensen squeezed my shoulder. I handed the bag over.

Under my nose, the guard tipped the loose contents of my bag onto the counter, including a banded stack of neatly clipped, letter-press letters from a mid-century gardening book I'd found at a library book sale: *L S A Q M W H*. He grabbed the stack with thick, pink fingers and flicked through it fast, like Michael's Mickey Mouse flip book, Mickey whisking his broom when you buzzed through the pages. I had spent hours razoring these letters from the page. "These are intellectual property," he said. He swept them over to his side of the desk and grabbed my cell phone.

I pointed to the letters. "I came in with those."

The guard drew my quill knife from my bag and lifted the blade to the light. "Ma'am, I understand."

I remembered the rumors that Q had a letterpress. How could I prove I hadn't stolen them?

He set the knife down on the counter. The brass buttons on his navy blazer sank into the mouth of my bag. Staring at the deep line etched across the fat part of his earlobe, I willed myself out of myself, holding my breath.

I had been searched before. The last time I traveled was a flight to Phoenix, a work trip I was anxious about not just because I'm anxious about convention centers swarming with twenty thousand colleagues, but because it was my last trip before Tristan left home, and it felt preemptory and wrong, me leaving him when we had so little time left together. On the way through the scanner at OAK, the signal flashed red; the chalk-outline body on the screen facing the agent glowed at the corners of my breasts. I'm not going to share with you the particularities of my anatomy or the way I've come to terms with parts of it, but a pair of blue gloves got more than some idea, lifting and swiping, while men in stockinged feet stepped around us to pull cases from the conveyor belt.

The Q security guard in his blue coat let my portfolio fall open in his open hands. Watching him press his thick, pink fingertip against the pale skin of the paper, watching the thick fingers heft the white curve of the page, my heart twitched, a rabbit snagged on barbed wire, thrashing to free itself.

Stars had begun to swarm my vision when the big tooled *A* on the leather cover caught Sandy Jensen's eye. It looked so much like the big, tooled *V* on the leather cover of the Silver Bible.

She thought I'd stolen the portfolio.

My phone buzzed on the counter, the ghost of Connie. And then, because I had something to prove, I said the only thing I could think of: "My wife gave it to me." The word *wife* blazed a white field across my mind's eye, or maybe it was the panic of having this thing I'd made, this expression of love and sadness, exposed for all to see.

A part of me wanted her to see it.

That was always the worst thing about the writing—wanting someone to see it. Wanting to be seen.

Sandy Jensen pressed the portfolio shut. She held it back over the counter toward the guard. "Can you sticker this?"

Just when I thought the worst had passed, she added. "Ms. Black is supposed to have a badge . . ."

I felt bad right then. I didn't know Sandy Jensen and would probably never see her again, but worse than knowing I was about to get caught was the feeling that I'd disappointed someone. That feeling had probably held me back half of my life.

The guard thrust out his hand. "License, please?"

Again, I looked frantically around, at the guard, the big open hall, the turnstile leading out of Q. If he hadn't been holding my portfolio, I would have made a break for it. As it was, I had no choice. Looking at the mess of my things spread across his counter, I fished through the flurry of cut cardstock, a pack of matches from La Cholita Linda, and my penknife, which I slid quickly up my sleeve, handed him the license and held my breath when he turned with it into the glass booth.

Sandy Jensen stood at my side, watching him, too. Things had turned so quickly from flirtation to incrimination. I wanted the flirtation back.

"Former," I swallowed. "Former wife. Years ago."

"Is that right?" Sandy Jensen tilted her hip against the counter. She had such angular hips, this movement was like a geometry equation. The guard emerged from the booth, my license and portfolio in his hand. He pointed to the shining coin of a fingerprint scanner and held his hand out for my thumb, like he didn't trust me to press it there myself. I expected him to mash it down on the scanner, like a detective booking me for a crime, but he didn't; he held it gently right on the surface of the glass.

I swallowed hard. But, as it had earlier that day, the scanner burped a happy *ping*. And then the guard handed back my portfolio, a silver sticker pressed across its back like the Newberry medal sticker on the front corner of the *Mixed-up Files of Mrs. Basil E. Frankweiler* I'd had as a child and given to Tristan. I felt like a plucky adventurer in a children's book right then, having snuck into the museum and gotten away with it. I was going to escape.

Leavened by my good luck, and not yet wondering how my fingerprint had scanned clear in Q's security system not once but twice that day, I felt my pluck bubble up inside of me. I turned to Sandy: "That would take some balls." I held up the portfolio. "Stealing a rare manuscript right under your nose."

She snorted. "I have no doubt that you've got 'em." Then we both laughed. Sandy gave her forearms a brisk rub; her shoulders swayed a few degrees in my direction. I'd noticed this before, the way recent, good sex atomizes off a person and draws other people to it, the confidence a signal to approach. The evening with Blue had limbered and loosened me and Sandy Jensen had sniffed the satisfaction on me, the heat that came from being desired. It was an illusion. But it was a nice one. Under my shirt, I was wearing Blue's tank top. I'd pulled it on that morning for luck.

I sifted through the pile of letters spilled across the counter, grabbed one and, fishing a ballpoint out of my bag, wrote out my phone number. As I did, I caught myself thinking about Blue, with her numbers and patterns and letters for numbers, the number 18. The world *Gematria* materialized out of some dusty, forgotten corner of my brain, but I couldn't place it.

I pinched my thigh and shoveled my portfolio into my bag. Blue was one night. A one-night stand. That was the extent of our arithmetic.

"Ma'am." The guard slid a badge across the counter. *Amy Black*, it read. *Vendor (Artist)*.

5 *Triple Letter Score*

MY FATHER LEANED OVER A TRAY OF SCRABBLE letters, his waxen cheeks shining in the lamplight. At his elbow sat a pad of paper and two Scrabble dictionaries, one of them large print. He may have been physically diminished, but he remembered the names of foreign currencies and he knew all the two-letter words beginning with Q. We'd been playing all evening. Every so often, I slipped my hand into my pocket to feel the sharp plastic corners of my badge.

It was my golden ticket to Q's Halloween ball, the seasonal extravaganza timed to coincide with the launch of the new algorithm. Artists would be performing at the ball, too, competing to become Q's new artist in residence. And I had a chance at the spot! A Q badge with my name on it. How absurd and brilliant was that? But many absurd things had happened in my life— Connie getting diagnosed with cancer, and then *choosing* to abandon me with a child. My energetic, industrious father, drooling and crumpled into a ball. So why not another, better?

Unbidden, I thought again of Blue. I remembered the weather patterns traced in ink along her hip, the warmth of her palm against my head. The way she said *You've managed something rare.* The entire velvet evening glowed.

My father pulled lettered tiles from the velour sack with trembling hands, sucking a string of spittle back into his mouth and failing. I let it soak into the green baize, subtracting by one from the thousand small humiliations of his disease. He laid an *S* at the end of the word T-R-A-P-E-Z-E. Double word score. He touched his finger to each letter as I counted out the points.

All my life, my father had been a man of commerce, an expert in precise and technical things. He left the house every morning at seven and came home at six o'clock, a pencil and a pad of paper in his pocket, iron filings spilling from the cuffs of his pants. When I was seven years old, he showed me how a pinch of iron dust could become a magnet when the magnet was gone. He was the magnet; from his brief contact, from his absence, our days found their pole. He'd traveled to every continent. In some ways, those days before I existed were the ones that loomed largest in my memory of him. A snapshot of him on a Pacific-island atoll: an orange polo shirt with wide lapels, dark glasses, his black hair brilliantined. The photo had yellowed in an airmail envelope that arrived months after it was sent. Places on the planet were farther apart then. You could go somewhere and be far away. You could go somewhere and miss someone.

I had never expected to have that kind of life, but I hadn't planned on being a single parent, either, with all the compromises it entailed—different compromises than the ones you made when you were with a partner, especially one with a comfortable income. But now—I touched the badge again—another door had opened, proof that there could be redemption.

"Dad?" In the confidence that comes with being chosen, I decided to ask my father an unspeakable question: "If you could have done anything you wanted in life, anything at all . . ." I glanced my father's eyelid, drooping on the right side of his face. My father's path to Golden Gate Tool & Die had been paved by chance—military service that led him to the Marshall Islands that led to a business deal. As a boy, he'd delivered papers, then driven an ice cream truck. But what had he dreamed of? Had he wanted to go to college? What had he *really* wanted to do? "What would you have chosen?"

I hadn't followed my dreams, either. I'd followed the path that let me survive. But maybe it wasn't too late for me. Unexpected good fortune had found me. Maybe my luck had changed.

My father fisted another clutch of tiles from the velour sack. He widened his mouth; he bared his teeth. I could only hear breath.

"Vocal cords," I reminded him.

He coughed for a few minutes, his cheeks blowing out, his skin nearly purple. I could see the letters in his rack, so many vowels. Finally, he coughed his own voice back up: "I took the best option." He sounded sanguine; even in his whisper voice, he sounded pleased with the results of plotting a life out moment by moment, based on the situation at hand. But what had he *imagined*? When he lay down in the grass as a boy and stared up at the clouds? My father had such dexterous fingers. What if he could have gone to medical school? He might have stitched nerves back together. My father with his loupe screwed into his eye might have traced the delicate filaments back to the place where dreams were born.

In the light of the desk lamp, I remembered lying in the Slumber Artist's bed, staring into the dark at the pulsing, visible shape of dreams.

My father looked up from the dark bruises that shadowed the backs of his hands; he was so fragile now, just being alive could kill him. "I saw what was in front of me," he paused. He was always pausing these days; I was always learning to let go of expectation, to sit with silence. "And then I made the right choice." His rough voice trailed off into a whisper, his head already turning away from the board.

My father refused help as he lumbered out of his seat and canted toward the bathroom more like a man falling than a man taking a step.

I found Michael in my bedroom (currently occupied by my father's loungewear and my mother's enormous suitcase), digging through my closet for Tristan's old cape.

It was almost Halloween.

Michael loved handing out candy to the kids, from the five thirty unicorns and jellyfish whose parents lingered behind them on the sidewalk and made them say "Thank you," all the way through the nine thirty crowd who showed up in their own clothes, grabbed fistfuls of Milky Ways, and shrieked "Is that your *face?*" as they fled. "Boo!" Michael, caped and fanged, would cry out, his own good humor elevating the cruelty of bullies to the spirit of the night.

He pulled the black scrap from a moving box stuffed with paper birthday banners and plastic pumpkins and tore it on one of the branches of a brass menorah. Seeing the tear, Michael yelped, a cry that could easily birth a wail. It wasn't just that the cape was ruined; it was also that it was Tristan's.

"Wait." I rummaged through a rusted coffee can for a needle and thread and put on my reading glasses. "I'll fix it." I tried to sew it up for him, but the cape was old; the velvet dissolved under my stitches. Connie was the one who knew how to sew; proficient in all the domestic arts, like making pie crust and soups, she'd stitched her way through half a baby quilt I'd finally packed away.

Michael's chest vibrated panic.

"What's going on?" our mother yelled out for my father. "Mickey?"

Michael snatched the ruined cape from my hands but we both went quiet. Our mother's face appeared in the doorway. She eyed the coffee can, the needle and thread. "Throw it away. It's junk!"

My mother, I think, was training herself to become unsentimental. She had already begun boxing my father's old suits and ties. Hearing my brother's whimper, she pressed a hand to his cheek: "We're guests in Amy's house. She doesn't have room for that."

I patted Michael's shoulder: "We'll get you a new one."

Michael's fingers trailed the floor, snagging the discarded cape. He brushed the velvet against his cheek. "Gap dot com?"

"Sure." I had landed a spot in Q's Halloween ball—and maybe from there a residency at Q, Department of Arts & Letters. Anything was possible.

My father was still in the bathroom.

Back at the game table, I switched my letters from one position to another, spelling out guttural complaint. I remembered the man with the tweed vest, his breath hot at my fingertips. The hour I'd spent with him now seemed eons past, a flicker, a murmur, a breath. The October wind slapping the alley door.

I wished I really were a witch. I wished I could summon him again across a Ouija board and ask him who he was. I wanted to ask him about Tal.

Under the lamplight, my fingernails tapped the baize.

Under the lamplight, my finger became his finger, tapping the initial capitals he had requested each time by tapping against the table. *Tap. Tap. Tap.* Suddenly, I remembered that he'd never said "initial capitals," nor let me say it aloud. Did he think someone was listening to us? Now it was so obvious: they were some kind of code he was tapping out just for me.

Maybe I did have a Ouija board.

I grabbed the bag of letters resting by my father's rack and dumped it on the table, picking through them for the letters I remembered with the clarity of my long labor over them alone in my room, the letters I had illuminated for him:

I M H A I S L T

These were the eight letters he'd counted on me to spend the most time studying. In my mind's eye, the illuminated *T* glittered almost painfully with beaten leaf. T for *Tal*.

A breath rasped: "Hey! That's cheating!" My father teetered in the doorway, gesturing dangerously at the table with his cane. "Help me." SHIMLAST, I tried. MISHLAT.

He crabbed his way over my shoulder. "Those aren't words," he whispered. Leaning into my back, he pushed the wooden chips this way and that across the felt: LAMISH he spelled, and SAMITHI. His breath wheezed behind my ear.

"You're not using all the letters," I objected, standing to pull the table away from the chair, so my father could fall heavily back into his seat.

He dropped his cane and jammed his hand into the pocket of his sweatpants, a far cry from the neat, wide-wale corduroys he used to change into on fall evenings, and pulled out the new phone my mother had recently gotten him. Picking up the huge magnifying glass he kept next to the *Official Scrabble Dictionary*, he poked at the screen until he'd found the app he was looking for, cleared his throat as he held the phone under his chin, and spoke into it: "Find words with I-A-M-H-I-S-L-T." He raised his voice as he spelled out the letters, baring his teeth like he used to when attempting French with the maître d' at Chez Panisse. The app was called "Scrabble Word Finder."

"*I'm* cheating?"

My father ignored me. "There are no words with all those letters."

"No words? At all?" It wasn't surprising that *I* couldn't come up with a word using a strange combination of letters, another thing entirely to suggest that, according to the world's greatest database of Scrabble words, there was no such word.

Michael appeared in the doorway. "What are you playing?" He sounded wary. We all knew he didn't like Scrabble, was easily frustrated by spelling, and strange words, and the demand that everything fit inside the squares.

"A made-up game." I pushed aside the big-print Scrabble dictionary and made space for my brother. "You can make up any words you want. But you have to use just these letters." I added, "Dad and I are stuck."

Michael looked at our father's phone and frowned. "*Sth*," he spat the letters out and shook his head. His thick fingers had already begun pushing letters apart. *I am* he tried *I am*.

I watched my baby brother with his involuntary frown, his thrusting tongue, his thinning hair. There were many ways Michael suffered in this world built by strivers, hackers, achievers. But at heart, he was one of them.

"I hadn't thought about making more than one word." I touched the wooden corner of the letter *I*, admiring his capacity for what tech called *disruption*. "That's smart."

I began experimenting with short sentences of my own.

I AM THIS L

I AM HIS LT

MATHS LII

"What does the Roman letter L stand for in numbers?" I asked my father.

TAMI LISH

TAL SHIMI

Tal. Tal *what?* I thought about the bearded man's sallow fingers, the smell of anise on his breath, the darkness of his beard. These were words in other languages, words unrecognizable to me, words I clearly wasn't meant to understand. I'd begun to doubt my hunch entirely, when my father laid out two words across the square marked Triple Letter Score:

MAIL THIS

6   *Tip Top Bicycle Shop*

IT WAS ONLY A QUARTER PAST SEVEN, BUT DARKER than midnight at the corner of 49th and Temescal Alley, a deep, smothering, velvet blackness that left my eyes straining for light. I hovered at the postbox where the woman I was sure was Tal had stood in her soft, green sweater and rested my fingers where her fingers had skimmed its cool, blue curve.

In my other hand, an envelope addressed only to *Tal* into which I'd slipped the note: *We need to talk* and my cell number. It seemed as likely to get a reply as a letter to Santa. But the man with the tweed vest had directed me here.

My phone buzzed: *Don't forget my birthday!* A color photo urged me to reorder a vase full of the palm leaves and red ginger Connie loved.

My thumb stroked my ring finger, the spot where I used to wear a red-gold posy ring twined with violets to symbolize "thoughts preoccupied with love." Connie's ring was inscribed *Amor Vincit Omnia* and dotted with bloodred rubies. I had worn other rings on other fingers. But this one was heavy, as if making up for the official title Connie would not accept without the Church. It took some getting used to the weekend after our return to the Mining Circle Building where we'd first fallen in love, the cool mass of all that metal slipping onto my hand under the domes suffused with milky light. Not quite a marriage, but. We were so young. It felt serious enough. I kept pushing the ring up and down with my thumb, a weight I could hardly imagine carrying across a page over and over again, all the years of my life. At one point, I wondered how I would tell Connie I couldn't bear it. And then I stopped noticing.

Connie was the one who'd wanted us to start a family. "As many as possible, as soon as possible," she'd said. Connie, who'd lost everyone, believed in the power of numbers. We were at Ocean Beach, our jackets wrapped tight around us, staring far out at the ships that passed through the Golden Gate; bonfires smoked the air, and the lights on the dark ships began to twinkle, all of us so far from one another, before they disappeared over the edge of the sea. Inside my pocket, I rolled the posey ring with my thumb. I wanted so badly to believe her.

The postbox handle radiated cold where the ring used to go.

I clicked *Delete*. I would not forget Connie's birthday and I would not send her flowers. Then I pulled the postbox handle, the envelope in my hand.

A voice echoed from deep in the box. "What do you want?"

Startled, I let go of the handle. The box clanged shut.

I studied the stolid little postbox, no bigger than a filing cabinet, no higher than my chest. No one could fit inside that mailbox. I'd dropped a letter in this box, my letter to Q, and it hadn't talked back to me then.

Wary, I tugged it open again.

The postbox barked: "What do you want?"

Determined not to be intimidated, I shone my phone's flashlight down the box's dark gullet.

"What do you want?" The voice repeated, insistent but bored, a young man's voice. This wasn't a recording. It was the voice of a Jack-in-the-Box drive-thru at midnight, a human voice.

I thought for a moment before answering: "I want to mail a letter."

A moment of crackling silence, followed by the sharp buzz of being rung into to a New York apartment. Then: silence.

My finger traced the side of the box, across the graffiti: *This is not a postbox.*

If Connie were here, she would have told me I was being pranked. (*Those aren't firecrackers!* Connie had pulled me by the hand through the midnight streets of East Oakland, leaving her friend Mirabel's midsummer night's party, *Those are gunshots!* I saw the world I wanted; Connie saw the world as it was.) But Connie was gone, a bouquet of red ginger on the screen of a phone. I caught myself stroking my unringed finger again and wondered what *Blue* would say. I remembered her bare skin, the Slumber Artist's bed, translucent jellies pulsing through our heads in the dark.

"Excuse me—" A bearded man hove out of the night, another pale face masked by thick, dark hair, a Paul Bunyan of a man with big shoulders in a plaid shirt and jeans. "What time is it?" He waited while I pulled out my phone, his thick, dark beard an oil slick under the light. He smelled like pine boughs and the gears of a machine, a smell that reminded me of my father. Like gears, the clock on my phone seemed to *tic tic tic*, even though it didn't make that sound.

"Hey, thanks!" the bearded Bunyan called out in a voice so friendly I hardly believed what was happening when his hand flew out to swipe the phone from my hand and, in the same smooth motion, tossed it to a skinnier bearded man in a plain white T-shirt and jeans who rolled slowly by on a shining chrome BMX bike.

The bicycle faded with a *tic tic tic* into the dark.

Cell phone thefts in Oakland were as common as early morning low clouds. "Fuck me!" I muttered, angry at myself for the foolish temerity that had put me out alone on the alley at night when the events of the previous night should have warned me away from this place.

"Fitbit?" he murmured, while the man in the bike looped back around the corner. Good things did not come into my life with bicycles. "Apple watch? Wearable anything?"

I held my hands up and shrugged. "Try Best Buy." I waited for him to run away. With Tristan flown, I was a little too unmoored in the world to conjure the appropriate terror.

The big man shook his head toward the bike, which disappeared at a walking pace toward Telegraph like a fish swimming deeper into the gloom. Then Bunyan began to walk away. With a stride like his, he could disappear in five steps. But he stopped; his big shoulders rotated toward me. "Amy?" He tossed his head toward Telegraph, the lamplight two shiny coins on his glasses like payment for crossing into another world. "Come on."

Even now, I wonder that I went along so easily, but isn't that how we're trained, to be pleasant, to be helpful, to submit, to be good?

I found myself hurrying to keep up alongside the big, bearded man in the plaid lumberjack shirt, his wake the pleasant scent of pine needles and cedar chips and something mechanical that I soon guessed, as he unlocked the door of the bike shop whose huge, glass windows fronted Telegraph Avenue, was bicycle grease.

Inside the Tip Top Bicycle Shop, the big, picture windows shone with high-handled street cruisers the colors of Easter eggs, pale peach and mint green, bubblegum and sky. Rugged mountain bikes and hybrids hung from hooks, their wheels great black gears turning slowly in the air. A chrome soda-fountain spigot offered *Air* and *Water*; an army of headless helmets hung in rows behind it like ranks of phantom soldiers.

The big man watched me taking it all in. "Do you ride?" he asked.

Michael and I had taken turns a decade apart learning to ride a sparkling purple, banana-seat Schwinn, fluttering pink and purple plastic streamers I stretched and tore as I ran alongside him holding him up, trying to let him go. Though I had loved that flying feeling of my hair streaming behind me when I was young and flat and twiggy, I'd stopped riding when everything about my body conspired to encumber me. Connie liked to ride, though. She biked to BART for work. Although she threatened that she would take me biking along the Embarcadero all the way to Crissy Field, we never did. And after what happened to Connie that spring evening on Market Street, I was done with bikes. "I don't really like bikes," I shook my head and wondered suddenly how it was that this strange man knew my name.

"That's too bad," he smiled, holding out his wide, callused paw and waiting for me to shake it. "I'm Arman, from the neighborhood. Come on upstairs."

With an odd, dizzying twin of the electric charge I'd felt following Blue up her floating stairs into the dark, I followed Arman behind the counter, where a door painted pale turquoise blended into the pale turquoise wall. The dazzle of the chrome and candy colors disappeared behind us. Inside the dark wood-paneled stairway, Arman took the steps two at a time.

We arrived at a landing two stories up, a floor higher than the building appeared from the street, at the entrance to a series of adjoining rooftop apartments that stretched the block. In the first, a red enamel teakettle sat whistling on a stove. In the open window, a white-haired man in pressed khakis crowded over the sink, beating a raw chicken flat with a brick.

We walked into another space, this one vast and undivided, the ceilings vaulted. Against the far wall, the full-moon face of a big, black Telechron wall clock peered out across the room. Underneath the clock glinted a wall of old-fashioned P.O. boxes, twenty across, their numbers stenciled in gold. Through the glass, I could see letters in white and blue envelopes, waiting to be picked up. I imagined slotting the man in the tweed vest's letter into one of the numbered boxes. "Is this a post office?"

Duke Ellington played on an old, wooden radio.

"You could say that." Arman led our way through a mountain of packages, parcels of every shape and size: brown-paper blocks, white cardboard boxes, tiny, tan cubes, a great wall of boxes in between whose bricks one could imagine tucked every consumer prayer and desire.

Beyond the wall of P.O. boxes, two rows of high, wooden tables stood in twin lines, three tables in each row. Across each table spread a neat, maroon blotter, and upon each blotter sat the same several objects, neatly arranged: a fresh block of white paper, a glass jar full of pencils, and a banker's lamp with an emerald-green shade. At each table perched a pair, a murmurer and a listener, and while all six of the murmurers were all of different skin colors and sartorial styles and body types, all of the listeners were older and white-haired and women, reading glasses pushed back from the tips of their noses; as each of those women listened to the person at her table, she blacked their words onto a white sheet with the tip of a pencil. Their murmured exchanges floated like clouds of soft vapor into the air above our heads. What was this place? What secrets were being exchanged under this high ceiling, what murmured words of love? "What *is* this?" First the library at Q and now this. I felt like I'd just stumbled into my own wildest dream. Why had the man in the tweed vest come to *me*, when there was this place in the world? Why had he sent *me* here?

Then I realized: It was happening. Sandy Jensen had told me: An artist's residency at Q led to big things: an agent, a gallery opening. *This.* In the middle of my life's journey, a stranger had found me and led me here.

I stepped closer to one of the tables. *The five-ounce bottle, not the eight-ounce* one of the murmurers said, while a mahogany-skinned woman with a neat white bun wrote it all down. I'd done the same thing with my father's letters from Golden Gate Tool & Die: the beautiful marriage of the sacred and the mundane.

I nodded at the women writing. "Who are they?"

Arman's beard parted to reveal surprisingly small white teeth. "We're a collective. A DNN."

I stared at his beard, willing something comprehensible out of his mouth. I didn't resent this culture and its LOLs and DTFs and ;) s. But what had happened to words?

Arman shifted his huge shoulders, as if they were heavy, even for him. "Sorry. A distributed-node network. We set this one up to protect people who don't want their buying habits profiled by Big Data." He nodded at the women with the pencils: "If you need a pregnancy test, or a price on a car, or a litterbox for your cat, you can come here and place your request." He pointed to the women jotting words onto sheets of paper. "Those requests get distributed randomly and anonymously to members of the network." He pointed to the mailboxes. "And the completed order, or the information, or what have you, gets returned here for the original requester to pick up. It's pretty sweet. Any one person's data is distributed across so many people in the network that it's meaningless as a profiling tool. It takes *just* a little bit longer to get what you want." He pinched his forefinger and thumb not quite together. "But people like the fact that they're helping each other. This can be quite a gathering place!" He laughed at that, a guffaw of pleasure.

I wasn't following. "Big Data? Cat litter?" I blinked from Arman back to the white-haired women with their coal-black pencils. He'd explained without mentioning the most important thing: "They're writing," I prompted Arman, "on paper. They're writing words." Arman nodded. "You have paper and pencils and P.O. boxes with letters in them. Women writing letters." I watched as a tiny, wrinkled woman in a black turtleneck licked the tip of her pencil before touching it to the surface of a plain, white sheet.

"Orders," Arman corrected me. "For the Neighborhood."

I did not realize he was saying *Neighborhood* with a capital N. "That's how we do it—on paper. Old school. It works pretty well."

It did work pretty well. It had worked well, I knew, for thousands of years: papyrus, sheepskin, parchment, paper. On calfskin curled around two wooden rollers had been tattooed the history of the world. Every human desire had at some time point sailed over the world's far edge, an absence made present, a fracture made whole, on paper. Across a shared room. Across lifetimes. It worked, sometimes, far too well. But I was surprised that this strapping hipster thought so, too, that he would find writing on paper useful, desirable, preferable enough to construct a world around it. I still had no idea what he was talking about really. But, could it be that, at last, I had found my people?

"We're all really excited that you decided to come help us out, Amy," he said.

I could hardly say how excited *I* was to have passed beyond the turquoise door into this secret world. Whatever this was, I wanted it. I wanted in. I stared unapologetically at the scribes with their flashing hands and white hair. "Is that why he sent me here? The man with the tweed vest?"

Arman's high forehead creased. "Tweed vest?"

A woman with a neat bun like a ball of white yarn folded the page before her into an envelope and tossed it into a basket at her feet. "I'm a scribe. That's why I'm here?" It was a question, but I was nodding and nodding and nodding.

"Yeah," my towering companion agreed, shaking his head at the same time, "No."

I stopped nodding. What did he mean: *Yes* or *No*?

"These women are really, really good at what they do. We call them our Invisible Army. Women over fifty! Right?" He laughed. I didn't. How old did he think I was? "So," he frowned, his cheeks flushing, "we don't need any more scribes. Obviously." Arman's smile flashed once again through his beard, but, as the smile disappeared back into the dark thicket of his face, he grabbed the beard in one hand and wrung it against his chin. "Not that you wouldn't be great at that!" he added quickly.

I picked at the hem of my shirt, aware of how empty my hands felt without my phone or my pen. Not being asked to scribe was a blow. I considered the women's hands flowing steadily over their sheets of paper, the postboxes lined up along the walls, the letters tilting against the glass, and I knew that whatever these people wanted me to do, I would do it, just to be a part of this. But Arman would have to understand that I would not let my hair go white. "So why *am* I here?"

Arman's head flew back, his mouth pouring out big gales of laughter, real *Ha ha ha*s. He laughed like I had just told him the world's best joke. Finally, he caught his breath: "I like that," he sighed. "That's good. That's exactly why you're here."

"Why?" *Anything*, I prayed. *Ask me to do anything.*

Arman's mouth contracted suddenly inside his beard, his eyes grew bright behind the bright lenses on his face. "They're in lockdown right now at Q, cranking out a new machine-learning algorithm. Predictive AI. Before it rolls out, you're going to blow the whole thing up."

All around me, above me, the air swelled with the swoosh of pencils, the hush of pages being folded into paper envelopes and floating down into baskets.

Anything but that.

I do not hate the Internet. Yes, I love real letters, paper and ink, black and blue tattooed across the skin of some organic thing. Texts, emails, and chats will never stand up to a fragile, warm-blooded human hand. But I am not a Luddite. Like most people on planet earth at this time in history, I rely on the web to get through my days.

I was not going to break the Internet. I would not blow anything up.

My real life was finally just about to start.

I didn't even know this man.

"Not the entire Internet," he corrected me. "Just Q. At Midnight, All Hallows' Eve."

I stared hard into Arman's face, as if by peering into the dark portals of his eyes I could find the person in there, as if I could really *see* him. "I'm sorry," I shook my head. "I think you have the wrong person." I didn't *think*. I *knew*. But this was part of being female. Feigning pale convictions. I also knew that it was not within my power to do what this man wanted. I didn't know anything about coding, or machine learning, or The Algorithm.

Arman crossed his huge arms, clutching each elbow in the palm of his hands. "Yeah," he nodded. "No."

There it was again, that strange artifact of speech, the Yes/No. Was the trick to remember which word came first? This is why people need writing. "You're Amy Black," he corrected me, as if I had denied being myself. "You have credentials at Q."

I turned my head from side to side, as if to better understand what he was trying to say. I was an artist. Not an engineer.

When I didn't answer, he nodded: "So you do. Have credentials. Good." He pushed his big hand into his beard again and wrung it out like a wet cloth. "You'll deploy the Kill Code and detonate the cloud." Arman set his teeth. "Or else a lot of people will get hurt."

Kill code? "No. Sorry. I don't know code." Apologizing instead of refusing. "And, I mean, why Q?" Q was just a social media app. Sure, Q could be a waste of time—FOMO, LOL, *#blessed*—but why would anyone want to wipe out terabytes of duck-lipped selfies and avocado toasts enough to hurt someone? Arman had threatened to hurt someone. Had he threatened to hurt me? I narrowed my eyes and tried not to think about my father, my mother, my brother, Tristan. *A lot of people*, he said, *are going to get hurt.*

Arman's beard glistened under the chandeliers. He grabbed it in his fist again, releasing a cedar-scented burst into the air between us, the smell of Tristan's guinea pig, Bogie, when I helped him clean the cage. Was it possible that Arman's life had nothing to do with wood, that he didn't spend his hours carving dovetail joints from the pink hearts of trees, but simply rubbed his beard in a cedar-tinged unguent? I tried to imagine dabbing my wrists, my throat, the soft indentations behind my ears, with a perfume called *Ink*. Connie had worn the scent of grass once, long ago. "First," Arman gave his beard a twist: "Q is *not* just a social media platform. Q is the largest repository of consumer data in the world. The social media platform is part—but not all—of how they get it. You're not the user. You're not even the product. You're the raw materials." He twisted again, twist after twist after twist: "They know more about you than your credit card company, than the big three credit agencies, than Match. com and Uber and Tindr combined; they know more about you than your mom."

That wouldn't be surprising, I thought. And then, *So what?*

Arman read the look of skepticism on my face, a skill I envied, would never master.

"Let me guess. You have nothing to hide."

I'm not sure I would have said that exactly. But, basically: yes.

He released his beard, then gripped it hard again: "First, no offense, but you're thinking the wrong way. You're imagining that you're a needle in a haystack. You're thinking as if individual people are reading your email. It's not like that. It's a machine, and it can read all of everyone's email, all at once. There's no haystack. It's all needles.

"Second, this is predictive AI. It uses all the data we each generate to make—and sell—guesses about what we're going to do next. Those guesses are big business. They're not just collecting raw data. They're using it to draw inferences about people. To give you a lower price—or a higher one. To predict what you want. To predict what you're going to do. And sometimes they're *wrong*." His eyebrows jumped up, as if he were waiting for my mind to consider the possibilities. And it did—the reminders to send flowers to Connie, which had started plaguing my phone now that it was October; the browser ads for Hawaii that followed me from device to device. But that was all so innocuous. And the fact that the browser had offered me an ad for a Medical Alert device, presuming as it did so many accurate things about my parents' situation without ever having been told—wasn't that a value-add? Did my parents *not* need a Medical Alert device? They did.

Arman dropped his chin to his chest and fixed his eyes on me. "The new algorithm is putting the crystal ball on steroids. They're gathering every piece of information about everyone, from everywhere. Email. Phone calls. Facial recognition data. Your location. Your *pulse*. Then they're putting it in the hands of the machine and asking it to make as many connections as possible. They're asking it to decide—" His big hands found his beard again and twisted violently "—who's a threat."

Arman stood in front of me, twisting his beard, smelling of cedar and bicycle grease. Everything he had said to me was preposterous. Alarming. But my pulse remained even, my breathing slow. I wasn't afraid of him. His ruggedness came from a bottle.

"*You*'re a threat," I pointed out. "Aren't you?"

Behind us, airmail-thin envelopes gathered slowly in the bottom of wicker baskets like drifts of snow. I could not quite reconcile what I'd just said with those white-haired women, their whispering pencils, the drifts of snow, which were all things I loved, achingly, the *fsh fsh fsh* that meant thoughts were turning into things you could see and touch.

I wasn't a terrorist. I was an artist. And I'd just gotten my chance.

"I can't help you," I told Arman, who was chewing on a cuticle. I really should have felt more afraid, but what I felt was my age, and Arman's beard-twisting earnestness, which reminded me so much of Tristan and his friends. His intentions were good. Surely, he could be talked out of doing something stupid. "I don't think you want to do this, either, Arman. And, anyway, you've got the wrong person." If it had only been about envelopes and letters and postboxes and a big room where women stood at tall desks to listen and write. For that, I would have been the right person.

"Yeah," he said, but started shaking his head. "No—" Arman pulled his finger out of his mouth, spitting the skin he had nibbled off with a quick *whht* to the floor. "You're the right person, Amy." Arman's voice softened around the soft sounds of my name.

For a second, the softness of his voice softened my resistance, the way I softened when a very old woman next to me said *Thanks, hon.* Then I remembered I had never told him my name. "How do you know who I am? Did the man in the tweed vest tell you about me?"

He shrugged. His big head wagged. He didn't know the man in the tweed vest.

"You have credentials. You're capable of creating a maskable virus the system will accept as normal data. And, if you get caught, you won't be able to point anyone back to us."

I crossed my arms. "And why is that?"

"You're face blind."

You think, of all people, you know yourself. But not necessarily. Not clearly. Not the way other people can know you.

When I was seventeen years old, I became obsessed with a girl named Lucia. This was after Heidi Chan. Lucia wasn't part of any crowd at my school. She'd started in eleventh grade, a transfer from Lick, a City girl. Lucia had her City past and her Italian name and her waist-length brown hair, joined to an at-first-charming insecurity that, as a new student in junior year, no one would ever accept her.

I accepted her. I lapped her up.

I liked the way she said her name, the Italian way she pronounced it, like she was biting into a juicy peach. Soon it was late-night phone calls and Lucia dragging me by the hand up to my own room.

You would think I would have understood this went beyond ordinary friendship. That, after the art supply closet and Heidi Chan, I would have had the words. But it was almost the opposite. Heidi had normalized "affection" between "friends." (Outside the art supply closet, we were never seen together, let alone friends.) Heidi had graduated without anyone ever finding out about us. Hooking up with Heidi, if anything, had thrown a cloak over my own self-awareness. I'd bought the lie myself.

Then something happened with Lucia that ripped that cloak right off my head.

We were at my house. Lucia *adored* the piano music that filtered through the house while my mother worked with her students. *Liszt!* Lucia exclaimed, breathless, at the first, dark notes of the Hungarian Rhapsody. I suppose Lucia found it dramatic, the delicate and stormy soundtracks that underscored life in our house, I suppose she found it perfectly suited to being a seventeen-year-old girl. For me, my mother's music was often too loud, too much, a noise I had to tune out to keep my hand steady on the page.

Lucia and I were in the kitchen, popping a bag of the microwave popcorn I knew my mother wanted me to save for Michael. Nuking it, I could picture her back ratcheting up straighter and straighter on the piano bench next to her student as the smell slipped under the door. Lucia was chattering—she usually did most of the talking, which I liked sometimes and sometimes found exhausting. She was talking, as she often did, about boys. (Because it was expected? The camouflage that allowed the hair petting and knee fondling? Or just what she was interested in? I heard through the grapevine after college that Lucia was bisexual, and according to her photos on Q, married to a man.) "Amy!" Lucia had a breathless, excited way of saying my name, as if she'd just run across the room to see me. "You should marry Brandon!" She folded into a fit of giggles that blotted out the *ding!* of the microwave when the timer went off.

Michael's high voice silenced her: "Amy doesn't marry boys." The popcorn smell had lured him into the kitchen. Michael was all of six-and-a-half—a little kid with an Elmo obsession and an appetite. "Popcorn!" he grinned, waiting for me to pour him a bowl.

Lucia had stopped laughing. Her eyes fixed on the door where my mother stood, silent.

That was the moment I realized: *Everyone knew.* Lucia knew. Of course she did. But my mother knew. And *Michael* knew. And I, who had learned how to unhook Heidi's bra with one hand in the dark—*I* knew, for the first time, right there in the kitchen, the hot butter flavor from the popcorn bag steaming my face. That's when I *knew.*

I blinked at the big, bearded man. Staring up at him under the lights of the chandeliers made it even harder to see his face, and now I could feel all the ways I had not been seeing other people, all that not knowing coalescing in the haloed blankness that was his face.

A *feeling* is different than a *diagnosis.* A diagnosis is a word. *Face blind.*

How had this happened to me. There were things I could not deny, recent things: The BART station. *La principessa* . . .

But another feeling bubbled up on the fizz of memory.

One night, late spring, Connie and I curled around each other in bed so tightly I imagined I could feel the roll of infant bones between us, though it was way too early for that. "What if it's twins?" I imagined people pouring out of the walls, small fingers dipping into pots of ink. I imagined an incursion.

Connie buried her head under her pillow and grunted. We had just moved to the house in Temescal, unfamiliar with the night sounds just off the avenue. Though it was after 10:00 p.m. and dark in our flat, voices buzzed through the bedroom wall. Connie found the music and laughter disruptive, especially now that hormones and strange dreams kept her up at night, but I could sleep through all of it, the heavy thump of the bass a heartbeat reassuring me that the world was alive while I slept.

I nosed my foot under Connie's calf, thick from cycling. I wanted reassurances that we hadn't asked for more than we could handle.

Turning to curl behind me, Connie slid the hem of my nightshirt up until I could feel the cool air against my skin, and she began to spell words across my back with her finger, one letter at a time: "It IS twins." Her fingernail dotted the last *i*. I gave her calf a shove and she turned over, already heavier, I thought, already bearing fruit.

I stared across the ceiling where the face of my watch threw a little circle of light. "Be serious."

"Don't worry," Connie whispered, hooking the band of my underpants and sliding it down with her big toe: "We'll have two or three or four and you'll make beautiful name tags for them so you can tell them apart."

Connie knew. Of course she did. She, of all people, did.

The bicycle shop floor tilted under me.

To counteract the sensation that I was falling off the edge of the world, I reached out a finger and poked this strange man Arman in his meaty forearm. "*Face blind*? How—?" I felt like I'd sucked helium from a balloon. I felt like I might float away.

His head tilted. "Shit—" he started. "You didn't know." He held his hands up in front of him, palms spread wide. "Dude—" he said. "I thought you knew—I mean—"

I found my voice. "How?" I poked him again. "How did you know?"

He stared at my finger until I let it fall from his arm. Then he held out his hands, palms up, like he was holding the murder weapon out for all to see: "Q."

I moved down the stairs in a new state of blindness, as if a dark, filmy layer had been added to my inability to see. *I'm blind*, I told myself. *Blind*. The ghostly silver bicycle *tic-tictick*ed to the curb and pressed my phone into my hands. "We'll be in touch," the cyclist mouthed, melting back into the darkness.

I was being melodramatic. I knew that. But I couldn't stop myself. For that, I needed Tristan, who had no trouble whatsoever telling me I was wrong.

My phone filled with Tristan's number as soon as I touched the letter *T*. (That's how it is to have a child: a whole world summoned in the first letter of his name.) I had no idea what time it was in southern Siberia, or the number of the youth hostel where he was staying. He hadn't bought one of those chips for his cell phone, or even brought his cell phone along. The whole point was to drop off the grid. Standing out there by the mailbox under the bright fall stars, the ink-dark sky, I imagined Tristan on the pale shores of the largest freshwater lake in the world, the angular set of his shoulders, his dark curls and patchy, dark stubble. The deep groove in the hinge of his elbow that matched the notch in his chin. But I couldn't picture his face.

I could hear his voice, then, casually naming the two friends who sat beside him, dismantling Oreos at the kitchen table, frequent after-school guests: "Mom. It's Jackson and Bella." His sweet, clear voice, before it broke, at his fifth-grade graduation, *Hello, Mrs. Ruiz*—identifying the principal of the elementary school he'd gone to since kindergarten. In the cereal aisle at the Bowl, at Back-to-School night in the auditorium, crowded against his classmates at the climate march, there he was, his voice in my ear, whispering names.

The realization washed in on a wave of nausea. I thought whatever was wrong with me had always been mild, had recently gotten worse. But it hadn't. For the past eighteen years, I'd had Tristan beside me, prompting me, whispering in my ears. It came so early to him, I doubt he even knew why he did it. And before Tristan, I'd had Connie. I'd had someone to help me pass. I had always been the same.

I stared at my dark reflection in the screen, the pad of fat under my chin.

If I could even reach Tristan, what would I say? *I can't recognize you in a picture. I'm afraid that when you come home again, I won't know who you are.*

I tapped open the Q app on my phone and, poking through my "profile" and "preferences" and "settings," tried to find the label Arman had discovered there, but turned up nothing. Still, just to be sure, I deleted my profile picture and then all of my "friends." What good was a social networking app for a person who couldn't read faces? Screen by warning screen, I made my way to the buried page posted in large red letters "Are you sure?" and deleted my Q account. Then I deleted the app from my phone.

7 *The Evening Mail*

HUMAN BEINGS HAVE ALWAYS LEFT BEHIND MORE evidence of ourselves than we have been aware of. In the state archives of Milan, across the pages recording all the plague deaths in the city in the year 1630, the traces of no fewer than six hundred proteins chronicle the tobacco, chickpea, rice, carrots, and maize enjoyed for their suppers by the city clerks, and record as well the skittering feet of the rats and mice who danced across the pages, leaving traces of plague. In the Folger Shakespeare Library, in Washington DC, a Bible from the year 1637 records among the *begats* the DNA of a scribe whose genes show he once had acne. Using the same science of proteins, scholars hope to gather from the pages of his memoirs Casanova's gonorrhea. The text becomes us and we become it.

According to Arman, most of the digital world, including and especially Q, exists to gather as much data about every person on earth as possible, and everything we click, browse, read, watch, like, and buy is another point added to the data constellation. When I pointed out to Arman that Q was not in the business of selling products, he brushed me off with a wave of his big hand: "Forget products. It's about ads. Almost every page of everything you see online has a tiny, invisible tracker on it, a single pixel that registers that you're visiting the page and where you've come from. That's not a secret, by the way. That's why you go to L.L. Bean and look at boots, and the next time you go to your Q newsfeed, you see an ad for Bean boots." With one big hand, he gingerly pinched an invisible pixel; with the other hand, he pointed at his boots. "Some people say that they get ads on Q for things they talk about in front of their phones— talk about a cordless fish tank vacuum; see an ad for the Norelco Cordless Aquariumvac 2000."

"What's wrong with getting ads for things you want?" I thought a little uncomfortably about the urging I kept getting to send flowers to Connie. Was that what I wanted? I didn't think so.

Arman turned both palms up: "Who decides what you want?"

Upstairs in my guest bedroom, I sat in the darkness and stared at the face caught in my windowpane and thought about Blue in the Slumber Artist's bed, bathed in gold light. Who, indeed? I was still wearing her tank top.

I walked to the window and pressed my face against the glass. All across the skyline, the rooftops were dark harbors in the pale glow that simmered up from the flatlands below. Feeling the heat in my chest again, I stepped out of my skirt. There was no point in wanting. That had been decided. I'd gone how many years of my life without even realizing that I lacked something as fundamental as the ability to recognize another person? How could I rely on myself to know what someone else was like? It all explained so much. I was *face blind*. I wasn't pitying myself. I had no right to subject anyone else to me. There was just so much I lacked.

Behind me, my laptop warbled, Michael's good night video call from the room next door.

Michael scratched his nose. "Are you sad?" How easily he saw the emotions that played across my face. I wondered again what that would feel like, to look at someone and know what they were feeling. It came so naturally to him.

"Just a little. *Wistful*." I watched the *W* spread its tendrils into tender blossoms.

"That's a nice word. Like *mist*." Michael smiled again.

I saw the letters spread and dissipate into wisps of gray, the sadness vaporizing with them, a fullness swelling. "Michael, I love you."

His mouth opened wide, his tongue and teeth showing. "I love you, Amy!" Then he yawned and looked at his watch. "Are the birds in bed?" He'd noticed the neighbor's pigeon hutch. If I saw him outside feeding them, I planned to ask the neighbor to show Michael his birds.

I carried the computer over to the window. "Sure. See?" The night was quiet except for the pale flutter of a forgotten pair of underpants flapping on a line, a glow against the navy sky.

The underpants cooed.

"Amy!" Michael squealed. Lowing quietly, the bird bobbed its head at the side of the coop, burbling. Next door, Michael's window lurched open several inches and caught on the safety. If I didn't go out, he would.

Stripped down to my underwear, I pushed my window wider. "I'll go."

The pain in my rump and shoulder reminded me I had fallen recently and was bad at it. Inelegant. Against my bare legs, the neighboring roof had the grit of rough sandpaper. There was a reason, besides being seen, not to leap out of the window half naked—though, once the scrape stopped smarting, the warm wind felt soft on my skin.

Out on the rooftop, the voices from the alley sounded far away. Down below, a car rolled by thumping *Just somebody that you used to know*. Down below, a man's voice called out: "Tomorrow!" It might have been the black-haired barber, closing up shop; it might have been one of the young men from the Neighborhood.

There was the sweet smell of pipe smoke and the dank stink of weed.

I wondered if Blue was down there somewhere and chastised myself for wondering. Elbows out, I peeled her tank top over my head, balled it up, and hurled it over the alley. The wind caught it; for a second, it flapped like a wild white bird, then sank out of sight. It was safer that way.

The wind was blowing, warm and clear and dry. To the east, the Oakland-Berkeley Hills lay dark and dormant, all the expensive houses invisible across their flanks, distant as another planet. The pigeon's voice, low and soft as a lover, felt very close. I padded to the hutch, a wire-fronted cage spattered with shit and bereft of birds—except this one, shy, mottled pigeon. She was soft, white and charcoal gray, her wings dipped in black. She peered at me, the dark bead of her eye bright with suspicion, suspicion burbling from her throat, low murmurs and innuendos that rippled the sheen of her neck, a lonely sound. A bird like that isn't meant to be alone. The pigeon bobbed her bowl-shaped head. I'd always liked large flocks of birds, the easy anonymity of them as they surged in dark lines across the sky.

Something glinted near the pigeon's leg. Probably a band. I looked more closely.

As I bent toward the bird, a light blazed up, a spotlight. I swung around. There was Michael in the window, his desk lamp turned onto the rooftop, smiling. The pigeon's neck glowed gasoline rainbows, pink and green. There was a band, but also: a small silver capsule attached to its leg, the size of an overlarge pill.

"Good girl," I cooed, reaching for the capsule, unscrewing it, unsheathing the rolled onionskin inside. "Good girl." A warm, October breeze rushed along the tar paper at my feet. *Shhhh.* I thought I could hear the soft leather scuff of cat paws across the asphalt, the whir of a Tesla gliding away in the night.

Then I heard my mother scream.

By the time I reached the living room, Michael had helped my father back to his feet. Blood seeped through the cuff of his shirt where his skin had torn, but he hadn't broken anything. "I'm fine. I'm fine," he brushed me away. But Michael was still holding him upright.

I glanced at the cane parked in the corner by a plant with waxy green leaves. I hadn't seen it leave that spot all day. "Dad, you need to use your cane. *All* the time."

My father nodded, but he whisper/shouted: "I'm fine. Your mother's here." Michael helped him back to the couch.

My mother stood at the piano, clutching the keyboard with bone-white fingers. "He was reaching for a pencil. And then he went back—" Her eyes fixed on the far wall; she was watching it play over again in her mind. "—just like that!"

Worse than my father falling: the possibility of my father falling onto my mother. My mother fed my father and helped him walk; she played him music and watched movies with him and made sure he remembered his pills. If something happened to her, what would happen to him? What would happen to all of us? Anxiety made me sound harsher than I meant: "Next time he could fall on you. Michael and I can't always be here." The fact that I could actually be there more than I chose to be wasn't something I wanted to think about.

My mother winced. "My goodness! You're bleeding!" It was odd for my mother not to address my father with an endearment. Then I realized she wasn't talking to him. Her eyes fixed on me; I was standing in the living room in my underwear. "What in God's name has happened to you?" The tar paper on the neighbors' roof had scratched fine red lines across my thigh; large bruises from the day before patterned my leg with thick, black blooms.

"It's nothing." I brushed at the scratches, grabbing a soft throw from the arm of the couch, wrapping it around my waist. "I fell."

I caught Michael's eye, expecting him to blurt out that I'd

jumped onto the neighbor's roof to tuck a pigeon in to bed, but he didn't.

On the way back upstairs to our rooms, Michael pulled at my elbow. "Was she carrying a message?"

I couldn't lie to my brother outright, but I shook my head. "Good night."

Back in my room, I unfurled the onionskin. Small as a fortune-cookie fortune on which a tight, neat hand had written:

Don't be fooled. She's dangerous.

8   *Soferet*

I HURRIED THROUGH Q'S WIDE ENTRANCE HALL, under the huge, curved tusks of the mammoth, wondering how and where I would set up my booth for the ball. On a giant LED screen map of the globe, like the one in the secret gallery, every single one of Q's currently active 2.5 billion users appeared as dots with colored lines springing from and connecting them, point by point, like the world's largest air traffic route map. Stopping for a moment to look, I watched what might have been my own face become a red circle, connecting to other red circles in the building, on the Q campus, in the City of San Francisco, in the State of California, in the continental U.S., out to the edge of the earth, each shift in order of magnitude revealing just how small we all were, here on this minuscule dot orbiting the darkness, and how vast the universe of Q, binding us all together, making us one. It was this, I knew, that Arman and his group found horrible: the connections between people made visible, threads in the great fist of Q. But I shivered at the sublimity of it: each of us, so small; the world, so large; Q aspiring to connect us.

That's what letters were, too, an expression of that yearning.

Years ago, I chaperoned a field trip Tristan's class took to the Contemporary Jewish Museum down in SOMA, a former power substation where the two Hebrew letters for "*Life*" now grow from the ground. There, inside a quiet gallery, spotlit in velvet darkness where she perched with her quills, sharpening and dipping, once scribed a *soferet*. (The word *book* transformed into the word for a person who scribes the book. I read this on a placard on the wall.) For over a year, the *soferet* leaned at her drafting table, transcribing 304,805 letters, not one more, not one less, calling each word by name.

The ends of her pigtails stuck out from under her knit cap like the bristles of brushes. While the children in Tristan's class scattered the gallery grabbing up dry erase markers, I pressed close enough to see the wet letters beading up, her warm hand, her firm faith. She was so beautiful, curved over her quill, whispering. I could never be that beautiful, that firm, that faithful. But I could be the hand who gave that longing a shape in this world.

I belong here, I told myself. *I am part of it.*

"The artist resides!" Jae Kim's long fingers cradled a *Lol Cats* mug filled with cereal the shape of cat kibble. He deposited it on the gridded paper cutter at my elbow, its blade as long as my arm. As he watched me rummage through the cabinets, he picked a freeze-dried pink heart from the heap and crunched it between his teeth, covering his mouth. The gift of food, his modesty in the midst of all this insane wealth and self-importance: I liked him for that. "It's okay for me to use this stuff, right?" Connie once told me I stole like a raven, gathering up glittery bits for my art, but it was important to me to incorporate pieces of the world around me in the bricolages that were my illuminated capitals—postage stamps, faces cut from photos, penciled family recipes.

"As long as you don't try to leave with them." Jae covered his mouth again and picked a fleck from his teeth. I'd barely gotten out the door with my own portfolio; I already knew that much.

"But I can get into most rooms around here, right?" I asked Jae, waving my badge, remembering that incredible manuscript in Q's secret library.

Jae's hand moved away from his mouth. "You haven't said. What is it you do?" *If I didn't know better, I'd have said he was suspicious. But how could he know anything about Arman or what he'd asked me to do? Anyway, I hadn't agreed to do anything. That wasn't what I'd come here for. That wasn't it at all.* Still, the heat rose to my cheeks when I told him the truth. "I write letters."

Jae looked me up and down. "Letters?" He propped his chin against his palm. "Sooo, you're a writer?" He sounded bemused, wary.

I shook my head. "No. I should have said—I'm a scribe."

I sounded like a pimply fifteen-year-old boy talking about elves and orcs. I frowned, feeling the heat rise up into my ears.

Jae's face tilted in his palm. "Scribe," he murmured. "Oh *my.*"

Instead of a sting, there was a softness to it, an echo of the sadness I felt myself at being something so ridiculous.

My phone buzzed. Another push reminder of Connie's birthday. *Ugh.*

Outside the art studio, up the cool, dark stairwell, rushed a chorus of voices, a faraway, schoolyard sound. Jae shrugged up from the stool, rising to his full height. "I'm an artist, too, you know. Or would be. I haven't done anything since I've been here."

I followed him upstairs. Sauntering to the pool table, he began racking up the balls, hefting each cool colored globe in his large hand as if it weighed years.

Before Tristan was born, I'd had a friend named Kareem. Kareem had started like me with ink-blackened fingers but had moved into multi-media, real birdhouses with medieval-styled birds, a representation of single motherhood in Black America; it was a kind of hagiography. And it was so beautiful. The thinness of the black lines, the saturation of the yellows, reds, and blues on the hand-pigmented birds. Kareem did what he loved for the love of it. He never compromised himself. And then he got picked up by a gallery, a really good one. He'd stepped into another room of his life; his hands moved in a different way through the air. Being seen had made Kareem truly lovely. I was not lovely. Unwashed, greasy, spitup-on, I had no energy for anything, no time in my life for art or for friendships that couldn't accommodate a baby. That was true. But, also, seeing Kareem was too painful. Kareem, his sail filling with wind, while the tide sucked me under. I've seen him in the *New York Times* Sunday Magazine. Still with the birds. And while I felt proud of my old friend, seeing his face in print next to his beautiful, intimate creations, I also felt as if one of my father's very small screwdrivers, the narrow, sharp one he used to help adjust the roller skates for my tiny mouse, had been plunged into my chest, where it turned and loosened some small screw that fell with an almost inaudible *plink* to the ground.

I wondered if that was what Jae was feeling now. I'd often thought about what I could have achieved if I'd had world enough and time. But Jae had been here forever, apparently free to do as he pleased, and what had he done? He leaned against the edge of the pool table, the eight ball loose in his fist. "4,748 days," he sighed. "Like *Rent*, but oh, so much longer." He slapped the black ball between the others with a crack. Connie would have had smiled at Jae's math. Connie could have verified the number down to the leap years.

"What kind of artist?" I knew how painful it could be to be reminded of a vocation you never practiced, to be asked what, after all this time, you had to show for yourself. But he had brought it up. I knew that loneliness, too; he wanted me to know.

The pool balls burst apart. Jae took off his glasses and wiped them with a square of soft cloth he pulled from the breast pocket beneath his sweater. "I'm a writer. Was." He planted his glasses back on the bridge of his nose and turned toward the pool table with a Vanna White smile. "I keep threatening to write a juicy tell-all about Q, but then I'd have to leave all this." We gazed at the shining Plexiglas silos of Lucky Charms and Froot Loops. "And, if I'm being honest, I never will." A dimple opened up at the center of one of his cheeks, a drain sucking away hope.

I could identify. But Jae protested.

"It's different for you." Jae looked down his cue at me. "Many of the artists who move through here get picked up by galleries and agents. Q is powerful. When you get picked to be a part of this, people notice. This is how they find you." I wasn't sure I had been picked. But I had gotten in. And I might be picked, if I found a way to step into this world for a night and make it my own.

I studied Jae in his butter-colored boots. He was still so young. "If you don't like it here, why don't you leave?"

A cube of blue chalk turned between Jae's fingers like a die he could roll to determine his fate. "Money. At the end of the day, I get a paycheck, and I stay."

At the end of the day—a phrase that haunted the halls of Q and the tables of the Hawk & Pony and the nooks of Temescal Alley like an elegy to all that is lost: *at the end of the day, at the end of the day, at the end of the day.* The words spooled out between us like a kind of prayer, one to mark the hours. In all the years at my own job, the job—there was no doubt about it—I would go back to as soon as the power came on—I'd uttered the same. But, in that wild moment, I looked around at the bright, colored pool balls, the colored cereals in their high columns pouring down from the wall, and I imagined not going back.

My phone buzzed again, and for no reason except that her name had been turning up on my phone a dozen times a day, I remembered a funny little song Connie—who was not a singer or a musician—sang for me on a borrowed ukulele, a breezy, plinking Hawaiian tune she had rewritten to make *Amy* rhyme with *slay me*, how her fingers went white at the tips where she pressed them into the nylon strings and how red they turned afterward—so red I had to suck them in my mouth, one at a time.

All her concentration puckered her mouth, so that, even in the funniest parts of the song, she didn't smile; I remembered her hiccough, after the last, sad note of her funny little love song. As I glanced at my phone, I wondered at the way people remain attached to each other far past the point at which it's any good for either of them. It's an art, knowing when to leave.

Jae glanced at my phone. "So, it's love, then?" The pool cue slid back and forth in the V of his fingers. "With your bearded engineer?"

Love? "God, no." I shoved my phone back into my bag. "I'm not—. Just, no." A whiff of that art supply closet smell rose up from the stairwell. I remembered walking into the art supply room with Heidi Chen, discovering LEZ BE FRIENDS scrawled across the door in pink chalk. I'd frozen mid-step. Heidi crossed her arms over her chest, turned, and raced out of the room.

"Of course." He glanced down at my long, curly hair and long black skirt down to my ankles, the black long-sleeved T-shirt that covered my pale arms down to my wrists, my chunky shoes. "I can see that. And I have also read your Q profile. Naturally."

Naturally. A bright spike of adrenaline hit my head, a chemical reaction when Jae's comment hit the residue of Arman's warning.

Jae and I were close enough that I could smell the marshmallow sweetness on his breath. He leaned long over the pool table: "Oh, the Q algorithm. How does it know what it knows?" Jae shrugged. "It's a mystery."

My stomach lurched with the seasick feeling that he knew so much more about me than I knew about him. But then I reminded myself: I had deleted my profile. Whatever Jae had looked up on me, it wasn't there anymore.

"Unlike that." Jae tapped my badge with a carefully filed fingernail. "There's no mystery to a Radio Frequency I.D. To answer your question: You've got a Vendor badge. You can't go anywhere with that."

9 *Ghost Bikes*

OVER THE BAY, THE SKY THROBBED WITH THE LAST of the day. Michael and I met near the trolley turnaround and headed toward the Embarcadero. A warm wind brushed our cheeks and whispered that night was falling fast, Michael murmuring with anxiety, "I don't want to go shopping, Amy. Let's do Gap.com!" as I hurried him along, pointing to the plastic jack-o'-lanterns glowing in Halloween displays, the green noses of witches.

It was the last Friday before Halloween and close enough to the Witching Night that costumed cowboys and warlocks ricocheted down Market Street, purling gin-warmed laughter into the wind. "Look!" I pointed out a bat-winged cape draped across the broad shoulders of a bare-chested man. "Do you want one that turns into wings, like that?" I didn't like the idea of my brother buying online—not because I believed Arman, exactly, but because I didn't exactly not.

Michael followed the man with his eyes and we both caught sight of it at once: a river of bodies streaming up Market Street from Justin Herman Plaza, a single, sinuous wave of cyclists surging through the streets—Critical Mass. They rode en mass through the City on the last Friday night of every month. That just-before-Halloween Friday they wore costumes, hundreds of vampires and caped crusaders and block-headed robots, the raucous human flood. The bodies blended together, a riot of color, reminding me that we're herd animals, masses of beasts rushing to sip from the river of time, not so special as we feel. It had often been a comfort, really, not to matter as a person quite so much. Over the years, I'd come to *like* the feeling of my own insignificance against the enormity of space and time. If what I did meant little, then what I had failed to do meant very little, too, in the great scheme of things. The sun would blow out like a candle. Even Shakespeare would vanish. This year, though, I had Q and the usual, nihilistic season fizzed with a sparkle of joy nothing could quench.

"They have a mammoth skeleton," I told Michael, bragging, as if what Q had was mine. (I had already decided I would see the Silver Bible on my own; no one knew more about radio frequencies than my brother and his friends.) "A whole one." The big model had impressed me. I knew it would impress my brother, too.

The wind lifted a feather of light hair off Michael's forehead. My brother had been born with thick, black hair that shocked me by dropping out, all in a heap, like pine needles, and then growing back milk-chocolate brown. It was a man's hair now, thinning. Michael nodded without taking his eyes from the stream of bicycles. "Woolly from Siberia. He's twelve thousand years old."

"What do you mean?"

"The museum wanted him. But Q got him. Woolly cost 645,000 dollars, Amy. He's real."

A real and complete, museum-quality skeleton in the halls of Q. I don't know why such extravagance surprised me, but it did, a breathless surprise at the vastness of history and of the cost and the very fact that the animal whose bones I'd stood under had, once upon a time ago, been alive.

The great, heaving wave of cyclists surged past.

The jingling, rolling chaos was disappearing into the dusk when a flotilla of skeletons bloomed in the darkness at Market and Pine: white skeletons on white bicycles, white frames afloat on the gloom.

Ghost Bikes.

Around the world, Ghost Bikes mark places on the road that a rider has died, the white-wheeled, white frames chained against light posts and street signs, a photo or plastic flowers in the basket. I stood stock still as they pedaled by, soft as wind, the whisper of their tires a white blur in the dark.

Connie used to bike to work on a silver mountain bike she described as "the Subaru of bikes," and secretly called *Lancelot*. She rode only at the times of the year when the sun rose early and set very late, because she had a problem with her eyes that made it difficult to see in the dark. It was that time of year, late summer, the birds shrieking us out of bed, the evenings cool and violet. That summer, our future so heavy with fruit, we'd turned back into simple animals, heavy and hungry and naked, orbiting each other in sheets flecked with crumbs. When she kissed me that morning, I could smell the sweetness of gardenia in the air; for once the lowing of the mourning doves did not sound mournful. "Baby. We'll continue this later." She was sipping a latte, her lips sweet with the dark chocolate chips she kept in a small baggie in her coat pocket, so proud of that new hunger. "Be safe." I stayed in bed, yawning like a kitten, listening to her unlock the bike, knowing she'd come home.

When the phone rang I was measuring black-eyed peas into a bowl, a bowlful of punctuation marks, that was how they looked when the phone rang, like pauses, like full stops—comma, period. "Am I speaking to Amy Black? You're the emergency contact." The nurse sounded skeptical. I twisted the gold ring on my finger like the top of a bottle; I was still holding a bowl full of black-eyed peas. I wanted to cast them into the sky like birds to bring Connie back home. "Ms. Black," the nurse measured out her words, "Ms. Austin has been in an accident. We're going to need you to come in."

I stared out the kitchen window. I could see Connie in the road, the tires of her bike gone to drunken O's. "She got hit," I murmured.

The nurse cleared her throat: "Ms. Black? Ms. Austin has been in a bicycle accident and broke a bone in her wrist." I could tell instantly than it was more than she intended to tell me, but my teeth had begun chattering, the frantic clattering of bone against bone. "We need you to come in. Can you do that?" Her impatience buzzed like an electric fence between me and Connie, a layer of static through which I could not see or understand what had happened.

"She broke her wrist? Is she getting X-rays? Why isn't she calling me herself?" A sudden scrim of cloud descended between me and the world. "Did something happen to the baby?"

The nurse paused, all the black-eyed peas in the bowl staring back at me. "You're going to have to come in."

Michael and I stood on the curb as the Ghost Bikes drifted into the darkness. Then Michael held out his phone, which had lit up with another one of those infernal ads for ginger flowers. "It's Connie's birthday. Halloween is."

I stared after the last of the white-framed bikes, floating away. "Yes," I agreed. "It is."

The Gap at Embarcadero Center was empty on a Friday night after work, the SOMA office crowd drained to Halloween parties and bars and the neighborhoods where they lived. But the lights were on and the preppy-looking store clerks in their pressed "Fall Fashions" were fluffing fleece vests and looking purposeful as we walked in, searching for the Halloween section, praying they had the same stuff in the store that they had online—a thought that hadn't occurred to me until I noticed that faux ermine-trimmed sweaters and neat black wool jackets were already on display for Christmas.

We were too late. Halloween wasn't even in SALE.

Michael, who hadn't wanted to walk into the store, and who was hungry, had started furiously rubbing his nose. I thought about taking his hand and walking back out, going to Beard Papa for a cream puff, going home and calling it a night. But then, among the women's black and charcoal winter suits, a piece of velvet drape caught my eye—a real cape, not something for a kid, or Halloween. I liked the idea of Michael in something serious, adult and formal, not a cheap piece of polyester, a costume. There was nothing fake about him. I imagined Michael at the door with the elegance of a real fifteenth-century Romanian prince, a person with a secret identity, a person with unseen powers, or at least someone who—when kids made fun of his face—could gracefully bend down and bite them in the neck. "What about this one?"

Michael, who had wanted to order his cape from the comfort of my kitchen, dragged at my hand like an anchor, and when he saw the skirts and scarves hanging in a black row around us, protested "This is the women's clothing, Amy!" But at the touch of the velvet under his fingers, I could tell he was pleased. I flipped the price tag between my fingers. Shocking. But it would last him such a long time. "Let's see how it feels."

On the day of Michael's bar mitzvah, my parents stood at the front of the synagogue and stretched out a prayer shawl, a plain white piece of fabric stitched with blue stripes. The strange letters edged the band against my brother's neck. Michael ducked under the gilt edging as the rabbi led him in the blessing, and when he stood with the white strip around his shoulders, I could see that they rose up higher. Michael had always reveled in the power of a cape.

I was just pulling the velvet around Michel's shoulders when the front doors clicked and a freckled redhead in tapered chinos hurried over: "I'm so sorry, but I'm going to have to ask you and your companion to leave the store." The clerk, androgynous in a neatly pressed Oxford and cardigan, was whispering, hurriedly, not to Michael, but to me, *about* Michael, an all-too-familiar dynamic that raised the pressure behind my eyeballs. "Please," they whispered again, though we were the only customers. Above us, the store sound system pumped out the old Cranberries hit, "Zombie." The clerk shifted their hips and glanced nervously at the guard, who turned from his post and headed toward us.

Michael began to whine: "I don't like going to the store. I don't like going to the store."

"What kind of problem?" I should have pulled out my phone and started recording this incident, I realized later; I should have dialed the ACLU. But I was too swept up by indignation and disbelief to think of it, and maybe, too, somewhere inside me, Arman's warnings about the power of my phone to work against me had planted a seed. I drew Michael closer to me, partly to calm him and partly to make it very clear that my brother was not a person I was going to conspire against with a salesperson who thought they could exclude him from a conversation.

The clerk's pale face flushed, as if this were a very humiliating episode for them. Their whisper dropped to a nearly inaudible level: "The Gap enforces a very strict shoplifting policy." The clerk's pink mouth tightened and the set of their hips, their crossed arms, their fierce whisper, suggested extreme discomfort.

I pulled the cape from Michael's shoulders and thrust it in their face. "We're trying on a cape. No one here is shoplifting anything. I assume trying on clothing is still allowed at the Gap."

The store guard, a wide Black man made wider by his black cargo pants and black rip-stop jacket, materialized at my side. "May I?" He was trying to be nice about it. The clerk nodded, and, blushing furiously, hurried back to the counter, where, with a push of a button, they unlocked the front doors.

"I don't like the Gap store," Michael complained as we threaded our way through racks of cashmere. "I like Gap dot com. *Dot com!*"

The burly guard explained: "They probably got him mixed up with someone else." He dipped his head in Michael's direction, "Someone who looks like him." *Looks like him* was code. Michael's genetic variation came with certain, typical features—the snub nose, the crows' feet, the almond-shaped eyes.

I stopped "Looks like him? Are there wanted posters behind the counter?"

The guard wiped his mouth with his broad hand and glanced back toward the counter, where the clerk glanced up to make sure we had really left. He turned his face away from them and kept his hand cupped above his mouth: "They scan your face. Not just you." He glanced, for the first time, directly at Michael, who quieted. "Everyone. That's how they do it now. They scan and then, if there's a match—" The guard poked his finger toward Michael's nose; behind his glasses, Michael flinched, but he didn't look away. "*Bing.* They got you."

"I work at the Academy," Michael offered. Michael got his job after he appeared in a news story about Moon Bounce Day under the headline *Oakland Boy Makes Music with the Moon*. This, though a.) Michael, twenty-four at the time, was hardly a boy and b.) the radio signals Michael and his ham radio buddy Jerry were bouncing off the face of the moon were not transmitting music.

The guard nodded, a little, deferential bow. "That's a very fine job!" Warmth softened his voice. "A good place to meet girls, too, I'm sure of that!" I winced a little, but I was used to it, still, the presumption of heterosexuality. And he laughed, the hearty laugh of someone who took real pleasure in other people's joy, a sound I hadn't heard much since my son had left our home, not at my job, not at the Hawk & Pony, not scurrying through the color-coded halls of Q. It turned down the temperature on my rage by half a degree; this man wasn't the enemy. He was a cog in someone else's machine.

The guard escorted us out into the windy fall darkness, the spiced perfume of the Gap still clinging to our hair and jackets, Michael's mouth folded into a tight, down-turned bow. "I told you I didn't want to." I hadn't listened to him and he blamed me.

"Hey," the guard raised his hand for a high-five that didn't come. "We're cool, right?" He turned to me. "Do you have pets? My wife has a little white dog, and she is always taking pictures of that little thing. *Snowball.* Isn't that cute? Every week or so the phone puts a whole lot of those Snowball photos together with a little song—all by itself—and calls it *Doggie Movie.* She's always bothering me when I'm cooking dinner. *Look, Ron. I've got a Doggie Movie.* I gotta admit, though. Some of those doggie movies are pretty darn cute." Michael's frown unfolded, his mouth opened a little, I could tell he wanted to see a doggie movie, too.

The security guard nodded. It was a dark night, windy and warm, the smack of a flag, the clank of the rope against the pole out there somewhere in the darkness. Outside the bright white box of the Gap, the darkness wanted to envelop us, to swallow us whole, but the security guard, with his dark, shiny nylon jacket and dark, satiny skin, attracted every beam and glow; the pale white lights through the glass, the traffic light between buildings turning from yellow to red, the yellow buzz of a streetlight, all wanted to polish and glaze him. "You know what else that phone showed her once? Gorillas. And you know what that was? Pictures of me and my kids. A whole lotta pictures of me and my kids."

I nearly burst into flame. Anger. And shame. Prone as I was to mistakes about faces, I lived in special fear of confusing Black faces. But I did. As a result, I had been especially timid about approaching people out of context, and so, out of fear of offense, had a thousand times doubly offended. Knowing now that my mistakes were at least partly neurological, did it make any difference? Neurology seemed like an excuse for something that moved through me, something much bigger than me. I was glad for the darkness then, the shadows that covered my mortification at the price of what belonged to me. It would be worth erasing all of history to undo that; if that was what Arman had asked me to do, I would have done it. This man had been kind to my brother.

We were standing outside the store, stories of office spaces above our heads, mosaic tiles laid out in circles at our feet. I stared down at the ground, the center of the bullseye.

We were all three of us outsiders there, but, among the three of us—the guard, my brother, and me—I alone could hide. The guard spoke directly to Michael: "It's not about you. You understand?" The guard towered above us; he had a good foot on me and Michael, who was small for a man not only because our parents were small, Old-World people, but by virtue of his divergent gene. He paused to make sure Michael was looking into his eyes: "Remember that. It's not about you."

I could tell by the jut of Michael's lip that it didn't make him feel better.

Our mother was in the hall before we'd turned the key in the lock. "Now both of you? My God, Amy. Have pity." I wasn't the only one who had regressed. Since Michael and my parents had decamped to my house, my mother demanded a degree of personal reporting that hadn't been required of me since high school.

My mother lifted Michael's pack from his back and hurried him out of his coat. "I left your dinner on the stove. Go serve yourself, Michael." To me, my mother said: "You know your father has to eat." I could hear *Wall Street Week* on the television in the living room. The house smelled like roast chicken, a warm, familiar, Friday night smell, the coats crowding each other on the pegs above the hallway bench. It was a night that felt suddenly like one of the Friday nights of childhood, the last of my mother's students hurrying through the hall where I pressed my nose against the cool pane, fogging it, while I waited for my father to come through the door, the dark smells of newspaper and aftershave and smoke stubbling his cheeks.

Then my father staggered into the hall in his gray sweatpants, his crooked body falling after his leg with every step. Once again, it shocked me: this gray, bent man whose spit dripped from his chin was my father now; there was no going back. Up in the hills, draped in the velvet blackness of outage, my childhood home lay abandoned and dark.

Halfway to the bathroom door, he turned and raised a trembling forefinger, the gesture he'd adopted to show he wanted something. His urgent finger brought me back to the moment, to the narrow hall shingled with coats, to the present from which all we could do was move forward. My mother and I went silent, waiting. His lips moved. His eyes moved from me to my mother.

"What, Dad? I can't hear you."

My mother lay a gentle hand against my father's back. "Mickey, darling?" she asked him. "Do you need help, my honey?" She rubbed my father's back and walked him into the bathroom. He could be in there for an hour.

I felt like shrieking. Some animal instinct possessed me with the desire to bolt back out the door. This was what their lives had turned into. And it would only get worse.

I slipped off my shoes.

On the shoe rack, I spotted a package I hadn't ordered. I picked up the box, which was big enough for boots. It was surprisingly light, and it rattled. It was addressed to my mother. The blackouts could end any day. I wondered what she could have needed that wasn't waiting for them at their house.

"Mom," I asked her back. "What did you order? I can pick up anything you want. I can go back up to the house."

My mother's hand fluttered in the doorway: "I don't know. Just a few things we needed." She shook her hand and, with it, shook herself free of the conversation. "Does it matter?"

My mother could be evasive, dismissive even, when she wanted to be. But this felt different. Either she was lying, or she didn't remember, and, studying the pinched skin on the back of the right hand that held my father's entire world in place, I couldn't decide which was worse.

10 Earth-Moon-Earth

238,900 MILES STRETCH BETWEEN THE EARTH AND the moon. Thousands of miles of blackness and silence. My brother does not see the distance between here and there. Michael sees the moon. Ever since he was eleven, Michael has been a ham radio enthusiast, a hobby introduced to him by our father, who spent a brief period interested in tremendous distances when he was stationed in the Marshall Islands and our mother, whom Dad had just met, was still a college student here in California. In those days before email and Skype and cheap long distance, the Marshall Islands were even farther away than they are now. But my father and his friends were switch-and-transistor nerds, the original Hacker/Makers; they spoke across islands via short wave radio and to them the moon on full nights looked like a big white satellite dish in the sky. It was off the surface of the moon that my mother, crouched next to the Anthony Chabot Transit Telescope "Rachel" in headphones and a wool pea coat, heard my father's watery voice triangulated from 4,500 miles west and 238,900 miles above the earth ask "Will you marry me?"

It's a romantic story but I've heard the way a voice comes to earth from the surface of the moon. Earth-Moon-Earth (EME) is the longest communications path any two stations on earth can use to propagate a radio signal. As a beloved member of the ham radio community,

Michael was invited to Cal Poly for World Moonbounce Day, a celebration of the fortieth anniversary of the Apollo 11 mission. It was in the papers and broadcast on a local interest segment of the local news. From the surface of the earth to the surface of the moon is a very long distance to travel, even for a sound wave, and the moon is not smooth, but a powdery, pocked cake of dust and rocks. On top of that, the moon wobbles. Voices bounced from the surface of the moon take an age to rebound to their target; they sound like words through water. The delay makes reciprocity difficult—*Hello!* You call out, while the other person is already asking a question. The way data returns from the lunar surface has been described as "weak signal communication" and also "colossal loss." Inside a lab at Cal Poly SLO, in front of the television cameras, my brother's cheerful voice left earth and, 5.4 seconds later, came back, a haunting, submarine echo.

238,900 miles—that's how far away it feels, when a child grows up and moves away, like they are radioing back from the surface of the moon. *Propagation, fluttering, loss*—I kept thinking of those many miles between the moon and earth, staring at the phone that Friday night, sitting in Tristan's room, thinking about my son and the new distance between us that was both no more than distance and everything more than distance—the beginning of a life in a different orbit. The soft powder kicking up between all of my words.

The air was still and cool in Tristan's bedroom, posters of ultimate Frisbee players and size 12 Nikes tucked under the edge of the bed, the lamp with the green glass shade on the desk. I clicked it on. It was the same kind of banker's lamp, the same golden light, that fell on the pages of the scribes over the Tip Top Bicycle Shop.

There had been no sign of the scribes or Arman or his *distributed node network* when I pressed my nose against the glass windows of the shop on the way home from San Francisco, determined to ask him what the fuck was going on and why my brother had turned up in a database of thieves. That night, the mailbox didn't speak, and I imagined that all of the desk lamps and the pencils and the white-haired women had vanished, a figment of my dreams.

Filled with thought of tremendous distances, my mind went to the dusk-violet pages of the *Codex Argentus* Sandy Jensen had shown me in the Q library, spangled with silver forms. Before the *Codex Argentus*, I'd never seen dyed vellum, not in the flesh, and it was magnificent, so vivid and so deep. It had gone missing so long. I needed to know more about that manuscript. I wanted to know where it had been all these years, and where it belonged now, and, most of all, I wanted to know how it ended up at Q.

But, the next day, I had to spend the long Saturday at home with my father while my mother went out to have her hair washed, her fingernails done, a quiet day without a fall or an intestinal distress, but without a visit to the Hawk & Pony or a trip to Q, without a word from Arman. It was six days from Halloween—six days from Arman's deadline, six days from Connie's birthday, six days from my Q debut—and maybe all of this would pass without my having to do anything at all, without my having to erase or remember. At least, that's what I told myself as I itched to find out more about a book I didn't have time to research.

Finally, my father settled in front of the TV and I went up to my room, spent. In the sunset hour this Saturday evening, *The Lady and the Unicorn* hung on my wall blushed like a Madonna weeping blood; the miracle appeared and disappeared in the span of ten minutes.

Michael's bedroom window lit up, a cheerful orange halo against the darkness. We had ordered his cape, the velvet one with black trim. His voice rattled the glass. "Ten-four!" he called to his friend Jerry. "Over!"

After a day with my father, I could understand why my mother felt so wrung out. Fifty times a day, he crooked his finger toward some want or need. He needed juice; he needed pills; he needed to get up or sit down again. I didn't know how my mother did it without losing her mind.

I opened my laptop and typed *Codex Argentus* into the search bar, but then didn't hit return.

Instead, I found myself remembering barred light on white sheets, the golden head of a daisy by Connie's bedside. Connie was on painkillers, her wrist bundled in black fiberglass—the laughably minor but most visible injury of her bicycle crash. She'd asked me to say a prayer. The words drooled from her mouth, her head dropping: *Pray for us. Please just this once. Say a prayer*. I curled the tips of her fingers in my fingers, which kept brushing the rough edge of the cast: "I don't know any prayers."

Could a quill's edge spill prayer, I'd have prayed. Wet ink. But whispered words? A Listener who changes fates? Connie whispered *If you loved me, you would do this*.

I was still sitting staring at the light fading from the wall when my mother walked in, her hair honey blond again and shellacked smoothly in place, her fingers painted blood red—*Good for you, Mom*.

"Dad said he had a good day?"

I nudged the laptop under my pillow. My mother had never been thrilled about my interest in medieval manuscripts; with all the shit she was dealing with in her own life, she wouldn't want to know that I was indulging in it still. "Quiet," I said, and told her again what he had eaten, and what he drank, and when he took his pills. When he went to the toilet, now, I had to help him on and off with a diaper.

"I'm sorry we're inconveniencing you. We'll be back home soon, I'm sure." My mother stepped closer to the bed. It was a small room; the bed nearly touched the standing desk; the desk touched the quilt hanging from the wall. I could smell her sticky hairspray, the lacquer on her nails. She reached out to touch the edge of the quilt and I was afraid she would say something about the hours Connie had spent piecing together that quilt from a basket of scraps she kept by her bedside, humming the French lullaby she loved, *Fait dodo, Colin mon petit frère*, with a needle between her lips and another needle in her arm, ignoring the discomfort by piecing together the future and the past.

I wondered if she was thinking of my own babyhood when she said: "You've always been a good girl, Amy. Do you know that? Since your brother was born, you've been such a love, such a help, letting him hold your finger when he was learning to walk, soaping his hair into little horns in the tub, drawing him pictures. You were so rambunctious on your own, such a wild little thing when you weren't scribbling." I winced inside but I didn't say anything.

"Do you remember the neighbor's girl, Mika? When you girls were fourteen, her mother stopped me in the market. Her hair was wild and her eyes were all red. They'd had to put a burglar alarm in the house, she said, to keep Mika from crawling out the window. She was sneaking out at night with her boyfriend and driving their car. Can you imagine! And the drugs. I almost felt guilty. I had nothing to complain about!" I chose not to remind my mother that she *had* complained, to me, about my oddness and my wildness and my fingers stained with ink, the cigarette smoke in my hair. It was better this way, the past in the past. "You were such a good girl. So devoted to your brother. And then with Connie—"

Connie. Connie's birthday. Always Connie. I cleared my throat. Six more days and then this would be past. For another year, this would be past.

"Well," she turned to the window, my mother at my bedside, my mother in the glass.

Michael's voice echoed up the stairs, a booming sing-song: "Louder, Dad! I can't hear you! I can't hear you!"

"Amy—" So much for the past staying in the past. I recognized this tone, this sharpening suspicion from the time I'd started having sex with Heidi, from the time before we finally told my parents Connie was sick. We hadn't been confidantes, but my mother always knew. "You've been coming home late—" I shook my head, but my mother put her hands up before I could answer. "I hear people coming in and out through the window at night. Are you sneaking people into your room that you don't want us to see? What's going on? Are you seeing someone?"

I almost laughed out loud.

"Are you embarrassed to introduce us to your *friends*?" She dropped her voice and whispered ferociously: "Are you meeting strangers for sex?" She whispered "sex" so quietly, all that was left was the stickiness of her mouth around the consonants, which I saw in the air between us: the curve of a woman's body around mine; the intersection of two lovers. My mind drifted to the gold globes in the darkness, the low voice like water, the lines etched across Blue's hips.

My face flushed hot and dry, but I wasn't sixteen, I wasn't Tristan, caught up here stinking of pot with his arms flung over the windowsill, legs on the other side. I was an adult. This was my house. I didn't have to explain. "Mom—"

She was shaking her head so vigorously, her perfectly set hair had begun to break apart. "I saw that black-and-blue mark on your hip. You were bleeding. For heaven's sakes, your skirt was torn! I'm *concerned*!" My mother whipped her cell phone in front of my face: a graphic ad for *scizr* blazed down the side of her Q feed, a woman's head at another woman's breast. "At first I didn't know why it was showing me all this. *Blendr, Grinder, Tickle, Fickle*. Please! I'm seventy-four years old!" My mother shook her head. "But then it showed me a pair of boots. *Your* boots. And then—" my mother shook the phone like it was a Magic Eight Ball, prepared to reveal the future "—a cape! Everything you do—" she shook the screen again: "—comes into my phone!"

I grabbed the phone from her hand. "Are you slut-shaming me?" Her face puckered. *Slut* wasn't a word her generation had reclaimed. "Are you trying to make me feel bad for enjoying my sexuality? That's all I have, Mom." My voice cracked. "Am I supposed to sit in this house with you and Dad and Michael, celibate now that my lover's gone, my child is grown? Am I supposed to become a juiceless old prune?" It wasn't my mother's fault. At every hot or lascivious or shameful thought these days, my face went hotter. I knew what that hot flush meant; my hormones were deserting me. But that didn't mean I wasn't mad about it.

My mother recoiled as if I'd slapped her. Then she pulled her head up and straightened her shoulders. Her voice went cool. "That was cruel."

"I'm sorry." I was. For most of my life, I wouldn't have been, but things were different now.

She stepped close enough to press her hand against my cheek. "You might not want to believe it, but your father and I were crazy about each when we met. Just because we weren't teenagers didn't mean that we didn't want to do all that." She shook her phone again. "But that's not what makes a relationship, Amy. Your father was always faithful to me. Devoted." Her voice became stern: "And I am faithful to him now, when many women would have put him in a home." She reached a thin hand to my shoulder. "You won't always be young."

The laptop pressed hard into the skin under my knee. I could still hear her chiding me, casting a side-eye at my boots on Christmas morning *You're a middle-aged lady!*

My mother's phone lit up in my hand with another advertisement for flowers. Down the hall, the toilet flushed and we could hear my father banging his elbows against the bathroom wall.

My mother tilted her head toward it, but her eyes didn't leave my face: "What if *you* need someone to take care of you one day? Sex won't get you that. That kind of care takes loyalty. It takes love." She kept her eyes fixed on me, bold accusers.

How could I tell her that sex was the best it was going to get?

Sex that was even that moment lifting me from the bed, leading me toward 16th Street Station, where Blue had told me she would be performing with her troupe. Suddenly, urgently, I needed to find her, though I had no idea how.

11 16th Street Station

THERE IS NO 16TH STREET STATION IN OAKLAND. (There's a 16th Street Station in San Francisco, in the heart of the Mission, palm-treed and reeking of piss. It's no place to throw a party.) But there used to be. Over in West Oakland, its back on the shoreline and the railroad tracks, the gray brick Beaux Arts station with its big, arched windows and neoclassic balustrade was once the Terminus of the Transcontinental Railway. Now it was abandoned, a victim of the Loma Prieta earthquake and the end of the railroad era. But like many old things, the hipsters had found it. Blue and her friends had found it.

On Saturday night, the wide cement yard stretching out in front of the station buzzed with light and bodies and vape, pale clouds that smelled of strawberry and mint. Giant sculptures rose over the crowd, shades of *la playa*. I recognized the giant papier-mâché dog from the warehouse, and the wire-framed dragon roared puffs of flame; at the center of it all, brass letters twelve feet high spelled out in tall, thin Art Deco capitals: YOU ARE HERE. They were latticed to let light speckle through.

It had been another warm day and the heat lingered on into the night, a warm breath on the skin, an impatient longing. Blue had said she was performing here tonight and I wanted to see her, if I could, without being seen.

I handed over six dollars for a red plastic cup of draught beer and wandered through the painted, half-naked bodies and let the beat of the bass move through my hips. Two women in black bodysuits were rolling a glowing ball between each other's arms and legs. With my eyes half-closed, I could feel the solid shape of the letter *S*, hard and warm and tasting of mango. I had no idea how to find Blue, and doubts about whether I should, but I was enjoying myself.

It had been years since I'd been out alone to a party. I met Connie when I was nineteen years old, and we'd gone out dancing together and with friends, throwing our hair, stripped to our T-shirts, sweating, grinding. And then. And then. And then. It was fun, dancing in the dark, the beat alive in my bones, knowing no one would recognize me, hoping someone would, gazing at the pretty figures moving in the colored lights, a beautiful rather than alien anonymity.

I emptied my cup and kept dancing until a figure wove through the crowd, a glittering gold tattoo on her forearm, and disappeared into 16th Street Station.

The main hall was vast, high ceilings and arched windows, ornate moldings and marble steps in their flaking shabbiness evocative of that greater Age of Rail. White pillar candles burned everywhere in great organ-pipe configurations. The thick, warm smell of wax bleared the air and warmed it. People milling at high tables drank blue liquids from real glasses. Pastry flecked dark beards and wide cravats. Everywhere, people had dressed for a fin de siècle Sunday in the Park of Frozen Brimstone: women wore high bustles and straw hats; men wore frock coats and monocles dangled from chains; but their smiles unveiled shining fangs and all their eyes were blue as veins. They were drinking and laughing loud, roaring, while blue-sequined Satans with forked tails delivered cool blue canapés. So many shades of blue but the one I wanted.

At a table near the door, I found a scattered stack of temporary tattoos: the nude suspended inside a leafy O against a spangled sky. *Press on with damp sponge*, the instructions on the back read. *Wash off with soapy water.*

I wandered back outside toward the old ticket window under the graffiti-splashed trestles, to a dank little room where a large metal sign offered *Fountain Souvenirs Cameras Films Sundries* in sturdy, early mid-century block capitals. Among the crowd, I felt more displaced than ever, the costumes and the colors and the laughter accentuating my own oddness, my blindness. But, down the old refreshment window, I could imagine myself somewhere else, some*time* else, alone at the start of a journey.

I stepped into the cool, abandoned space where travelers once bought newspapers, peanuts, and popcorn. The room echoed with dripping water, though I could not see water anywhere. Light spilled from the farther doorway and I followed it.

A floodlight blazed up the tiled phone vestibule, the telephone long ago ripped from the wall; at an eagle-gilded lectern stood a woman with dark, radiant skin, and a halo of hair spangled with silver glitter. She wore a shimmering white robe on which great, feathered wings had been mounted at the shoulders. From the darkened door behind her podium, I could hear laughter, echoed voices.

"Settle down, y'all!" she yelled out without turning around. "I'll be there in two *freakin'* seconds." Then she pulled a bottle of Perrier from under the lectern, and with a hiss brought the bottle to her lips until all the water was gone. "Whew." She wiped her mouth with the long sleeve of her robe and murmured, "Just let me find the damn script." She shook her head and a cloud of glitter materialized around it before shimmering down into the dusk. "Everyone always has some new plotline to add to the damn script." With a huge sigh audible over what sounded like the hammering of metal, she tucked the bottle back out of sight and began to turn away, one big wing brushing the side of the lectern. "And tonight is sup*posed* to be a party."

I stared a moment too long. Before she stepped into the darkened doorway, she spotted me and turned back.

"I'm sorry—" the Archangel glittered coolly on her perch, eyeballing my black skirt and top. "Are you lost? Witches are meeting up on the train platform—" she shook her robe up to her elbow and tilted her wrist awkwardly toward the light, revealing a thin, gold watch— "fifteen minutes ago."

Her voice, her cadence, the little gold watch against her dark, supple skin reminded me of a woman Connie danced with once to spite me. We had just won a new right in the courts. We were at a backyard party at Connie's friend Mirabel's new house, an early-midsummer-night's eve, and the yard was striped with rainbow ribbons for a potluck barbeque to which we'd brought the leftovers of an argument about whether it was too soon for Connie to try to get pregnant. That hadn't been our plan; Connie's desire came on suddenly, and threw off what I thought I'd agreed to. Connie had an ability to put on a happy face in the midst of conflict that I always found bewildering, but that night Connie stayed angry at me when we were in public. "If you're in, you're all in. We've been together since we were nineteen, Amy. How much more time do you need?" It was warm out, glowing, summer dusk, and Mirabel's band was playing salsa. When people started to dance, Connie thrust her paper cup in my hand so hard the alcohol splashed out onto the front of my dress. "If we wait too long—" Her words trailed behind her as she picked up the polished fingers of a woman wearing a watch just like the Archangel's, a thin gold band on an arm that was soft and round, and they danced while my face burned in the dark. It was the meanest thing Connie ever did to me, running away from me once we'd started something, dancing with a woman that beautiful. It should have been a warning.

"I'm not a witch." I stepped closer to the lectern. Even as I said it, I felt hysterical, witchy laughter bubbling up in my throat. With my steel blade and my bag of inks, my dark desires and my hobnailed black boots, of course I was a witch. Wasn't that why Arman had wanted me? To cast a disappearing spell? I strangled a laugh. I'd had more to drink than I realized.

The Archangel cleared her throat and cocked her head. Next door in the high-ceilinged station, the heavy notes of an organ had begun to play a gloomy tune that echoed through the walls the way the rumbling of the trains must once have echoed. There was a screech, and more laughter, and then the laughter died away.

I raised my voice. "I'm looking for Blue." I'd started out confident, but by the time I articulated her name it came out with a question mark, because Blue, like the Archangel and the organ music and the dying laughter, had begun to feel like a dream.

From somewhere above us, the organ wheezed into a stream of whirling, colored, funhouse notes.

"A Google search about a color. I like that." The Archangel pulled her fingernails through one of her large wings. "Some people would tell you to look that up in the Encyclopedia, but I will not. It's Saturday night and the middle of a party, but here you are, aren't you? Curious about the colors of the rainbow!"

I started to protest. But she pulled a sheet of paper from beneath the lectern and pushed it toward me: "Just fill this out. Can you write longhand? That's the best way. Just fill this out, take it down to the nice ladies at the farmers market—" She paused to appraise my jet-black hair streaked with silver, my black combat boots. I could tell she still wasn't convinced I wasn't a witch. "Tell them you know James Franco. You got that? Go to the ladies at the farmers market on Sunday morning and they'll help you get started."

Longhand? I stared down at the form, but it was too dark to see; I didn't have my glasses. I was about to ask her what she meant, but laughter roared again from the hall next door and echoed through the chamber, which had begun to throb with flashes of green light from the room beyond; a walkie talkie crackled below the lectern. I was having a vertiginous feeling, like I had come to the party to enter Blue's world and wound up in Arman's. "Is Arman here tonight?" I asked, wondering immediately if I had said something I shouldn't.

"Arman?" She looked me up and down again, as if nothing in the way I looked could explain my relationship to him. Her great white wings shook as she squawked into the walkie talkie. "Someone's here for Arman." Between the noise of the music and shrieks coming from the door behind her, I couldn't make out the reply, but she pointed up and said, "He'll meet you on the platform. You have a good night, now." As she turned to go, I saw the beautiful reptilian ridge of scales trailing its fearful symmetry down between her feathered wings, the scaled, forked tail.

I clomped up the stairs to the elevated platform, the first elevated tracks west of the Mississippi, the old sunken track beds where freighters on the Southern Pacific line once passed through Oakland, heading across the Mississippi carrying punches, die sets, jigs and fixtures forged and ground at my father's own Golden Gate Tool & Die. I looked down into shadows wishing I could see him in their depths, young, healthy, standing straight and tall. Then I propped my hands up on my hips and looked out at the Bay.

The party throbbed below, but milder from this distance, a familiar heartbeat—but one that masked the sounds of footfalls.

"Amy!" Arman appeared, panting against the night, his big, pale body outlined by the sparkling lights of the bay. "It's Arman!" He touched his chest, which was bare. He wasn't wearing his glasses. I didn't recognize him—glasses or not—but he knew that. That was the point. Green-white grease paint covered his thick shoulders, which were draped in furs. A flap of fur folded down at the back of his neck, and when the light hit it, grinning teeth glinted back. Perspiration sparkled through the body paint. "Oh wow," he sighed, finally catching his breath. "You're here. Okay. That's terrific."

Arman being there was so preposterous that I almost protested *I'm* not *here*. But, of course, I was. Why was he there, too?

He shook his heavy head, more bearlike even than the head draped down the back of his neck. "You're in." His dark eyebrows began to wriggle and jump. "So the next step is the Kill Code. We think we know who's got it."

Though I had no intention of helping him, still, after the incident with Michael, I was a little intrigued. My own son was an idealistic young person; I wanted to know how Arman thought he could pull it off, a big, friendly guy dressed like a caveman, screwing over one of the most powerful men in the world.

According to Arman, Hack had a mania for control, and wanted to be able to exercise an option to destroy. "There's a cypherpunk rumor about an urban legend at Q Engineering that some friends from Hack's Tigertone days remember him boasting that he wanted to take over the world with his code, and he planned to build in a back door, so that, if he wanted, he could also destroy it." Arman shook his shaggy head and poked a finger at the glasses that weren't on his face. "According to the legend, the Kill Code is carried around at all times by somebody at Q, somebody from Hack's way back. Some people say there's a capsule slipped under the skin of an arm; some people say a chip inserted into the brain."

I had turned to face Arman and now I could see the party, boiling over from the station onto the patio where I'd been dancing what already felt like a long time ago. "A story about an urban legend about a rumor?" The *legend* sounded like another ingenious bit of code Hack had devised to run and keep running through the ranks, the flex of a bad boy willing to burn down his seventy-eight-billion-dollar house, a lie told to keep everyone guessing.

Standing on the elevated platform, looking out at the letters spelling YOU ARE HERE, I had to laugh at Arman, and at myself. "I wish I could help. I really do. But an opportunity has come up for me. The chance of a lifetime. Among other things. And I can't just—" A flash of orange light announced a fireball sent up from the spectacle. "It's just not something I can do."

Arman shook his hairy head. "Is it the face blindness?"

I flinched at the word, which was still so new.

He was almost talking to himself. "Is it the face blindness that makes you so self-centered?" That stung. "No offense," he added. Tristan often did that—say *no offense* as a prelude or postscript to an insult. "I mean, it makes sense, doesn't it, if you can't really see other people, if you can't understand their emotions."

I wanted to scream in his face: *I'm not selfish! I raised a son! I wipe my father's ass!* But Arman had suddenly turned a bright light on something unspeakable in me—the times I had hidden in the car reading a book instead of making small talk on the sidelines of a soccer game, the times I had chosen the corner by the fireplace and a box full of notes in Connie's nineteen-year-old's handwriting over the translucent plastic tubes streaking ghost lines next to her bed. I had believed that, without the live wire of written words connecting me to another person, I could not know intimacy. But was I in fact incapable of *loving* someone, or capable *only* of living in a world I could see on a page? The lumbering thunder of freight cars rattled my bones, though these tracks didn't carry trains anymore.

"Hey," his voice softened. He could see that I was upset—another thing I couldn't do. "There was another application of facial recognition software that could really help people like you. Did you know that? A cross between facial recognition and emotional recognition software? From 436 points on the human face, the computer can tell if the person is happy or sad, or conflicted or lying. They developed it at the MIT Media lab to help people with Asperger's. Open source, developed for the common good. You could've used something like that if they hadn't ruined it."

I didn't know that. I tried to imagine it—a special pair of goggles I could wear, like a hearing aid or a translation device. Something that would have let me see more of the world than I saw. Would that have given me more access to life than I'd had, or taken something special from me, the deficiency that had caused me to grow my own, secret sense, the touch and taste of letters? I suppose I might have liked to find out.

But Arman shook his head. "Once the lab released that software, guess how quickly someone discovered they could make a lot more money using it to decide which ads people preferred for Diet Coke? Now your next employer can use your job interview to tell how much money you're willing to accept."

I wanted to believe him. But a gear turned in my mind: "Is that what you did to my brother? At the Gap?" It made perfect sense, Arman creating a reason for me to hate Q as much as he did, a threat to my brother. I didn't know how, but I also didn't know how I'd come here to find Blue and wound up talking to Arman. I was blind. Blind!

Arman squinted. "What happened to your brother?" When I told him, Arman brought his hand to his face and gave his beard a violent twist. "I'm sorry. Look, I don't know why that happened, but are you sure it's never happened to him before? Have you considered the possibility that things that seem to be happening all of a sudden are things that have been happening all along?" Greenish-white grease paint streaked Arman's beard and the little streaks of green paint in his dark, thick, hair looked so much like mysterious words in another language, I found it difficult to focus on the rest of his face.

Arman's body paint glowed ghoulish in the dark. "We're not making these things happen, okay? That's the point. They're *happening*. They're *designed* to happen. And they're dangerous." He raised a finger to scratch his nose. "Even if you're innocent—especially if you're innocent. They can ruin people's lives."

He sounded so convinced, but that's what people did, when they wanted to change your mind. I didn't have the ability to read his face. I couldn't tell the difference. And if I couldn't tell the difference, how could I trust him? After all, he was asking me to commit a felony.

Grease paint smeared Arman's fingers. A splice of skin showed through on his nose. Whatever he'd started out as—the Green Knight?—his twenty-first-century-self had begun to show through. "Did you know, they can already tell that a person is pregnant, just based on the things that you buy. And when you stop being pregnant, too." I shuddered. When Connie and I had been trying to get pregnant, ending a pregnancy hadn't been a crime.

Arman shrugged and the bear's head nodded against his back. "Look. We're not a terrorist group. We're a neighborhood. We help each other. We're asking you to help us. Maybe to help yourself, too."

But that wasn't the way I needed to help myself. Not by destroying Q.

The wind swirled up, carrying dead leaves and gum wrappers, a flattened plastic bag. Down below us, the deep roll of timpani had begun to beat the air. Arman straightened up, shook his shaggy head and sighed. I got the sense that he was done with me, and for a second, I couldn't help it, I felt rejected. He pulled the fur head up over his own head; he had become a towering bear. "Amy? What are you doing here?" The wind ruffled the tufted bear's fur where it stuck up between the ears. He spoke more softly now, cocked his head: "No. Really. I didn't stage this party for you. I didn't ask you to come here." He spread out claw-tipped, fur-covered hands. "Why *did* you come here tonight? What did you come here to find?"

What had I come to find? Blue. Blue, whom I didn't know at all, and couldn't recognize, and who was no more than the fantasy of one, perfect night.

"Have a good time at the party," Arman sounded like he didn't really mean it. Then he jogged back down the stairs, his animal teeth grinning wolfishly behind him.

Up on the platform, I closed my eyes and hugged my chest and let the wind wrap my hair across my face, black streamers against pale skin.

When I opened them, I saw figures down below perched on the brass letters twelve feet high spelling YOU ARE HERE. Three figures in pale, shimmering body suits; spandex hoods held their hair away from their faces. They were swinging flames: a baton, a blazing brazier, a burning hoop. They hissed through the black October night, flames whirling faster and faster until they spun sinewy ropes and twists of fire that appeared like solid figures, gold and orange letters painted onto the darkness, *L* and *O* and *V* and *E* spiraling off into an infinity, liquid gold against the dark page of night. The one with the hoop held still then, head tilted, birdlike, into the night. *Tal!*

I'd been chasing Blue. But Tal was the reason I needed, and the reminder. Tal was part of the world in which letters mattered, the only real world I know, a world on the other side of a glass. And so was Q—a world with magical things inside it, a world I wanted to become part of. I needed to deliver that letter, like I needed to get inside that library. I needed to make words that mattered.

"Tal!" I cried. But I was too far away.

12 Prayer Tower of God

TWENTY YEARS AGO, CONNIE'S BEST FRIEND MIRABEL bought a home of her own just east of Fruitvale, the Iglesia de Dios on one corner, Prayer Tower of God on the other, back when a woman buying alone in that neighborhood looked like madness and today looks like genius. Mirabel was all that and more, tattoos of the Virgin Mother and a one-eyed French Bulldog on her drummer's arms, a brand-new job in corporate at B of A. The parties at Mirabel's were legendary then, cars double-, triple-parked in the road, tea lights sizzling, Mirabel's band growling "Strike It Up," while street racers burned black donuts onto the asphalt, *O*s opening to a world you could enter for a little while to be free.

Then Connie got sick, and, with everything that happened, I hadn't stayed in touch.

That made Mirabel the person I most needed to see.

I was in the kitchen with my parents, brushing my father's hair. Once a sea of thick black waves, it had dissipated to a summer fog, soft and white and shapeless. He slouched at a kitchen chair, submitting, while my mother pulled a bottle of apple sauce from the refrigerator for his pills. On the counter, the radio murmured the daily news: ethnic Uighurs were being reeducated in China; in Washington, M. David Hacker had been summoned to testify on Capitol Hill about Q's data-sharing practices. I felt relieved hearing that. It made me feel better for not helping Arman. It was all being sorted out through the official channels. It would all be all right.

But what about my parents?

A trio of Crest White Strips lined up in shining silver boxes along the side of the fridge. They'd appeared one at a time, day after day, as if my mother had bought one, forgotten, and bought one again. How many would she buy this way? And why did she need her teeth so white?

"I've always been self-conscious about my smile." She leaned into the fridge, not talking to me, but to the applesauce and the small yogurts and the fizzing bottle of grape magnesium sulfate that gave my father terrible, explosive diarrhea, all the strange, soft, sweet things they now required. "Just because you think I'm old, doesn't mean I don't have a right to look decent."

"But three packages?"

My mother kept her head in the refrigerator. She had perfect pitch, and she told me once that the inside of her refrigerator hummed an F sharp. I wondered if she was listening to the music of the spheres in there. I wondered if she was losing her mind.

"I'm going out for a bit," I told her. "Will you and Dad be okay?"

I stepped back to study my father's head. The pale bird's nest had become a winter field ploughed with curving furrows. His head bobbed, his breath wheezed. "What, Dad?" I glanced at the clock. From inside the fridge, the plastic bottle of sauce appeared, a slush of yellow flesh. I fished in the drawer for a silver teaspoon. My parents now observed their own private Book of Hours, measured out in spoons of applesauce and pale yellow pills.

My mother's voice echoed from deep inside the vegetable drawers: "The car has been making a terrible noise. You really need to get it seen."

To my mother, a terrible noise could mean an augmented fourth. Or it could mean the engine is about to go. The real question was whether my mother should still be driving. She'd never been a good driver, swerving theatrically away from oncoming traffic, stomping the brakes like piano pedals, cursing like a sailor. Was she worse now? It was hard to tell the difference.

"I'm not taking the car." I shook four pills from the amber bottle into my hand. My father wheezed and spat. "Just hold on. I've got your pills." In his incapacity, my father had managed to become both meek and mild *and* impatient and demanding. When I was alone with him, he summoned me to his side for water, eyedrops, getting up, sitting down, a snack, a napkin, a wipe. No wonder my mother was exhausted. I dipped the spoon into the applesauce, sprinkled the yellow slurry with pills, and deposited the spoon into his mouth. "I'm taking the bicycle."

The bicycle was Connie's bicycle, the only bicycle we had, since Tristan had sold his to help pay for his trip. It hadn't been damaged, not badly. Connie had gone over the handlebars. The front wheel had needed to be tightened—that's all. I would ride it, and why shouldn't I? It was just a thing, a thing that had been allowed to sit and soak up so much weight and meaning, it had ceased to function as a thing. Two *O*s , two *V*s, an *I* on its back.

My mother reappeared from inside the fridge, her yellow hair cool as a ring of Jell-O. "The bicycle?" she said. I had wondered about her mental state, how tuned in she was to reality, how close to the mother I had known when I was younger. But now she came rushing back; her voice bled dread and pity. "Oh, *Amy*."

I wasn't thinking about Connie, though, but about the data trail Arman said I left everywhere I went, when I wheeled Connie's old bike out of our basement, pumped some air into the tires and started off toward MacArthur Boulevard, where I boarded an eastbound bus and paid with a handful of change to ride all the way to High Street, where I hitched up my skirt, threw my leg over the seat and pointed the bike down High with my hands on the brake.

I hadn't been on a bike in over a decade. *It's just like riding a bicycle*, I reminded myself.

My legs wobbled with nerves and the cars whizzing onto and off the ramps, but by the time I emerged from the shadows, I began to enjoy the feeling of floating. I could see why Connie had liked this. I liked the *tic tic tic* of the gears, a sound that reminded me both of Arman's request and of time passing, of the moments that had passed since this bicycle had driven me and Connie to the outermost edge of our happiness, moments that had passed and would keep passing until the pain was a small, bright spot very far away. Arman was not wrong that those two things were joined: how much easier to let go of Connie if my phone would stop remembering her every year on her birthday; but it wasn't worth blowing up the world for, either. Arman wanted a believer. And that wasn't me.

The bicycle rolled faster and faster, past crumbling bungalows and stucco apartments with names like *The Royal-Hi*, the sky open and blue, flat and palm-feathered. Hanging out the third-floor window of a three-story apartment building, a woman threw water down to the sidewalk from a red paper cup. She was holding a blue bowl in one hand, and the cup in the other, and she dipped the cup over and over into the bowl, scooping up water and pouring it out onto the clipped green hedge below, scattering it like holy water. She might have been crazy. She might have been bored. But it looked to me as the bright droplets arced into the sunlight and splattered that she was performing a ritual, exorcising something, maybe; maybe making her own luck. I wondered what my life might have been like if I had inherited something like that, if I could have believed.

Connie grew up in the Church, a fact that was somehow entwined with her winding up in the front row of Professor

Donoghue's class the spring we met; I think she was hoping to meet a girl entranced with the same candle smoke and incense that had flavored her childhood. Instead, she found me. Church wasn't something she talked about at first because being with a woman meant she had to leave it. But when we went back to Tucson to gather her high school yearbooks and her mother's ashes from the white stucco house with a bare spot on the wall, Connie took me around to the places she'd loved growing up: a dry creek bed where she used to watch shooting stars; the swing set next to her old middle school where she used to get high with a stick-skinny girl who let Connie kiss her a few times; the big desert mission church with its wedding-cake tower and bell. It was a Thursday afternoon near the end of the winter, high-desert cold, when Connie pulled me to the steps of the church and put her hand on the heavy wood door. I thought we might be there to expiate her guilt about what she'd said about her mother, that she would never forgive her, a jagged shard of rage that had flashed when we walked into her childhood home and not spoken of again.

In medieval times, the Church was a sanctuary for murderers and thieves.

Connie and I stole across the marble floor, but instead of taking shelter in the pews, she pulled me by the hand to a dark stairway at the back of the nave, up to a high gallery at the back. From up there, the stained glass glimmered like wet jewels in the watery winter light. "I always wanted to get married here," she confessed.

I stared across the high ceiling at the powder blue paint circling the frescoes of the saints, mesmerized by the color, the light, not really listening. "It's pretty."

She shook her head. Connie pointed to the little gate that separated the rest of the church from the altar, a cross inlaid in the marble floor below a fresco of Jesus and his friends. "I'm serious.

White dress, everything." I couldn't help it: I laughed out loud. One big guffaw at the thought of Connie, *my* Connie tarted up in satin and tulle like a *girl*, asking for a blessing from some sinful old man in a long black dress.

The Connie I knew was not a church girl from Tucson. My Connie was a person of science, her faith reserved for creation, not a Creator. A sexy nerd in a tie-dye Chem. Club T-shirt and sandals. But Connie wasn't laughing. Inside the pale, colored light of the church in those same sandals, red dust on her feet, I could see, suddenly, that she was a pilgrim, staring into the space between the gilded arches as if something else were there with us, something I couldn't see. The stale air smelled like old breath. It was cold up in the gallery, sunk in the dark. Cold pebbled my arms and, under the drugged-out, beatified gazes of saints, they started to itch. I remembered that murderers and thieves could only claim mercy in the church but then they had to give up all their worldly goods, and head out to the port, abjuring forever the realm. I wanted to go.

At the time, I reminded myself that Connie's mother had just died, that her family was gone, and that sort of thing pulls you back to religion, if you have it to begin with. But later I understood it wasn't that. Connie believed something special could happen in a place like that, even a place that would exclude us. By the time she slipped a ring onto my finger years later, without the blessing of a rabbi or a priest, I knew it was not what she wanted. In some way it would never be enough.

Constance. Her name meant faith.

Oh, how she'd surprised me with that. How I'd surprised her, with my gilt-haloed saints, my ink-stained fingertips and small crackling Book of Hours, my infidel heart.

The rubber tree in the front yard had grown up to the eaves and the jade plant was dead, but Mirabel's bungalow was still painted yellow and blue—*Go, Bears!*—and it didn't occur to me that, in twenty years, she might have moved until a long, thin teenager in pajama pants and a sculptural afro answered the door. When the boy howled into the house: *Mo——om!* I mumbled apologies and turned to go. The street was quiet, a tiger-striped cat sunning in a front yard scattered with pink plastic toys, an electric BMW with two different ride-share stickers in the window.

"Energy company or the Kingdom of God?" A silver cloud floated into the doorway of Mirabel's old house and had begun speaking to me, a nimbus of glittering curls.

I started to apologize: "A friend of mine used to live here . . ."

"A friend?" the silver nimbus asked, but wasn't that the same bat-eared dog Mirabel used to have on her forearm, the same Mary, mother of God? "Is that what you call someone you never see, you never call?"

"Mirabel—" Were there no limits to my blindness? Of course she'd gotten older; what had I thought? Connie and I had decided to have children; why hadn't I remembered that Mirabel had, too? Up until this moment, Mirabel had lived only in my past. I fixed my eyes on the sad-eyed dog and remembered something else I'd forgotten about Mirabel: She could decide to love you or hate you in an instant. "Mira, I—"

"You should see your *face* right now!" She yelled into the house, over her shoulder: "Jessie, come see her face!"

"Mama," the boy's deep voice called, "don't be salty."

That old musical laugh: "Amy Black, where have you been?" She reeled me in and crushed me to her chest, those drummers' arms. "Don't answer that."

Mirabel had Jessie set me up on a bar stool while she made us cups of tea.

I typed *Codex Argentus* in the Duck Duck Go search bar on Jessie's laptop while Mirabel called to me through the kitchen pass-through. "The kids don't use the word *lesbian*, but look at all this tea, AB, what other word can you use?" Mirabel always used to call me *Ay-Bee*, my initials, because she knew how much I liked letters, and she'd fallen right back into it, even though I hadn't stayed constant, even though so much had changed; dirty lacrosse sticks cross-hatched her entry, tubs of protein powder crowned the fridge; but maybe Mirabel needed it, too, the relief of recognition. She held a library card catalog drawer up to the counter and I picked through her selection of teas. I chose a black tea with licorice notes and handed back the long wooden box. I'd given it to her myself when she'd moved into this house. How strange. "Still drumming?" I nodded at Mirabel's still-impressive arms, lean and brown, if softer than they'd once been, the saucer eyes of the small dog wider and sadder.

She nodded at Jessie, who sat on the coffee table in front of the television, earbuds stuffed into his ears, his fingers and thumbs flicking over plastic buttons on a game controller, a sound like the dancing feet of little birds against a plastic pan; it reminded me of Tristan. "I play; he plays. We've got a band." I sensed she wanted to say something else, wanted to ask about Tristan, but didn't.

Water pounded into the kettle.

Mirabel had been generous inviting me in with no questions, acquiescing to my request to use a computer without so much as a *Power down at your house?* That's how it had always been: no conditions.

Mirabel nodded at the computer. "You gonna click on that?" She swept her silver curls into a rope with a twist of her hand, a gesture I remembered from long ago. Mirabel never clipped that rope up, just twisted it and leaned her head toward Connie or over her newspaper or a pot of sauce until the twist unfurled. "I wouldn't ask, except that you showed up here out of the blue after twenty years just to use my computer." Jessie's fingers fluttered over the plastic buttons of his game controller. "When, to think, you could have gone to the library."

A memory came back to me then of Mirabel out in her back yard the night of that party, the midsummer night Connie dropped my hand and went off to dance with someone else, the night she was so angry she couldn't hide it; that night she was possessed. She must have told Mirabel we were fighting. And why. Or maybe Mirabel watched from behind her drums while Connie danced with a woman who looked like the Archangel. After she and her band played a set, Mirabel came to find me with a fresh drink in her hand, a virgin piña in a thick glass with a dipped blue rim. "AB," she threw her leg over the bench where I sat staring into the thick fingers of a palm. "You look like the loneliest girl in the world. And you are definitely not alone." She laughed, that *do-re-mi* laugh, and threw her arm across my shoulders, the rope of hair chasing it.

I let my head fall on her shoulder, though I wasn't usually that way: "She wants to get pregnant. Or else she's not sure why we're staying together." Connie hadn't said that directly, but there she was, dancing with somebody else. Someone tapped the mic *one-two-three* in time with the hot drops hitting my arm. Mirabel drummed a finger lightly against the side of my head: "So what are you going to do about it?"

I'd forgotten that. How insistent she could be. How intolerant of indecision. A minute or two later, Mirabel left the table and Connie came over, and I remembered the knot of resolve that formed in my chest before I told her *okay*, the bright breaking open afterward, when Connie stood up and punched the air *Yes!* and kissed me, her dance partner forgotten. Suddenly, everything felt easy. But it was Mirabel who'd brought me there. Mirabel, who—afterward, way afterward, I'd heard, I did the math, was already pregnant with the boy before this one in pajama pants— who wanted us to come along with her. And that was why, after

Connie flew over her handlebars into a hospital bed, we stopped seeing Mirabel.

Now she perched on the bar seat next to me and, as I clicked the magnifying glass and the page filled with search results, she waited for an explanation. "Why didn't you? Go to the library?"

I jiggled the mouse and watched the cursor zip around the screen. "Someone told me that everything I do online is being tracked. Not just me, I mean. Everyone."

If anyone could confirm or deny Arman's claim, it was Mirabel. The same week Connie got her diagnosis, Mirabel slid her dog tattoo under a button-up and blazer and took a position in fraud at B of A. She'd stayed, a VP in cybersecurity now. (I'd Googled her once, but it was ages ago.) She knew more about online privacy and theft than most people in the world. This was part of her world, as much as the tattoos and tough talk. Her heels hooked over the rung of her stool, Mirabel glanced down the page of innocuous-enough-looking information about another ancient manuscript. "Someone was correct. And I guess that's why you're sitting in my living room."

Mirabel and I had never been friends online. We hadn't been photographed together or uploaded together into social media. No Q spiderweb spun threads between us. If I searched for information on her son's laptop, no one would tie the information or the search back to me. Mirabel's braid flicked in her hand, heavy as a snake. She had already done the math herself. I was using her and the eighteen years we'd spent apart; that, as much as the silence of those eighteen years, was unforgivable. I thought about getting up and walking out the door.

But Mirabel just sighed and dropped her hair. "Well, okay." I don't know if she'd decided to forgive me, or just decided not to talk about it right then, turning away into the life she'd made without me: "Jessie set you up on Tor, right babe?" She launched herself from the stool and went back into the kitchen.

Jessie grunted.

"*Tor*? What's that?" I imagined Norse gods hurling lightning bolts at the algorithms tracking me across the web. I was glad to have this strange word to interrogate, a better subject than me and what I was doing in Mirabel's living room, the same living room I had sat in and laughed in and ate in with Connie. A room I had last been in *with Connie*. There could hardly be another room of which that was true, that the last time I was in it, I was with her.

I watched Mirabel through the pass-through as she opened her cupboard full of teacups. "Acronym. The Onion Router. It's a browser that makes it harder to track where a request is coming from—not impossible, but harder. I let him surf the Dark Web. He needs to know what's out there." I followed her eyes to Jessie, still flicking away at the game controller, and imagined Mirabel zipping him into a Teflon suit and goggles to walk around the Dark Web.

"I caught him and his brother searching for their donor once. Poor knuckleheads were way too young. They didn't find him, but they found a fourth cousin on my side." Mirabel dropped tea bags into two blue teacups as big as small pools. "Weirdly, Xav was in Little League with their kid. One whole century, two continents, three generations later and we lived four blocks apart. They kind of looked alike." I wondered what that would be like, to look at a distant relative—or anyone, really—and see a resemblance. Mirabel sniffed. "The parents turned out to be assholes. There's a reason people lose touch." It was out of her mouth before she realized the implications, or maybe she did realize, maybe she was telling me we were having tea, sure, but I had ghosted her for almost twenty years. I thought about the friends I had made since Tristan was born, a revolving series of women happy to help out with a pickup or a playdate, coffee now and then, all the talk about insomnia and perimenopause, people I liked well enough but didn't love and who didn't love me back, who didn't turn to me when a spouse had cheated on them or their parents got sick, people I didn't turn to, friendships nothing like this one had been, even though Mirabel had belonged to Connie first.

Mirabel held the big blue cup in front of her mouth. "Your friend was right. We shed data like fingerprints, all over everything we touch. But *most people* don't give it a second thought." It sounded like an accusation. It sounded like a question: *So why are you?*

Why was I? There was something about the *Codex Argentus* that intrigued me. Something I wanted to explore and savor in private. I wanted to know more about that manuscript and I didn't want Q to know I wanted to know—and, for the first time I had the sense that if I Googled without protection, they just might.

If Mirabel really wanted to know why, she didn't press it. She just stepped back into the kitchen and let me do my research.

The *Codex Argentus* was an incomplete translation of the Gospels into the Gothic language, by the Gothic Bishop Wulfila ("little wolf"). He invented his own alphabet for the task, an adaptation of the all-capital Greek—and how uniform and beautiful it is. The Bible, which was carbon-dated to the sixth century, was most likely commissioned by the king of the Ostrogoths, Theodoric the Great. When Theodoric died in 526, the Bible disappeared from Ravenna, the capital of the Ostrogothic Kingdom in Northern Italy. After that, there is no record of the *Codex* in inventories or book lists for a thousand years. The Silver Bible reappeared in the Benedictine abbey of Werden, German, one thousand years later. How did it get there and where did it go in between? That is "the Mystery of the Thousand Years."

After the *Codex* resurfaced in the mid-1600s, it moved across Northern Europe as the booty of the Thirty Years War, until, finally, it landed at the Uppsala University Library in Sweden. An attempt was made on it there in 1995, when parts of the book on display were stolen. But the missing folia turned up again a month later in a storage box at the Stockholm Central Railway Station—with no clues about the thief.

Today, only 188 of the *Codex*'s original 336 folios remain. The surviving pieces include the final leaf, folio 336, which was discovered in October 1970 in Speyer, Germany, in the Saint Afra chapel, rolled around a thin wooden staff, tucked away with the bones of the saints. The Speyer Fragment was the last discovered folio. "*Until now.*" That's what Sandy Jensen had said. But there was no record of the discovery of the remaining 148 folia, which was surprising, given that the Silver Bible was the most valuable book treasure in Sweden, and one of the most important manuscripts in the world. The *Codex Argentus* belonged to the UNESCO register *The Memory of the World*. So how did the world not remember its fragments' discovery?

Officially, the missing folia hadn't been found. But it was almost like they didn't *exist*. If the museum in Uppsala didn't have it, where had Hack borrowed it from? Could Q unwittingly be holding a black-market manuscript? Wouldn't they need to find out?

Outside, an ice cream truck slid by on its music-box tinkle.

Mirabel came back around to the dining room to peer over my shoulder, her stray hairs tickling my ear. "Pretty book. Love the color."

Suddenly, I remembered that Mirabel and I shared an illicit love of grape soda, how Mirabel used to sneak me a half-can's pour in a tall coffee mug so Connie, who didn't understand the appeal of junk food, couldn't see it. How she and I would stick out our tongues at each other when Connie wasn't looking, would compare how purple.

I had purposely not thought about walking out of Mirabel's life and not coming back into it, about how I had dropped her completely, about doing that when we were both alone with small children. Now, with Mirabel's hair prickling the back of my head, I *was* thinking about it, sizzling with shame. But not only shame. I glanced over my shoulder at Mirabel's broad cheek. How easy it was to imagine a life with these people in it, Mirabel and her boys, making up for lost time, reclaiming all the things I'd lost when I'd lost Connie—real friends, a chosen family of my own.

Mirabel tapped the rim of her cup. "Find what you were looking for?"

"I'm not sure." I swilled the last of my tea. "How hard would it be to find out about a black-market art sale?" If Q was in possession of a stolen manuscript, that was something Sandy Jensen should know about. But it was tricky. I couldn't say anything unless I knew for sure. I didn't want her to know I'd been overly curious.

Mirabel started clicking windows shut on the computer. "Real art objects aren't so easy to unload. Nine times out of ten, the guys who get ahold of them end up using them as a bargaining chip when it's time to get sentenced. But something big? Rare? Expensive?" Mirabel shook her head. "You can't just sell it." Mirabel lowered the clamshell shut. "A book like that would stay out of sight."

The ice cream truck had stopped in front of the house. Every few bars of the now insufferable tune, a computerized female voice called out, "Hello! Hello!" I waited until the truck started up again and the music-box tinkle slid down the block. "The book I'm looking for isn't out of sight. I mean, I've seen it." Inside me, the bronze bird threatened to burst into song, crying out the location of the secret library, telling Mirabel everything. I pressed my lips shut.

Mirabel twisted her hair into a rope. "Well, is there any way you can *un*see it? Because black market art dealers aren't the kind of people you want to start meeting online. Even on the Dark Web. Because it's just not that hard to find you. Will you create a new email address? Will you disguise your location and ISP with a VPN?"

The letters broke from her lips, sharp snaps, and floated off into the air, finding purchase where they might, one *P* bubbling to the windowpane and sticking, the *S*, as esses do, curling around my boot.

"Even if you do all that stuff, and more, you're shedding data everywhere you go—in the real world and online. Your phone location data, Amazon shopping, even medical tests. Deanonymizing that shit—that's nothing to the bad guys." The way Mirabel talked about Bad Guys, I pictured cowboys in black hats. She let the heavy rope of her hair fall against my shoulder.

"But you already knew this, right? It's almost impossible to be anonymous online. Isn't that why you came here?" I watched that word *here* brighten and float into the barred sunlight gilding the credenza. The droop-eyed dog smiled sadly on her forearm. "When you came in here asking to use a computer, talking about distributed node networks and shit, I thought you'd become an internet sophisticate, AB, but you're still a babe in the woods!" I watched Mirabel pull the plug from the computer and stuff it in the credenza.

A speech followed, about how Mirabel did her best every day to keep credit safe, about how there had always been bad guys, about how the web made for so many more bad guys, a speech I guessed from Jessie's dramatic sigh was one she had given before. "I wouldn't worry about it, though," she said at the end. "Just because some library doesn't know about your book, doesn't mean there has to be a crime. Private dealers, rich people. They can do a lot of things and no one else is ever the wiser."

That was the thing, though. The Silver Bible was part of the Memory of the World. The Uppsala Library *would* know about it. They would have to. So why didn't they?

The wind had begun to kick up again. A gust pressed the windows close, rattling palm fronds against the purpling sky. I brought my teacup into the kitchen, rinsed it out and set it in the sink. "Hey, Mira—" Since those old days in this house, the epic parties with Mira's band, so much had changed, but so much had stayed the same. "Do you ever wonder what your life would be like if instead of work you'd chosen art? I mean, if you'd really made a go at it."

"Uh. Broke! Probably homeless." Mira threw her head back and laughed, but I didn't.

When I didn't say anything, she held her palms to the sky. "AB, have you been listening? The canvas is broader than you think. Cybersecurity *is* an art and I'm fucking good at it. I have my music, too. It's enough. But we're not talking about me, are we? We're talking about you." This was a habit Mirabel had always had, reminding me that she knew me better than I realized.

"No, you're right," I said, but I was stepping toward the door.

Mirabel's head tilted back toward the other shoulder, testing the tensile strength of the thought in her head. "You know, Amy." Mirabel switched back to my real name. "Connie—"

She pulled the word out like taffy, sticky, opaque, pale pink, like the very beginning of something, viscous enough for me to cut her off before the next one. "I need to get going." What had been soft and impressionable and pink in me had hardened in an instant, the stale wad of gum that was my heart. I didn't want to hear one more word about Connie.

Mirabel held up a palm.

But I was already leaving. Mirabel had been Connie's friend. She would always belong to Connie. My bike helmet dangled from her fingers, and I took it.

"Let's get together. Catch up. We could meet for coffee. Downtown? Preservation Park? Where are you working these days?" she said.

Pressing the helmet into my hair, I paused. I admit it: I wanted to impress her. "I'm an artist in residence." It wasn't true yet but as soon as I said it out loud to another human being it had the distinctive ring of truth. Words did that. Made things real. Feeling suddenly as if I'd arrived somewhere, I found myself trying to remember the very last time I'd stood in this house, at this front door, gazing through the panes of glass that looked out on the rubber tree and the red steps and the street. Had it been the party that night, a new resolve thickening in my super-saturated blood, that we would go all in, that Connie would get pregnant? I remembered: there was a sweetness in the air, the warm darkness—. It wasn't the party. It was later. Dinner at Mirabel's. Fresh strawberries and cream, a celebration, because Mirabel revealed that night that *she* was pregnant. That night at the party, she'd been pregnant, encouraging me, goading us on. The strawberries were small and wild, *fraises du bois*, bright and tart, little bursts of surprise that was both joy and betrayal because all along, Mirabel had been holding this back. I clipped the helmet under my chin. "Artist in residence. At Q."

I had expected to impress. After all, despite her drummer girl tats and East Oakland digs, Mirabel worked for The Man. But she blew out her lips: "Shit, Amy. Don't tell me this missing book thing has something to do with them. I can only imagine the releases you had to sign. What did you give up—fingerprint, facial data, iris scan, intellectual property, right to sue them, NDA, DNA?" Mirabel saw me flinch. I hadn't given Q permission for any of those things. But I'd made it through the fingerprint scan, so who had?

Mirabel crossed her arms over her chest. "I *know* these people." She paused, a blank space in which the logo of the bank she worked at unfurled between us, blue and red. "And they do not play nice." Mirabel glanced reflexively at her son, and at the television to which he was tethered. He was murmuring, talking to someone else playing the game with him somewhere else in the world. "If you know something they don't want you to know, I'd think twice about being connected with them. I'd think seriously about giving the residency up."

I stared at Mirabel, her arms crossed over her navel, her wild cloud of silver hair, and I wanted to shove her. She was just like Connie that way. Righteous. I wanted to shout: *You hypocrite! You work for a corporate bank!* Instead, my fingers closed around the door handle: "I love you Mirabel." The words tilted behind me as I tripped down the stairs and picked up the bike, *tic tic tic* down Mirabel's street for what was certainly the last time, though I did love her, I missed her, I would never have a friend like that again.

"What did we do to make you so mistrustful?" My mother lay on her bed, a score for Schubert's *Standchen* curled in one hand.

When I'd rolled up to the house, I'd discovered two bearded men waist-deep under the hood of my car. After explaining that they weren't stealing it, but fixing it, one of them rooted a blackened hand through his pocket and handed me the O'Reilly's receipt for a coil pack, alternator and four iridium spark plugs neatly folded around my mother's credit card.

It was worrisome, her sudden familiarity with strangers. (I'd lived on this street for nineteen years. I didn't know those people.) "I'm not mistrustful. I'm careful." I turned toward the door of my bedroom, brushing the toddler bed rail that held my father in bed at night. I'd always been careful. Ever since I'd had Tristan. I'd chosen a life of duty. What other choice did I have? And just because Tristan was gone didn't mean I was free from that now. Mirabel had scared me enough to remind me of that.

In the living room, my father tilted against the couch cushions, asleep in front of a documentary about a notorious Gold Rush counterfeiter. I watched for a minute as the narrator explained that the circulation of paper banknotes was forbidden in California in 1850. I kissed his forehead under the lip of white hair, which smelled like shampoo and baby powder, and for a second I wanted to shrink him down to munchkin size and put him in my pocket.

From upstairs I could hear Michael and Izzy choking with laughter up in Michael's room, watching *Pirate Radio* for the twenty-fifth time. "I will broadcast from this boat until the day I die!" Michael roared.

"Amy!" my mother called; my mother hated television. "It's getting late. Can you take Michael's girlfriend home?" Hiccoughs of laughter spattered the hall; Michael and Izzy loved to be called *boyfriend* and *girlfriend*, ticklers for an outsize joy that fizzed between them, sweet and pure. Suddenly I remembered an afternoon at an outdoor jazz concert, *Peanut Butter and Jazz*, something silly like that, blankets spread out on the grass at Crab Cove next to people we didn't know at all, Connie calling me *my wife*.

Girlfriend, Wife, Brother.

Trust was a luxury I didn't have. I had my father, my mother, my brother, my son. I was responsible for them. That was why, even if I'd wanted to help Arman, I couldn't put my family at risk.

But the *Codex* was different. I'd been careful, and the only person I had to trust was myself.

Upstairs, I grabbed the phone I'd left behind on my trip to Mirabel's and texted Sandy Jensen. *Lunch?*

I remembered the sound of her laughter when I tumbled out of the nap pod—little waves lapping the shore, pink and orange and aquamarine highlights, scattering brightness. Sandy Jensen was the kind of person who felt at home in the world. Who *did* trust others. The kind of person who chose light instead of shadow. I began to imagine that we could be friends and that, somewhere in the far distance of our friendship, I could tell her about the time I had for just a minute "borrowed" her identity and we would wade into that sparkling light and laugh and laugh.

Downstairs, my mother played a few bars of Schumann's *Fantasiestück*. In my room, the blinds opened on the hutch burbling with birds. Over the past few days, the cage had begun filling slowly with pigeons carrying duplicate messages. *She's dangerous. She's dangerous.* I'd learned from Michael's *History of the U.S. Signal Intelligence Corps* that pigeons were sent knowing they could get lost. They could be shot out of the sky. In the watery mid-day light, two restless figures bobbed outside the cage with gasoline rainbow throats.

I wanted to know where they came from, who was sending these birds to the rooftop outside my window. I imagined an open window somewhere in the dark city, gray bodies streaming out across the sky. I'd asked Michael's ham radio buddy Jerry if we could source them, glue a GPS tracker on their little drumsticks and follow them back to where they came from. But Jerry said *They're homing pigeons. They only go in one direction: Home.* There was something terribly sad about that word to me—*Home*—and something that made perfect sense in the idea that you would be far from it, only able to send messages back, tiny papers curled tight.

When I landed on the rooftop next door, the pigeons burbled and gossiped, but didn't flinch when I fingered open the little capsule on the larger one's leg and pulled out the scrap of paper tattooed with ink: a scrawl of black ballpoint written in Arabic.

13 *Autumn Flame*

I KEPT THE NOTE CLOSE IN MY POCKET WHEN I went to the farmers market the next day. It was late for peaches, but the new weather threw everything off—strawberries in January, watermelon in November, passionfruit all year long. The woman at the farmstand handed me a brown paper sack fat with peaches so ripe they throbbed.

It was crowded, the smell of hot oil and burnt sugar and popped corn in the air, the rows of bright canvas canopies lined up in the DMV parking lot stretched out like circus tents. Clutching the paper bag full of peaches, I debated handing over the curled slip of paper tucked between my knuckles. I wanted to get it translated securely, and the way to do that was through the Neighborhood. The woman at the Red Hen Farm booth, willowy and brown, took my money and slipped it into a red cooler.

While I waited for her to turn back around, I eavesdropped on the murmured conversation the other woman at the farmstand, stocky and blond, was having with a young child and its parents. "I understand," the blond woman said to the child. "Your sister messaged you that she missed her period. And now she's been picked up by the Sherriff back in Texas. Is that right?" The child whispered ferociously to the parents, the family huddled together like hostage negotiators. They were all dark-haired and small, a woman in a pink tracksuit and a barrel-chested man in tight jeans and cowboy boots, a small child in brown footie pajamas with a hood and ears of a bear. Now the child, the mother and the father were all nodding their heads, so that when the woman from the farmstand spoke next, she directed her eyes to the parents: "I am so sorry to have to tell you this. I really am sorry. But we can't help you with anything regarding remediation. Do you understand what that means?" The child stood, rubbing a finger back and forth over the fold of the nubbly brown ear of the bear hood. All the members of the family had gone still. "Remediation. That means, once Q has picked up a data point and added it to your profile—" She spoke slowly, turning her gaze to the mother, "we can't fix that. We can *prevent* things from going on your profile." Her eyes shifted to the father, "But we can't take them back." At this—the phrase *can't take them back*—the mother's voice rose up in a terrible cry that she suffocated with the heels of both hands. "It was nothing, though!" the mother cried. "It was just a mistake!" The woman from the farmstand put a hand on the mother's shoulder but didn't actually touch it: "Ma'am. Sir. I'm so sorry. Next time you need to research a medical condition, or buy pills for someone, or wire someone money, come to us first. *Before* you search."

Is this really what things had come to? The scrap of paper stuffed in my hand had started to feel very small. I was still standing there, frozen, the paper going damp between my fingers, when a hand fell on my shoulder.

I flinched.

Then I saw the rings, ring after ring after ring, stacked in the places where the white stripes had been. "Blue."

"And here I thought you might pretend not to know me." I panicked. Had I run into her and not recognized her? But she was already threading her fingers through my fingers. My pinky pressed hard against my ring finger, pinning the note between them. There was no way I could ask for the Neighborhood now that I wasn't alone.

Blue and I fell into step, shoulder to shoulder through the crowd, through jogging strollers and people picking at dark, ruffled bundles of kale. I noticed the way our bodies fit; we were the same height, like Connie and I; I would have said we saw the world from the same vantage point, except that I had been proven wrong on that count so expressly it left me breathless. So, instead of focusing on the familiar, I noticed the way her hips moved, her shoulder beside me, bare in the honey-colored autumn light, remembering the rest of her skin, remembering the spot where tattoos rippled out across her thighs. I forgot about the bag of peaches, heavy in my hand, until my fingers pressed four wet prints into their flesh.

As we left the DMV parking lot and stepped on the path next to the creek, I offered her a bite. She made her mouth wide, her teeth animal in a way that reminded me of other animal motions she'd made. A slow drop traced the line from the corner of her mouth. Her tongue came out, pink and feline, to lap it up. Her fingertip flicked over the knot of my pressed fingers, also tonguelike and feline, closer and closer to the slip of paper tucked between my knuckles. "Want to make out?" I wanted to distract her from the little slip of paper, but I also suddenly wanted that pink tongue in my mouth.

She threw the remains of the peach over her shoulder into the ivy-lined creek. "Sure."

I tugged her through the blocks of Temescal, suddenly enflamed with lust like I hadn't been since I was fifteen. I was looking for a make-out spot when we crossed the ghost bike on 51st Street trimmed with plastic flowers. Ever since her crash, those bikes reminded me of Connie, even though it wasn't the crash itself that ended our life together. The bike was tied to a pole between the rushing cars, like the memory of Connie there to interrogate me: Was I going to drag a stranger into the house where my father was slouching toward the TV and my mother was mixing up another slurry of applesauce and pills, up the stairs to the guest bedroom that shared a wall with my brother's?

Clutching hands, Blue and I hurried on until I saw a large shipping container parked on the grass outside a brightly muraled school. It was painted gold; black letters stenciled on the door spelled: *A PORTAL*.

I tested the door and she pulled me through a heavy curtain, inside.

Egg-carton foam silenced the walls and ceiling, a giant screen at the far end of the room playing the plotless scene of a rainy street corner scattered with pigeons. In a second I had her pressed hard against a wall, my knee between her thighs, working the buttons of her jeans. I still had the slip of paper clamped between my fingers, damp now and curling, and, desperate to find somewhere to put it without taking my hands off her body, I tucked it in the tight watch pocket of her jeans.

I was the one leading this dance, but it didn't feel voluntary, didn't feel like I was the one leading my hands across the curvature of her surface, which was drawing all my desire toward her without any will at all. Maybe that's what those lines across her thighs meant, those soundings, the mapping of a future shipwreck.

The air around us ripened with the animal smells of sweat and sex and there it came again, the heat creeping into my neck and chest. Hot flash, flashback. A hiking trail near Tucson, our legs cool to the thigh where Connie and I waded in the shallow pool at the foot of a trickling falls, our faces burned, the baking heat of a giant boulder behind our backs, Connie's warm, dry hand in mine. *Glad you're my girl.* The quick flash of her smile, white light leaping off the water. We were twenty years old, putting her old life to rest, claiming our new one.

But you're not here anymore, I told the Connie in my mind, and wanted to believe it. "Don't stop," I pushed my hair out of my eyes. "Sorry. Don't stop."

We were both breathing hard, though the egg crate took the sound of our breath away. Blue pulled the damp scrap of paper from the watch pocket of her jeans. "What is this?" she asked. "A love letter?" The paper unfurled in her fingers like a flower.

On the screen beside us, the pigeons wobbled and cooed. The words *Love letter* rang in my head like a bell. "Maybe."

"What does it say?" Staring hard into my eyes, did she also hear the note from that bell, the deep vibrations spreading out across the air like the waves on a quarry, spreading outward on all sides, when a boulder calves? The slow possibility of drowning.

"I don't know. It's in Arabic."

Those worrying fingers that liked to count rings, count bones, drew the line of my jawbone, the curve of my ear. In the same way that each line she traced ran straight to my groin, my thoughts traveled from the twisted slip of paper to the man in the tweed vest to Arman and Q. And because my mouth was open, the words poured out: "It might say to burn down Q."

And because my hand had slid to the smooth spot at the top of her jeans, under her shirt, she murmured back, "So. Burn it down."

It was one of those things sex makes people say. Hot, provocative words, meaning nothing. But there was something so appealing about her certainty. I imagined her warehouse full of musicians and dreamers, the Archangel in her feathered glory, the fire dancers with their literate flames all behind me on All Hallows' Eve, performing with me at Q, burning it down.

I don't know how long we'd been kissing—long enough for the kiss to become a slouch to the floor—when voices emerged from the far end of the room, and applause. "Hey guys!" someone called in a thick German accent. "Get a room!"

What the *fuck*? Twisting toward the screen, we saw that the street corner freckled with pigeons had become a crowd of people. As we turned, they began waving. "Hello! Guten tag! Hello from Berlin!"

We hadn't walked in on an experimental film. This was a PORTAL and it worked both ways.

Jesus fuck. Here I was talking about blowing up Q on a live video feed broadcast around the fucking world. How much had they heard? Behind us, the velvet curtain whispered open—the portal attendant saw my shirt untucked, Blue buttoning her jeans.

"Go," Blue flicked her fingers at me. Before I darted out, she pressed the curled paper from the pigeon's leg into my palm. "*Azizam*, it's Farsi, not Arabic," she whispered into my ear. "It says *Meet me at the library*."

14 *Little Birds*

I SET UP A DRAFTING TABLE IN THE ATRIUM directly on top of the area reserved for holographic games of chess and midnight covens of witches. The virtual game board just happened to sit not far from the hidden door to the marvelous library. I liked the idea of being close to the Library of Books That Don't Exist; my own portfolio of work seemed in an essential way to belong to it. Behind that door, the missing pages of the Silver Bible would be my touchstone, a hidden source of power. I tapped the pocket of my skirt for my talisman, a copper coil Michael's friend Jerry had dropped into my open palm.

The guard with curly hair and creased earlobes—the same guard who'd tried to confiscate my portfolio— carried out two high stools and a sloped desk fitted with wire hoops for my bottles of ink, and Jae emerged from his den long enough to transform the game board into a wide pool of water that splashed around your ankles. When I protested that a medieval market scribe was not the same thing as a monk or nun, that I shouldn't be sequestered, Jae countered: "It's not really water, okay? And it makes you seem hard-to-get."

I wasn't sure I wanted to be hard to get. The ball was my qualifying performance, and, as far as I understood, whether I became the artist in residence or not depended at least in part upon the number of partygoers I drew to my table. They would sit and dictate letters they wanted to send, and I would transcribe them. Based on my experience in the real world, handwritten letters did not tend to draw *likes*, and I wasn't sure people who spent their lives making sure no one ever had to write a word by hand again would see the appeal of sticky ink. I did not know if they would speak to me. (*People don't write. People don't draw.*) But I counted on them to know what it meant when something was available in limited edition, like Q's disappearing posters, and to want one for themselves.

A lard sculptor and art purist (who had applied unsuccessfully to the Q residencies for ten years running) would tweet that I had *perverted the name of art* with my *crass commercialism and aspirations toward permanence*. (His politician/bovine chimeras were elaborate grotesques he mounted in direct sunlight.) *Art* magazine would exclaim with glee that my work was a commentary on the way tech companies turn our most personal interactions into commodities for sale. (By the time the article was written, the *commercialization of data* was a phrase on everyone's lips.) Interpretations of art belong to the viewer, so I won't call any of these reactions *wrong*, but they were not my intention, either. Writing for the medieval court, a secular scribe was a pen for hire. I already had a portfolio full of letters no one had seen and nobody wanted. To create work that had value—as far as I was concerned, there was no shame in that. As far as I was concerned, that was the reason I was there.

A half hour before lunch, I was still finishing up my preparations, carving my dulled quill back into shape. Sharpening a quill is not unlike paring a toenail, shaving the keratin along curve and point into the perfect angle to produce a sharp, clean line. That day, though, I was no mere toenail parer working late at night in my bedroom by the light of the swing-arm lamp. Q had given me an identity as an artist, a place to work and a people to serve. I swept the waxy shavings into my hand and there was Jae, in navy shorts dotted with miniature white palm trees: "*Hey,*" he called. "How's it going?"

"Let's find out." I slid a ruled sheet of vellum in front of me. "So, what's it going to be? A *Dear John* letter to your old friend Hack?"

His chin resting on the flat of his hand, Jae glanced down at the page, a long, slow look. "Of course not," he drawled. His lashes knit closed: "What if I win?"

All of the partygoers who came to my table and asked me to create a letter for them had to give consent that *their* letter might be chosen to be scanned into Q's digital archive. I'd gathered from Sandy Jensen's tour, Q liked to keep a record of what artists produced here. It was good PR, proof that the company wasn't *only* a tech behemoth devouring everything in its path. And it would be a record for all of posterity. Of course, Jae didn't want Hack to see his. But maybe Jae needed him to.

I inked a small black bird in the upper right-hand corner of the page, a pigeon. "What if you do?" Jae seemed like a prisoner in need of a cake with a file baked into it, a stick of TNT. As much as I wanted to be a part of this place, he wanted to leave it.

Jae blinked. In the margin of the page, ink pooled in the bottom half of the bird and dried there, heavy and dark. I thought about Connie's long days in the hospital, the fluids dripping in and out of her veins, draining away our life together. But this is what ink was for—to draw out the sadness. It helped.

"It's not like Hack will see it." According to my father's *Morning Joe*, Hack was in Washington DC preparing to testify before Congress, even while back here on campus his worker bees buzzed with the pink neon *Lockdown* sign, hurrying to launch the next *iteration* of the Algorithm.

"Won't he?" His Adam's apple bobbed up and down the skin of his throat. He flourished his fingers vaguely toward the almost-hidden door that led to the library. Had he been in there?

Did the people at Q know about it, or care? It was the most wonderful room on the campus to me. I wanted to go back inside and sit near the bronze tree, and stare at the violet pages of the Silver Bible. "Won't some machine read it for him and let him know that his golden pigeon wants to fly the coop?" Under the small bird in the margin of the paper, I lettered *pigeon* in small, black capitals. I remembered the scanner in the library reading the musical notes on the illuminated manuscript and playing them, the sweet, piping sound of the little birds scattered across the page.

I still didn't understand the force that held Jae here when he was obviously so unhappy. Money? Really? But that was what had held me in place for so long, too.

"Would that be the worst thing? You'd be free."

Jae waved away the idea of freedom with his fingertips. He sat and watched me hash lines into the bird's small feet. He circled his eyes over my table, the paper, the ruler, the quill knife, the inks. "We'll see."

I dipped my quill and pressed it to the page: _ear Hack, I wrote, leaving space where the *D* would go for a decorative capital. With a pink slip I had found in a drawer in a copy room—an actual, old-school termination of employment slip—I planned to fashion a curving flamingo, balanced on one stick-like leg, the beak tipped with a single drop of India ink.

Jae was shaking his head. He'd been slouching at the stool the way tall people do when they grow up not wanting to be seen. "You are *not* going to submit that!" His voice rose in protest but it sounded like a question.

"No. I'm not." I dipped the pen again and traced a tendril along the margin, two tendrils: branches.

"That's very pretty," he said. His suede lace-ups tilted back and forth against the bottom rung of the stool. Every time I saw Jae, he looked like a catalog model. I wondered if this was *why*

Hack kept him here: with his long, bare brown legs, he was their United Colors of Q. He ran a finger along the lines of purple-black ink, not touching them.

"Thanks." I switched quills and dipped this time in silver ink, outlining clouds.

"Ooh. Silver," Jae sighed.

I angled my quill for the finest line I could manage. "There's a manuscript here written in gold and silver ink, one of the rare manuscripts on loan to the library."

"On loan?" Jae reached for the sheet and tilted it back and forth in the light, admiring. "Hack doesn't borrow, my dear. He steals." He lay the sheet back on the table. "Speaking of which—" A rolled poster materialized at Jae's fingertips. "I thought you might want one of these." He handed it to me. It was the 1960s-style concert handbill, the capitals fat and warped as clouds of weed smoke, announcing the Q *All Hallows' Ball*, the one I'd seen on my first day at Q, the ball at which I would be performing.

"Limited edition," Jae traced a finger along the Q. "You like?"

I loved it.

He tapped it into a poster tube and pressed his thumb against a silver sticker, like the one the front desk guard had affixed to the outside of my portfolio, so I could get it past the guards. "I stole it, of course."

"Of course."

Jae leaned forward over the letter that lay between us. "That's not what I call him." He tapped the table next to my hand. "I call him David. '*Dear David*—'"

Sliding out a fresh half-sheet, I listened and wrote.

Fifteen minutes later, I blew the page to dry it. "I'll add the illuminations later," I promised him, drawing Jae's eye from the thicket of letters which spelled out his defection. "I'll make it really beautiful." I would help him say goodbye.

I'd had a friend like Jae at my first job out of school, an easy friend, a fellow traveler. Cris was a gay boy who had answered phone calls at the desk next to mine while I slid rejection letters into thin white envelopes, a boy with a shock of black hair and a penchant for doodling Popeye on the Dean's letterhead. Cris went home one afternoon not feeling well, took some over-the-counter asthma medication and died. The funeral was in Santa Barbara, where his mother and sisters lived, in the whitewashed adobe of the old *Mision Santa Barbara*. It was three days after Christmas, the nave of the old mission chapel bloodred with poinsettia flocking Cris's open casket, where he lay, beautiful and still under the outspread arms of Jesus. *Crisanto*, the priest kept murmuring the name Cris never used, and reassured us, crowding the hard pews, that Cris was safe now in the arms of Christ. While the sisters keened and the mother sagged in their arms, I imagined Cris at the back of the chapel, doodling a naked cartoon Christ. It was this funeral that Connie remembered and said she wanted, a Christmas funeral in the big desert mission church back in Tucson where, as a girl, she'd dreamed of being married. She was lying in the hospital bed at the foot of a window blazing with light, one bright line leading into her arm, white light glazing her face, her arms, the fluttering print-out of the ultrasound bleached white in her white, slinged hand. *Don't be ridiculous*, I said, remembering the bright scent of the Christmas greens. *You can't choose death*. I pulled the fingertips of her other hand to my stomach and noticed when she flinched, her face blanched by the light.

I slid Jae's letter into my portfolio before he could tear it to pieces. "So, you'll leave?"

Jae stretched his arms over his head and yawned, tilting his head to one side and then the other, cracking his neck. "I don't think so."

My phone chimed. "Oh, fuck me. I'm late." I capped my bottles of ink, swept my portfolio into my bag and hurried Jae with me through the halls. "I have a lunch date with Sandy Jensen."

Jae's eyebrows rose. "You have a lunch date with Sandy Jensen?"

We stopped under the wide, glass ceiling of the main entry hall, under the bones of the mammoth. Of all the red dots moving through the entryway, the LCD screen snagged on me and Jae, began to zero in on and multiply our connections in this world, a widening web of ties. "You know her?" I asked him.

"Do I know Sandy Jensen?" Jae raised his long arms like Moses at the sea. On the screen behind him, the intersecting webs of our connections stretched across the planet, where they were visible from space. "Go! Go!"

15 *Wind Telephone*

THE Q CAMPUS WAS LARGE AND LOVELY AND surrounded by walls past which you couldn't see the homeless encampments at all. It was ten acres if it was one, landscaped like a private college or Golden Gate Park, with cactus gardens and hidden grottoes and wooded groves stretching to the edges of real, running creeks. I'd have needed a map to find her if Sandy hadn't dropped a pin at her precise GPS coordinates and texted them to me.

I discovered her in one of those bucolic recesses, on the grassy slope at the edge of a creek I could hear but not see, reclined on a striped lawn chaise. "Hello! You found me!" When I went to shake her hand, she stood and did the side-hug thing instead. I wasn't used to casual affection. It had been years since Tristan threw an arm around my neck and leaned his head against my shoulder. It was nice, nice in the way the dappled light was nice, and the sound of the water running in the creek nearby, and the muscle memory of writing *Dearest* on a thin, ruled page.

The nice feeling stilled the conflict between how it felt seeing Sandy Jensen and what I knew I planned to do, and, given the sunlight and the water and the basket of picnic foods at her side, I decided to let the nice feeling win.

Sandy motioned me to sit and fell back into her own chaise longue, her long arms and legs stretched out like chopsticks. She was tall and thin in khakis and a tailored, densely patterned shirt, in that Banana Republic size-model, everything-fits-her, tomboy sort of way. (There was not a single item of clothing that fit me exactly, and definitely not a pair of pants.)

I tugged my skirt down over my knees and stretched out too, and tried to remember the last time I had put my feet up in the middle of the day.

Next to us, a glass-paneled kiosk glinted in the mid-day sun. The water running below it and the eucalyptus trees swaying above it cast their reflections in the glass; every time the wind blew, they shifted like reflections in a broken mirror. The wind was warm and dry, and the kiosk, which was all white, from its antique wooden frame to its fanciful white roof, seemed to sway with images from the world around it like a figure in a dream.

"There was a man on the coast of Japan who built a structure like this, a glass telephone phone booth he'd built for survivors of the tsunami," I mused, remembering the little shock I'd felt at the idea of someone building such a monument to loss, meant not just to remember, but to *undo* the loss. The phone booth stood at the edge of his fields on the edge of the Sanriku coast. Outside, the wind whips around it. Inside, the wind is all you can hear when you pick up the handset of the black rotary telephone to speak to the dead. I could hear the wind around us now, the violent toss of the trees.

"I knew you'd know that!" Sandy exclaimed, smiling.

"It's a Wind Telephone?" I shuddered a little. Moving across its surface, the water and the leaves looked like faces in the glass. I had no desire to speak to the dead.

Sandy had pulled a bottle of Perrier from her basket and offered one to me. She banged her chest with her fist and burped. "Definitely not. No, nope. It's the *opposite* of that." She leaned back and took another long drink.

The opposite of the Wind Telephone? Like the Library of Books That Don't Exist was the opposite of all other libraries? "Is everything here the opposite of something else?"

Sandy sputtered. She was fizzing over with laughter. "I like you," she said.

I sipped my drink.

"Q has a phone booth like this at every campus in the world. It's totally random where it rings, who picks up." She fished out another dripping bottle and cracked the top. Normally, I would have felt judgy about co-opting a powerful cultural symbol of grief and turning it into a tech-world prop. But the late morning sky was a shining, stained-glass blue, the wind as warm as breath; the world inside Q's walls was like a Technicolor picture. "I used it once. The people who picked up were engineers in Berlin; it was midnight there, they were all fantastically drunk; the whole thing was hilarious. '*Na? Na?*'" There were those bright chips of laughter again, peeling off toward the water like glinty waves. "When the rest of them roared away into the night, the last engineer confessed that he'd left behind the man he was in love with. He asked me if I would be his 'confederate.'" Sandy scratched the air with two fingers. "Virtual things wouldn't do, he said. They messaged each other all the time, but it wasn't the same. It had to be as if he were here. It had to be old fashioned."

Sandy Jensen knew how to use the conditional tense. "Old fashioned?"

"A cassette tape in a cassette recorder in the middle of his lover's bed, a trail of red rose petals." *Cheesy*, I told myself. "A paper love letter." *Hm.*

The wind lifted our hair. Some small grain of something dead—pollen, leaf, insect wing—scratched at my eye. This was a place, too, where people could be lonely. Maybe it was more than irony, giving people a phone they could pick up and know that somebody, somewhere, would answer.

Sandy stretched her bottle toward mine and clinked: *Cheers!* "I read a poem at their wedding in Rome." I tried to picture Sandy Jensen reading from a sheet of paper that had been folded and unfolded many times. Instead, I pictured my gangly eleventh grade physics teacher calling the laws of thermodynamics out across the Spanish steps. In a good way. An endearing way. Sandy Jensen was anyone's best buddy. Sandy Jensen had wriggled through an old rubber doggy door clutching a sack of rose petals and a love letter. If she knew what I wanted, she would probably say yes. She handed me a finger sandwich and nodded at the telephone booth. "Give it a try?"

I smiled, eyes closed, into the sun. "No way. Not after that." I took a bite of the sandwich—pesto and sundried tomato, some kind of cheese, three colors spreading warmth across my tongue. Working, preparing Tristan for his move, I hadn't spent a single summer day slathered in 100+ SPF, baking by the public pool. Though it was a restless autumn warmth, I kept my eyes shut and let the heat sedate me. Techies got a bad rap, I thought. Some of them, like Sandy Jensen, were really quite nice. "It could never be that good."

There was a crinkle of paper, a sound like Sandy Jensen collecting her jackpot winnings from a slot machine and offering a coin to me. Salt welled in my nose—a bag of potato chips. "You never know what you're gonna get."

The chips were golden and shiny with grease. "Why did he ask you?" I squinted at the phone booth and then at Sandy Jensen. Sandy was staring straight ahead, toward the hidden creek, her elbows stretched above her head. "The guy in Berlin. He must know plenty of people who work here. Why didn't he ask a friend?"

Sandy rolled to her side to face me, her hands tucked under the side of her face, prayer hands, like a little girl. "I don't know. I don't think he planned it. The phone rang. And I was right here. A door opened up."

"*A door.*" I rolled onto my side and stared at Sandy Jensen's eyes, inscrutable to me. Studying the lines fanning out around her eyes, I wondered why I wasn't attracted to someone like Sandy Jensen, with her romantic stories and her tricolor sandwiches. Why did I have to make things so complicated? But I knew why: I couldn't make sense of the color of her eyes. But maybe a door could open up. Maybe it was up to me. I was on the verge of asking her outright for what I wanted.

Sandy offered a ginger cookie the size of my face and held it while I broke off half. "I hope it hasn't been too weird, coming here. I hope no one's given you a hard time." She sank her teeth into her half of the cookie with the unselfconsciousness of a shark.

"What do you mean, a hard time?"

She gestured toward the world outside Q's buildings. "When people find out that you do things at Q—things can get weird. People assume you can do things for them. They want things. It sort of comes with the territory."

I felt the heat rise up in my head. I felt accused.

"'Erase every picture of my ex,' 'Erase every nude pic of me,' 'Delete all the women.'" She counted off requests on fingers she bent back with a violence that was almost sexual. "'Mark everyone in the entire world *safe @ homosexual.*'" At this last, she threw her head back and laughed again, her sandy hair streaming. She made everything that had happened seem so harmless. "'Fire Hack. Marry Hack. Kill Hack.' At some point, I'm sure someone here actually considers doing one of these things. I have. But it usually makes new people uncomfortable."

Could Sandy know about *Arman*? Could she possibly know that a bearded hipster with a 1940s mail room and an army of white-haired women had taken me to the top of a bicycle shop and asked me to blow the Q database to smithereens? My throat and face flushed with heat. "I can imagine."

I slowly folded the cookie into my napkin and dusted my hands against my skirt. Could she know I was planning to let myself into her library?

While we had been sitting there, eating our sandwiches, the only sounds were the water and the wind and the crinkling of paper—quiet, childhood sounds. But now an old-fashioned factory whistle blew; a garbled male voice carried over the PR system. The whole apparatus of Q was winding up. Relieved, I tucked the wrapped cookie in my skirt pocket, then remembered Tristan wasn't home waiting. "I should go. I've got to prep for the ball," I said, though I didn't.

"That reminds me." Sandy Jensen reached into the basket from which she'd pulled the cookies and sandwiches and drew out her fist. She thrust the other fist out beside it. "Pick a hand." It was silly. I'd seen the hand that dipped in and out of the basket. The silliness was a relief. I tapped the back of her hand. Sandy turned it over to reveal a small glass bottle shimmering with liquid the color of blood.

A gift. For me. I could feel my face flush with happiness, a feeling I quickly deflected. "Human sacrifice?" As soon as I said it, I panicked a little, remembering the priest with his bottle of holy water, the chalice of wine he called *blood*.

Sandy smiled. "Close," she said, tilting her hand back and forth. A silver pearl of air slipped back and forth in the crimson liquid like the bubble in a spirit level. Bloodred wax dripped over the cap. A square label, smaller than a postage stamp, white on black, read *Scroll & Quill: Vermillion*. In smaller print: *Mercuric sulphide, white of egg, gum Arabic*. "For miniatures."

Miniature doesn't come from the Latin word for *small*; it comes from the Latin *miniare*, to color with red lead. But the word is confounded. The illuminations that gave rise to the word, drawings heavy on red—red knight, red cross, red flag—*were* minute.

So small that the word for *red ink* and the word for *small* blended into one.

If Sandy Jensen could have bottled all of her cleverness, her thoughtfulness, her desire to impress upon me that she valued my work and spoke my language, this is what it would have looked like: a bottle of red ink, sealed with red wax, for making *miniatures*. That was a real act of friendship, and right there on a bright, windy fall day on a chaise longue at the edge of a hidden creek somewhere near a demented Wind Telephone on the edge of Q's campus I dared to imagine a future in which Sandy Jensen and I could be friends.

For me? I mimed. I stretched out my hand and Sandy Jensen leaned over and set the bottle in my palm.

I reached out to hug her. "Thank you," I said into her hair. "Really." And I meant it. Sandy's ID badge, the one with which she had swiped us into one restricted area after another, dangled between us. As I brushed it with the copper coil tucked into my other hand—the coil Jerry had given me to pick up the frequency of Sandy's radio ID badge—, I believed that Sandy Jensen was generous and kind; and even as I slid the coil back up my sleeve, I believed that, even though she didn't know it, she was offering me another gift.

16 *Herbs and Tinctures*

THE HISTORY OF ILLUMINATION IS THE HISTORY OF pigment. Blue *azurite* crushed from stones rich in copper was second only to red in frequency of use in medieval manuscripts; *ultramarine*, the purest and bluest of blues, passed hand to hand on camel train from Afghanistan to Europe, was more expensive than gold. But gall inks were the mainstay of medieval writing, bold and permanent inks whose ubiquity and tendency to oxidize to colors between deep black and blackish purple have left us with our tradition of signing documents "legally" only in blue or black ink.

An oak gall or an oak apple is a perfect, hard brown ball that forms when a wasp injects its venom into an oak leaf bud, creating a safe home for her larvae. Empty oak galls—a hole marks the point at which the young wasp crawled out—were gathered, crushed, treated with rainwater and left to steep in the sun, a pale, bitter brown. It must have been a forager-scribe with a rusty spoon who discovered the trick: iron transforms the pale brown ink to black. The work of a scribe is full of transubstantiations, and born in alchemy.

Connie and I disagreed about these terms (we disagreed, never argued). Connie called the formulation of ink from iron and oak and gum Arabic simply *chemistry*. I knew how to mix a simple oak gall ink and Connie had taught me that, pulling a fist of acorns from her pocket. Brewing up pigments and dyes—that was the kind of thing Connie was good at, chemical reactions. Swirling the drops of ferrous sulfate into the jar, Connie held it up to the light: "Iron sulfate plus gallotanic acid equals ferrotanogallate, babe." The top of her cheek and her eye, seen through pale brown liquid, disappeared behind a jar of night. But I was sure this was more than chemistry. This was thaumaturgy, nature turning into art.

Could Connie really argue? Connie with her transubstantiations, the priest with his cracker and Dixie cup beside the bed, a touch on the forehead with oil and ash. Maybe this is why she was willing to let go of her own life to make another one. Connie and I disagreed about the terms but on this we did agree: quite suddenly, one thing becomes something else.

Bottles quivered on every shelf of the Apothecary Shop in Temescal Alley—wide-mouth jars of dried mugwort and nettle; brown, stoppered bottles of feverfew and spikenard, sweet dreams and calm. They shivered as I moved among them, running my fingertips over hand-dipped candles, pink, purple and green.

In the ancient world, the purple-magenta dye like the kind that tinted the pages of the Silver Bible came from sea snails, the spiny *Murex brandaris*, a single drop of dye per snail, extremely dear, extremely rare. Prized by the Minoans of ancient Crete because the color did not fade, but became brighter with light and time. To become more vibrant instead of fading: anyone would want that.

I did not have spiny sea snails, or chemistry, but I had an imagination and a will to try.

I took my time next to the rose stone and quartz, hard hearts cracked open and glittering. The crystals and the bottles, the smell of wax and herbs, reminded me of that night in Crimson Horticultural Rarities; I stopped and closed my eyes and breathed sandalwood and thyme and imagined I could pull Tal to me on the stream of my indrawn breath.

So much had happened since that night just a few days ago: Blue, Sandy Jensen, Arman. The Halloween ball and a residency at Q. Something was happening, as if by transcribing that letter for the man in the tweed vest, I had walked through a door into someone else's life. A door—that's what Sandy Jensen had said. I had stepped through it, and now I had to keep on going.

I picked up books on essential oils and black magic and set them down again. I wasn't sure what I was looking for until a bright spark caught my eye through a window set in the far wall. Visible through it, a person sat in the adjacent stall, setting fires and pinching out fires with the tips of their fingers under a sizzling blue neon sign that read TAROT.

The door creaked as I pushed it open, and the wind whipped in, hot and frantic, stirring a swirl of blue dust across the countertop. A woman with small shoulders and a cap of dark hair stood behind the counter, pinching blue powder into a glazed, black mortar with blistered fingertips. I glanced around the walls at oversized photos of Tarot cards: a watercolor Adam and Eve taking the first slow steps of exile; a pitch-black card engraved in silver with grinning faces of sun and moon. The room smelled of sage and gunpowder, smoke and fire.

"Hello again." She held my gaze for a long second before turning her attention back to her crucible, scattering some volatile element into the bowl. It blazed and sparked with a blue light which bathed the origami folds of her face when she smiled or frowned.

"Blue." A pale, yellow word with a thick, creamy taste to match the thick clot of anticipation and desire that rose in my throat.

I stepped closer, close enough to smell the contents of the little glass vials lined up next to the bowl—phosphorus and aluminum dust—the smell of lab days when Connie and I were still in college, Connie memorizing the periodic table of the elements, writing the letters and the numbers in an invisible grid across the palm of my hand. That was the best poetry she could give me, the poetry of her love of the world and the things it was made of—those afternoons on her hard, narrow bed, the arches of her bare feet pushed against my shins.

I blew a strand of hair off my hot forehead.

In the end, it came down to chemistry. Cisplatin, Doxorubicin, Paclitaxel. Drugs with ugly, trademarked, unpronounceable names. Names that struck at the hot pulse of cells in Connie's Catholic soul. If she'd been offered Vincristine, would she have been more willing to pump it through her veins? Would she have been willing to halt everything growing inside her?

Just that day, I'd received three more urgent reminders of Connie's upcoming birthday. If I went through with it, if I sabotaged Q, the reminders would stop; Connie would really be gone.

My father still read the newspaper, the driveway confected each morning with crinkly parcels wrapped in red and blue. Since Arman's request, I had started reading the pages aloud to my father, noticing for the first time that others were asking the same questions as Arman. In the European Union, people had sued for "the right to be forgotten"—to be purged from internet searches. That was what Arman wanted, too, a right to have our online history forgotten by the companies that were stripping it from us, click by click, without our knowing or caring. *Never forget* is the mantra my parents' generation grew up with. But forgetting can be a kindness, too.

Blue beckoned me closer until the cool, blue light bathed my face. Staring with her into the ash, I considered the taut skin at her neck, her clear, broad forehead. I looked up at the bottles lined up along the walls, the illegible, hand-inked labels. What would it mean to erase the past? What would it mean to really start over?

I picked up a deck of Tarot cards from the counter and flipped one over: a young man facing the horizon, three tall, leafing branches at his side. I recognized Tristan, my young seeker with his will to green the world. Or could it, possibly, be me?

"What are you looking for?" Blue asked.

I wasn't sure. I hoped I would know it if I saw it. I flipped another card, the Devil. Blue flame crackled in the bowl. I thought of Arman standing on the old train platform in his bear head, pleading the case of the moral universe, shaking sweat from his face, the bear's wild teeth flashing. I thought of Sandy, long limbs stretched on the chaise lounge by the creek, who believed the connections Q made between people were the story of love. How could I know which one of them to believe, when I couldn't even trust myself to tell them apart? "How can I know what I'm looking for if I can't trust what I see?"

Blue's hot fingers gripped my wrist, muscular as a python. Fear gripped my throat. I felt like I should run. But the suddenness of her grip, her firmness on my wrist also brought me back to the warehouse on the night we met, my arms pinned tight behind my back, her mouth hot against the bones at the top of my spine. The whole room closed around me, hot and dry and salted with strange chemicals.

Her voice went low as a struck match: "You can trust me."

There are certain people for whom you would do anything, say anything, go anywhere. It makes no sense at all. Most of life, you forget what that's like until you're in it, irrational, crazy love for someone you barely know. I wondered if the bottled herbs had been drugged. I wanted to climb over the counter, into her skin. Whatever she asked me to do, I would have done it. It was dangerous, to want so desperately to believe. But in the hot moment of wanting, nothing could stop me. I pressed five white half-moons into the skin of her wrist. Then her hold loosened, her restless fingers worrying tarsals and metatarsals as if she could scry the future in my bones.

A scar seamed her chin. I hadn't noticed it before—or maybe I had noticed it but failed to integrate it, like so many other things, into an image of her face. "How did that happen?" We were playing at trust, so I brought my finger close enough to her face to feel the heat. I wanted intimacy, something from her, some piece of her I could take with me. It wasn't a reasonable thing to want. I knew that. But I wanted it anyway.

"I split my chin. Doesn't everyone?" I didn't answer, but drew my finger to my own, scarless chin. "Okay. This is the place I fell down in my uncle's carpet shop." Now the thin white line looked like the spot where the universe could split and where it had already sealed back up. That's the way I felt when I was with her, like I was still floating through the Slumber Artist's depths. "My uncle was an importer. My brother and I liked to pretend the stacks of rugs were trampolines." She shrugged. I could hear the thud of sneakers, see the clouds of dust billowing up. "My brother jumped into me and I fell, and that was the day we discovered the rugs sat on a wooden frame. Blood *everywhere*. My brother screamed. My uncle screamed. I had stained a hundred-year-old handwoven carpet!" She raised an eyebrow. "There was one consolation: a young ER doc with long hair in a braid down her back. Very pretty. She thought I was a boy." Her face half-folded, a secret smile, but she was sharing it with me. Her hand cupped the bowl, covering the ashes. I wanted to touch the back of it, where the veins traced green lines beneath her skin. I *wanted* to trust her.

Blue raised her fingers. They were touched with black, and they startled me; they reminded me of Connie in a hospital gown, the priest smearing her forehead with ash, a reminder of the dust to which we all return. She wrapped her hand around my hand

and, with her usual worrying motion, began to stripe my skin. "There's something I need to tell you." I heard an urgency, and it scared me.

"No." I set the cards back on the counter. My throat constricted. Whatever it was—a boyfriend, a wife—I didn't want to know. I turned from the counter.

She gripped me harder. "Wait."

"Amy!" Michael's squat figure darkened the doorway; his face, taking this in—me, Blue, our hands entwined—was bathed in eerie blue light. Seeing his face that color, pale blue, made me shiver with fear. He'd been that color when he was born.

My wrist broke from Blue's grip. "Michael." I rushed toward my brother. "What's wrong? Is Dad okay?" Images of my father splayed across the tiled kitchen floor, orange juice and shards of glass around his face. Of my mother pinned underneath.

My brother frowned. The tips of his hair were damp, his face smooth; he smelled like shampoo and aftershave. "Mom and Dad are fine." This close, I could hear the quick whistle of his breath as he craned around me, his eyes darting back and forth over my shoulder. "Who is that? Is that your girlfriend?"

I felt an instinct to hide her from him, from everyone. I scrubbed the ash from my bones. "No one," I said grabbing his arm, pulling him out of the shop without looking back.

Any reluctance Michael had to move on evaporated as the sun fell on his face. "I came out to get ice cream. Now you can help choose!" The late rays of sun lighting up Michael's hair threw me back into my parents' kitchen fifteen years gone—Michael, Tristan, and my father surrounded by graters and whisks and puddles of cream, licking the blades of the ice cream machine that had lived since my childhood on the top shelf of the hall closet. I strapped Tristan into his car seat sticky and sated and never told my parents that he threw up three times that night in his bed. It was impossible to imagine my father doing anything like that now—measuring liquid in a cup, standing up at the kitchen counter, taking care of someone else. "Mom said to because we're celebrating." Another smile lit his face, a smile like the autumn's lemon-gingersnap light.

"Celebrating?" Now I felt fixed in place, my boots rooted to the alley as I wondered if my parents knew about Q. My mother had scolded me when I pulled out the letter I'd scribed for the man in the tweed vest, had scolded me long ago for the idea of pursuing a passion so impractical, but maybe they were old enough, finally, to be happy for me. "Is that what Mom said?" I wondered if we had time to pick up a bottle of champagne. It wasn't hard to imagine the words my mother might say at last: *We're proud of you.*

Behind Michael, pale oblongs of ice cream glowed in the case. "Mom said I shouldn't tell you until we're at the dinner table."

"*Tell* me?" In the corner of my eye, a flash of silver-gray struck a quick, cold dagger of fear into my chest. But when I turned, the blond men in their tight gray suits were nowhere I could see. My mind must be playing tricks, telling me to be afraid. Telling me not to trust happiness. "Tell me what?"

My brother straightened his shoulders, which were solid and round, dependable shoulders. "Amy!" He was so happy his eyes rolled shut. "I'm getting married."

Everything went quiet. The wind slapping the sandwich board outside the ice cream shop, the creak of the chain swinging the red and black Coffee Shop sign, the boisterous voices of the crowd—all of it muted. In my vision, black spots multiplied and overlapped, converging into a large, Gothic letter M. I grabbed blindly for the sleeve of Michael's shirt. Thinking I had meant to hug him, Michael reached out and grabbed me close. He was squeezing me hard and my words of betrayal fell into the folds of his neck. "Married? What do you mean?"

He pushed me away. He was going to marry Izzy. And leave Mom and Dad. His friend Jerry had an in-law unit he would rent them for under market. It was all planned. "I'm a grownup man, Amy," said my baby brother, and there was an edge to it; I had underestimated him, like so many others.

I wanted to protest: Of course I hadn't underestimated him. I was the person who wanted everything for him! I was the one pushing him on the purple bicycle, running and pushing and letting him go!

Years ago, when Michael started dating Izzy, we joked at first about the two of them getting married, and then we talked about it seriously—my parents and I, privately, about whether the two of them could live on their own, whether they should. But then my father's back bent in the shape of a question mark, and it was my parents we talked about—whether they could live on their own, whether they should. With Tristan gone, my parents and Michael were the only family I had left, the four of us together, the original constellation. It had never occurred to me for a second that my baby brother would want to *continue on with his own life and leave me.*

Before it all ended, Connie scratched out a line from a poem on a slip of paper by our bed. They'd stopped placing IV lines in her arms by then, had installed a port straight over her heart. Connie was never one for poetry but one of the nurses had a crush on her, read her love poems, which should have made me jealous, but by then I begrudged her nothing. Once when she was sleeping, I'd picked up the book, stiff pages, spine cracked, tented at the side of her bed, and the note fell out, one line in Connie's crabbed blue spider web: *Save yourself*, it said, *Others you cannot save.*

I licked my lips, which were so, so dry.

"It's your party," I pushed Michael toward the pastel ices. "You choose." Across the way, inside the barbershop, the chrome chairs sizzled under the lights; a small clump of hair dotted the floor. Spotting it, I realized: the man in the tweed vest had walked right by me. He was the man with a pale, freshly shaved chin who'd pressed past, smelling of shaving soap and limes, a neat white line cut into the hair at the nape of his neck.

How blind I was. Oh, how blind.

No one knows more about radio than my brother Michael and his ham radio buddy, Jerry, a retired, forty-nine-year-old Space X pilot who lived three blocks away in a house with an enormous antenna and two fat orange wind socks fixed to the roof. That night after dinner, Michael and I met Jerry in Jerry's converted garage.

The room smelled like metal and glue and a musty wool area rug. Gleaming coils of copper wire and licorice-colored spools of red and black hung like tribal masks against the inside of the old garage door. Along the wall, custom-built shelves displayed Jerry's collection of antique radios: a boxy, teal General Electric 914D transistor with a big gold analog clock face; a brown leather Zenith "Transoceanic" whose case opened flat to an array of shiny disks and small glass vacuum tubes. On the second shelf, Jerry's impressive collection of ham radios with their digitized buttons and glowing wave displays looked like alien spacecraft touched down in a rubble field of scattered transistors. Just being inside Jerry's converted garage felt like time travel, a possibility I wouldn't put past Jerry, who had gazed back at earth from the blue-black water of space and skimmed the planet's bright skin like a stone. I had never been inside Jerry's house before, and I wondered about the other rooms of it, about the granny flat where Michael and Izzy would live, and what kind of strange magic lay in wait for them there. Though I also already knew: Love. Independence. Companionship.

"Do you have the cloner?" Jerry held out his palm, the thumb of his left hand scored with a white half-moon where he'd sliced it trying to hack a piece off a frozen Snickers with a pocketknife. I knew because Michael had warned him not to and shook his head every time he saw the scar. He was shaking his head a little bit right then, and he caught my eye and we both laughed. That was the thing about being together in the same place. Little things—a look, a laugh. I had already lost that with my son. Just being together.

Michael would never move in with me.

I dropped the plastic card and the copper coil that functioned as its antenna into Jerry's palm, remembering the way the warm metal felt in my hand as I passed it over Sandy's badge without her knowing.

Jerry attached a USB cord to the cloner, a flat, plastic card studded with electronics, and plugged the cord into his computer, a sleek, black tower glowing with red lights that Jerry had built himself, and which he said had no connection to the internet, *because you never know who wants to come knocking.* Suddenly, I wondered if Jerry could be part of the Neighborhood, if he would think they were geniuses or if he would think they were nuts. Jerry fiddled some buttons on the machine. I decided not to ask. Jerry was a person who had willingly left earth's atmosphere. And he hadn't asked me why I needed to clone a Radio Frequency ID. Jerry gave a thumbs-up. "Successful transfer. I'll just switch this into transmitting mode and you're good to go." He dropped the card back into my palm, now a functioning copy of Sandy Jensen's Q ID badge.

"Blackberry picking?" Jerry asked, eyeing the purpled tips of my fingers.

"Something like that," I said.

17 In Flew a Sparrow

SANDY SAT AT MY DRAFTING TABLE, WATCHING ME trim temporary tattoos from a sheet. The tattoos were a cheat, a way to apply detailed illumination without mastering the art, but all of my art was a cheat, an approximation of something more long-lasting and real, but purposely so, a reflection of our transitory nature. It was meant to exist in the world, like us, and also, like us, to die. I loved books and manuscripts that had lasted centuries, like the Book of Kells or the Lindisfarne Gospels or the astonishing, violet-and-silver *Codex Argentus* hidden away in Q's library. But my work did not aspire to centuries. Over time, and not too much of it, my tattoos would peel and my bricolage would flake from the page until all that was left were the letters inked on paper. That was the point. That was enough.

The tattoo I was clipping was a line-drawn *hamsa*, the Middle Eastern hand common to all three religions of that region, drawn to ward off the evil eye. Sandy had "waded" across the holographic waves to my table, pant legs rolled, shoes and socks in her hand, and watched as my Xacto knife rounded the edges of the stylized fingers. I was glad to have her sitting at my table, watching me, a shift in the balance of power between us. Since the moment she'd pulled me from a nap pod, I'd been off-balance around Sandy Jensen, a guest in her space. Now, at least in some way, she was a guest in mine. I liked her like a brother. I wanted her to like me back.

Sandy cleared her throat: "Protection from evil. That's always wise." Impressing me, once again, with the breadth of her knowledge. She pulled back the rolled sleeve of her shirt and offered the pale skin of her forearm. She smelled like sunscreen and salt. "Got a spare?"

I chose a small tattoo for Sandy Jensen, a gold, black and blue *hamsa* she could cover with her sleeve. I held her thin arm in one hand, aware of holding her limb like the soft, thin leg of a horse, with care for the animal life within it, but nothing more. Pressing the hamsa onto her skin, it was hard to believe Sandy Jensen, *Evangelist*, with her big brain and bright laughter, needed protection from anything. From the day I'd met her at Q, Sandy Jensen had struck me as easy, self-confident, lucky. It was hard to believe anything could phase her, let alone seek her out for harm. And it was very hard to square Sandy Jensen with the claims Arman had made about Q in the nighttime bicycle shop, the murmured secrets over whispering pens. Sandy Jensen didn't seem to want to ruin people's lives. Sandy Jensen was a *nice* person, a person who smelled like a day at the beach, a person whose pale arm sat smooth and cool and trusting in my hand.

I touched my damp sponge to the back of the tattoo paper. "You don't believe in evil."

The bright ruff of her hair shook under the glass panels of the atrium as she threw her head back and laughed. "You kill me." The fingers of her other hand brushed my arm.

I wondered what I looked like to Sandy, through her curtain of laughter and light, my black hair and black boots, small, dark, hidden. Hiding.

Carefully, I peeled the wet paper backing from the back of Sandy's forearm. The fine lines of the *hamsa* had transferred perfectly to her skin.

"Why are you so easygoing?" I considered the shoes clutched under Sandy Jensen's armpit, at her bare feet and rolled pant legs. "And why do you smell like the beach?"

Laughter splashed from Sandy's mouth, her face open and bright. "I thought you'd never ask."

Did I worry just a little bit as Sandy took my arm in hers and led me through the wide, windowed hallways, through a little locked door onto a courtyard at whose far edge turquoise water murmured over a pale, pebbled beach into which Sandy waded barefoot; as I unlaced my boots and socks and waded into the water beside her, did I worry about what it meant that she was so much a part of this place I envied and wanted to possess and had been asked to destroy?

I did not.

A blink, a forgetting. A cleansing as simple and pure as the water at our feet.

I wiggled my toes in the warm backwash of the liquids that cooled the great underground farm of servers. "Tell me the truth. You're Wonka, aren't you?" Over the courtyard, the big belly of the wind pushed the lacy fingers of steam from the surface of the water, lifting our hair and tossing it up like streamers. Over the vast, empty courtyard, the boxed square of sky blazed wide as eternity.

"Maybe I am." Sandy dipped a long, thin finger into the water. Her hands were nimble, her fingers long and dexterous, hands that would be capable of taking apart the minute springs and screws of an antique watch and putting them back together again. She pressed the tip of one of those slender fingers gently against the surface of the water.

For the first time, I wondered: Did Sandy Jensen feel lonely? It was hard for me to imagine that the thin, blond *Evangelist* at the world's most famous social networking company, a person who was certainly friends with Hack and his inner circle; who undoubtedly knew by name and face a ridiculous number of the engineers and product managers and even service workers who cruised the rainbow buildings of Q; a woman with capable hands and an easy smile, would have any opportunity at any moment of the day to feel lonely. But, glancing at our shadows against gently rippling water, I knew that I knew better.

I peered down at my reflection and thought about how Q would map my connections—Sandy and Jae, my mother and father and Tristan, Arman and the man in the tweed vest and Blue. I knew well enough that the number of people didn't matter, or felt like it didn't, if there wasn't one who mattered most. I remembered cupping my hands around Connie's belly, the feeling that I was holding the entire world in my hands. I wondered where Blue was and what she was doing right then.

I stretched out my back, which had begun to get cranky over small things, and gazed out over the courtyard walls at the brilliant blue sky, a sky that might have been poured from a vat to match the rainbow buildings and the picture-perfect world they were trying to make inside them. I wondered if this was what it could feel to be at the center of creation.

It struck me again within the cloistered walls that perhaps this was the point of Q in all its webs of connection: from the vast chaos of limitless data, to make meaning. My eyes fell to the light shining off the water, the blue pool. Could I be converted? It felt like it would be so easy to just believe.

"This is the thing you believe in," I commented, more to myself than to Sandy.

I had failed a believer before.

I don't think she heard me.

She'd asked me a question. She'd asked me: *Will you come to the ball with me?*

My first reaction was regret. I wished that holding Sandy Jensen's arm didn't fill me with the same tender feeling as wrapping my hand around the leg of a dog. My second reaction was: *What is wrong with me?* What had *been* wrong with me, that I stood here with a smart, thoughtful, accomplished person shedding tangerine peals of laughter and let my animal nature discard her. My animal body wanted heat and thunder; it wanted showers of sparks. They had been the only thing I felt capable of, after Connie—moments of incandescence. After Connie, without faces, without letters—I had only my body to connect me. Only the strike of bone against bone. Only moments of heat in the darkness. But what had heat in the darkness produced?

Her feet were long and pale and bony, in the water beside mine, waterbird feet.

I could not tell the difference between excitement and fear, guilt and terror in the hard rush in my ears when I said *Yes*.

I *was* Sandy Jensen.

It felt as innocent as pulling a fresh T-shirt over my head. Swiping into the Q Library with her cloned badge, I remembered Sandy's dry lips pressing mine against the rough stone wall of the courtyard. But it was Tal my blood was beating for, the shadow at the postbox, the dark figure swirling with flames. In my pocket, the note scribbled in Farsi: *Meet me at the library*.

It was a frenetic time at Q—even an outsider could feel that: the *Lockdown* sign sizzling over the quad, engineers madly at work on the newest version of the Algorithm, while Hack flew back and forth to Capitol Hill, testifying that Q did not need to be contained. On monitors clinging to the walls of campus, you could see his calm demeanor in a tailored suit but only read his lips. And all the while, the ball was being planned for All Hallows' Eve, the night when all of it would swirl together: the Launch of the Algorithm, the Return of the Hero.

Before Sandy left campus herself—her job as Evangelist summoned her to distant locales—she told me she would pick me up Friday night. "Look your witchiest," she'd laughed that jingle-of-golden-coins laugh that was the opposite of witchy, kissed me again chastely and said *Be good.*

Ha.

The cloner worked. My blood throbbed in my fingertips against the plastic card Jerry had given me that mimicked Sandy's ID. I swiped it past the sensor and the green light flashed and I walked through the white door set in the white wall. Inside the smooth white eggshell, a distant claxon screeched calamity, but I had been in this room before and recognized the sonification of climate change. I moved through the portal to the darkened passage in which Sandy had shown me the video screen of the entry at Q where the giant mammoth bones hung and watched for a minute as it caught one of the passersby and started spinning out a web of connections. It was strange, a god's-eye view; that was why Arman hated it and why Sandy loved it and I guess why I was indifferent to it: I had never longed for an all-knowing god, and I didn't see the threat in it either, especially when the "god" was a bloodless machine.

I moved easily into the library, past the glassed-in scanners speaking and singing and labeling the sheets and folios under their gaze; past the clockwork bird ticking away on its branch. I glanced up. Q had cameras scanning most of the halls of campus; in the library, they did not. The smell of smoke, which had begun permeating the air, filtering down from fires somewhere far in the north, persisted here as a vague hint of campfire and toast.

I felt my pocket for the scrolled note. But the library was empty, Tal nowhere in sight.

Of course.

But, of course, it wasn't empty at all. It was full of scrolls and codices, letters and words. At one of the glassed scanning booths, the robotic arm reached for another manuscript lined on the shelf. I watched how delicately the arm squared the leather-bound *codex* atop the pedestal, lifted the cracked cover and peeled back the first page. Above it, an antique title page appeared on the screen; the text was written in what looked like Arabic, and was accompanied by carefully sketched orbits of the sun and moon. On the screen, the orbits suddenly animated along the trajectories the illustrator had drawn twelve centuries before. *Hijazi*, the comment read beneath them, *9th c.*, *The Movements of the Planets*.

It was as much confirmation as I needed that not everything that happened here at Q was bad. Some of what happened here—I turned to look for the silver-spangled, purple pages of the *Codex Argentus*—was magical.

On a library cart, I recognized the spine of the *Codex*, whose cover looked so much like mine. Close enough to its scan date on All Hallows' Eve, it had been moved into the queue. Slipping on white gloves, I lifted the manuscript out of its slot, untied the leather thong holding the thing closed and let the cover fall open.

There were the watery depths of the deep violet folios shimmering with silver script like a span of the Milky Way. There was the mysterious Gothic script a human hand had penned fourteen centuries earlier. Gently, gently, I carried the *Codex* to a library table where I could study it under a bright pinpoint of light. The manuscript pages had turned up after centuries somewhat worse for the wear. Curved and wrinkled, they had sustained damage—words had been rubbed clear of the page, the vellum had torn, and some of the pages stuck together along splashes of wine or blood. But it was magnificent. Even more than magnificent. The vellum warm as wine-blushed skin, it glimmered against the deep purple dye made from those rare, ancient snails. When I turned the leaves, I thought that I could smell the sea.

The folia were unbound; they had probably changed bindings a number of times over their history, and were easier to scan that way.

I examined the leather cover, letter tooled into its front in its Gothic font. Sandy had called it *cheap*, but they couldn't have picked it up at Walmart. It really was stunningly similar to mine—but for the slightest difference in color, in the *A* on my portfolio's cover versus the *V* on the *Codex*'s, in the silver radio sticker Sandy had asked the guard to affix on the back cover of mine so that I could remove my own work from the building. Except for that sticker, and my own first initial instead of the *V*, even I would have trouble telling them apart.

Removing one sheet, I compared the deep violet of the *Codex* with a recent page of my own, dipped in a dye I had cooked up with ingredients from the Apothecary shop and some wildflowers pulled from a vacant lot. The color match wasn't bad.

Squaring up my own blank purple sheet and taking out my ruler and quill to practice my hand at the strange letters in silver and gold, I fell into that beautiful state of being that only comes with paper and ink. Copying the characters from a sheet of the original *Codex*, I wondered again about the Mystery of the One Thousand Years, and the faces these letters had seen, the hands they had touched, the solid capitals outliving their speakers: a landscape of distant fields, low buildings, candle flames.

The letters were the only ornamentation on almost all of the Bible's pages, the language illumination enough. Baffling though it was to me, that was what Connie, too, had seen in this story: certainty, salvation. A truth worth giving up everything for.

According to the Venerable Bede, writing in the eighth century, this certainty was the reason for which King Edwin sought Christianity:

> This world is like the feast hall in which you sit with your aldermen, the fire kindled, the hall warmed, while it rains and storms and snows outside. In comes a sparrow, flies through and out again. From winter he comes and to

winter he returns. Such is man's life, the briefest interval; what comes before and what comes after, we cannot know.

In the rain, the storm, the snow, Christianity offered him knowing. Offered it to Connie.

Not me.

I was a sparrow. I was just passing through.

And the *Codex*? Where had these pages gone for all of their unaccounted thousand years? Things this beautiful and rare had a way of disappearing between the strata of time. So much darkness and silence. So much time passed.

I thought of all the things I had lost, all the pages torn from my own Book of Hours: the Hour When Love Has Left Me; the Hour With a Child Who Has Just Cut Teeth; the Hour Desperate for Solitude and the Hour of a Soft Warm Body Clutched to the Chest; the Hour of Fever and Flush and Hair Sweat-Stuck to the Forehead; the Hour of Naps; the Hour of Cheerios; the Hour of Sidewalk Tantrums and the Hour of Underpants Worn on the Head; the Hour of *Blue's Clues*; the Hour of Soccer and the Hour of Farm A Little League; the Hour of Swimming Lessons and Goldfish; the Hour of Homework; the Hour of Driving to the Next Thing and then the Next; the Hour After He's Gone to Bed; the Hour and the Hour and the Hour after that; the Hour of Solitude and the Hour of Longing; the Hour of Pimples; the Hour of Shaving his Upper Lip; the Hour of Condom Wrappers in the Trash; the Hour of Handing Him the Keys; the Hour of My First, My Only, Leaving Me; The Hour of Being Alone Again.

Each page had disappeared so eagerly. Three years of Saturdays on the sidelines of the baseball field, screaming *Be a hitter!*, rust-red dirt on the back of his pants—You tore out the one page and then it was gone. And this was only one human life! A decade or two! You put these things somewhere for later and they just disappeared.

Imagine a hundred years! Imagine a millennium! Imagine how much a whole culture could lose. I could picture it: some ancient anchorite or priest wrapping one of the *Codex*'s purple, word-spangled pages around a staff as a charm to ward off decay, tucked into a box for all of eternity like the holy bones of a saint. And all the other lost pages, each a bright butterfly in its chrysalis, waiting. How had they been found again? That was the mystery, wasn't it—not loss, but return.

Watching the page dry, I considered my silver penmanship against the folio leaf. Not bad. Not to an untrained eye.

I set the original leaf back next to the 148 folios that made up the remainder of the complete manuscript. *Once we scan these pages, the* Codex Argenteus *will be complete again for the first time in a millennium.* A complete, digital original. And it was all happening at once, on All Hallows' Eve: the ball, the Algorithm, the manuscript. Hack clearly had a sense of ceremony. And he liked nice things.

Turning the pages over carefully in both hands, studying the portfolio cover, I looked for a loan slip from the lender, something to indicate where the priceless folia had come from, but found nothing there. *They must digitize the records*, I decided. But there was no radio ID sticker on the portfolio, no bar code, no tracking number of any kind. My eyes traveled the shelves.

All around me, scrolls and codices and books tilted and huddled along the rows. Even with a database, there was no way to keep track of them all without *some* kind of marking attached to each physical item. Without tags, the entire library was a jumble, impossible to return to the lenders.

But who was the lender?

I closed my eyes and sucked in the must of old parchment; the odd bronze bird rioted to mark the hour. What a strange place this was, this new Byzantium, this library of books that didn't exist. What an ambitious collection.

A *whoosh* sounded behind me as a manuscript was lifted off the scanning block and dropped into a slot in the wall. So much care laying them out for the scanner, so oddly little care as each rare article made way for the next. Though the library was sealed and climate controlled, the distant smell of smoke rose in the air, a faint tinge of burning wood and flesh.

I skimmed a gloved finger across one of the deep-dyed pages of the Silver Bible, half-expecting the halo of cotton fuzz around the tip to come away purple, but of course the dye had set too long ago for that. The pages of my own portfolio lay loose and scattered, the cheap purple-dyed simulacrum of the *Codex* and the brilliant original strewn across the wide oak table, both tooled leather covers discarded like empty clothes.

I started stacking purple pages together, separating the originals from my own, the heat blooming on my cheeks, understanding and resolution gathering at once in my chest: Hack didn't just *like* rare things. He liked to *own* them. To *collect* them. Like the mammoth in the atrium, the laddered scaffolding of ancient bones, rare and complete. I could hear Michael in the crowd on Market Street, spelling it out for me: *The museum wanted him. But Q got him. Woolly cost 645,000 dollars, Amy. He's real.* And I could see Jae's mouth, moving behind his hand: *He doesn't borrow; he steals.*

I looked around the Library of Books That Don't Exist and I knew: Hack had found a way to find rare books before anyone else even knew they existed. He was *that* rich. I doubt he would have purchased anything stolen. That would be obviously illegal, and tawdry, and derivative. But—if he thought he was *disrupting* the normal order of things in a cool, subversive way by snapping up something extraordinary—he might steal it himself.

The *Codex Argentus* wasn't going to be returned anywhere to anyone. That's why it didn't have a loan slip on it. It was staying at Q. Not because it had a history here, or a curator to care for it, but only because Hack *owned* it. Did he even come down to look at these things he collected? The *Codex* was a manuscript among manuscripts in this library no one knew existed. And if Hack had it his way, no one would ever know.

But I knew.

I walked out of Q that day in a strange state of elation, my mood lifting on the gusts that stowed into the atrium every time the big glass doors whooshed open, so high on adrenaline that I didn't flinch when the guard who searched my bag pulled out my portfolio and scanned the silver sticker on the back. I made sure to leave my hands out on the counter, so that against the dusky edges of the pages he would see the purple-stained tips of my fingers and know that I had been making art.

Thus, I walked out of Q with the fifteen-centuries-old *Codex Argentus* in my bag. I wasn't stealing it. It was a library book and I was borrowing it. I had until All Hallows' Eve. As collateral, tucked into the *Codex*'s portfolio cover, I had left all of my life's work behind.

I stood in the kitchen, swigging kombucha, sticky and satisfied. My brother was out shooting hoops in the driveway; my mother was in the living room, prying apart my father's eyelids, dripping in cool drops. *There, my darling. There.* I leaned against the kitchen counter, the punch and echo of the basketball reminding me of Tristan, and peered into the looking glass of my mother's phone to find proof of my new existence.

Sandy Jensen had been true to her word. I was getting noticed. Promoting my appearance at the ball, someone at Q had written me up, a short news post I read on my mother's Q feed. In the photo, the top of my head tilted over the top of my desk. I didn't think of myself as vain, but the caption "Artist Recalls Bygone Era" sent a flash through my veins as cool and fresh as the kombucha. It was just two sentences and a photo, but it already had 121 views and two shares.

I cannot lie. My face flushed at that word under my picture, *Artist*.

Scrolling down to see if there were any COMMENTS from Jae or Sandy, I spotted something oddly familiar. A sponsored ad, looking very much like a regular Q post, a photo of a shiny red birdhouse painted like an iconic country barn, topped with a hand-feathered bird. I didn't have to read the caption to know what I was looking at—*who* I was looking at. Kareem, my old art studio buddy from before Tristan was born. Kareem of the lovely, *New York Times*–worthy medieval-manuscript-stylized birdhouses of Black motherhood. At forty-five years old, he was having a retrospective!

And here I was, imagining myself on the brink of something. Imagining *shares* and *likes* and maybe even fame. That was the other thing Q did, though, wasn't it? The thing people *actually* talked about: Q made you compare yourself; it made everything you did feel small. It used its great treasure troves of data to do that, too.

I hadn't talked to Kareem in eighteen years, and yet here he was in my mother's phone. Not just any artist. Him. I remembered my mother flashing me ads for *scizr* on her phone. I realized: Q had never deleted my account. Not really. Or, rather, it had deleted my account, but it had never deleted my *data*. That would be like deleting money from Q's bank account. And why would Q ever do that? And what had been in my account connected me to my mother, and on and on. Just like Arman had warned me, I, too, was caught up in its sticky web.

Really, if I couldn't take the FOMO, I could simply never log onto Q again. But I'd already seen myself reflected in its screen, and what I saw, I didn't like: A little person, scrabbling for a little, torn gold leaf of fame. To be someone—for a moment. But that was not what my art was. My art was the art of people who were never meant to be known. The medieval monk, cramped in his cold cell, squinting by the light of a candle. The one-thousand-year-dead nun, sequestered and secretly writing, lapis staining her teeth. Their art was not about themselves. They were merely vessels. Their art belonged to time. Like the *Codex Argentus*. To the Memory of the World.

What was it Mirabel had said? *The canvas is broader than you think.* Blue had said it the night we met: *Your work has meaning to someone outside of you.* At least, it could have.

I clanked the kombucha bottle down on the counter. I might have knocked it just as hard over my head.

I'd been thinking *so* small. About what I could achieve for myself. When my son was out in the world trying to save it for all of us. When the guard at the Gap store with his little white dog, a compassionate man who was kind to my brother, couldn't even search for his own face in his photographs, because the algorithm thought he was an ape. When Michael feared going shopping because the store—not people! the store!—called him a thief. When so many people lived in terror that a missed period recorded by an app could mean the end of the world.

There were so many things out there in the world, happening without our knowing. It all seemed so innocuous, if you hadn't done anything wrong. If you *thought* you hadn't done anything wrong, because what was "wrong" was constantly changing. And by adjusting the facts just so, the truth could be made up. That was Arman's point: You assumed you were safe, but you just didn't know. What was out there, coming for Michael, or Tristan, or someone they loved? What if I'd had the chance to save them, and all I did was save myself?

Because, let's be real, I'd never believed that Q wasn't suspect. We all knew that it was. It's just that, mostly, nobody cared.

But if I didn't care, then I wasn't any better than Hack with all his beautiful, purloined things. Was I even an artist? The big canvas wasn't writing love letters for database engineers. (Though actually that wasn't nothing.) It was anonymously penning the letter that would rattle and shake the throne of the world.

"Amy!" my mother's voice rushed in. "Will you get Dad's pills?" From the other room, I heard her reassure my father: "Darling," she crooned, "Amy will give you your pills."

I put down my mother's phone and concentrated on the cold weight of the applesauce jar in my hand. It felt good against the tendonitis in my fingers from working on letters all day. I stared at my hand and traced the beautiful lines of pain, the flesh callousing my knuckle, the grit of gum Arabic under my nails. I examined my hand, this sinuous thing that had the power finally to earn my parents' pride—or to throw their lives into chaos. (If I got caught, Q would blow our lives to bits.) And, finally, I knew which one I'd choose.

"Amy?"

For a second, I was seventeen years old, in my parents' old house, waiting for Lucia to come save me, shaking, my mother screeching down the hall to my father: *She's wild!*

I'd always thought that was my mother, misunderstanding me, when I spent my hours so quietly pressing a quill onto a page, so focused on my art. But those quiet lines were only part of the art. There was that other part, the part that wasn't afraid of what would happen next.

It turned out my mother was right.

18 Kill Code

WITH A DIAGNOSIS, THINGS HAPPEN QUICKLY.
Decisions are made. Cells die. Cells split and divide. All
that sticky, red multiplication swarming under the wet
cover of blood. Connie, eight weeks along and diagnosed
with uterine cancer, did not want to give up her baby. She
lay on the couch at home, her lips pale and chapped, a
cold cup of tea and a can of seltzer at her elbow. Already,
our home felt different, the way the light crept across the
crocheted blanket, fuzzy and pilled, the way it lit up the
side table that would soon fill with bottles and glasses,
pills and tonics. Connie dragged her nails against the
rough fiberglass of her cast, pleading: "This is the only
chance I'll get." That stung, a swift blow that made a
quick, hard knot of my womb. That she needed so much
for something to be hers, she would die for it. Hidden
inside their aluminum tube, the bubbles ticked against
the can of seltzer. I tapped the dimple at the center of
my belly, "But we have more than one chance." Then I
started to cry.

I left a letter in the postbox. That was all.
    For seconds at a time, the bridge of my nose went
numb with the horror of what I was going to do. Purging
Q's database would cause more material destruction to
the world's largest collection of consumer data than if I
were to douse all of Q's beautiful buildings in kerosene

and set them on fire. The Kill Code would spread its trail of flame right up into the Cloud, purging it of every *Like*, purchase and facial twitch, and from the Cloud it would backwash into the servers of the companies that used Q's for data storage like a great lick of flame rushing from the barbeque up the stream of lighter fluid back into the can. Online stores, insurance companies, police departments. I would erase histories of illness and false "patterns" of gang affiliation and ex-lovers and troublesome brothers and facial "recognition" that couldn't tell Michael from a thief. Purging the Q database went way beyond the Neighborhood, way beyond a thousand neighborhoods. I didn't fully appreciate it then, but the Kill Code had the potential to tank the entire global economy. A city like San Francisco might topple and burn—but also, Minneapolis, Austin, Bangalore. Oh, how fucked we would be. The scale was beyond my reckoning. (Or, maybe, my child newly fledged, my parents perched on the edge of the void, the scale did not match up to my reckoning, to the scale of the loss as I already felt it.) I told myself it would just be a blink, a forgetting. A reclamation of all of our loves and our memories and our choices. And then things would return as they were.

But that is never how these things go.

I was summoned to the barbershop on Temescal Alley.

Nickel bell lights blazed above each station, bright bowls of light thrown hard against the window. Outside, the barber pole spun its ribbons, lazy and blue. Inside, three tall, dark-haired men clustered at the farthest chair—a pair of butter-yellow Timberlands braced against the footrest. The shop was closed. All the short hairs had been swept from the penny tiles, the air brisk with the scent of juniper, the gin cool of the men's thickly pomaded hair. I thought of him then, the man in the tweed vest, of the night he vanished; I saw him in their narrow backs, sweating through silk-backed vests; and again when a straight razor whispered in one of the men's large hands, swept back and forth across the strop, flashed against the pale brown bulge of a throat stretched back, a sharp, bright gash where the overhead bulb struck the razor's edge.

"Jae!" I screamed. He lay back, the straight razor at his throat. All three men turned. It is possible that one of the tall, bearded figures was Arman, and equally possible that none of them was. They looked at me and they turned to look at the man pressed into the barber's chair as if they had just discovered what they were doing.

"If you don't fight it," said the biggest of the men, "this won't hurt a bit."

"He doesn't have anything to do with any of this! Let him go!"

The man holding the razor let it fall against his thigh. "He wants to do this."

If I thought about it, I had known that Jae was depressed—disappointed, resigned to a comfortable, second-choice life.

Pulling the lever at his side, Jae sat up. "It's true. This is what I want." Jae and Hack had been freshman roommates and unlikely friends, Hack a schlumpy but wildly ambitious Jewish boy from New Jersey and Jae a tall, handsome, wildly ambitious young writer; both of them wanted to devour the world. Hack's big break, famously, came quickly, so young he still believed in things like blood brothers, and controlling the thing he created. "The Kill Code was never a joke. Hack sort of knew he was on the verge of this huge thing and the Kill Code made him feel like he wasn't selling out because he knew he could always destroy it. And, to cement our friendship forever, he gave that power to me." Jae would be Hack's deputy, his Number 2. Never mind that Jae had different ideas about his future. "How could I ever explain it to my immigrant parents? *Your roommate wants to make you rich and you want to write stories?* It just didn't make sense to them and, in the end, it didn't make sense to me, either. Except."

Except that the heady first days of a shared house with a pool and late nights playing *Doom* gave way to cubbies in a cement-block former Walmart, blazer-and-golf VC bros and a whole lot of coders. Hanging around wasn't fun anymore. But he couldn't leave. "Hack trusted me. More than anyone." It's possible Hack knew that Jae had always been a little bit in love with him. "It was a *very* long time ago."

Jae swiveled the chair with the tip of his boot. "He's afraid of me, but he also doesn't believe I could ever do it. My title? *The Cueist?* That's his joke, you know. I'm the one who can cue up the apocalypse. But he knows I won't." Jae ran his fingertip along the edge of the straight razor, then licked his finger and sighed. "*Knew.* I've been David's little bitch far too long. This is my bridge to burn."

It was a grand gesture. But Jae's big flourish was about freedom, and that was as good a reason as any of us had for wreaking this havoc—freedom from all the symptoms we'd Googled and the exes we'd stalked, freedom from our browsing and buying and watching, freedom from all of our mindlessly rendered history.

The men huddled around Jae's chair looked at Jae. "Ready?"

Then I was alarmed again as they tilted Jae back into the sink and brought the razor to his face. His voice floated up from the bowl: "After this, there's no way back."

"Jae!"

But one of the bearded men was already threading his thick fingers through the thatch of hair at the top of Jae's head, getting a grip on it, as if Jae's head might drop to the floor.

My chest tightened. What was I here to witness? What had I done?

Jae's voice burbled up from the sink: "Freshman year, David and I both took ancient Greek history. When David learned that the Greek tyrant Histiaeus had tattooed a message on the shaved head of his slave and then waited for his hair to grow back before sending him off, he became obsessed. He wanted desperately to send a message of his own. As soon as he came up with the Kill Code it was obvious what message he would send, and who he would send it to. Himself." Jae's Adam's apple bobbed up and down. "Making me the slave. David thought it was hysterical. A joke I would be in on, and, shame on me, I was flattered."

The silver buckle on the back of the tallest man's vest glittered as he pressed Jae's shoulders back down against the chair. The heavier-set man bent closer to Jae's head and angled the razor. "Hold still."

"Don't kill the messenger," Jae drawled. He didn't sound scared.

"Don't worry. This razor is *very* sharp."

I'd handled penknife on parchment and quill and I knew what he meant: a sharper blade was less prone to mistakes. But it didn't sound like a comfort.

Then there was the slow sound like silk tearing and the man with the razor stepped back, a bloodless square of black pelt dangling from his hand. "We've got it! We've got it!" A nauseatingly flesh-backed patch of hair flopped into the bowl.

I did not think I could be forgiven for this.

The tallest man waved me over. Afraid of what I was going to see, I stepped forward.

Sweat, cologne and raw animal scents hit my nose like smelling salts, pricking me to life. The world's most sacred scrolls were animal skin and stank of death; sometimes skin was the price.

The square at the top of Jae's head looked clear-cut, a pale chessboard square-sized patch of skin in the middle of a dark thicket. Across the pale, light-starved, sub-layer of skin, a deep blue blot spread like a bruise. Slipping on my reading glasses, I saw that it was not a bruise, but an initial capital—or something that looked like one: an indigo letter M set in the center of a blurred field. The tallest of the bearded men slipped a large magnifying glass into my hand, and the blurred field came into focus as a matrix of dots. The dots also been hand-inked, but carefully, according to a long-erased grid. Stick-and-poke work, very neat. Jae picked up a hand mirror and tilted it toward the top of his head. "He hadn't come up with the name for Q yet, so he used his first initial instead." He ran an almond-shaped fingertip over the top of his skull. "It took three days. He'd dragged me out to his parents' house in Jersey and, for the first week he wouldn't let me leave the house. A beanie wasn't good enough. I had to stay hidden *from the world* so no one would know what little M. David Hacker, who was famous for nothing, was up to." Jae smoothed his palm across the top of his remaining hair, murmuring, "I should have asked for a trim."

I got out my quill, my penknife, my bottles of ink.

"It was fun, though. We stayed in his room watching rom coms in our socks and he fed me heaps and heaps of deep-fried pork rinds." His hand flew up to cover his mouth, the habitual gesture. "He said the fat would make my hair grow faster. But all it did was give me the shits!"

I laughed. Then I apologized before touching my fingertip to his naked scalp, counting the rows in the invisible grid. "Sorry. If you could just—"

They all watched quietly while I lined a forty-by-forty-row grid across a loose sheet and started to copy. Unmagnified, the dots were not much larger than the black, stubbled silos of Jae's roots, and I appreciated Hack's genius in choosing blue for his work instead of black, just dark enough to blend in, but distinct enough, if you knew what you were looking at, to tell them apart.

While I worked, the middle-sized bearded man murmured over my shoulder. For the next half hour, he and one of his companions read out the position of each dot on the grid, comparing the pattern on the top of Jae's scalp with the marks on my page, a strangely serious sound, like a game of Battleship being played by accountants. I wasn't used to having company while I worked, or having my work checked against a source, but instead of annoying it comforted me, reminding me of the dark *soferet* in the Jewish Museum murmuring over her sacred words. It was the law of the Jewish scribe to recite every word before transcribing it, a law of fidelity. Because the text was more important than the scribe. That was our tradition.

My mind skipped and hummed and I had to scrape a blue dot from the wrong place in the grid and ink it again.

At the next station over, the tallest of the three men was carving a wolf's face into a piece of wood the size of a small Lincoln log. Watching me ink the final dot on the sheet, he slipped his knife into the pocket of his Dickies, tugged my page off the drafting table with the longish, sharpish nail of his thumb, held the page close to his face then farther away and, nodding, tore the sheet into a thousand pieces. Then he gathered the pieces into a metal tray on the counter in front of him and set them on fire.

I sucked at my writing callous. "What the fuck?"

The ball of light flared and collapsed. At the same moment, watching the flame double itself in the mirror, I thought I saw a face in the glass. A face capped by a knit cap, lamb's-ear green. By the time I turned around, the pale blur was gone.

Jae stared at the pile of ash, cupping the bald spot on the top of his head. "Yeah. Seriously. What the actual fuck?"

The tall man pointed at my quill and dipped his head. "Smaller."

He wasn't wrong.

I studied the top of Jae's head again through the glass, noting the position of each dot while another man called out its coordinates on the grid. Connie, who was good with math, and logic, and the periodic table, would have recognized each position by heart. Sandy Jensen, who was smart and funny and knew what micrography was, reminded me of Connie, of what my life would have been like with Connie still in it, sunny and familiar and rooted. Barbeques in Hawaiian shirts, friendly heated arguments about charged particles, or conversion rates, dart-throwing nights and *South Park* and guys named Kev. A glass of water on each side of the bed. In the warmth trapped under the comforter, a hand to hold in the dark.

But, dotting each speck of blue along the cage of the grid, I couldn't help myself, I imagined them seeping and spilling into pools and ripples, waves washing out across the parchment skin of Blue's open thighs.

The tallest man studied my copy against the Kill Code tattooed against Jae's pale, shaved skull. When he nodded, another of the men picked up the small, square pelt they had cut from Jae's head and began spreading glue across the back. "Scribe." The taller man cleared his throat. He was talking to me. "Do your thing and don't improvise. And, whatever you do, don't go into that library."

It was nearly midnight by the time I stepped back out onto the alley. Too late for the little stall next to the apothecary shop to be open, but there was the sizzling blue sign that read *Tarot*. The shimmering reflection of a shape in the window froze me in place. I watched in the glass as the two blond men in tight gray suits slipped through the barbershop door, and then I slid into the night.

I found my father in the kitchen scooping vanilla ice cream straight from the carton. It was reassuring to see him in his white undershirt, his mouth laden with cream. A delicate man, able to tighten the tiny screw in an eyeglass frame with the tip of his nail, when it came to his meals, my father had always mauled and devoured. It was good to see that, even in his illness, his appetites hadn't left him. "Mom said you were upstairs," he coughed.

"She did?" Forgetting that she had just taken a yogurt out of the fridge was one thing. Imagining me moving around upstairs when I'd been out on the alley was something else. Which was worse, having your mind wiped clean of memories, or filled with ghosts? I didn't want to talk to my father about it and I don't think he wanted to talk to me about it, either. I nodded at the ice cream carton. "Don't overdo it."

I kissed his stubbled jaw and left him there, licking cream from his lips.

Upstairs, the shadows moved. Then they spoke: "It's very pretty."

The dark pages of the *Codex Argentus* stacked on my drafting board flickered purple and silver. My heart glittered with terror.

Then I smelled the sulfur on her. Blue. I was better without faces. I saw more that way. Neither one of us reached to switch on the light. "Didn't anyone ever tell you not to play with matches?" I should have been afraid. I should have wondered why and how and what she was doing there. I should have asked myself if I was doing what I was doing to impress a woman. Instead, I reached out in the dark and spread my hands across her eyes.

"That wouldn't be much fun, would it?" She smiled vaguely in the half-light of the window, her eyes still covered, as if we, two, could play at this game of blindness, as if she were as comfortable at it as I was. Maybe she was.

A warm wind rushed at the open window, rustling the pages. I pulled my hand free and gently closed the portfolio's leather cover. *A for Amy. A for All Things.*

"You never told me," she said, "what sort of things you write. Besides love letters."

"All kinds of things," I told her. I put my fingers back against her skin. "All kinds of letters. Books of Hours." She tilted her head. "Books of prayers and psalms you could carry around and recite at the different hours of the day, so an ordinary person could live their life in the contemplation of God. Like a monk or a nun."

"That doesn't seem like the kind of thing you should be doing." She put her hands over my hands and starting tracing the tendons as they webbed out from my wrists. "Living like a nun." I laughed. But I felt guilty. I remembered the last time I saw Blue, Michael pulling me out of the stable beside the Apothecary shop, asking me who she was, telling him *Nobody*.

I lifted my hands from her face. "I'm sorry."

She opened her eyes. "What for? Something you did, or something you're going to do?"

She moved to the guest bed I had been sleeping in since my parents' arrival. My narrow, single bed. "Both," I said. She kept looking at me, long enough to make me think that she knew what I had done and that it hurt her. Then she patted the bed next to her and said, "Tell me everything."

I told her that I may have stolen the Silver Bible.

I'd meant to return it, but how could I? After the Kill Code, there would be no residency. I was destroying the one thing I'd expected to save me. "I think I need it," I said.

In the next room, Michael laughed in his sleep.

I tried to explain. "They have a library. An incredible library filled with incredible things, rare manuscripts like nothing you've ever seen before." She blinked. She had seen. "Like nothing *I've* ever seen before. Tinted vellum, gold and silver ink, pages that have been missing for centuries." She shrugged, like what did a library have to do with anything. "Like the Library at Alexandria."

She bit her fingernail. "Didn't the Library at Alexandria burn to the ground?"

"That's the other thing," I said. "There's a database," I said. "I'm going to destroy it."

Did she look impressed or horrified, or neither one? I couldn't say.

"Hmm." She was wearing her rings tonight, pale circles of luminescence she worried like beads up and down the base of each finger. Then, just like that: "I'll help you." The night outside the window was black and warm, a gust every now and then billowing the glass. I felt my chest flush, my thoughts scramble.

I hadn't asked her to help me.

I didn't trust *help*. When Connie talked me into having babies, she had sworn that she would always be there to help, that, even if she worked and I took care of the children, I wouldn't have to do it alone.

"Did you hear what I said?" Blue's quick fingers worried my knuckles, that thing she did, counting and measuring and reading my bones. "I'll be there."

"Be there?" I felt my heart flapping wildly like one of the pigeons across the way, struggling to get out of my grip. But I moved toward her, felt the currents of the air shift and swirl like the glowing dark above the Slumber Artist's bed, the stuff of dreams opening and circling to draw us in. Her fingers pressed cool lines and circles against my face. I could see the shapes behind my eyelids lighting up like bits of silver foil. She had that power to summon the whole alphabet of desire.

Already, I felt the thrill of it: Blue's dark shape slipping through the shadows along Q's quadrangle, dipping in and out of neon pink, taking shape and disappearing. The promise of disappearances, which was all that I had learned to count on.

Then I remembered Sandy Jensen.

Blue couldn't come to Q on the night of the Halloween ball. Because Sandy Jensen. Because bright slaps of laughter against the jellybean-colored pods. Because flared hip bones and storkish legs. Because a head of sandy hair, tumbling down her neck like a thick trail of feathers. Because *micrography*. Because *miniatures*. Because a bottle of ink, the color of blood.

It was one thing to wash the Q database clean while going to the Halloween ball as Sandy Jensen's date. It was another thing to do it with Blue. To choose Blue. A flickering heat in the dark and that was all. I didn't even know her name.

"I'll return that for you." She nodded at the Silver Bible. "No one will have to know."

"I can't ask you to do that." It was tempting. I'd been told not to go back to the library, not to leave a trace. But Blue hadn't. Still, I couldn't risk it. "Anyway, the library is locked. You can't get in." I doubted there were very many even at Q who could get in. I hadn't run into anyone when I'd snuck in with Sandy's cloned key card—just the mechanical bird, chiming the hours. If I were Hack, secreting away the world's rarest manuscripts and keeping them all for myself, I wouldn't want too many people to know.

Blue had already started taking me apart, unbuttoning, unhooking, unzipping. "So, how did *you* get in?"

I pulled off her shirt. "I got someone's card key." I pulled the lanyard over my neck and threw it on the bed.

She tossed my shirt after it. "Who?"

"Hmmm?"

I wrapped my leg around her hips.

"Whose key?"

I looked down at the card key, flat against the bedspread, and thought about Sandy's bony toes beside me in the shallows warmed by the servers. "Nobody."

Blue's hands went loose on my waist. "Right," she said.

Pulling my shirt back down, I struggled to protest, but what could I say? I'd called her *Nobody*. Now I was calling Sandy Jensen *Nobody*. I was already erasing people. No wonder the Neighborhood picked me. When it came to disappearing people, I was a pro.

19 All Hallows' Eve

SANDY SENT A CAR TO PICK ME UP. A DRIVERLESS TESLA.

I told my mother I was going out and immediately realized I'd forgotten to buy candy. With Tristan gone, I had planned to pull the curtains and shut out the lights until the whole wretched nightmare of Connie's birthday was over and done. "You don't have to answer the door," I told her.

Though it was a Halloween ball and many people would wear costumes, I'd dressed in my usual witchy black from head to toe. She looked me up and down, the habit of a lifetime. "Are you going to a party, too?"

Michael, who loved to stay in on Halloween night, was going out with his fiancée. His life was changing. Mine might still, too.

"It's a work thing," I fudged. I hated denying my mother the small pleasure of knowing I was finally going to achieve something with my work, but I was shielding her from danger. If anyone investigated, she couldn't know I played a role. (Would anyone investigate? I tried to believe what Arman had told me: that once the cloud servers blew, no one would know it was me.)

The lines around her mouth fanned out. "That's a shame." She picked at a thread on the faded purple zip hoodie Tristan had left on the rack by the door, and which I'd worn every night for the first three weeks he was gone. "Don't get angry at me for saying so," she paused to look me in the eye, "but sometimes I worry that you've never gotten over—" I shook my head too violently to prove her wrong. "Amy," she dropped the purple thread, "Is it so wrong that we want you to find happiness?"

I shook my head again, more gently, but I didn't tell her about Blue, or about Sandy Jensen, because I knew she would get too excited about Sandy Jensen and warn me too sternly about Blue. My mother waved a spotted hand. "We'll be fine."

An hour before the ball, the neon *Lockdown* sign fizzed against a molten sky fading to black. The baking late-October heat hadn't left us, and neither had the wind. Sparks leapt from my fingertips when I brushed the car door, a reminder of Blue in the Apothecary shop, pinching bursts of fire between her fingers. Heat prickled my chest thinking about it, little shocks of fear that she might after all show up tonight. I couldn't have her here, not with Sandy Jensen. I hurried toward the buildings, glad that night was falling.

The Quad was thick with people streaming in for the party—more black beards than usual, and more women, too—and if the men in grey suits were among them, I couldn't tell. It wasn't until I spotted the giant papier-mâché dog and three women stilt-walking in long, striped pants, juggling fire, that I realized some of these were the performers who lived in the warehouse where I'd slept with Blue. I felt that kick in my chest when something big is about to happen and you don't know if it's terrible or thrilling.

It was Friday night, Halloween night, Connie's birthday—maybe the last birthday 1-800-Flowers.com would remind me of—the night of my debut and my finale, the night the new Algorithm launched, the night of the Kill Code and Sandy Jensen, the night of the summation of everything.

The entry hall vibrated with people—people in striped pants and velvet smoking jackets and people in chinos and fleece vests, the artists getting ready for the show and the engineers crunching for the Algorithm to launch. I felt anonymous moving through the halls in my black uniform, until I turned a corner just past the floating bones of the woolly mammoth into a barbershop quartet singing a four-part harmony of "Sweet Clementine," four darkly bearded men in black bow-ties and pink candy stripes, lips pursed in their beard-masked faces. Were they the men from the barbershop or different men? *Oh my darling, oh my darling, you are lost and gone forever, my darling Clementine.* The shortest one seemed to follow me with his eyes.

In the wide atrium near the library, my drafting table had been set up on the holographic play space the way Jae and I had planned it, the virtual water already lapping the foot of the table, lapping at my stool and the stool where partygoers would sit to pour the contents of their souls into my black ink. That night the water looked dark and cold. Mist floated on the surface, gauzy white tongues licking my knees, wrapping them in ghosts.

Crossing four holographically wet stepping stones, a parallel part of myself waded into the real, warm server water next to Sandy Jensen, my bare feet squat and crooked next to Sandy Jensen's long, bony feet, our shadows rippling next to each other in the shallows, sunny and companionable and easy. If I got away with this, I was already persuading myself, Sandy would never have to know.

The Kill Code, after all, was just another bit of bricolage I would weave into one of the letters I scribed that night, like the night heron from an Audubon calendar, the ticket stub from an A's game. It was part of the Artist's agreement that one work I produced there would belong to Q, a piece that would go to the library that night to be scanned. I would have nothing to do with it. Sometime during the evening, someone the Neighborhood selected—not one of them, but someone like me, someone who would never be seen again—would sit down at my table. *Forget I said anything,* they would say, the secret words. And I would weave the Kill Code in. That was all.

Climbing onto my stool, I was thinking less about what I was there to destroy and more about what I was there to create. I put the bottle of red ink Sandy Jensen had given me *for miniatures* out where everyone could see it.

The honky klaxon bleated through the halls, *Awooga! Awooga!* A pale rush of submariners in white bell bottoms and white sailor shirts raced past. We were diving, or rising up from the depths, the party was starting, the engineers were cranking, it was all hands on deck.

I could hear the barbershop quartet but not see them, so thick was the press of bodies, the brush of velvet and fleece, the smell of alcohol. Next to me, a group of men dressed in white was carrying in boxes, setting up a stall just six feet from mine, but once they stepped into place, I couldn't see what they were doing, but only hear an *Ohhh!* and an *Ahh!* from the crowd. More stilt walkers flung swords back and forth over our heads. Far above, a trapezist in sparkling black spandex floated below the glass-paneled sky, tossing fistfuls of glittering powder. Maybe by the end of the night we would all be high. I stuck out my tongue. The flecks that fell on it burned sour and sweet—Pixie sticks powder, the fizzing kind.

Once I picked up my penknife to sharpen my quill, once I dipped and pressed the first dark bead against the vellum, people began to cluster at the margins of my little lake, talking quietly and drinking, pointing as if they'd never before seen pen on paper. I was so quickly engrossed in the feeling of ink sliding across the page that I barely noticed. I didn't want an audience, but a supplicant, someone whose raw feeling would run warm into the warm canals of my ears, to the sharp tip of my quill and onto the page. I smiled. I wasn't a witch. I was a vampire.

I reached into my bag and pulled out the pasteboard sign I hadn't touched since that night in the back of Crimson Horticultural Rarities. It still smelled of wax when I put it at my elbow: *Love Letters, Hand Scribed*. There in Q's big hall, I felt echoes of that dark, warm night in the storage closet, the hush of the velvet curtains when the man in the tweed vest parted them, as the first bold partygoer stepped across the water to my table.

He was a wiry man in jeans and a polo who spoke in such a low deadpan I was sure at first, as he dictated a letter to *Calla Lily*, that he was mocking me. It didn't matter to me if he was. I was a conduit, a pane of glass. Only my hand moved more quickly or slowly across the page, dipping, scratching. The wiry man's voice grew higher, tighter. Calla Lily, the dog, had died. This *was* a love letter. He stared hard into the mist at our feet while I affixed a pink, vintage postage stamp from the Romani Posta to the spot where the C should be—C for Calla Lily—and transformed it into an illuminated capital that was sweet and wistful and fit for this man's best friend. When he waded back across the wet rocks, he clutched the letter to his chest.

The pace picked up—an engineer who confessed to loving eighteenth-century French epistolary novels, a product manager who confessed that she loved marking her reports with colored highlighters (I shuddered to think what my letter for her would look like after I put it in her hands), a woman from Operations who confessed that her aunt had always dreamed of a passionate lover and would be thrilled to get a letter in the mail. It turned out mine was a discipline of a thousand confessions. A very tall blond with a thick Russian accent asked me to illustrate only in black the letter in which she told her husband "Enjoy your stupid meet-cutes with Frankie. We're done." An anti-love letter;

it counted. Only one person pressed a nail against the page where an illustrated capital would go and said: "You could do an angel." The ink was still wet; he received a copy of his own fingerprint. There were shopping lists and thank you notes and even a will. (I had to remind the writer, a heavy-set man in a pirate blouse and eye patch, that I could not produce a legally binding document, but he seemed to feel it was sufficient for his African Gray parrot and cookbook collection. The parrot, beady-eyed and sharp-beaked, eyed the page dangerously, singing "My Heart Will Go On."). My script, not quite the court's *chancery hand*, tipped and swirled. That was partly the point—speed, not perfection, not the slow hand of the monk sealed in his scriptorium, but the quick stroke of marketplace scribe, a hand for the people. In the first hour alone, I drew down two entire pots of ink.

People wanted letters. Here in this digital place! Inside, I was flying.

The hours passed in flakes of gilt, paper tattoos and postage stamps, Lira notes and antique wallpaper, glitter and ink and photos of strangers sold by the box. The sinuous flow of ink into shapes soothed some deep itch I didn't even know I had, a purring sense that all was right with the world. Letters slotted in my mind like bricks, rough and solid; letters drifted into place like fallen petals, soft and delicate and mild; letters curled against the pressure of my quill like hot iron being twisted—all of this as real to me as the hot lights overhead and the white noise of the crowd in my ears. There were colors—blue and yellow and red—and a waxy lightness, like the shavings of a crayon, a fragrant smoothness. It was the most wonderful thing in the world.

I was just capping a tube of cinnamon powder when the next supplicant sat down, a dark-haired person in a sport coat rolled to the elbow. A low voice said, "Are you ready?" and then, without waiting, started to speak. There was a contraction of the air around me at that moment, an intensity of focus like the moment when the man in the tweed vest had started to speak, a sudden hush and then the warmth of breath, the urgency, intimacy, speaking to me, through me.

Azizam, I don't believe in the soul, or forces that seek our happiness. Or fate. The world we have is beautiful enough. There is an entire universe in its surfaces.

Massaging their way across the drafting table's surface, five tawny fingers encountered the edges of a pencil, picked it up.

When I met you, I was not looking for more than surfaces. So—

A sudden silence fell. I looked up and instantly I felt that tug that happens when you stare long into someone else's eyes, an intimacy that is only there because the eyes hook up to nerves that pump out hormones that tell the brain *This means love*. A simple, primate reflex, but, still, it's strong. I tried to keep my eye on her pupils, the little mirror of light in which lived a little shadow me, my small hand with my small quill. But I was drawn in.

She swallowed and cleared her throat and went on:

—It was a surprise when I liked you. When we just clicked. No offense, but it's true. Someone tells you they've met your match—some algorithm cranks out a connection—two cherries—but what are the odds?

I heard it before I saw it or felt it, the whisper of the pencil scratching at the edge of the vellum. I started to tell her that she couldn't do that; we were being watched; this was still a competition and the marks on the paper had to be my work—but as I watched the contour lines spill and spread across the margins of the page, I felt my heart start to race. "Blue," I protested. She wasn't supposed to be there but she was there. My eyes darted to the top of the letter. *Azizam*. She had called me that, a word that bracketed the alphabet. She called me that and she could get whatever she wanted from me. I would be powerless.

"It means *Dear One*." In the long moment that she held my gaze, the noise of the room pressed closer to the space between us, but did not rush in. I resolved not to break contact with those dark eyes that pulled at me like black holes, a pull stronger than anything I had felt since Connie, but my face glowed with heat at the effort; my fingers itched to dive back into the dark cool ink.

"I told you I would be here for you," she murmured in a voice not meant for the page.

A pop drew our eyes to the air above our heads, an indoor firework spilling its shiver of glitter. Inside my chest, shivers of glitter were also breaking open across a darkness more vast and deep than I had realized had been inside me all these years—Trails of sparklers showering down, spelling *Remember, remember,* tingling the top of my head.

Her warm finger tapped the back of my hand. "Forget I said anything."

The tails of those glittering comets splintered, not fire but ice. It was a cold moment before it hit me: This was the code phrase. *Forget I said anything* was my signal to paste the Kill Code into the letter, right here in front of everyone, where no one would think a thing of it. *She* was the messenger. For a second, my sight darkened with confusion: *She was the messenger?*

The barbershop quartet had migrated into the room; they were singing a four-part harmony of "I would die 4 u." I could feel their voices pressing closer.

This was the moment.

I didn't have time to think about why it was her, or what it meant that Blue had said those things to me and then unsaid them, or whether it meant anything at all. My fingers were shaking as I pulled the postage-stamp sized Kill Code square from its tiny white envelope and with shaking hands I almost glued it to the page facedown.

Affixing the letter in its spot, more careful now about how it aligned with the letters beside it, slipping into that relaxed, alert state of mind in which the world became a field of letters, I felt the soft hum of the Kill Code's *M* taking its place among the other letters, the beginning of a long journey. At some point, M. David Hacker had had a first name, but he'd attached it to the Kill Code and let it go—some part of himself he'd lost or given away to become who he was now. Touching the page around the Kill Code with thin lines of silver leaf, a delicate shimmering web, I wondered if some part of him wanted it back.

Under my quill, lines of silver filigree spread out from the edges of the *M* like the rays of the sun, a delicate clockwork in M. David Hacker's Book of Hours. Here was the prayer for the Hour of Creation and here the prayer for the Hour of Dropping out of School; this hand the Hour of First Round Funding, and here the Hour of the First Million Users. Here was the Hour of the Assumption, when all the data went up into the Cloud. And this thin tick of silver the minute before midnight, the Hour of Extreme Unction, the Kill Code the prayer for the Hour to Put an End to it All.

I held the glittering clockface to the light and it was beautiful.

Blue watched quietly, no longer fiddling the pencil, and I didn't look at her, didn't want to find myself in the pull of those eyes again. "This is going to have to dry," I told her, which was true, because of the adhesives I'd used, and the deep indigo ink I was touching to the lines she'd traced along the sides of the page, and also because, whether or not she'd meant these words, she'd written them to me and I wasn't ready to get rid of them yet.

Words of love would always be my weakness.

A server waded over to my table, lithe in a white pantsuit and feathered wings that reminded me of the Archangel. Twin goblets sparkled on the tray in her hand. I shook my head. I was working. But Blue nodded; the angel waved a smooth, dark hand and suddenly the cool, clear liquid welled with blue flame. I felt it in my blood, the way the flame wavered over the liquor, undulating like water. "A living person needs life," Blue urged, holding the glass to my mouth, and I wanted that—to be alive. She was all liquid motion, water and fire, and I watched the slow motion of the flame before it ran down my throat.

My throat was still hot with liquor when a lanky figure in plum-colored jodhpurs took Blue's empty seat at my table, a ringleader with a plum-colored tailcoat and top hat. The ringleader startled me by leaning over the table to kiss my cheek, then picked up the bottle of bloodred ink. Two bright coins of laughter spilled onto across table. Sandy Jensen. I panicked a little, wondering if she'd seen Blue, if she smelled the alcohol fresh in my mouth, and was surprised that those were the things I was worrying about more than the Kill Code in plain sight on the letter on the table behind my back, which I would hand later to the Q archivist who asked me to select one letter for scanning.

Sandy stretched out her long, thin legs. Little waves lapped at the pointy toes of her boots. "I'm here to write the letter."

I was flustered and a little buzzed. I fumbled a sheet of vellum, which sliced my finger, a sharp, shallow cut I had to suck before picking up my pen. "The letter?"

Sandy tapped her finger lightly against the tabletop. "For the library," she said, leaning so close I could smell her breath, which smelled the way Tristan's used to when he had a fever, my father's when he didn't have enough to drink, the smell of a body digesting itself. I pulled my finger out of my mouth. "I wouldn't want you to use someone else's letter for the official Q record of your work. So I'll write one, and you can use mine."

It took every muscle in my neck not to turn around and look at Blue's letter. There was no way I could peel the Kill Code off the page, and no way I could reproduce it correctly here, not under these conditions. And no way I could make a switch if Sandy Jensen wanted to make sure that her letter got scanned for the library.

A great flare rushed across my chest, raced hot and itching up into my neck and cheeks. I felt caught—not once, but twice: I'd betrayed Sandy (though she didn't know it) and I would betray the Neighborhood, too, if the Kill Code didn't get scanned by midnight. Signs of my guilt were everywhere. And still a part of me protested: *I haven't done anything wrong!*

Sandy saw the heat in my face, the telling flush. "Don't worry," she sat up very straight on her stool, the rare tall woman who didn't slouch, "I won't make it racy." Then she laughed. And her laughter, as it always did, put me at ease.

I slid out a sheet and picked up the bottle of red ink. "For miniatures." I raised the little bottle up like a shot glass. Planning a special character would give me an excuse to consider the problem of Sandy Jensen's illustrated capital letter after she had gone.

If the letter Blue dictated at my table made every hair on my arms and neck stand up, the words that came out of Sandy Jensen's mouth smoothed them down again. She was smart, articulate, reassuring—steady. *Like Connie*, I thought but didn't want to think, the alcohol making me soft.

> There are a lot of creative people around here. But life has gotten a whole lot more interesting since I met you. Not just because you're the only other person I know who knows *micrography*, or the etymology of the word *miniature*—

She tapped a long, thin finger against the cut glass bottle that had quickly become our talisman.

You're just . . . different. There are no coincidences. But sometimes there are surprises. You're one of them. I like you.

It was sweet. A sweet letter that made me think once again about what it would be like to be with someone who had a job and friends and a life I could be a part of. Sandy perched on the stool in her riding boots and tail coat and it was so easy to envision something more. I bet she made coffee fresh from whole beans, took delivery of the Sunday *Times*.

"Is that a stamp?" Sandy was peering over my shoulder at Blue's letter, directly at the silver lines radiating out from the clock, the Kill Code at its center.

Fifteen years ago, I got vertigo. It was the day I tried therapy with a woman who in our first session called Connie a *bitch*. That night, when I rolled over in bed, the whole world swam around my head. When I launched out of bed to vomit, the floor tilted and hurled me into the wall. That was how I felt in that second, totally unbalanced, tossed from my comfortable fantasies of life with Sandy Jensen, crashing fast into the hard fact of my perfidy; I clamped my jaw over the urge to throw up.

"Mmm." I shuffled a pile of colored stamps out of a small manila envelope at my elbow, the two-kroner head of a well-coiffed queen, the twenty-franc flag of Cameroon. "I like to use stamps." My tongue felt thick in my head. "They feel official, even when they don't have any real value."

"But they do, implicitly." Sandy Jensen pressed her finger against the face of the queen and slid her toward the flag like an advancing army. "They represent an entire system of value."

The air around my face prickled with dread at what she was about to say next—about Q and its system of value, about the terrible thing I had been planning to do.

"*And* sending things through the mail." A third stamp appeared under her fingertip like a magic trick. It wasn't one of mine. I had it under my magnifying glass before she released her finger.

It was old looking, pale cream paper with sepia-toned engraving on it, a line-drawing of the same prism that was on the inside of the man with the tweed vest's pocket watch. On the stamp a silver beam spread from the center of the prism—not silver, but holographic. It tilted with the colors of the rainbow. Nothing old-fashioned about that. At opposite corners, a single *Q* appeared where the value would be. Another of Sandy Jensen's impressive courting gifts. "Limited edition," she said.

"A Q stamp?" With the stamp in the spot of the initial capital, Sandy's letter looked a little too much like Blue's for my comfort, but I squared the stamp against a larger square of purple foil and set about inscribing the whole thing with twining leaves and vines. "Is there mail service here?" As far as I'd seen, Q was paperless—no interoffice mail, no printed forms, nothing except for the occasional throwback piece, like the posters. Certainly, no communication on which this empire depended. And yet, for all Q's investment in a paperless future, there was some force here deeply invested in the analog past.

Sandy tilted her head back far enough for the rim of her top hat to brush the back of her coat, "Maybe. If we end up having a scribe around. You never know."

You never know . . . The vowels floated to the ceiling, bubbles rising into the rafters where the tightrope walker danced on a string, so high, every breath in me rising with them, expanding, shining. Everything felt possible then, Sandy Jensen in her ringleader's top hat spotlit at the center of a Big Top I could see from up above, waving: *Make it so! Make it so!* I wondered if she could see it in my face, that joy, bright as blood, bright as the red ink exploded against the tabletop when I knocked the bottle over.

"Wonder how the scanner will interpret that." Sandy stretched to her great, thin height, even higher now with the hat on her head. "I'll come back just before midnight to pick you up."

I hadn't counted on Sandy Jensen dictating, choosing, and delivering the letter to be scanned. That wasn't a scenario the Neighborhood had planned for and it sent my mind spinning. But I had no time to figure it out.

The air warmed with the burnt sugar smell of cotton candy and the yeasty breath of beer; a great orchestra was massing at the shores of my private lake, playing long glass tubes that looked like bongs and sounded like bassoons; and the roar of laughter filled the hall all the way to the ceiling high above; it was high time for revelry and mirth. "Oh, this is so much better than the one next door!" a woman at my table cried, clutching her letter, dismissing with a sniff the station next to mine—no doubt some other artist, competing for a chance at artist in residence, but the crowd around the table was too thick for me to see who it was or what they were doing. And, anyway, I had too much to do. There were letters and more letters and foil glittering red and gold; I was performing like I had never performed in my life.

It was a quarter past eleven when Jae plunked an iced latte at my elbow. I recognized him by his cashmere sweater and sage green chino shorts. "Where's your costume?" I cranked off the lid and took a deep swig. My head was starting to hurt from the drink I'd had with Blue—a quick rush, running fast to its unhappy conclusion.

"I'm wearing it." His large hand made a flourish up and down his body, then pushed his dark hair back from his forehead. "Same as you." I glanced down at my own outfit—black shirt, black skirt, black boots—my old witchy guise.

"Right." From where I was sitting, you couldn't tell a patch of his hair had been cut down to the skin.

His fingers grazed the top of his head. "It itches like you would not believe." His eyes traveled across the letters spread behind me on the table, Sandy's and Blue's. "So. I've fulfilled my function," he sighed. After tonight, there was no alternative: Jae would have to disappear.

Around us, a cheer went up from the crowd, followed by the lurch of a mariachi band. For a second, I thought about Maribel and her drum set and her dog tattoo, and knew that there was no way we could be in each other's lives anymore, either, which made me sad, even though I was the one deciding. Was Jae's choice much different?

"Enough about me." Jae nibbled his thumbnail. "How *is* Sandy Jensen? Is she in love with you?"

"Don't be ridiculous." I put the bottled latte down. "She's just being nice." But it was more than nice, and I knew it.

Jae slid his hand again over the top of his head. "Hmmm. I'm sure." He smiled, his eyes narrow. "But you like her?"

"Definitely, I like her," I said. I did. I just didn't lust after her. I could see our two pairs of feet waving through the lapping waves of the vent water, solid against the white cement, like statues. But who said I couldn't develop lust, with time? Fidelity was what mattered. Trust.

Blue had just been a messenger.

Jae's knees rested against the edge of the table. He hadn't missed a trick. "You should think about it, you know? Because you could do a lot worse than Sandy Jensen. And she usually gets what she wants."

I smiled. I liked the idea of somebody wanting me so much, she wouldn't stop until she got me. Jae picked up the bottle of red ink and turned it gingerly in his fingers, then put it down again. My face filled with warmth. Bottles of ink made just for me. It was almost too much.

Jae tapped the bottle, a little chiming sound to wake me from my reverie of Sundays in bed, fresh toast, oranges on a plate. "Unless . . . there's somebody else?"

The bedsheet flew from the imaginary bed, sent orange slices flying, Sunday morning flung into the dark space filled with music, the ceiling rattling with wind, pale thighs, tattoos—a dark night and then an empty bed.

Jae did a slow double take to show me he'd seen it all. "Oh my! There *is* someone else."

I tried to deny it. Who was Blue? A burst of sparks, a fizzling dream. A person who turned up in unexpected ways, who disappeared again. Someone who couldn't be counted on. An operative from the Neighborhood.

"Who is she?" Jae studied me intently.

I shrugged, but my clothes clung to me like sunburn, itchy and hot. I didn't even know her name.

Jae sat up straighter, folded his hand under his chin. "Let me get this straight. You're being *courted* by Sandy Jensen, *Evangelist*"—he stretched out the word *E-VAN-gel-ist!*—"but your loins are on fire for a mysterious stranger." I nodded. There was no flaw in his accounting. His head tilted to the side, his mouth open. Then he said in his oddly formal way: "I have to say, I am impressed. Not one woman, but *two!* I didn't realize you were the type!"

Ink blotted my fingertips, black and indigo and sepia. "Don't be ridiculous." For the past eighteen years I'd been nobody's girlfriend, nobody's lover, nobody's wife. "I am definitely *not* the type."

Jae rose from the stool. His head framed by the dark glass of the ceiling above, he looked down at me from what seemed in that moment like a very great height. "You are now." Then he leaned to air-kiss my cheek and very quietly, under all the noise of the musicians with their bouncing strings and the stilt walkers with their distant cries and the partygoers with their chiming laughter, he whispered in my ear, "Goodbye."

My head felt strange and hollow, flushed with heat and light and drink, unmoored.

I checked my watch. It was thirty minutes to midnight.

I needed to figure out how to get the Kill Code to the scanner before Sandy Jensen returned. The barber had forbidden me from returning to the library. I couldn't be seen anywhere near it. But if I could get Blue's letter to the scanner, I could get back in time to scan Sandy Jensen's letter with her, too. She would never have to know.

I twisted behind me for Blue's letter, left to dry on the table.

The letter was gone.

As mist rose up from the water at my table legs, twining around the tip of my boot, I started having a haunted feeling. Jae was right. After eighteen years of no one and nothing, suddenly: two women.

There are no coincidences. That's what Sandy Jensen said.

What are the odds . . . That's what Blue had said.

What *were* the odds of my having stayed single for the past eighteen years and then, suddenly and without much effort at all, finding myself with not one but two suitors? I started to have a terrible feeling.

I saw it all again in my head: First, the man in the tweed vest showed up, leaving behind a letter, and then the Algorithm offered me Blue. I chose her—I thought I did. But that was Arman's point. The Algorithm gave you things so well chosen to match your profile you thought you actually wanted them yourself. You felt like you were choosing. I remembered those times Blue had just shown up out of nowhere—at the farmers market; in Temescal Alley, near the apothecary shop; in my dark bedroom last night. Every time I had felt doubt about what Arman had asked of me, she was there. Encouraging me, egging me on. She was here tonight.

I had made a terrible mistake.

Through the wide, crowded hall, a gong began to chime. Far above, in the reflected light off the glass ceiling, two trapeze artists in black and silver stripes were swinging away and toward each other, toward each other and away. The slender, short-haired one held a mallet; the other held the gong.

It was thirty minutes to midnight.

I still had time.

20 *The Library of Books That Don't Exist*

SANDY JENSEN'S CLONED BADGE STILL WORKED. The party's chaos gave me the perfect cover to enter the library unseen. The hall was so crowded that when I swiped myself through the library door, a tipsy woman in a spaghetti-strap camisole tumbled in at my back; I had to push her out again. *Whoopsie!* she screeched. *Whoopsie!* When the door closed, the screeching and the laughter disappeared behind it. Inside, climate change began its slow progress through the centuries, innocent as birdsong. In the entry to the vestibule, the livestream display of Q's entry hall exploded with connections, a furious tangle of webs leaping off eyebrows, lapels and teeth, tying them to each other and to people in the world beyond, so many people. I paused for just a second, hovering my finger above the screen, each of those faces the size of a fingerprint, and wondered what it was like to see an identity in each. That's what Q did for people, after all—connect faces to names, people, histories. How ironic that the person who destroyed it should be a person like me.

As I grazed the surface, a red line leapt from my fingertip to a face on the screen: a person standing before a large, photorealistic cut-out of the moon, the shadowed Sea of Tranquility. Before I saw the name on the screen I registered the vest, the corduroys, the overhead earphones: *Michael Black*, the screen read. My brother was here in his museum clothes, running his radio off the moon. How on earth he'd been pulled into this—by Blue? By the Neighborhood? By the man in the tweed vest?—I could hardly fathom, but I knew it wasn't good. Michael was a fundamentally decent person. He didn't suspect anyone of anything. He would always try to be of help. I wanted to rush to him. I wanted to pull him out of the crowd and push him out the door. I wanted to intercept his voice on the face of the moon and throw it back to him: *Go home!*

But a chime was sounding from the library, a strange, tin cry, and I knew it was the mechanical bird, chiming the march toward midnight, and I knew that if Blue had brought the letter with the Kill Code on it to the library, it would be any moment until it was scanned, and I knew that I needed to stop her.

The late-night library had been transformed into a winter forest. Darkness settled between the racks of manuscripts and scrolls, bare, leafless trees among the aisles, and snow—pale flakes of holographic snow—whispered between the branches, freckling everything in specks of light. The shelves, too, looked almost bare. Beside them, the metal bird finished its complaint, tilting up and down a metal branch in a golden halo of light; the dark windows on the courtyard framed a grand tableau of night.

Inside, light from the scanning booths blanched the edges of the room. Behind the glass, mechanical arms plucked pages and scrolls and codices from the library carts and gently splayed them on the platens; musical notes and gilded Gothic capitals and pale blue birds darting from a margin appeared above them on a screen. Q was busy bringing the world's most precious books that did not exist into digital life, and this, too, carried on with an urgency that went with the late hour and the midnight ball and the Algorithm, though I did not know why. *The Algorithm*—my mind snagged on the word, letters looming into shapes, angled, sharp and glittering—

There was something else glittering, a glittering figure at the front of the room, neither angled nor sharp. A figure spangled in brightness, head covered in a spandex hood. Her head tilted, birdlike, looking, listening, peering into the darkness. *Tal!* How long had she been here in the library, waiting?

"Do you like fire?" she asked. She pursed her lips and unfurled a purl of flame. A dark hoop in her hands caught fire, spilled gold.

I gasped. We were surrounded by rare manuscripts, the rarest manuscripts in the world. So rare, that if they disappeared, there would be no record they'd existed at all. With one illuminated *O* she could erase thousands of years of history.

"Stop!" I cried.

The irony, me telling her not to. Behind her, the fine silver web of the clock face glowed, waiting to be plucked and scanned. The Kill Code—*she*'d taken the letter I'd written for Blue. I wanted to tell her she'd gotten it all wrong: She was trying to destroy the man in the tweed vest by destroying the thing he'd created—this Algorithm—but it would only make him forget her. *Don't!* I wanted to say. And yet how could I tell her she was wrong?

Everything felt muddled, the ghost of the liquor swaying in the swaying light of her hoop. She had begun twirling it fast around her hand.

The light broke across her body in a million tiny pieces.

I stepped closer, my hand toward the blur of golden light. But I couldn't stop it. It was so hot. He'd warned me: She was *dangerous*.

"Don't be afraid," she said, whirling the hoop high over her head. It stretched toward the ceiling, a blazing circle of light.

Something in her tone snagged on one of the bare branches in my mind, a snatch of bright fabric. Between the liquor and the fire and the quick glimmer of her suit, I couldn't catch at it. I couldn't catch at anything, but watched the flaming circle rise above her, burning *O*, shape of surprise, desire.

A voice behind me cut the silence. "So, this is awkward."

I spun around to a tall, thin witness, her pale face made paler by the light from the scanners. In her plum-colored tail coat and top hat, it could only be Sandy. Staring at me in the Q Library, staring at Tal swinging a burning hoop through the air, the Kill Code behind her.

Well, *fuck me*.

There were so many ways I'd been caught. I'd broken into the secret library she'd shared with me; I'd scribed the Kill Code that sat there in the queue, poised to destroy the company she loved; and I was there with a woman whose very name struck longing like a match in my chest. It was this last that felt strangest—being caught with Tal, whom I didn't know at all, I felt that I'd been caught cheating.

Suddenly I realized: Sandy Jensen wasn't dressed up as a ringleader. In her plum-colored coat and top hat, she was Willy Wonka, promiser of wonders. I'd called her that. I flooded with guilt—for flirting with Sandy and sleeping with Blue; for neglecting my parents all week and spending it at Q; for using my creative power to destroy something someone else had created; for having created so little; for resenting others for what I had failed to create—my parents, Tristan, most of all, Connie.

Sandy looked from Tal to me and back again, her pale face the great magnifying lens of my failures to everyone who had been decent to me. This was why I had stayed single all these years. Not because I couldn't trust other people. Because I couldn't trust myself.

Connie told me once to go to hell. She was blind with rage at the time. But I considered it—the ways I'd betrayed and disappointed her: Maybe I *should* go to hell. Maybe that would be fair.

"Sandy—" I started. But what else could I say. "*I can explain*"?

The bonze cuckoo went still. The hoop whispered with the sound of fire-eating air, the scanners whirred their mechanical arms and, out of the headsets hooked to each scanner, whispers and chirps and musical notes chattered and buzzed.

Sandy licked her lips. The thing I'd loved about Sandy Jensen were those bright beads of laughter bubbling to those lips. She wasn't laughing now. "I came to pick you up, but you're already here, aren't you? With one of the performers from the party." She dipped her head at Tal. "But she's not just a performer, is she?"

I could feel my breath hitching. I didn't know what was coming.

With a flourish of her long arm, Sandy pried the top hat from her head and flung it into the shadows. I'd half expected doves to flutter out, but instead out flew the damning facts against the woman gleaming in the darkness, holding a flame to the library at Q.

"She may look like a circus freak, but this woman is a mathematician, a good one. Good enough to have received inquiries from Iranian intelligence and the FBI."

Tal had become a statue, the blazing hoop rotating in hands that never seemed to move, spinning a bright *O* like an exit to another world.

Sandy's glasses blazed. "Ask her. Tehran wants her to come home."

Home. The word broke from Sandy's lips like a bubble filled with flame.

Was that what the man in the tweed vest had meant when he said that Tal was *dangerous*? Was she a spy?

"One week ago, an engineer named Daniel Khalili ran a simulation of the Algorithm on a small data set from within

Q. Standard stuff before a launch. But it wasn't standard. The Algorithm turned up something. That's what the Algorithm is meant to do, you know. Make connections. And we believe the connections it made to Daniel Khalili did not look good."

The word *Khalili* looped and whorled, whispers of ribbon spinning. Such a soft name, soft like the tawny hands of the man in the tweed vest.

"He scuttled the run, deleted the Q data set and cut out before we knew what he was up to. But we can derive the data set again—it's only a matter of launch. He knew that. That's why *she's* here." Sandy Jensen laughed a little, but these sounds were dull and colorless, weathered chips of wood.

I was thinking *No, she's got it wrong. Tal isn't here to save the man in the tweed vest—Daniel Khalili. She wants to destroy him*—when Sandy tilted her head at Tal and said—

"Professor Maryam Khalili."

Khalili. Then the ribbon's loop caught and pulled tight. Drawing the two of them—Daniel and Maryam—tight together and cinching tight around my throat. It reminded me how little I knew about either of them. I had imagined myself into their story—helping him, rescuing her—but they were connected to each other, already, in ways that I was not. It made no sense, but envy seared my face. It was ridiculous: I'd wanted her. I, myself, had wanted to make her forget him.

Was there some small shift in me, the set of my shoulders, the stretch of my neck, giving me away?

Sandy stared at Tal-Maryam—sparkling in her sequined suit. Then she whipped toward me. "And you. You're fucking her."

Fucking. The word slapped me like the flat of her palm and I knew that's how Sandy wanted me to feel. Stung.

I hadn't slept with Tal. But I'd never been the type of person to explain myself, and, anyway—what if I had fucked Tal? Sandy's possessiveness irritated me, a sharp flare of annoyance. But then

I heard the hurt in it, the betrayal, and I knew that part was true: I had betrayed her. Was it the light on her glasses, or were those tears glittering in the corner of her eyes?

Then another thought: The frenzied searching of memory. Had I slept with Tal? I *could have* slept with Tal—any one among the many I had found on *scizr* after Tristan left home. And I wouldn't know it. There was something—the way she moved her hands through the hair, the tilt of her head. The heat from the burning hoop felt hotter and closer, crisping my face, flirting with the loose strands of my hair.

There are things we can't see and things that we won't.

Inside the scanner, the mechanical claw turned the last page of the manuscript on the platen, a robot arm moving with the tenderness of a nurse.

Above Maryam Khalili's head, the hoop spun flame, slicing perilously close to the edge of a rolled manuscript.

"Be careful," I pleaded. There were so many things I didn't know about this woman I thought of as Tal, but I knew this: I didn't want her to burn down the library.

Tal spun the hoop like a flaming portal between us and looked through the flames straight at me. "*They* burn them," she said. Her voice stretched out between us like a stream of fire—familiar and warm with the low roar of flame. I didn't trust it.

"What do you mean?"

The fire trembled. "Haven't you noticed the smell?"

I had noticed a smell, the distant campfire smell of Q's library. I'd thought it was coming from over the hills, the wind and the wildfires, but how would those smells enter a sealed room like this?

Behind Maryam Khalili, the robotic arm scooped a thin book with failing leather covers from the scanning platen onto a steel tray, rotated it 180 degrees, and fitted the tray into a slot in the wall. I'd seen the scanner complete a scan before, depositing the manuscript into the slot behind the wall. This time, though, in the darkened library, before the slot in the wall slid shut, I saw a glow.

I swallowed hard. I remembered the glass crematory door after the paper box slid in.

Sandy Jensen must have seen that swallow, must have registered the set of my jaw. I expected her to tell me this was preposterous. Burning books? I expected her to deny it.

In the short time I'd known her, she'd always been solicitous—ready to share a novel experience, a story, a gift. Now when she spoke, there was a hardness to it, as if she could quell my rising confusion not with generosity or kindness but only with violence. "That's right," she said. "The originals are destroyed. And if she wipes the database, all the scans will be wiped with it." Her fingers fluttered in the direction of the emptying shelves: "All the manuscripts that have already been scanned? Wiped. The manuscripts are gone. Ink, paper, dust."

What in God's name was she saying? Q *burned* all the manuscripts? Of the books that didn't exist?

Sandy's eyes blazed. She would say anything right now to hurt me. And she was terrified of losing the database. Still. What if it was true? What if deleting the Q cloud meant deleting centuries of human art and history and culture? It was unthinkable.

And there was something else, something much smaller but much closer to home. Something I had not, it occurred to me, given enough thought to at all before this moment: Myself. When he asked me to deliver the Kill Code, Arman had assured me there would be no risk of danger, not really, because the Kill Code itself would erase the record of the crime. It would leave no trace. But Arman hadn't said what would happen if I tried and failed to use the Kill Code. He certainly hadn't imagined Sandy Jensen catching me with Tal, the Kill Code in the scanning queue in a letter written in my hand. Destroying Q's intellectual property would not just be a fine. It would be jail. How many times had I warned Tristan that it was easier to do something dangerous when other people were doing it, too; being part of a group made dumb things feel safer. That's what the Neighborhood had offered me—the safety of a group, and a sense of anonymity, too—and because of it I'd done something that might cost me my son, my parents. Tristan was on the other side of the world, deep in the heart of Russia, but I was the one who had gotten in trouble.

Behind Maryam Khalili, the scanner's robotic claw hitched toward the letter I'd written for Blue, the Kill Code framed inside the gleaming face of Time.

Sandy Jensen lunged.

With her thin legs and long body, she launched like an arrow into the air, an arrow aiming straight through Tal at that letter. But Tal was quick. With a quick pivot she advanced on Sandy. The burning hoop slashed the air.

Stepping behind it, into the shadow, I snatched up the letter.

Tal whirled toward me. Maryam Khalili. "Think about the world you want to live in," she whispered in my face, a whisper that made every hair on the back of my neck stand up, because it was close and warm and because I knew it, knew the timbre and the tone and the smell. It was Blue. Of course it was Blue. And she knew it was me. She'd always known. I felt gutted. I'd been used. Blue eyed the letter but she didn't try to take it from my hands. "I made my choice," she said. "Now you have to make yours."

In the short time I'd known her, that low voice, so full of self-confidence, had always reassured me. It might have worked again this time, if the pain of betrayal weren't so sharp and so fresh.

Behind Blue, Sandy's coat sleeve curled with flames. By the time I reached her, she was already stamping out her coat, and Blue was already gone.

It was fourteen minutes to midnight, and Blue had left the Kill Code in my hands. Now I had to choose.

Over the past eighteen years, I had been many things—angry, lonely, overwhelmed, determined, and even contented—but not once, not ever confused. Not when I walked out of the hospital alone with a newborn Connie had convinced me I wanted, fumbled at the complicated buckles in his bucket seat; not when I tied my hair back from my face and took the job I'd had as a student, respectable, regular and dull, and kept it to keep my kid and my house, too tired at the end of every day to write or draw; not when I wrote a letter to Q and dropped it in the mail and not when a man appeared at my table and then disappeared and by some miracle I'd wound up here. Not when I first saw the lines radiating across a stranger's thighs in a strange bed, or when Arman had asked me to burn this place down. I'd been many things, but not confused.

Now uncertainty washed at me from every side, threatening to suck me out to sea. *Overwhelmed* because *wielmas* are waves and this was drowning. I had been betrayed by Blue—Maryam Khalili. Used. She'd seen me that night at Crimson Horticultural Rarities and lured me to her on *scizr*; she had played on my wish to see myself as an artist, encouraging me to play the rebel, to destroy something for her.

But also, there was Blue, her voice in my ear, the golden globes of light floating above us, telling me I belonged in the world; Blue, pressing me against the wall in the portal, her mouth sweet with peaches; Blue, a pencil between her fingers, limning the edge of the world.

I studied the letter in my hand; its silver fretwork had dulled now that Blue's fire had gone.

Sandy Jensen was asking me to choose, too. Sandy, whom I'd betrayed by not wanting her the way I wanted Blue—even now—Sandy whose world I'd set upon destroying. The Sandy who had shown up that night in the library in her top hat and velvet coat had said ugly things, horrific things. She gathered her coat, which smelled of burned plastic and cloth, and picked up her hat from the aisle between the shelves; long, thin, she looked and smelled like a chimney pipe. There was nothing of the bright beads of laughter now, no wading in water clear enough to see the small hairs on the backs of our feet. I could barely recognize her.

But that was my problem, always.

I'd trusted Blue and been tricked. And I'd taken Sandy herself for granted. She'd taken me to see this library, for fuck's sake. She'd made me a picnic and shown me the Wind Telephone and brought me a bottle of ink. She'd *invited me here*. And what had I done? Scribed out the Kill Code and wrote a love letter from Blue. No matter how angry and strange she'd been tonight, I reminded myself, Sandy Jensen had been good to me, decent and kind, and I had not repaid her with kindness.

I felt like I owed her something.

Sandy slung her coat over her shoulder and turned toward the door. "Let's go." She was giving me another chance.

I looked around the library. Inside the glass booths, the robot arms gently turned pages, the white lights blazed and the scanners scanned page after page after page. Scanned and destroyed. I could have slipped the letter back into reach of the robotic arm, but I didn't. I kept it.

But before I followed Sandy back to the party, I spotted the tooled leather cover that had held the Silver Bible and now held my portfolio, queued up and waiting to be scanned, and swiped it from the shelf. My life's work. Q didn't get to burn that, too.

21 *The Automata*

IN THE VAST HALL, PEOPLE CLUSTERED UNDER THE shining black panels of night, watching acrobats above their heads, twirling hoops and braziers and batons of fire. It was possible that Blue was among them, but something about her last words made me think she had left Q and wasn't coming back.

Once in a while, a splash of fire would drip from one of the braziers and the crowd would roar and ripple out of the way. I glanced at my table. I remembered that Michael was out in the front hall with his moon-to-earth radio and I wanted to grab my things, gather him up and go. I wouldn't be getting the residency now, and I'd failed the Neighborhood, but at least I'd saved the digitized manuscripts.

And then there was Sandy. She hadn't said a thing about the Kill Code, though she must have known that I was responsible for it.

Sandy folded her arms across her chest. The top hat had molded a ring around her head, denting her hair. She hadn't changed out of her plain, white Oxford, the kind we used to wear in high school with the little plastic buttons at the tips of the collar. Now with the fabric pulled between the sharp points of her shoulder blades, she looked more like the old Sandy Jensen I'd known at Q, a little awkward, a skinny girl who had grown up funny and smart. I felt bad for the ways I'd hurt her.

"Look up," she said. She gestured at a swinging acrobat, a streak of fire through the air. She wasn't angry. She was trying to put it behind us.

So when Sandy Jensen held her hand out toward me, I took it. And I might have held on long enough to go home with her that night, long enough to try to explain, but then two things happened.

First, I noticed that the station next to mine, which crowds had mobbed all night long, had emptied, and, finally, I could see what had stirred up so much excitement: At a low table not unlike mine, outfitted with an inkwell not unlike mine, with a quill in its hand not altogether unlike mine, sat an artificial boy, pale and uncanny as a porcelain doll with his painted mouth and glassy eyes. With the tick and scritch of a gear, the boy's eyes began to slide back and forth, the hand began to glide up and down across a paper card, and the quill began to draw. These were not meaningless chicken scratch, but real letters, strung one by one into words, written in India ink. He was an automaton. I'd seen an automaton like this before in a YouTube video, a complex machine created two and half centuries before by the Swiss clockmaker Jaquet Droz and programmed to scribe words on paper. For all I knew—and by then I knew well that Hack liked to collect rare and expensive things—it was the very same one.

On the corner of the table where I had worked all evening sat my cardboard sign, *Love letters, hand-scribed.*

On the corner of the table next to the wind-up boy, a paper sign read *Love letters, hand-scribed.* It was written by the boy.

Something peeled loose in me; a piece of tape that had been holding many pieces of belief together for me tore violently free. That night had been no demonstration of my skill. I was being mocked by a toy.

And then suddenly I could see that I had been placed in that hall on Halloween night as an exhibition that had nothing to do with language or art and everything to do with the midnight unveiling of the Algorithm. The boy and I both were exhibits in a museum of extinct creatures, quaintly laughable steps on a journey that led only, inevitably to Q. Hack was fascinated with the things he would annihilate. Had turned the halls and rooms of Q into the museum of an extinct civilization. He took his conquest so blithely that some of the rarest manuscripts in the world—the remaining physical history of entire civilizations— were being fed to an incinerator.

There was something monstrous happening here. Something monstrous in the way Sandy Jensen had hissed *Tehran*. Something banally evil. That was the first thing.

Then Sandy swung my hand, her fingers threaded through my fingers, and she said: "I knew you wouldn't do it."

That was the second thing.

Sandy Jensen and her Algorithm might know that I sometimes drank Starbucks lattes from a bottle; she might know I bought my boots from eBay and binge-watched MTV; she certainly knew I was face blind, and that I had two parents and a brother and a son; she might even be able to predict, from the boots and the videos and the eighties music that one day I would take out a second mortgage or blow all my savings on a ticket to Umbria.

But Sandy Jensen had no idea what I was capable of.

Once upon a time, when we were young and in love, and Connie had a good job and I had a meh job and a dream of something better, Connie wanted us to have a baby. Naturally, because I had the meh job, and because she said I was her goddess and an artist and could create entire worlds, Connie wanted me to have it. I wanted the something better. I wanted time. But I also wanted Connie to have everything she wanted. We were young and in love and I said yes. There was the donor with the same eyes as her brother, and the steel tank holding the vials, chilling the floorboards, Connie putting on Guns 'n' Roses and holding my hand. And it turned out Connie was right about one thing: It was easy for me. We were going to have a baby.

And then that wasn't enough.

Connie had always been competitive. As a woman in science, she'd had to be—first in her class, first to complete her dissertation, first to land a post-doc. She marched through the world with her shoulders back: first, first, first.

I was not even halfway through the first trimester when Connie set a mason jar full of Brugmansia by my side of the bed. The big, pink-edged trumpet flowers flared in the faint yellow light of the bedside lamp, spilling sweetness. "I want to have a baby," Connie said, pressing her hand against my belly. I covered her warm hand with my hand and pressed it tighter. I meant to show her: *It's here. Your baby is here.* But that wasn't what Connie meant. "There's still time," she said. She meant: for us to have babies at the same time. It would be so much easier that way, she said.

And suddenly I saw myself in dirty sweatpants, my hair a rats' nest, my face blank with exhaustion, becoming a ghost while Connie went to work and won prizes and came home clean and bright and kissed us at the end of the day.

That's what we were fighting about that night at Mirabel's party, midsummer's eve, the night Connie danced with the woman with the shoulders of the Archangel. The night I told Mirabel that I thought that if I didn't agree, Connie would leave me, and Mirabel drummed a finger lightly against the side of my head *So what are you going to do about it?*

What else was I going to do about it? I loved Connie—loved the self-confidence and the sweetness and the heft of her. I wanted nothing more than I wanted Connie.

Mirabel left the table and Connie came over, and I remembered the knot of resolve that formed in my chest before I told her *okay*, the bright breaking open after, when Connie stood up and punched the air *Yes!* and kissed me. Suddenly, everything felt easy.

Connie got pregnant too. Then Connie kissed me goodbye one late summer morning, jumped on Lancelot, the Subaru of bikes, and ran into a car. Of course she'd demanded an ultrasound—though she was only four weeks along, nothing to see. Except the same cancer that had killed Connie's mother. Very rare. Very deadly. The doctor looked down at us over the black frame of her glasses. Night had fallen, and Connie's bed was dark, lit by the blue glow of the nurses' station.

Connie always looked so strong in her clothes, chinos with the right leg clipped, the blue windbreaker she wore, no matter whether it was hot or cold.

She looked small in the bed, stripped down to the pale, sterile wrapper.

The doctor turned to me. "You're the wife?"

I wasn't. Connie hadn't wanted to do that without the Church. The doctor glanced at my belly, which had started to bowl out. I nodded.

The doctor looked at me, hard. "We need to take it out." The ultrasound had been followed by a biopsy. "All of it."

It was as simple as this: Connie could not carry the pregnancy to term and live. We would have to choose.

For Connie, there was no choice.

We were back home, not the same home she had left that morning, not the same two people. Connie stretched across the old blue couch. Though it was summer, she had swaddled herself in sweatpants and socks, as if she needed to be a little more careful now with all the parts of her. Her right arm hung in its sling, the finger of her left hand touched to the grommet at the top of her sweats, a little brass navel. "You know I can't," she said. "You know I can't."

I set a mug of jasmine tea down on the table.

I knew Connie believed she couldn't. And that was something I had never understood—ever since that Tucson afternoon in the pale winter light of Connie's childhood church, the dry cool air stale with candle smoke. I never understood how Connie, who knew the chemical formula of both the slipperiest and the hardest substances on earth, believed that wine could turn into blood. From up above the altar, the gilded trim along the lectern looked pretty. But the smoke and the water and the oil—what did any of that have to do with what rushed through our veins? Maybe Connie and I were always too different that way. Maybe when she refused to marry me until she could marry in the Church, I should have known. But that night I wasn't thinking about the differences between us. I was thinking about my friend Cris, angelic in his open casket in the Christmas mission, pale against the bloodred poinsettia.

I knelt by the side of the couch and drew her fingers from her waistband into my hands. "I need you. We need you to be alive."

She let me pick up her hand but she didn't move. This wasn't my Connie. My Connie picked up trash from Temescal Creek with the neighbors on Saturday mornings; fought her graduate department chair to get the more-qualified, less published woman hired instead of the inevitable man; when a neighborhood drunk used our driveway as a toilet, she went out with a shovel to clean it up. She never accepted a bad situation for what it was. Now she was limp, lying down on the couch to die, all because of a faint pink line. I could not accept that. Connie had the cancer that had claimed her mother and might claim her, too, and there was nothing I could do about that. But Connie not doing anything to save herself—I could not allow it.

I pulled her hand closer to my face, a swimmer clutching a lifeline. "I need you and this baby needs you," I told her. And then I said the thing that we had never spoken of, not since that blanched winter afternoon in Tucson, crouched by the big plate glass window her brother went through, when Connie told me about how her mother abandoned her emotionally after her brother died. *She left me. I will never forgive her for that.* I squeezed her hand against my cheek as if trying to pinch blood back into it. I wanted so desperately to bring her back. "Don't abandon the one you have left."

As soon as I said it, I wondered if I'd made a terrible mistake. After taking me to Tucson, Connie never spoke about her mother again. Her rage and disappointment were a darkness in her that didn't fit with how she saw herself in the world. "We have so many privileges," she always reminded me whenever I complained.

Prone on the couch, Connie went stone still. For the first time ever with Connie, I wasn't sure what she would do—take that same shard of glass that had come out of her brother's neck and stab me with it, if she could. But she only blanched. Tears smutched my hand but they were mine, not hers. She nodded.

Sandy Jensen had no idea what I was capable of.

When it came to protecting someone I loved, I was willing to kill.

The clop of hooves through the great hall gave me a reason to disentangle my fingers from Sandy Jensen's. I had a brother and a son, and a mother and a father, people whose lives were so tenuous and fragile and dependent on mine. I had made promises to people whose lives would hinge on what I did. *That* was the true social network. A duty of care worth more than all the art in the world.

Eight riderless horses pranced in, glossy and shining. They strode in, heads high above the crowd, smelling of hay and horses' silk.

Sandy clasped her hands together under her chin and laughed, finally, that bright, burbling laughter I had missed all night.

When she did, I slid the letter with the Kill Code between the pages of my recovered portfolio, just another leaf hidden in plain sight among the leaves. And when Sandy's eye was fixed on the shining eye of one of the horses, I tucked the bottle of red ink she had given me against the leg of the desk where no one would find it until later. I didn't want it anymore.

The horses shouldered their way through the crowd to drunken shrieks of laughter. I really thought some idiot might get trampled, but the big, calm animals stepped to the spot underneath the acrobats and stood perfectly still while the performers rushed down on silks, falling fast but never touching the ground. As soon as they reached the saddles, the horses lifted their large heads, whinnied, and clomped away. The acrobats stood atop them, waving. The crowd trailed the horses from the building.

Sandy gestured and I didn't hesitate to follow.

I planned to lose Sandy in the crowd, but she kept a hand on my shoulder, steering me along. It was ten minutes to midnight and the Algorithm was about to launch. I had heard that phalanxes of engineers hadn't left the campus for weeks and, loosened by alcohol and the late hour, there was a sense of barely suppressed mania in the crowd, a giddiness that anything could happen—fireworks or colored fountains or money tumbling from the sky. They were loud and jocular, the ones in witches' hats and capes, the ones in fleece vests and chinos. It wasn't hard to imagine them rushing to burn someone at the stake. That feeling was swelling in me, too, a desperate feeling that I was about to be burnt, and that I was the one doing the burning.

The horses' hooves echoed fantastically through the great entry hall. I looked around frantically for Michael. He was standing under the bones of the woolly mammoth, before a cardboard cutout of the moon, his headset on, staring up through the glass ceiling at that big satellite dish made of rock and powder. For a treasonous moment, I wondered again if Blue had brought him here, if this was another way she'd betrayed me. Thinking about it, I felt the heat rise again in my face and my chest, a mix of hormones and rage and shame and the liquor returning, the desire to burn and be burned.

Watching Michael at his receiver, I wanted grab his arm and pull him away with me. But I knew I couldn't. Michael wasn't the kind of person who tolerated sudden changes. He had an uncanny ability to become a deadweight when he didn't want to be moved and he might well throw a fit. Instead, I followed Sandy and the crowd flowing toward the exit turnstiles as the horses clopped through.

The crowd bottlenecked at the security checkpoint as the wide pool of people narrowed into two lines. Queuing up, Sandy finally dropped her hand from my shoulder as we shuffled forward.

Through the big glass face of the building, we watched a stilt walker in electric blue put her hands in her coat pockets and turn out six white doves. Their wings glowed in the night as they wheeled away. I imagined them coming to rest outside my window, burbling secrets, and longed more than ever for home. Two blond men in surf shorts slouched near the doors, watching the birds, as if they, too, longed to be somewhere else.

The line ahead of us moved forward. Almost no one was carrying a bag, though some had red plastic Solo cups and one man was fiddling a klezmer tune. The fiddler got stopped on the way through the turnstile and was asked to turn over his fiddle, at which the crowd booed wildly, and again when the man was asked to remove his large black overcoat, which the guard inspected carefully, turning it inside and out. It was the younger guard, the one who had called me *Miss*.

When the man finally retrieved his coat and fiddle, a great cheer rose up and, with the cheer, two doves rose into the air. The guard shook his head, but the fiddler was already out in the night.

I envied the birds their freedom. I was more and more desperate to escape from Sandy. When I noticed someone ahead of us in line, a tallish person in a flared plaid coat, carrying a large bag, I waited until Sandy was looking away and dashed sideways into the second line. By the time she noticed I was gone, it was too late. She was trapped in the crush of people before and behind her. When she caught my eye, I smiled and waved. *Here I am.*

My line moved faster. It was almost my turn to go through security when the person in the plaid coat ahead of Sandy stepped to that guard's desk. As I expected, the guard demanded first the large leather bag and then the flared plaid coat and then even the straw hat topped with a flower. The young guard was pulling yards and yards of colored silks from a pocket of the coat, spooling them around his fist—orange and houndstooth and purple and green—and pulling more.

The whole of Sandy's line was still cheering for the endless scarf when I stepped up to the guard in front of me. Immediately he asked for my bag, and immediately pulled out the largest thing inside it: the fat leather portfolio, tooled with the letter *V*. The guard eyed me. It was the older guard, the one with the creased earlobes. He knew I had a hand-tooled portfolio. But maybe he'd had enough of the partygoers, and the fiddlers, and the clowns, and of being at Q until late into the night. Instead of passing it over the counter to me, he flipped the portfolio over, front and back. I knew what he was looking for: a sticker with its radio frequency ID indicating that this portfolio was mine, free to come and go. I also knew there wasn't one. He'd stuck it on my portfolio himself—the one I'd used to smuggle the *Codex Argentus* out of the building.

"There's been a mistake!" I cried. "That's not my cover, but it is my work!" It wasn't a lie. It was the portfolio of my own years of pages I'd swapped for the *Codex*, tucked between the

Codex's covers—the one without the radio ID. But they looked so much alike.

Sandy was still trapped where she was, but she heard me and she called out to the guard: "Mario!" Then she gestured with her head and he lowered the portfolio and opened the cover. A dusk sky, winking with stars—the rich purple field of the deep-dyed page, twinkling with silver letters. My purple, practice pages. Pale imitations of the *Codex*. But Sandy didn't know that.

Silently, Sandy motioned with her hand and the guard picked up the phone. Two other guards were already rushing toward the security gates in their blue coats.

Sandy didn't even look at me as she waved her hand.

She knew I knew what that meant. The library and the scan and then the furnace. I was sure she meant to punish me—but maybe I was wrong; burning handmade things, ancient things, rare things, didn't mean the same to her as it meant to me. Her fingers snapped, two quick pops and the two guards rushed away with my portfolio, wrapped in the *Codex*'s cover. Sandy herself was trapped, but as soon as she got free, she would accost me. Guards would rush forward. Things would happen.

In that moment, though, as I watched the two guards hurry away with the portfolio full of my father's letters and my secret prayers and my purple-stained pages inscribed in imitation of the *Silver Bible*, Time slowed down. The guards and the drunken crowd and the clown with the fake daisy in her hat and even the wheeling doves all went still. Time blew through the turnstiles and the passage and the high ceiling. From the great entry hall, the woolly mammoth bones tinkled like wind chimes. Crowd, birds, woolly mammoth, we were all part of something vast and deep and slow, and a tiny piece of that slowness was inside those portfolio covers, my requiem for all the lonely hours, my devotional, and it was being carried away; everything I had devoted myself to in order to save myself was about to be burnt. I lost many things when Connie left me. I had learned to accept loss. But I had not learned how to forget.

Perhaps, now, I would.

A flash of color and the world rushed in again, the clown stuffing ten yards of colored silks back into her bag, shrugging on her plaid jacket. Sandy stretched her long neck, impatient to push forward. In a minute she would slip through the turnstile and double back.

I was fucked.

My fuckedness started manifesting as a noxious roar. By the time I realized it was actual roaring—skateboard wheels against the ground—the two blond surfers were at my side. "Come on." Thick arms bristling with blond hair lifted me onto a board.

Zipping out of Q with two surfer boys in Hawaiian shirts felt no more or less miraculous than anything else that had happened that night. One of the men pushed the door open with a meaty hand and I sailed through; I was floating, my heart filled with gratitude for the artists and the freaks of this world who had the power to open doors where none had been.

It was midnight. Fireworks crackled over the courtyard and the pink *Lockdown* sign fizzed out. The fire dancers were there, spinning their hoops and braziers. I knew she wasn't here though: Tal, Blue, 18, Maryam. Whoever she was. I could feel the strangeness of these bodies to mine, and knew in feeling the absence that, even though I hadn't known it, I had always recognized her. At the last stroke of the gong that chimed the hour, the fire dancers converged and we all watched as brass letters twelve feet high spelled out in tall, thin Art Deco capitals lit with fire: TAL.

A great cheer went up—a particular kind of cheer, a *bruh! bruh! bruh!* not from the acrobats or the clowns or the stilt walkers in long, striped pants, but from the men in chinos and fleece vests—the engineers. That's when I got it. They were cheering the algorithm.

The Algorithm.

I saw the letters break and reassemble.

Tal.

Tal was The Algorithm, like Tor was The Onion Router. Because engineers loved their abbreviations. They were creating an artificial intelligence. *The AI*, they had called it, until too many people mixed up the capital *I* for an *l* when they typed it, and a beloved nickname was born. Everyone and their brother had an *Ay-Eye*. But *Tal* belonged to Q.

Make Tal forget me.

The realization blossomed like fire: Daniel Khalili hadn't been talking about a woman. He was talking about The Algorithm and he was talking to *me*.

And I had done what he asked.

I had slid the letter with the Kill Code in it between the pages of my portfolio, the one in the *Codex*'s cover. Pages a robotic arm would right then be lovingly turning, one by one on the platen, and scanning, and performing and making part of this place.

Inside the halls and servers and lines of code, the Kill Code M. David Hacker had written to destroy his own work was blooming like fire, unfurling its tongue, worming its way through the vast sums of data in Q's great cloud—names, faces, places, things, connections, connections, connections—burning them all away.

The man whose broad back I clung to stopped the skateboard with his foot. "Did you do it?" His friend turned to me, reached into a pocket of his surf shorts and pulled out a thick brass badge. "FBI," he said. The men in gray suits. They'd changed their clothes and become different people to me. He shook his badge in front of my face the way he had shaken the photo of Daniel Khalili under my nose, demanding recognition, wanting answers. "Ms. Black," he said, "we need to know: did you or did you not destroy the Q cloud database?"

22 *The Party's Over*

MY PARENTS WERE PACKING UP THEIR THINGS. The power was back on in the hills. They wanted to go home. "It's time to get on with our lives!" my mother crowed.

I wished I shared their enthusiasm to get on with my own.

My mother was in the kitchen, gathering up my father's pills. His medications had arrived in a cardboard box that had once held a pound of tangerines but had spread across the kitchen tiles and swarmed the old push-button phone. "We like our privacy," my mother said, pill bottles rattling in her hand. "And I'm sure you want your own house back."

I slid the poster for the ball, and the letter rolled inside it, back into the poster tube Jae had given me and popped the top back on. Did I want my own house back? I'd spent so much time escaping from my parents while they were here, I didn't want them to leave. I'd betrayed Sandy and been betrayed by Blue. My parents were the only constant and I'd wasted my time with them. The suddenness of it all surprised me.

The lack of news surprised me, too.

Waking, I'd expected darkness to blanket the entire city, the telephone to go dead, the markets to crash. I'd heard Michael complaining this morning that Q was down; he couldn't see photos from his Earth-Moon-Earth exhibit last night at the ball. An angry Twitter thread demanded to know when people could get back into their Q accounts. But that was it. Whatever repercussions there were from what I had done hadn't yet hit the wider world's awareness.

"Did you get your whitening strips?" I asked my mother, scanning the top of the fridge for the Crest White Strips that had been massing there since my parents' arrival.

My mother's head disappeared into the fridge, emerged with a half-empty jar of apple sauce. She set it in the tangerine box, considered it, and stuck in back on the shelf next to the milk. "I don't know what you mean."

I glanced up at the top of the fridge again, though I knew the whitening strips weren't there. "You said you felt self-conscious about your smile?"

She straightened a towel and hung it on the oven door. "Did I?"

My mother could always be evasive, fiercely jealous of her privacy—that smack when I discovered her letters in the hat-box, the sharp retort when I asked her who she was going out to dinner with—*A friend*. I felt the old shame rise in my throat. Was she working with the Neighborhood, I wondered. Had she been five steps ahead of me all along? I watched her open the refrigerator a second time, pull out the apple sauce, place it in the carboard box, consider it and return it to the fridge again. I shivered a little. I wanted to believe my mother was still canny and sharp and capable of gaslighting me, but I had begun to fear that she was losing her mind. I feared for my parents, then, for their future together, and I feared what it would mean for me when it became impossible to deny.

I closed my eyes and pictured the letter I had written for Blue, which had gone back to the library last night between the pages of my portfolio, and wondered if, by deleting the past, and all the connections in it, I had robbed my mother, too. But the worry didn't last long.

"It's *your* smile that worries me." She pulled the tangerine box close and counted off each pill bottle with the tips of her fingers. She had always been able to count that way—not with one finger jumping from object to object but with all her fingers spread out, rolling through the numbers like keys of the piano. She hadn't lost the knack. I wondered if that was something Blue could do. *Maryam*, I reminded myself. *Maryam Khalili.*

"I didn't see anyone come pick you up last night. That was strange. Sending an empty car like that. It's lonely, isn't it?" I shrugged. I'd thought it was extravagant, sending a driverless car, a kind of show-off, really. But my mother wasn't wrong, either. Her fingers drummed the pill bottles. Her lips moved silently with each touch. "Eighteen." She looked up. And with that piercing way she'd always had of reducing me to my failures, she said, "Almost nineteen years is a long time to be moping for someone who left you, don't you think?"

Connie did not die and leave me a widow. She lived and left me.

I didn't think I was moping for Connie, not anymore.

I was moping for Blue. What I'd heard the night before had stunned me, a letter opener through the heart. I kept going over it in my head—how she'd seen me at Crimson Horticultural Rarities the night Daniel Khalili disappeared. How she grabbed my hand in the warehouse and pulled me up the stairs without saying a word. I felt outraged, but it was an anger that shook with other things, the thrill of following a stranger up those stairs into the dark. The body is a blunt instrument, easily fooled by strong emotion, shaking legs, a racing heart. I remembered her showing up at the farmers market, following me inside the Portal, whispering into my mouth, *Burn it down.* The way she'd shown up in my bedroom at midnight and said "I'll help you." At every turn, she'd just appeared. At every turn, I felt sure, though it was hard to put my finger on it, she'd tried to persuade me. I'd just been her means to an end.

And yet—there was something else about Blue. I was sure there was. Something rippling out from those fingers worrying every bone in my hand, rippling out from the warm cave of her mouth, from the unselfconsciousness of the way she picked up her pencil, fell into her trance, and drew her doodles at my elbow. Something stronger between us than mere expedience.

Fishing my house key from the green glass bowl by the door, I decided my mother was right. I'd wasted an awful lot of time already and I wanted to do something about it.

Temescal Alley the morning after Halloween was quietly stirring, the air brisk with pomade. A chocolate lab leashed outside the barbershop read the day with a wet black nose. Across the way, the Apothecary shop was shut. I pressed my nose against the window, close enough to read the signs on the big glass jars: *Lobelia, Marshmallow Root.* No one was inside.

And it was dark inside the stall where I had found Blue setting small fires. Empty and blank. There was no sign of the sizzling blue sign that read TAROT, no oversized photo of Adam and Eve departing the garden. Even the counter where she had shed sparks from the tips of her fingers was gone, the glazed black bowl. Staring through the pane at the empty space, I felt dizzy, as if in the night a great time had passed without me.

"Excuse me!" I tugged the sleeve of a woman licking the cream from a donut. The dog's fat black nose twitched, hopeful. "Do you know what happened to the Tarot shop?"

The woman picked up her coffee cup. "That's an art gallery," she shrugged. "Show's over."

I was at that same spot, still staring at the blank windows of the gallery, wondering at Maryam Khalili's perfidy, clutching a tepid, half-full coffee, when a hand fell on my shoulder. I didn't recognize the arm, or the calf-length cardigan, which smelled like the cream-colored angora sweater my mother used to have in her closet, a warm, rabbity smell. It goes without saying, I didn't recognize the face. "Hey," she said, and sat down next to me, long legs in black pants. She thrust out a fist. "I think you forgot this." And there like a magic trick was the bottle of red ink.

"I didn't recognize you," I confessed to Sandy Jensen. What I meant was: in this different place, in those terrifyingly beautiful clothes, I would *never* have recognized you. I said it with a feeling of dread because I would rather Sandy Jensen never recognize me, ever again.

Sandy leaned back on her hands, so that even though she was sitting down, she looked tall, commanding. We may have been near my house, but we were still on her terms, as, come to think of it, we'd always been. "Remember when we met?" Her gaze followed mine to the blank windows of the empty gallery. "You were in the nap pod and I had to pull you out?" She laughed, and there again were those bright waves, the colored tubes, her strong hand pulling me from the darkness.

"I remember," I said.

"And how I took you to see the library," she said, stretching her head back like a cat, her neck so long and slender I imagined slicing it with a knife. "All those manuscripts no one else had ever seen."

My hands had gone cold, my face hot. I didn't want to talk about the library, or what was in it, or what had happened there last night. I studied Sandy Jensen's long legs and knew I could not outpace her if I ran.

"The *Codex Argentus*. I thought it was magical," she said. "Didn't you think it was magical?"

I did think it was magical. Like the Wind Telephone and the bottle of ink. The sandwiches, the bottles of fizz. It was magical how she always knew what I liked. It felt magical to be seen and appreciated by someone like that, magical enough to make me feel like, when she kissed me, I should kiss her back.

That great ruff of blond-brown hair moved around her head. "Not magic, though," she said, plucking the sleeves of her luscious sweater down over the knobs of her wrists. She looked around the alley, up at the bulbs strung between the buildings, down toward the barbershop and back toward the crowded green windows of Crimson Horticultural Rarities. (I noticed: the blue postbox was gone.) "Are you one of those people who sees things in the stars?"

This was going to be about Sandy and me, I realized. Not about what I'd done at Q. Along with relief, a different kind of guilt flooded my mouth, a particular dread. *Here we go again with the old romantic lie*, I thought, but I was thinking bitterly of Blue.

Sandy wrapped her sweater over her knees. "The constellations, I mean. Do you see pictures in the stars?" I shrugged. I'd *depicted* things with stars, a field of blue pricked with silver flecks. But constellations? Tristan had had a phase, but we couldn't see many stars in Oakland, and I could never keep them straight. "Humans have been looking for meaning in the stars for thousands of years. It's an expression of one of our deepest drives: to find patterns, to look at a thousand points of light spattered across the sky and find meaning there."

Sandy Jensen had never struck me as the sort of person who believed in fate or things written in the stars and she didn't sound like that now. She was doing that thing she did that had made me like her in the first place—saying smart things, sounding confident. For a moment, it was easy to forget that she was angry. "The positions of the stars are meaningless," she sat up and grabbed her knees in her hands. "But the search for patterns is not. Q is built on that—the deepest of human desires. And, unlike human beings staring at the stars, Q *can* find meaning in a thousand data points. Ten thousand. A hundred thousand million. Last night, Q was on the verge of making sense of all of it. Imagine a photo of someone at a birthday party in Brooklyn leading to the diagnosis and treatment of a rare disease. Q can do that. Imagine a purchase from Williams Sonoma stopping a terrorist plot." Sandy was staring into my eyes, her hands reaching out between us as if offering me a pile of riches. But I was remembering the sad family at the farmers market, agonizing over a text message sent between sisters, a search for a prescription. Those were the connections Q made, too—invasions and interpolations that were almost impossible to prevent and had the power to destroy a family's life. If Sandy had really been looking at me, she might have seen the concern tweaking the corner of my mouth, my eye. But she was swept up in the grandeur of Hack's Big Idea. She sounded like she was in love with it. "When it comes to seeing far and deep, the Hubble has nothing on Tal."

It was the first time I'd heard Sandy refer to the Algorithm by its nickname. Hearing that word, *Tal*, stirred a wave of longing in me for the night with the man in the tweed vest and his letter, a longing that was all the longing I had felt since my life with Connie ended, a longing that had seemed to find an answer in my life all at once, standing at the postbox, a silhouette in lamb's-ear green. I wondered if Sandy, too, was grieving this ideal Tal she had lost, though it meant something entirely different to her.

Sandy spread her pale hands out wide. "When you have enough data, there are no coincidences."

Because of Connie, I understood: Big Data was like a God to Sandy, a way of making sense of the mess of our lives, pulling it all together, giving it meaning. If *someone* knew everything, if someone *could* know everything, there was no reason to be afraid. I also knew that thinking you knew everything could lead to terrible things. Those terrible things had motivated Arman and his white-haired scriveners and barbershop quartet and a secret army of people—my Neighborhood—to wipe the whole thing clean. It had motivated me, too. My son had a right to have a life without always being tracked, without his idealism being used one day against him.

Sandy's hand drifted down to my kneecap. "Did you know you were the last person to see Daniel Khalili before he disappeared? The very last one before his cell signal went dark. And then," she turned and smiled at me, "the very next day, you showed up at Q. That's odd, don't you think? Of all the people in Temescal Alley that night, do you know how many also showed up at Q the very next day?" I didn't know. "Twelve. But the rest of them worked for us. Me being there outside those nap pods, ready to grab your hand, that was *not* a coincidence."

Nearby, a barber slid his push broom across the threshold of the Temescal Alley Barbershop, clapped it against the sidewalk and turned inside. For a moment, the cloud of dust and stubble caught the light. It rose and swarmed, bright as embers.

Sitting next to Sandy Jensen, watching the short hairs shaved from the back of someone's neck flare and fade, I had the horrifying realization that she was not a kind person, caught up in a warped system. She *was* the system. "Hack knew everything," Sandy said. "You didn't wipe the database. He did. You were just his instrument. You couldn't have done anything unless he allowed it to happen."

Could that have been true? My meeting with Arman, my decision to act—could all of that really have been orchestrated by M. David Hacker? That's exactly what Arman had warned me—that the ability to track us was not only about knowing our past and our present, but about coaxing us to do what they wanted us to do.

"This isn't a bad thing, Amy. It's a good thing. For most of human history, things have happened by coincidence. But not anymore. Now, we have Data."

I stared at Sandy's hands, the same hands that had passed me a sandwich from her picnic basket, and I was stunned. How close had I come to going home with her? To reading the Sunday paper in her bed?

"Don't you get it?" she said. "I forgive you."

Sandy's lips were still moving, but I could hardly hear what she said. I was going over every one of our meetings in my mind, the time we met by the creek next to the Wind Telephone, our date in the server cooling water. I was trying to find the signs, trying to make sense of it. Sandy Jensen knew I had sabotaged the database. Sandy Jensen had shown me the shimmering pages of one of the rarest manuscripts in the world and also calmly explained that it would be shoveled into a crematory. All of it made sense to her. It was all part of a pattern.

I never really appreciated it before Connie: For thousands of years, people had prayed to an all-seeing, all-knowing god, being good because they always felt seen. They *wanted* it. Now we really *were* seen. And, no matter how much knowledge that gave us, that didn't sit any better with me.

I wasn't like King Edwin. I had never been afraid of the rain and the snow and the darkness. I had always thought the dash of the sparrow was enough.

I crushed my paper cup in my hand, cold coffee dripping over my fist. "I'm not a believer," I said, standing up. "I've never been a believer."

Connie had been the believer, and I wasn't. That was the story I'd always told myself about what happened. Connie was dying and we had to choose, and Connie couldn't do it. Was she really going to let herself die in order to protect the *idea* of a baby? "I'm going to die anyway," she protested. And she probably was. But I needed to try to save her. And she needed me to be the one to choose.

They didn't bother with an abortion. She was only a few weeks along. Two days later, the surgeon removed Connie's uterus and ovaries and a number of other things you couldn't even name. *Scrambled egg*, the surgeon said. Her uterus had fallen apart as soon as they opened her up. Unsaid: There was no way on earth that baby could have come to term. "If there was a baby," the surgeon put a gloved hand over my hand. Sometimes, in cases like this, the test result was just an artifact of the disease.

But Connie and I hadn't known that. In that moment, I only knew that I had to choose Connie or the baby. I chose Connie. And for that, Connie never forgave me.

Last I'd heard, she was married to someone else.

Shaking cold coffee from my fingers, I realized I'd gotten it wrong. I wasn't a *believer*, but I had believed—I'd believed in Connie's vision of our lives more than my own. I'd let her want it enough for both of us, and I'd believed she would always be there to take care of me.

I flung the paper cup in the compost bin. And now I started to walk away.

"Hey!" Sandy started up from the bench. Suddenly this woman whom I had perceived as so easy, so smart and adaptable, so mild, was towering over me, her angora sweater flapping. "Are you kidding me? Are you seriously choosing *her* over me?"

"I'm not choosing anyone," I said.

Around us, people had stopped to stare. A man in cuffed jeans was whispering in the ear of his companion, pointing, like he knew who she was.

"She's an *adjunct professor*," Sandy spat. "And a circus freak!"

An adjunct professor? I didn't say: *Didn't you say she was an Iranian spy?*

I didn't say anything, though, and it infuriated her more. She hissed: "Do you have *any idea* how much *money* I make?" Her mouth went very wide when she said it, and I imagined that if I were a different person, I would have said with confidence she looked like a wolf.

A woman with a cell phone was recording the scene. The sight of the camera was all it took; Sandy gathered her sweater around her and strode away.

A chill ran through me when she stomped off, cursing, a trembling wire of terror.

And then a shimmering thread of joy, when I realized: *She doesn't know.*

Sandy Jensen knew many things about me and about everything else. But she didn't know I had the *Codex Argentus.*

23 *Deep Blue*

I WAS TOO TIRED TO CHANGE THE SHEETS ON MY BED where my parents had slept, so I went back upstairs to the guest bedroom hoping to collapse, and sleep, and forget. I'd been right about myself. I'd tried to imagine I could put the past behind me and find someone to love, but I couldn't read people for shit. Sandy Jensen, who'd seemed so nerdy and mild, was a megalomaniac in love with Big Data. And Blue—Blue was either a fire dancer or a spy, a math professor or a circus freak, but, whatever she was, she hadn't come into my life for me. She'd done it for Daniel Khalili. I threw my boots in the corner but even my stocking feet thumped too loudly through the empty house.

The wind was blowing through the stairwell, but it wasn't that hot, devil wind anymore. It was November and it was cold. The bedroom window was open wide, and as I stepped in the doorway, a person fell through it. I raised the only object I had: my bare hand.

"What? Are you going to slap me?" a low voice drawled.

"Blue!" I hurried to pull her up. I realized a moment too late I probably should have called her Maryam. *Or 18.* "You're here?" *I thought you were gone*, I thought, *I thought you left.*

Her hand, as always, was warm in my hand, fingers of fire.

I had a sudden memory of finding Connie downstairs in the kitchen, blending shortbread dough with her fingertips. "Go back to bed," I told her. By that point, my belly loomed large and hard under my shirt. By that point, Connie spurned me for my caretaking. "It's not the same as love," she said. But the truth is that I never loved Connie more than when I was taking care of her. For the first time since we'd started talking about children, I didn't doubt the kind of mother I would be. Connie didn't move from the kitchen table, where she sat in a chair, her fingers ghostly with flour. "It's perfect. You can't blend in butter with warm hands, and mine are like death." Her hands might have been cold, but she was getting better. The tumors, which failed to respond to treatment in 93 percent of patients, were shrinking. In a month, she would leave me.

I dropped Blue's hand and she dropped mine. "I didn't think I'd see you again."

"Because I'm an Iranian spy?" Her voice glimmered with sarcasm, anger, and hurt.

"Because you used me," I said. "I wrote that letter for your—" I hesitated. I didn't want to guess what he was to her. "For Daniel. And then there you were. And then you messaged me on *scizr*. And then you were here in the alley. And at the farmers market. Here in my *room*." I shuddered. I didn't like the idea of being watched. "You can't deny it. You've been watching me."

She leaned back against the windowsill. "I can deny it. I came to Crimson that night because Daniel texted me. He told me it was urgent. He wanted to tell me something, but then he didn't show up. And that night you came to me—you found me on *scizr*. *You* messaged *me*. You wanted to see me right away. I'm an artist. I had a show in the alley. I shop at the farmers market. I like fresh fruit. Maybe you're the one who's been watching me."

I hadn't been watching her. That was ridiculous. But I felt confused, and I couldn't tell if what she said made sense or if she was just bewitching me again. She was wearing her rings, silver loops up and down each finger, and she was doing that thing she did, quietly worrying the ring along one knuckle, spinning it between her fingers, the glittering hypnosis of her hands. I looked away.

"Come on," I protested. "You were at Crimson." Blue wasn't Tal, but she *had* been in the shop when the men in tight suits appeared, standing very still among the plants. I remembered the way her eyes flicked away from mine, little bits of tinsel. She'd been the woman tilting her head in the dark, touching her fingers to the mailbox. And she'd been my *scizr* date that night at the warehouse. "But, when I saw you that same night, you asked if I wanted to have coffee and you didn't say anything."

"Exactly! You showed up at the warehouse and you said right away you didn't want to talk. You talked about Daniel as if I hadn't been there at the shop. I thought we were playing a game."

Her hands started making shapes that matched the shapes I had seen her draw on paper, and with fire. I could almost see them light the air. I could feel, if this conversation turned just so, I would be burned.

"That night," she said, "Daniel asked me to meet him at Crimson Horticultural Rarities, which was right near his house. And then he didn't show up. At that point, I didn't know anything was wrong. Even when those agents appeared, I didn't know it had anything to do with him." Her mouth folded down. "But then he never texted me back. And I realized something had happened. People had warned me about Q, about being too close to someone there. Then Daniel vanished. And then when you told me you had a position at Q, I wasn't sure if I could trust you." People in the troupe, I suspected, must also be part of the Neighborhood. Blue could be part of the Neighborhood. I could. Anyone could.

The side door to the bicycle shop was locked and the talking blue postbox was gone. I imagined the top floor of the Tip Top Bicycle Shop empty, the Telechron clock still ticking on the wall, the devils and the fire dancers and the white-haired women a circus that had packed its tents and moved on. I felt a lightness about it, the relief of a letter folded up, slipped into an envelope and sent away.

Daniel Khalili wasn't a spy, and neither was Maryam. Daniel was an engineer; Maryam was a graduate student and an artist. An adjunct professor. Q could make data say anything.

"My god—" She blew a stream of imaginary smoke from her lips. The sky outside the window had fallen dark. An explosion in the street announced the death of a garbage can. "To think you were spending your time with Alexandra Jensen!"

"*Alexandra Jensen?*"

Blue sucked a blister at the side of her finger. "Author of *Do It, More*? Chief Operating Officer of Q? M. David Hacker's right-hand woman?"

I sat down on the bed. "Sandy?" Her badge had said *Evangelist*. "I thought she was in marketing."

Blue moved across the room and sat down next to me. "You're funny."

I *was* funny. But not in that way.

Blue thought I'd deliberately chosen not to say anything about seeing her earlier that first night when I showed up at the warehouse. I hadn't. I hadn't recognized her. But she didn't know that. Between Arman and Sandy and god knows who else was involved in all this, Blue was the only person who didn't know that about me before I did.

Blue hadn't deceived me. I'd deceived myself. And not just because I couldn't recognize her. Because I hadn't trusted her. In the gallery stall, under the sizzling *Tarot* sign, little bursts of fire at her fingertips, she'd tried to tell me something, and I'd said, *No. I don't want to know.* Now I needed to tell her what I'd never told anyone.

"I'm face blind."

"What does that mean?" She picked up my hand and started tracing lines across it with her finger. She was making another one of her maps. I could see the lines ripple out across the inside of my skull. I had the sense that she was doing it to me again, her subtle enchantment.

I explained to Blue what *face blind* meant. "I see other things, though." With my free hand, I started to draw letters in her palm. "Letters, but I don't just see them. Every letter has a texture, like sugar cubes or teardrops or hot wax." How to explain that the letter *V* had always felt green and ferny, redwood fronds in rain?

At *hot wax* she twisted toward me with new interest. "Really?" I nodded. "Some people have that with numbers, you know. Color/number synesthesia."

I remembered her screen name on *scizr*—18, under the profile photo of her hand—and how when we met and she'd said *Call me Blue*, I'd understood right away that the color stood for the number. I didn't know how I knew that, I didn't see it the way she must see it, but I had, and it was a tie between us.

Avians, salamanders, some claim even the smaller mammals, possess a sensitivity to the earth's magnetic fields, which they use to orient. This mechanism is best, if still poorly, understood in migratory birds, who, at the proper time of year, cluster anxiously in the southern corner of their cages, poised for flight. Blue and I squinted together out the dark window, over the next rooftop where the homing pigeons murmured inside their hutch, as if with enough concentration we, too, might see magnetic lines as patterns of color or light. I might not know anything about Maryam Khalili, but Blue and I saw the world through different versions of the same filter, colors becoming numbers becoming letters becoming smooth and sharp and rough. And something about that was bothering me.

"Sandy Jensen came to see me today. She told me that everything that happened at Q was planned—her meeting me, the

Kill Code, your choices, my choices, everything. She said that, when you have enough data points, there are no coincidences." It had sounded like a loser's boast, but all the signs pointed to Sandy Jensen being right. Earlier that afternoon, Q had made global headlines with the announcement that they had expunged all of the company's user data—the largest trove of such data in the world—and were moving to a subscription model. *Moving fast, breaking everything!* the *Tech World* headline read, hailing Q for resetting the bar for the entire industry. Q dubbed it *Data Liberation Day!* Hack was off the hook with Congress. He was off the hook with the FBI. Hack would go on to start a data mining company named after one of the Lords of the Rings.

"The FBI?" Blue crossed her legs on the quilt.

"Those men in gray suits." After they'd scooped me up on their skateboard and demanded to know if I'd torpedoed Q's database, they'd explained that I wasn't getting arrested. They *wanted* me to do it. They'd wanted *Daniel* to do it, but couldn't find him. "They've been trying to get at the database for months. You know how every site and device encourages people to log into it with their Q login? Q sucks up all kinds of data that way. According to the U.S. government, Q sucked up enough fitness tracker GPS data from American military personnel to give away the locations of several secret bases. The FBI wanted it purged. Q wouldn't budge. And neither would the courts. So they were willing to . . . get creative."

I'd gotten creative, too, I reminded myself.

Blue's mouth folded and unfolded. "I understand wanting to be able to destroy the thing you create. It's pride. But why didn't Hack just do it himself?"

I traced *B*, liquid wax, across Blue's palm and winced, thinking about my portfolio. I'd been trying not to picture it, the claw lifting it to the platen, the flash of the scanner, the short drop into the crematory. Years of my life, burned to ash. The only surviving copies of my father's letters from Golden Gate Tool & Die. An era erased. I reminded myself: The Library at Alexandria, too, had burned to the ground. "This way, no one will ever know exactly what happened at Q, and I think, as much as he loves data, when it comes to himself, Hack prefers for people to guess."

One of those people was Jae. Would Jae ever have left Q on his own? He said he wouldn't have. But releasing the Kill Code the young M. David Hacker had tattooed on his head with his own hand—that was unforgivable; that was the one act that Jae knew he could not take back. I popped the top off the poster tube Jae had given me and slid out the poster for the ball. Rolled up inside of it: the letter I had written for the man in the tweed vest. For Daniel Khalili. Jae had pulled it from my bag the first day I showed up at Q and read it. He'd known what it was. It was his sign that it was time. As hard as it was to believe that altruism was part of Hack's toolkit, he may have wanted to set Jae free.

Blue studied the letter. "Oh." Her finger hovered over the shower of swallows, the thumbnail moon bright with silver leaf. "It's exquisite." She moved her warm hand to the side of my face. "And it worked."

I pressed the hand to my cheek. I wanted to believe in this closeness. But how could I? "It's just temporary," I said. In the end, what had I—or we—the Neighborhood really achieved? Q may not have their user data, but they'd proven they controlled everything. It was just like Arman had said. They didn't just *know* everything. They didn't just *predict* everything. They *caused things to happen*. I remembered the spidergram on the monitor outside the library, the gossamer threads tying all of us together. What should have been a triumphal moment wasn't. Because Q owned those threads, and, once people started subscribing, they would again. They were pulling the strings.

This was the thing I could not get over. "If you agree that algorithms are dangerous and wrong—" I rolled the letter and tapped the top back on the tube and knew I would never open it again. "—how can you trust a match picked by an algorithm?"

Blue picked up a scrap of paper and started testing out my quill, dipping it into different colored inks. "An algorithm?"

I picked up my phone. "*Scizr.*"

She took my phone from my hand and dropped it on the bed. "The algorithm didn't put us together. My brother did. He saw you writing your letters, and he thought of me."

"Your brother?" I wondered if he was the man at the back table of the Hawk & Pony who always ordered an almond croissant. I wondered if he was one of the two people who followed @illuminated on Twitter.

Blue scratched the tip of the quill against the page, paused to watch indigo ink pool and darken. "Daniel." She gestured up with her chin. "Those are his birds."

In the darkened window, our faces floated over the single bulb that hung near the wire hutch. In the twenty third century before the common era, the king of Akkadia ordered his messengers to carry homing pigeons. If the messenger was about to be captured, he released the bird, which flew back to the palace, alerting the king that another messenger should be dispatched. How many messages had I missed for want of a system to alert me of my shortcomings? Daniel Kahlili was my neighbor. Daniel Kahlili was Blue's brother. I had seen him outside the window on his rooftop, tending his flock, touching his cap to me.

I blinked, remembering the bit of fluff that had floated out of his watch case when the man in the tweed vest sprang the latch, an oval the size of a fingerprint, a feather.

"Twin," she said. She never stopped her drawing, colored lines whirling like thumbprints. "He watched you and he knew. I think he asked me to meet him at Crimson that night because he wanted me to meet you."

I closed my eyes and saw Blue in the corner of Crimson Horticultural Rarities, picking up bottles and putting them down again. I saw her in her silver suit, spinning threads of fire. I saw her hips moving up the tenuous stairs, and through the velvet curtains of the portal. And I realized that I had not missed everything. I knew her. I knew the way her hands moved through space, the burn mark on her fingertip. The way she spelled words with fire. I knew her voice. I had not missed everything. "I knew," I said.

She put down the quill, screwed the caps shut tight on the bottles of ink, wiped her fingers with a rag. "I know," she said, pressing her mouth to my mouth. "I knew, too."

Then she said: "Hack didn't know everything, did he?" She was looking at the portfolio on the desk. The cover was closed, leather tooled with the letter *A, A for Amy, A for All Things.* Inside it was the *Codex Argentus,* the dusk-colored pages twinkling with the light of distant stars.

"No," I confessed, smiling at the very rare, very valuable book I had stolen from Hack's Library of Books That Don't Exist. "He doesn't know that."

Hack was so convinced he had the power to know everything, to predict everything, to determine everything, he forgot I could actually make choices of my own. I didn't exist for him, and the *Codex* didn't either—not really, not as anything more than something *priceless*—and because of that, I'd managed to walk off with something more precious and lasting than anything Hack had created, or ever would create. *The Codex Argentus.* A living piece of the Memory of the World. Even though I'd joked about stealing the *Codex,* Sandy Jensen hadn't thought me truly capable of a gesture like that. She thought she and Hack with their data collection and their predictive software and their three-billion-dollar valuation were the only ones who could see more than one step ahead.

In the security line, Sandy had seen my attempts at purple pages in the front of my own portfolio, covered in the portfolio cover they'd used for the Silver Bible. At a distance, she could only think I'd stolen the manuscript and that she was saving it. And after the Kill Code ran, there was no evidence to the contrary. "I knew that the Silver Bible was incredibly rare and that it belonged somewhere else, to someone else." I remembered the Speyer fragment, rolled around a thin wooden staff, tucked away with the bones of the saints. I touched the manuscript cover with my fingertip. "Some things are not meant to be forgotten."

All that was left of my own work was the portfolio cover Connie gave me, but I was ready to let that go, too.

Blue ran her hands through my hair. "There will be more work. Take it from a fire dancer. Each specific thing you create doesn't matter. What matters is the work. And there will always be more work." She pulled a knot of hair tight at the back of my neck, drew me close and kissed me. Then she picked up her coat. "I have to go."

I watched her move toward the window. "Go where?"

"To the library. Daniel won't be touching digital devices. He won't know it's safe to come home."

"The library?"

"The Haskell Free Library and Opera House. It's right on the border between Vermont and Quebec. It's a neutral zone, so a person in Canada can go there to meet a person in the U.S. and neither one crosses the border. Iranian families have been using it for years." She tapped the window frame. "That's what the message meant. *Meet me at the library.* The message was for me." She pushed the window open wider and climbed onto the sill. There was no need to come in and out of windows anymore, but I didn't tell her that. I wanted to see her against the glowing skyline. I wanted to see her disappear.

"What about you?" she said. "What's next?"

I tilted my head toward the *Codex*. "Uppsala," I said. "Special delivery for the King of Sweden." I'd thought about it. There was only so much time before my parents would need me and I wouldn't be able to travel. And I had never been to a real rare books library. There were still things I wanted to do. Tristan was at Lake Baikal. "I'm going to see my son."

She nodded. Whatever she felt about my going halfway around the world, I couldn't read it on her face. Her mouth folded and unfolded in that way she had.

But she could read my face. "Write to me," she said.

24 *The Memory of the World*

THE RIGHT TO BE FORGOTTEN MEANS THERE ARE things we should not know. Burning a hole in me: that I would never know whether I'd really been invited to Q as an artist, or whether I was just a pawn of Hack's and Sandy Jensen's. The day I stowed away on the Q shuttle and pressed my thumbprint to the scanner, it was already in their system. Sandy could have done it; Daniel could have done it; someone from the Department of Arts & Letters could have done it, too, and I would never know. And the worst thing was: I cared. (*You can't write; you can't draw.*) But, also, a part of me understood that never knowing, always doubting whether you were good enough was, sadly, the way of people who create things. At least, the way of people who create things for love instead of money. And I knew that I would spend all my life trying to believe the creating was enough.

"Happy birthday, Dad!" Michael and Izzy, my mother and I crowd close enough around my father's cake to hear him whisper-talk. He's eighty-five years old, older than his father ever was. His back is a question with no answer. His silver hair tilts over the pale, soft stem of his neck. A dandelion. "What do you wish for?" Michael asks him.

Squinting hard, we hear with no mistake: "Eighty-five more years!"

I wish he could have it. As it is, neither the Kill Code nor the Algorithm will have much impact on my parents.

They're the ones who've lived a life of freedom—moving through the world unrecorded, living private, unrecorded lives. *See?* I try to remind myself, *anonymity can be a comfort, too.*

"Mickey, honey, would you like a slice of cake?" She points at the plate smeared with frosting at my father's elbow.

When Michael was still in school, I sometimes came home early to find my mother in front of the bathroom mirror, standing in her bra, the way she used to "put on her face" before performances. But she wasn't putting on makeup. She was pursing her lips, staring for long moments at her face. I often wondered what she saw there, or who she was looking for. The artist who had given up her art? Or the mother she'd become, despite herself? Sometimes I wonder still.

The world leaves it marks on us. Fame. Heartache. Dirt under the nails. At the place where we touch the world and the world touches us is an alchemy that changes both.

A medical researcher studying starch in ancient diets and a microbiome specialist in ancient oral bacteria were examining teeth from the first millennium. Ancient teeth swaying polyp-like along a jawbone porous as bleached coral. The scientists scaled off a bit of plaque cemented there when saliva met the remains of bread in that mouth ten centuries before. Washed, crushed to ultrafine powder, the plaque gave up a secret: brilliant bits of blue.

The teeth belonged to a middle-aged woman, a nun at the female monastery of Dalheim in Germany, alive and then dead sometime between 972 and 1100 CE—her life a bat's lash in the great stretch of Time. But here were her teeth, and in her teeth sparks of lapis lazuli, the same powder that produced the rich blue pigment *ultramarine*.

In the tenth century, lapis was mined from only one place in the world, a single region of Afghanistan. Worth more than its weight in gold, lapis traveled over four thousand miles to Europe on the Silk Road to the brushes of medieval scribes and painters of the most priceless illuminated manuscripts.

Monks were scribes. Not women; men. *Women can't write; women can't paint.* But she did. She wet her brush with her lips and used her tongue to shape the point. That we know this took ten centuries and belongs to a bit of lapis powder caught between the teeth.

My mother is playing her fingers against the kitchen table, humming. My father licks his fork.

The donut shop has long moved away, and the Hawk & Pony shuttered. The portal and the Apothecary are gone. Whatever happened or didn't happen there has already been erased.

"One more time!" The cake is half gone, but Michael begs and Blue blazes the candles up again. I study the shape and color of her blisters as she strikes the match.

We become what we encounter. That's what it means to live in the world. A tattoo. A scar. A bit of blue between the teeth. Not everyone is meant to live in public. But if we're lucky, if we stay at our private labors long enough, if we work at the thing we love, only for the thing itself, we may finally be seen for who we are.

ACKNOWLEDGMENTS

This is a work of fiction many of whose most marvelous and terrifying elements are real. Algorithms with the power to single us out, quantify us, and shape our choices are not a dystopian fantasy. They are the silent infrastructure of the way we live now. For insight into the terrifying power of the algorithms that influence us every day, I owe thanks to many brilliant pieces of opinion and reporting, including but not limited to the *Reply All* and *Note to Self* podcasts, the columns of Charlie Warzel and Shoshana Zuboff's brilliant *Rise of Surveillance Capitalism*. If you're interested in what you can do about it, look into the work of the Electronic Frontier Foundation. With the planet on fire and autocracy on the rise around the globe, the workings of technology to limit our freedom and shape our choices without our knowing can feel far off and less urgent, but these issues are not unrelated.

Similarly, many little wonders depicted here, both ancient and modern, really do exist. These include micrography, the sonification of climate change, nap pods, Earth-Moon-Earth radio, the writing automata of Jaquet Droz, reading of DNA left on ancient parchments, a *soferet* scribing an entire Torah inside the Contemporary Jewish Museum in San Francisco, and the Blenheim nun whose lapis-flecked teeth millennia later revealed her identity as a scribe. For these and other interesting facts— including the poetry from Connie's bedside, which comes from "Snapshots of a Daughter-In-Law" published in *Adrienne Rich's Poetry* and reprinted here with the permission of W. W. Norton

& Company, Inc.—I have thanks to more magazines and books than I can list. (The translation of Bede's account of the conversion of King Edwin in this book is my own, with thanks to the late and inimitable Professor William Alfred, whose house kept perfect time.)

For help with this book, broad and particular, I certainly have more people to thank than I can say. But I will do my best, knowing this list is incomplete. Timothy Schaffert and S. J. Sindu dreamed a beautiful dream and invited me and my book to be part of it, for which I will be forever grateful. Dr. Erika Dreifus led me to it. Many thanks to the entire, talented, and enthusiastic team at Zero Street Fiction and the University of Nebraska Press, including Courtney Oschner, Rosemary Sekora, Anne McPeak, Abigail Kwambamba, Tayler Lord, and the talented design team at UNP who made this book into a thing of beauty, and many others. Galloping love and adoration to my cover designer, Gil'i Zaid. Cheers to Eric Schnall, who comes next.

For time spent thinking and talking about writing, my thanks to the Tin House Writers' Workshop and the Sewanee Writers' Workshop, and to Alexander Chee, Jill McCorkle, Steve Yabrough, and Jess Walter. For the sustaining friendships formed at these and other places where writers gather, my deep appreciation to: Leslie Absher, Camille Acker, Kevin Allardice, Anna Lena Phillips Bell, Melinda Blackorby, Rachel Borup, Emma Burcart, Dani Burlison, Chris Cander, YZ Chin, Tyrese Coleman, Lee Conell, Sarah Cypher, Karin Cecile Davidson *and* her mom, Pat Dobie, Molly Dumbleton, L Feldman, Lisa Fernandez, Jennifer Fliss, Craig Foster, Janet Frishberg, Karin Lin-Greenberg, Georgia Kolias, Chaney Kwak, Rachel Hall, Lois Leveen, Rachel Maizes, Avvy Mar, Jane Mason, Michael Mechanic, Nayomi Munaweera, Denne Michele Norris, Crystal Reiss, Meredith Rose, Amy Rowland (who is so humble that I must acknowledge her twice), and Tara Weinstein. I realize it's terribly unfair to thank Tara Weinstein, because she knows how to do absolutely everything. In fact, she could have raised a couple sheep, built a loom, hotwired an Edison bulb and a typewriter and thus saved me heaps of time writing this book.

Thanks also to Salem West and the team at Bywater Books for our continuing friendship.

Thanks to David Way and the Tip Top gang for letting me reinvent the place, and to the real Crimson Horticultural Rarities, which lives in a parallel universe to the one depicted here. Also to Zach Sabin and Art and John for showing me the top floor. The Ghost Bike on 51st Street is a memorial to Bruce Russell, whose name shall live in these pages. For the comment that black is a tone and not a color, and for a name dear to them, thanks to Aviva and Michael Black. Thanks to Sharon Lipping, for informing Mirabel's thoughts on cybersecurity.

Thanks to Annie Bloom's Books, East Bay Booksellers, A Great Good Place for Books (and especially to Kathleen and her team), Pegasus and Pendragon, Violet Valley Books, Weller's Book Works, the Rockridge Library, and the Melrose Branch Library for being a friend to writers. My heartfelt thanks to Charlie Kim. Your work makes art possible.

For help understanding the experience of prosopagnosia, my thanks to Eaton Hamilton and Lynn Wander.

For help understanding most things, my thanks to Rachel Adams, Shona Armstrong and Zac Unger, Karen Augusta (z"l), The Augusta Family and Barbara Boardman, Cheryl Krisko and my pal Steve Onishi, Jessie Austin, Agi Ban, Judith Barish, Cantor Sharon Bernstein, Ginger Bisek, Joel Boardman, Judy Chang and Mark Davis, Mitch and all of the Cohens across the sea, Congregation Sha'ar Zahav, Rabbi Mychal Copeland, Mavis Delacroix, Carrie DeLucchi, Elizabeth Gessel, Francoise Giguel, Alissa Giusti, Hugh Groman, Blake Howard, Paula Hurley, Sarinah Kalb, Nancy Kates, Anna Katz, Lily Khadjavi, Cherry Kim and Rhonda (z"l), Nina Klose, Jed Kolko and Eric Rice, Janine Kovac, Camille Landau, Dora Lee, Deborah Levi (z"l) always, Steve Marylander, Jamie Mayer, The Oakland Tech College Essay Mentors, Rebecca Pollon, Jennifer Robinson, The Ross Family, Rob Saarnio, Deborah and Michael Sabin, Mo Saito, Anne Schmitz, Diana Selig, Tanya Spanier, Connie Sommer, Adrian Staub, Sara Sulaiman, Lisa Sutton, Mike Waters, Anke Weiss, Amy Weston, Jessie Williams, Raymond Wong, and the Zaid Family—especially Shirley and Gerald Zaid (z"l), Gavin and Angelica Zaid, Blaine Zaid and Carmel Kadrnka and my nephews, who are very sweet young men.

Nancy Han, Tami and Jim Herzog, Joanne Manning—thanks to our families Gemstone, Kallahan and O'Mannion, who have filled our lives with wordless, limitless love. To our Best Boy, always.

To Soph, our best addition. Most of all, to Lauren, who sustains me, and to our boys, who are the most wonderful, most beloved young men in all worlds, real and imagined. Everything, always—for you.